The White Chariot

by

Richard Denning

The White Chariot
Written by Richard Denning
Copyright 2016 Richard Denning.
First Published 2016.
ISBN: 978-0-9564835-9-1
Published by Mercia Books

A catalogue record for this book is available from the British Library

Book Jacket design and layout by Cathy Helms
www.avalongraphics.org

Copy–editing and proofreading by Jo Field.

Author website:
www.richarddenning.co.uk
Publisher website:
www.merciabooks.co.uk

Dedicated to the readers of the Northern Crown series without whom I would have no one to write for.

The Author

Richard Denning was born in Ilkeston in Derbyshire and lives in Sutton Coldfield in the West Midlands, where he works as a General Practitioner.

He is married and has two children. He has always been fascinated by historical settings as well as horror and fantasy. Other than writing, his main interests are games of all types. He is the designer of a board game based on the Great Fire of London.

Author website:

http://www.richarddenning.co.uk

Also by the author

Northern Crown Series

(Historical fiction)

1.The Amber Treasure

2.Child of Loki

3. Princes in Exile

4. The White Chariot

Hourglass Institute Series

(Young Adult Science Fiction)

1.Tomorrow's Guardian

2. Yesterday's Treasures

3. Today's Sacrifice

The Praesidium Series

(Historical Fantasy)

The Last Seal

The Nine Worlds Series

(Children's Historical Fantasy)

1.Shield Maiden

2. The Catacombs of Vanaheim

Britain 606 to 610 A.D.

Picts
Dal Riata
Gododdin
Strathclyde
Bernicia
North Rheged
Ynys Manua
Deira
South Rheged
Elmet
Lindisware
Gwynedd
Mercia
Middel Engle
East Engle
Powys
Builth
Brycheiniog
Hwicce
Thames Valley
Middel Seaxe
East Seaxe
Dyfed
Guenta
Celemion
Cantia
Glastenning
West Seaxe
Suth Seaxe
Dumnonia

1. Degsastan
2. Catraeth
3. Eoforwic
4. Godnungingham
5. The Villa
6. Wicstun
7. Licitfelda
8. Tamwerth
9. Legacaestir
10. Deganwy
11. Clynogg Fawr
12. Trer Ceiri
13. Ogwen
14. Augustine's Oak
15. Pengwern
16. Ruthin
17. Meifod and Mathrafal
18. Doric
19. Garinges
20. Suindune
21. Calleva
22. Badon
23. Sarisburie
24. Wintanceastre
25. Hamwic
26. Percestre
27. Fisborne
28. Cicestre
29. Belesduna/ Pengingaburnam
30. Readingum
31. Basingstoches
32. Wochinoes
33. Lundunne
34. Cantwareburgh

Names of nations, cities and towns

Here is a glossary of the main locations referred to in The White Chariot and what they are called today.

Aemelesworp – Emsworth. A small village in what is now Hampshire.

Augustine's Oak – Possibly the village of Rock near Kidderminster.

Badon – The city of Bath.

Basingstoches – Basingstoke, a large town in Hampshire.

Belesduna – Lower and Upper Basildon in Berkshire.

Bernicia – Anglo-Saxon kingdom in Northumbria.

Boseham – Bosham. A coastal village in West Sussex.

'The Family Villa' – Cerdic's home at Cerdham - modern Holme-on-Spalding-Moor.

Calleva – Roman city of Calleva Atrebatum or Silchester.

Cantwareburh – Canterbury in Kent.

Catraeth – Catterick. Site of a signficant battle in c 597.

Celemion – Caer Celemion. A British Kingdom. Capital was Calleva.

Cicestre – Chichester - a city in West Sussex.

Dál-Riata – Kingdom of the Irish Scots from Ulster in what is now Kintyre, Argyle and Butte.

Deganwy – Ancient hill fort in the modern town of the same name near Conwy and Llandudno.

Degsastan – Battlefield in 603. Uncertain location. Possibly Dawstone in Liddesdale.

Deira – Anglo-Saxon kingdom north of the Humber.

Din Eidyn – Ancient capital of Manau Goddodin - modern Edinburgh.

Dogfeiling – A minor subkingdom in Northern Powys.

Doric – The town of Dorchester on Thames.

Eoforwic – York.

Elmet – Welsh/British kingdom around the modern day city of Leeds.

Garinges – The town of Goring on Thames.

Godnundingham – Site of Deiran Royal Palace. Possibly modern day Pocklington.

Gwynedd – Ancient Kingdom of North Wales.

Legacaestir – Chester.

Manau Goddodin – Welsh/British kingdom around what is now Edinburgh.

Mathrafal – A fortress in Powys and probaly the capital once.

Meifod – Small village near Welshpool, Powys. Once a major religious site.

Peginganurnan – Pangbourne in Berkshire.

Pengwern – Probably Shrewsbury in Shropshire.

Percestre – Porchester, a small port in Hampshire.

Powys - Ancient Kingdom of Central-East Wales, covering what is today the modern county of Powys but also at times Shropshire and Cheshire and Flintshire.

Readingum – Reading - a large town in Berkshire.

Rhufoniog – A cantref or subkingdom in Gwynedd.

Ruthin – Possible capital of Dogfeiling. Now country town of Denbighshire.

Salisburie – Salisbury.

Suindune – Swindon.

Tamwerth – Capital of Mercia, modern day Tamworth

Tre'r Ceiri – Iron age hill fort near Nefyn, Llyn.

Wicstun – Market Weighton.

Witanceastre – Winchester, capital of West Seax (Wessex).

Wall – Roman town near Lichfield, Staffordshire.

Wochinoes – Woking - a small town in Surrey.

List of named characters
* Denotes historical figure

Aedann – Once Cerdic's family slave but now his companion.

Áedán mac Gabráin* – King of the Dál–Riata Scots.

Aelle* – Former King of Deira.

Aethelberht* – King of Kent, Bretwalda

Aethelfrith* – King of Bernicia.

Aethelric* – Late King of Deira.

Aidith – Cerdic's wife.

Aneirin* – Welsh Bard and Poet

Augustine* – The first Archbishop of Canterbury

Bertha* – Queen of Cantia (Kent).

Boyden – A lord in Wessex.

Breguswith* – Princess of Sussex.

Bronwen – Aedann's wife.

Cadfan* – Son of Iago, Prince of Gwynedd

Cadwallon* – Grandson to Iago, Cadfan's son.

Cenred – Father to Cerdic. Lord of Wicstun and Earl of the Southern Marches.

Ceolwulf* – King of West Seax (Wessex).

Coerl* – Lord in Mercia and one day king

Cerdic – Main character, Lord of the Villa and son of Cenred.

Cuthbert – childhood friend of Cerdic.

Cuthwine – Cerdic's older brother, died in 597, also the name Cerdic gives his own son.

Cynan* – King of Powys

Cwenburg* – Princess of Mercia

Edwin* – Younger son of Aelle.

Eduard – Childhood friend of Cerdic.

Felnius – Captain of the Scots.

Frithwulf – Son of Guthred.

Grettir – Cerdic's family retainer.

Guthred – Former Lord of Bursea to the south of The Villa.

Haiarme* – Scots Princess and Queen of Powys.

Harald – Former Earl of Eoforwic, advisor to Hereric.

Hereric* – Son of Aethelric, Grandson of Aelle.

Hussa – Cerdic's half-brother.

Iago* – King of Gwynedd

Kadir – Irish guard of Haiarme.

Lilla – Bard and friend of Cerdic's family.

Mildrith – Cerdic's younger sister.

Pybba* – King in Mercia

Ricberht– Leader of a Wessex company.

Rolf– Friend and Huscarl of Hussa.

Rowenna– Woman from Witanceastre.

Sabert – Earl of the Eastern Marches.

Selyf* – Prince of Powys.

Tysillio* – Welsh Abbot and later a saint.

Wilbur – Friend and Huscarl of Hussa.

Chapter One
Independant Command
Autumn 606

Hussa sat on his horse and gazed across the wilderness. Rocky outcrops dotted the landscape, and moor and bog lay in between. A single path wound its way across; a narrow route for an army to traverse perhaps and yet that was his way. The skies overhead were heavy with rain clouds. It was cold and wet and he shivered despite wearing a linen shirt, a thick wool tunic and a heavy cloak. *'I am a long way from home,'* he said to himself. The thought made him laugh, but it was a hollow, humourless laugh.

Home. When had he last felt at home? That hovel in Deira had maybe been home. Yet she that had made it so had died years before. He had rooms in Aethelfrith's clifftop fortress of Bebbanburgh as well as other houses and strongholds. None, however, quite felt like home.

He thought of his halfbrother, Cerdic: now he had a home, despite being an exile far from the scorched remains of the villa where he had been raised. Cerdic had a family and children and belonged. Yes, that was the word: *belonged.* Did Hussa belong? He commanded five hundred men here in Manau Goddodin and was answerable to no one but the king. Indeed, in Northumbria his power was eclipsed only by that of Aethelfrith. Yet did he belong anywhere?

Did that matter? He waved his thegns forward and the army was on the move at his command, shield companies to the front. He would conquer more lands and subvert more people to yield to the power of his king. His own fame and power would rise.

So did belonging really matter? Was the knot of tension in his chest secret acknowledgement that it did, or was it just annoyance that he found it hard to dismiss such thoughts? Cerdic! Why did he always end up thinking about Cerdic? He needed a distraction.

"Attack at once," he ordered his second in command, who had ridden up beside him.

The campaigns north of the Roman wall continued to expand Northumbria's power. Two fortresses held out like breakwaters against the tide. In the West, Alt Clut, that rocktopped castle of the kings of Strathclyde focused resistance against Aethelfrith's drive further that way. Here in the North it was the mighty Din Eidyn that sheltered the Gododdin. From their hilltop fastness their foot soldiers and the remnants of their cavalry sortied forth. Aethelfrith had decided a year or two before not to mount a direct assault against it. Even with two or three thousand spears at his beck and call, the fortress would be impossible to capture by main force. Yet the king had not given up on it.

"One day it will be mine, Hussa, one day!" Aethelfrith had told him. Then the warlord had outlined a strategy that involved absorbing Manau Gododdin in stages – village by village and valley by valley. That was what Hussa was doing here in this godsforsaken wilderness. This was just another worthless dung heap of a village he was heading for; there was little glory or chance for wealth here. As he kicked in with his heels and trotted his horse forward between the shield companies, he shrugged. Not every day would bring glory or wealth. Yet these days were all part of the plan to see Northumbria become the most powerful kingdom in Britannia one day.

They reached the end of the path where the marshland gave way to fields surrounding a pathetic little settlement of no more than a dozen hovels. Lined up in front of the village were forty men, illequipped with old weapons and rusty armour. Hussa examined them for a moment and then dismissed them. A single one of his companies would destroy the villagers' defence in a matter of moments. However, he would prefer it if they would surrender. Aethelfrith wanted workers for the fields. A kingdom took a lot of wealth to run and the more people he had under his control, the more taxes he could raise.

Hussa rode forward accompanied by half a dozen of his huscarls. He reined in about thirty yards from the villagers' pathetic attempt at a shield wall that now presented itself to him. Despite the hopelessness of their situation there was defiance in many faces. There was certainly no glory to be had this day for Hussa and his army, but it was clear that some of these villagers believed they could earn it for themselves by resisting him. Would he have to knock the pride out of yet another rabble? Did he have to kill them all? He sighed, knowing there was little hope they would surrender and spare themselves. Still, he had to try to make them see reason.

"I am Lord Hussa," he shouted, "Lieutenant to King Aethelfrith who claims all of these lands and, indeed, all lands as his own. Surrender to us this day and your village will become part of Northumbria. You will return to your houses and to your fields. You will be unharmed." Hussa waited for a response.

"We serve the King of Gododdin. We belong to Din Eidyn!" An old man shouted from the centre of the company – presumably the headman of this village.

Hussa shook his head. "This is your last chance. Lay down your arms and you will live to see the sunset. Fight us and all of you will die."

The villagers looked on with stubborn expressions. "Long

live the Gododdin!"The headman shouted, sealing the fate of his companions.

"So be it,"Hussa replied and turned his horse away.

He rode back to the Northumbrian lines and gestured to Tamtha, the commander of the nearest company. "You will lead the attack. Second company will follow up in reserve should you require any assistance. "

The captain smiled at him. "That won't be necessary, Lord Hussa. The job will be done in a few moments."

With a curt nod, Hussa turned away. He had no appetite for watching the slaughter. It was not that he could not stomach the battle, nor did he lack courage in combat, but he did not enjoy killing as sport. Besides, what would follow here was hardly a battle. As he waited for the attack, he noticed a messenger galloping up the path towards him. Riding over to intercept the horseman, he heard a sudden roar behind him. His captain had rallied the first company and was leading them forward. Spears and swords were hammering against shields, telling the villagers that the Northumbrians were coming for them and that shortly they would die on spear and blade.

Hussa glanced briefly over his shoulder and saw a pathetic sprinkle of slingshots directed towards his men. Not one of them was wounded. Turning back to receive the message from the courier, he heard his captain bellow the order to charge. In moments the villagers were shouting and screaming as they died, and from the village came the highpitched cries of anguish from their families.

"What is it, messenger?"Hussa said, losing interest in proceedings.

"Instructions from King Aethelfrith, my lord. You are to return to Bebbanburgh at once, bringing only your personal guard.

4

You are to leave your senior captain in command here. The king said to tell you he has an important task for you in the South."

Hussa turned and shouted out an order. Soon two dozen men had assembled around him.

"What is it, lord?" One of them asked.

"Rolf, tell Tamtha he is in charge of the expedition until the king sends him fresh orders. We are leaving."

Rolf nodded and galloped off.

"Where are we going, lord?" Another man asked.

Hussa glanced at him, "South, Wilbur, a long way south."

"How long will we be away from home?" Wilbur asked.

Hussa frowned at the word 'home' and the feelings that came with it.

"I don't know," he said.

Chapter Two
Cantia
Winter 606

L ooking back, I suppose the rot first set in during that winter trip to Cantia. It was the end of a quiet couple of years and we Deirans had settled in Gwynedd perhaps a little too easily. It was becoming familiar to us. We were starting to treat it like home and had begun learning to speak the language of our hosts.

My family and I, along with my companions and a number of the villagers for whom we had been responsible, had arrived in the Welsh land of Gwynedd two years before. It was not, however, our native land, for we were not Welsh but Angles from the land of Deira in Northumbria. We were a party of around fifty who had accompanied into exile the two princes of Deira: Edwin and his nephew, Hereric, with whom we had been forced to flee our homeland when the king of the neighbouring AngloSaxon nation of Bernicia had attacked Deira and killed our king, Aethelric.

We had managed to secure a new home in the Welsh kingdom of Gwynedd and had gained the protection of King Iago and in particular his son, Prince Cadfan, who had adopted Edwin as both son and godson. Despite this, Aethelfrith of Bernicia was still a threat. He had sent Hussa, my treacherous halfbrother, to demand that Iago hand us over to him, but King Iago had refused. Failing to secure our capture in Gwynedd, my brother had ridden away emptyhanded, shouting threats that his lord, King Aethelfrith, would not be long in coming to wreak revenge upon us.

In the first few weeks after Hussa had gone we expected an attack at any moment. But as the spring of that year, 604, turned into an idyllic summer and was followed by a golden autumn, news finally reached us that Aethelfrith was busy fighting up beyond the great Roman wall again. Our friend Lilla, a bard and poet who travelled around visiting the courts of kings where a bard was always welcome, carried the news to us. He was able to report that the Bernicians were taking longer than might have been anticipated to absorb our land of Deira and also to pacify and suppress the British of Manau Goddodin.

We had been more than ready to face him that year, but when he did not come, nor in the year after that, we begin to relax. Prince Edwin had argued again for taking the fight back to Northumbria, but even he could see that with only fifty men that was impossible. So we kicked our heels and waited. I think it was Edwin's continual moping that in the end annoyed our hosts to such an extent that King Iago found land for us. It was along the border with Powys; good land too and fertile. I was happy because for the first time since leaving my family's villa in Cerdham, we had land of our own on which we could grow our own crops and raise our own animals. So we did just that; we became farmers; we worked the land, we harvested it and we feasted. My family expanded and I was content.

It was at harvest time in the year 606 that a message from Prince Hereric arrived. Edwin called me into his quarters where, looking tired, wet and dirty from travel, there stood a young man in his early twenties. After a moment I recognised him as Godric, one of the sons of Guthred – my onetime neighbour back in the land of Deira and now Prince Hereric's chief advisor. Godric was standing at one end of a long table. At the far end, illuminated by a single candle, sat Edwin, a halfeaten plate of food abandoned in front of him. Also in the room was Earl Sabert, Edwin's most elderly lord and his respected advisor. He stood over by the brazier rubbing his hands to warm them. He looked up as I came in then addressed Godric. "Tell Lord Cerdic what you just told us. "

Godric frowned slightly as he turned to regard me. His father and I were not friends. Indeed, I had broken off the arranged betrothal between my sister, Mildrith, and Godric's older brother, Frithwulf. I had then added insult to injury by allowing Mildrith to marry the man of her choice, who happened to be my childhood companion and close friend, Cuthbert. Guthred's family had never really forgiven me for that decision.

Back in the year 604, the princes had agreed that while Edwin would continue to pursue the alliance with Gwynedd here in the north, Hereric would go south to Cantia to seek an alliance with King Aethelberht, the so called *Bretwalda* or overlord of the Saxons, who might be persuaded to help the princes regain their Northumbrian homeland. It had been an obvious decision for Guthred and his family to accompany Hereric and for me to remain with Edwin. Hereric seemed to trust Guthred more than he did me, and while Edwin and I had not always seen eye to eye on all matters, we had reached an accommodation that appeared to work.

"Godric, what is it? How are things in Cantia?" I asked, coming forward and offering my hand.

He hesitated and then shook it. "Well, as you know, we accompanied the party of Archbishop Augustine on his return to Cantwareburh, so we were welcomed into the Christian court of King Aethelberht. Doubly so because Hereric took my father's advice and agreed to be baptised. The ceremony took place in the church Augustine was building there."

"Is he any less arrogant than he was at that meeting when he angered the Welsh so?" Sabert asked with a wry smile.

"Actually, he died not long after we arrived. There is a new Archbishop now, called Laurence. It has not really changed anything as he more or less carried on where Augustine left off, "replied Godric. "It was Laurence who actually baptised Prince Hereric. We have heard that you have also been baptised, my prince,"Godric observed, turning to Edwin.

"Yes he has, "I growled in disapproval, earning me a stern look from Edwin.

"I know how you feel about the old gods, Cerdic… "Edwin started to say, but I interrupted him.

"My prince, I am sorry, but why do you talk about the 'old gods'? It is clear to me that by using that phrase you have abandoned them. Can it be that you have already forgotten Tyr, who gives us victory; Thunor and Odin, who watch over us in our times of danger and Freyr, who blesses our harvest?"

"Cerdic! "Sabert exclaimed, his face an angry red. "I think you forget to whom you speak. Edwin is your prince, not some humble fyrd to be so spoken to."

I bowed hurriedly to Edwin. "My prince, I am sorry. I meant no offence."

Edwin got up from his seat and came over to me, placing his hand on my shoulder. "No offence taken, Cerdic, I know how you feel about the… gods. Trust me when I say I have not abandoned them. I still worship them but this…" he waved his hand about, "…situation requires careful handling. If praying to this Christ gives me support from Cadfan and Iago, then so be it. It can't do any harm surely?"

Godric coughed. "My prince, I have heard that after he visited Cantia, King Redwald of the East Angles had two altars built in his temple – one for the old gods and one for this new one."

9

"Spreading his bets is he?" I asked.

Godric glanced at me and shrugged.

Returning to his chair, Edwin indicated that we too should sit down.

"My apologies for the interruption, Godric," I said with a wave at the young man. "Please continue."

"Well, as I was saying, things were going along nicely. Aethelberht invited Hereric to go hunting with him and it seemed our hopes of an alliance were looking good. But then, a month or so ago, a familiar and fully unwelcome face arrived at Cantwareburh and since then everything has gone wrong."

"Who... who was it?" I asked, fairly sure I knew what he would say.

Godric gave me a sharp look. "It was your brother; it was Hussa."

"Thunor's bones! "I swore. "Bastard never leaves us alone does he?"I muttered, glancing at Sabert, who shook his head but said nothing.

"What is he up to now?" I asked Godric.

"A bastard he may be, and a traitor to Deira as we all know he is, yet he is a cunning man too and has a silver tongue that one. He has been using it to insinuate himself into Aethelberht's company. He has been feeding the Bretwalda stories about us, telling him we are cowards; that we retreated to Deira before the battle of Degsastan and fled Godnuningham before the attack where the king died. Anything to make us look craven."

I looked at him sharply. "Did no one argue against him?"

Godric's face went red, but it was with anger not embarrassment. "Of course we did, what fools do you take us for? Earl Harald was swift to counter Hussa's lies, but Hussa always has a reply and of course, neither Hereric nor Harald were at Degsastan."

10

"Nor was your father or Frithwulf as I recall," I said.

Godric flushed a deeper red, but maybe this time there was some embarrassment. As Earl of the Southern Marches, I had called out the fyrd to march north at our king's command, on the road that took us to that fateful battle north of the Roman wall, the battle where we had crushed the armies of the Picts, the British and the Scots of Áedán mac Gabráin. We had not fled, indeed we had been at the sharp end of that battle, but Guthred and Frithwulf and his retinue had not been there, having refused my summons because of our personal dispute over Mildrith. As a result neither had they been at Godnuningham when it fell to Aethelfrith's invading armies.

"No, they were not," Godric said. "Hussa is sharp enough to know this and so... "

"So he was able to say you could not know the truth of it," I finished for him, turning to look at Edwin. "What we need to do is send someone, a lord I imagine, who was at Degsastan as well as at Godnuningham when it fell and could set the record straight..."

I trailed to a halt at that point because they were all looking at me.

"Woden's balls!"I cursed again, because my mind had just caught up with my tongue. Sabert had been at Degsastan but he had been away from the king's hall the night it fell. Only Edwin and I out of the princes and all their lords here in Gwynedd or down in Cantia had been at both battles. We would not want to risk having both princes in one place so... it would have to be me. "Aidith is not going to be happy about this!" I said lamely.

The fastest way from anywhere to anywhere around Britannia is often not along the roads. Many, of course, are Roman built and even after two hundred years are straight and still pretty good. However, the Romans had ruled over a single province. Their legions had protected the roads and kept them open. Britain in AD 606 had more than twenty kingdoms. Without the escort of Augustine's holy men to lead us across them, most of those kingdoms were hostile or at best ambivalent to us. Many roads were plagued by bandits and leaderless men. The seas, on the other hand, were generally empty. So it was that about a week later, a seasick bunch of Angles sailed into Doverre harbour after a hellish journey on the rolling autumnal seas around the west and south coasts of Britain. The sun was just coming up as we edged into the port past the ruins of a tall stone tower, which Godric told us was once a lighthouse built by the Romans to prevent ships from floundering on the sandbanks.

"I wonder if men will ever be able to build such things again, "Aedann, my former slave, a Welshman and a Christian, but for a long while now my friend and close companion, muttered as the lighthouse fell astern. I shrugged. The Romans had built such wonders as I had already seen: the great wall and the city of Eboracum; my own family's villa itself in fact. Yet the Romans seemed almost legends to us; far removed from our life of mud huts and dirt and our fight for survival. However, it was an intriguing thought: could man ever get back to the glory of Rome, I wondered?

"Maybe one day, "I said.

I had brought with me my three closest companions: Cuthbert, my brotherinlaw, who was sharpeyed and agile, a natural scout as well as being an accomplished archer; Eduard, my other childhood friend, huge, strong and the best man with an axe that I knew, and finally, Aedann, who was a great swordsman. In addition, Edwin had sent half the warriors at his command: twenty of the veterans that had followed him out of Deira. You might ask what I was doing bringing with me a band of warriors on what was supposed to be a diplomatic mission. Well, let's just say, I liked to be prepared.

Godric was returning with us to Cantia and we sailed back in the same Cantiash ship that had brought him to Gwynedd. From Doverre we rode on the main road to Cantwareburh. It was a typical Roman road: wellbuilt and straight, but now, two hundred years since the legions had left, it was breaking up and becoming overgrown with grass and weeds. Even so, it was better than most other roads I had seen. The day was cool but dry and with our horses rested from the sea voyage we made good speed along it. We passed great swathes of farmland dotted with dozens of settlements from which smoke could be seen rising. The fields were now empty as it was past harvest time, but I could tell they were fertile. This – the oldest of my people's kingdoms in Britain and which, according to the old tales, Hengest and Horsa themselves had first settled – was a fine land indeed.

The sun was now dropping in the western skies behind the low hills that had run parallel with our journey all day. Ahead of us I spotted a much more substantial settlement. We could make out decaying city walls. Beyond them would be the corpses of Roman buildings – always intimidating – now overgrown with ivy, the tops of trees poking out above their walls. Clearly the Angles and Jutes who inhabited this land of Cantia were as reluctant as my own people to dwell in such places. As we approached I saw that I was right. Wooden and thatched huts and hovels were clustered on the land outside with only a few visible inside the city through gaps in the walls.

"See there," Godric broke the long silence of the journey. He was gesturing away from the road to the north. We could see two construction sites. At one an old stone building dating

13

back to the Roman occupation had scaffolding around it and it appeared that an attempt was being made to restore the stonework. The other site was being constructed in wood – something a lot easier for us Angles to understand.

"What am I seeing? "I asked grumpily. I was tired and still fed up with being so far from my family.

"Remember I mentioned that Augustine was building a church here? "

I nodded.

"Well, rebuilding, I guess would be more accurate. The Romans built that centuries ago. It's a bit of a mess, but Laurence and his churchmen are restoring it. "

"What about the other one?"I asked.

"That is going to be an abbey church," he replied.

"A what?"

"By abbey I mean a church belonging to a monastery – where monks live. A whole bunch of them in those dreary brown gowns all moved in soon after we arrived. Bastards have services all the way through the night. Damned bells ring out all the time, or so it seems."

"You seem to know a lot about churches all of a sudden, Godric," Eduard commented, giving the lad a sideways stare.

Godric shrugged. "We have been here two years now. The king's main hall is here and so this is where Archbishop Laurence is based. As a result there are churchmen all over the place. We try to keep out of their way but have to go to some of the services occasionally. Woden's buttocks, but they are dull affairs!"

We rode on past the distant church and abbey and arrived at the houses outside the city walls. There were some shops and a blacksmith's, now closing up for the night. We could hear music and laughter coming from a lively tavern. Passing it by with

14

some reluctance, we came to a wooden bridge across a deep ditch, which was clogged up with weeds, brambles and tree branches. A couple of spearmen stood guard on the bridge and we halted briefly until they recognised Godric and waved us on by. Clattering over the bridge and through a crumbling stone gateway, we emerged inside the ruins of Roman Cantwareburh.

Looking around I could see that in some ways it was like York: a large city with well laid out streets. Residences were located on the outskirts, shops and workshops further in, and finally, in the centre, the civic buildings. Yet unlike York, this place resembled a graveyard or mausoleum. Whilst in York the Britons lived on in the city, here they had long gone and no one had come to live in these haunted stone tombs. I reflected on the fact that my grandfather had been unique in having chosen a Roman villa in which to live. These Cantiash Angles, like most of my own people north of the Humber, avoided them. The largest building of all was a vast circular structure with curved sides. It stretched up three stories and had tall, wide arches all the way round at ground level. Now though, a forest seemed to have taken root inside and oak trees thrust out of the windows and above the structure.

Godric saw me looking at it. "One of the monks told me it used to be a theatre for stories and plays. Says there are many left in Italy."

For a moment I imagined the theatre in its former glory. It must have held hundreds of Romans watching the stories of their gods and their conquests. To have sat in such a place one must have believed such glory could never end. That evening it seemed such a sad old ruin as we turned away from it.

"Aethelberht's people have only just started clearing the ruins and settling here these last ten years," Godric said, his gaze flicking over the decaying stones houses we passed as if expecting to see a ghost. "Before then the city lay empty for two hundred years, I am told."

Beneath the shadow of the giant ruin the land had been left to itself, but not far away was evidence that my own people were staking a claim to it. Saxon settlements stood along the remnants of the old roads, and the gardens of once rich Roman villas and town houses had been turned into fields where the ground had been dug over after the end of harvest to await the next spring sowing.

It was here, alongside the old city wall, that we came to a large hall. It was surrounded by a wooden palisade and ditch, which had been dug in a semicircle out from the city wall. A single gateway allowed entry and we headed for this. Once again, we were stopped by guards who, having recognised Godric, nevertheless enquired of us our identity. Apparently satisfied, they allowed us to enter, directing us to a large building in which to stable our horses. Leaving our men to see to them, I and my three companions followed Godric out of the stables.

Standing outside were two men we recognised: one in his midforties, baldheaded, tall and muscular with a closetrimmed, dark beard flecked with touches of grey. This was Earl Harald, formerly Lord of Eoforwic. The other man was slighter of frame and more agile and lithe. He was younger too, around thirty, with blond hair and striking blue eyes. Unusually for a Saxon he was cleanshaven; a vanity that I suspect he believed made him look younger than he was, which it did. It was Lilla; a man as skilled with his tongue and his lyre as Harald with a sword. We all embraced for we were firm friends and had shared many dangers and adventures in the past.

"I have missed you, Cerdic... and your companions too,"

said Harald. "Guthred is decent enough but he doesn't have your sense of humour – especially Eduard's!"

Eduard grinned. "My lord, I have a new joke about a miller's wife, a rolling pin and…"

I held up my hand to stop him. "Save it for later, Eduard, "I suggested.

Harald nodded. "Yes, maybe over a few beers. Come through to the hall, Prince Hereric is inside. "With that he turned and led us toward the king's hall. I fell in beside Lilla. "Is my brother here? "I asked him.

"Yes, somewhere about. Guthred was all for killing him when he arrived, but Harald suggested that it would not look good to the Bretwalda."

"I dare say he's right. Shame though. For once Guthred had an idea I would agree to. So, anyway, what is he like, this Lord of Britain?" I asked.

"He is a wise king. He deliberates and weighs up much before he makes a choice. If I felt he chose wrongly when letting in the Christian mission of Augustine, I knew that at least he would have thought it through. In the end the thing to bear in mind, Cerdic, is that he is keen to get into men's minds and their souls to see what manner of men they are. Apparently he did that with Augustine and he will with you. For this to go well you need to persuade him that you… indeed, that we are *all* worthy of his support. Well, it's time to see for yourself, here is the hall," Lilla said, pausing at a huge pair of wooden doors.

Aethelberht's royal hall was not unlike Aelle's and Aethelric's had been: a long bulky building with a single dining and audience chamber occupying most of the space. Smaller rooms led off at the far end, which were the private quarters of the king and his family. Fires burnt in several fire pits dotted here and there, around them groups of warriors and nobles warmed themselves while exchanging gossip and chatting about politics, warfare and the harvest. In short, we were on familiar territory here and the language was, of course, English.

Half way up the hall Hereric and Guthred intercepted us. The prince was now around eighteen years of age. The last time I saw him his face had been all but hairless and he was struggling to grow a beard. Now his whiskers, which he kept short and neatly trimmed, grew thickly on his upper lip and chin. I noticed that he was filling out around the shoulders and chest. He was becoming a man. Indeed, he was perhaps a little older than I had been at Catraeth. I gave him a short, respectful bow and he smiled at me and taking my hand gave it a strong squeeze.

Guthred, on the other hand, treated me to his usual scowl from under his dark eyebrows. "Cerdic, your bastard brother is causing trouble," he said by way of welcome.

"So I hear," I replied.

I would have said more but at that point Hereric waved a hand in front of my face. "There will be time for that later," he said. "Come, let us introduce you to the king."

We followed him up the hall. At the far end, beyond the high table where the king and his most honoured guests would eat, was a highbacked, chairlike throne. Benches had been arranged in front of it. Seated on the throne was King Aethelberht, the most powerful king in the lands of the Angles, Jutes and Saxons. He was in his late forties, a tall man with auburn hair and a well-trimmed beard. He wore a simple golden crown. Beside him, in a similar but smaller chair, sat a lady of much the same age.

"That is Queen Bertha," Lilla told me "wife of King Aethelberht and daughter of the King of the Franks. She it was who persuaded her husband to allow Augustine and his churchmen into

Cantwareburh nine years ago. Take a look at her, Cerdic. Not much to look at perhaps, but that lady may just have changed our future – if Augustine's followers have anything to do with it."

I did now take a closer look. Whilst not exactly stunning, Queen Bertha was pleasantly attractive, with hair that was once deep brown now turning grey. Perhaps sensing she was being observed she glanced up at me and locked her gaze with mine. In the end it was I who broke away. I was left in no doubt that she was sufficiently strongwilled to have done as Lilla suggested.

I looked back at Aethelberht. The king was holding court: deliberating on legal matters: "I am satisfied that you, Eadric, freeman of this city, did enter the premises of your neighbour, Alfred, and took from there various items to the value of three shillings. I therefore judge that before Yuletide you will pay to Alfred the compensation of nine shillings."

Eadric, a gaunt fellow with a tatty, wellworn tunic, bowed and then turned away from the king, his face now grim. Another man, more well attired, presumably this Alfred, also bowed but as he turned he flashed his neighbour a triumphant smile then moved over to a group of his friends who were cheering as he joined them.

"Silence!" bellowed Aethelberht and the cheering died down. "Next case!" the king called.

Before another case could be introduced, Hereric had drawn the king's attention. Aethelberht waved him forward and we followed. Once we had arrived in front of the Bretwalda's throne we all bowed.

"Your Majesty,"Hereric said. "May I introduce to you Earl Cerdic son of Cenred, and his companions. They have travelled from distant Gwynedd in the lands of the Welsh to answer claims and accusations raised by Hussa of Bernicia."

Aethelberht studied us closely before addressing a guard. "Send for Lord Hussa," he said.

As the guard ran off to fetch my brother Aethelberht looked me up and down. "So, as I understand it, Prince Hereric and his uncle, Prince Edwin, claim that their throne was usurped by Aethelfrith of Bernicia?"

I nodded. "Yes, your Majesty, it was."

"And furthermore that they are looking to challenge Aethelfrith and regain their throne," he continued as if I had not spoken.

"We will do one day," I said.

"Perhaps, but as of now you have what, fifty warriors?"

I nodded.

"Not exactly an army to inspire fear in Aethelfrith?"

"No, sire," I had to concede.

Aethelberht tapped his fingers on the arms of the throne. "So, as a result, you seek alliances to further the princes' ambitions. An alliance with the Welsh of Gwynedd I hear, and maybe one with my kingdom of Cantia?"

"We believe it is in your interests as well as ours, sire."

Aethelberht gestured at Hereric. "So have your prince and his companions argued. They reason that if Aethelfrith is able to expand further he will be a threat to all the Saxon lands, even, maybe, my own. Whereas if I support your claim and your campaign is successful, so that one of the Deiran princes is enthroned in Northumbria as an ally of Cantia, then my own position as Bretwalda will be enhanced."

"Exactly so, sire," I responded, relieved that the conversation so far was going rather well. Somehow, though, I knew something would come along and change all that. Then I heard a familiar voice behind me and realised it might not be something but someone who would spoil it all. I turned and saw that my halfbrother had come into the hall through a side door and was moving towards us.

"Do not believe anything they say, King Aethelberht. They would lead you to disaster if you fought my king." As he spoke Hussa glanced at me and gave the slightest tilt of his head in acknowledgement.

"Do not believe them," he repeated. "There is little honour or strength in their blood and no glory in their spirit. Aethelfrith has both. Send these cowardly Deirans under guard to him and he will be steadfast in his loyalty to you."

Aethelberht considered this for a moment. "Lord Hussa, you have argued that there is no honour in these men and the princes they follow. Yet the tales I hear are that this man, "he now pointed at me, "has honour and courage in abundance. Is this not the same Cerdic who held the gate at Catraeth and who slew King Owain? Is this not the same man who helped destroy the Scots at Degsastan and later led his own princes out of danger and into exile?"

Hussa shook his head. "Stories grow with the telling, sire. There is little honour in his blood."

The king looked surprised. "Really? But I thought you shared the same blood."

My brother, discomfited, blanched at that. "Some, your Majesty, some, it is true..." he faltered into silence.

Aethelberht got to his feet. "So then, we have a quandary: how to determine who tells the truth? In other words, how am I to tell if the Deiran princes, Hereric and Edwin, are worthy of our active support?"

21

Queen Bertha moved out of her chair to stand by her husband. She carried a large book which she held out to him. He took it from her and lifted it up.

"This is the Holy Bible that Archbishop Augustine gifted to me when he came to Cantia. Will either of you place your hand upon it and swear in Christ's name that what you say is true?"

Hussa and I exchanged a look. Then my brother stepped forward and placed his hand on the book. "I swear in the name of Christ that what I have said here is true."

He stepped back and the queen turned to me. "What about you, Lord Cerdic?"

I glanced at the book. I did not believe in this Christ. That being so, I asked myself, would there be any harm in taking the oath? Then again, what if this strange new god was real. It never did to anger the gods. Furthermore, my own gods would be jealous and angry. I stepped back.

"I will not so promise, my lady, because I believe in the gods of my fathers: Woden; Thunor; Heimdall; Freya and the others. I will not abandon them nor will I slight your Christ with a false oath in order to gain favour here."

Aethelberht shook his head. "How then can we learn if you are truly worthy of our support?"

Now Lilla's words about Aethelberht desiring to know what manner of men we were came back to me. Somehow we had to prove it.

"Test us, sire. There must be something we could do to show our courage and our honour?"

The king inclined his head as he considered this suggestion. Returning the book to his queen, Aethelberht helped her back to her chair then seated himself on the throne once more. Waving his hand to my huscarls to indicate that they seat themselves on the benches, he continued to gaze at me. After a few moments a smile came to his lips. "I believe I do have something you can do to prove your worth."

I glanced round at Harald and then back at the king. "What task would you have us do, your Majesty?"

Aethelberht's fingertips tapped at his throne as he regarded me in silence and I wondered with increasing trepidation exactly what he had in store for us. At last he spoke.

"To the west of my realm lies the forest of the Weald. Beyond it is the kingdom of Suthseaxe: the land of the South Saxons, whose king is Cissa. Cissa is an ally of mine against the rising power of West Seax, which borders Cissa's land and also mine. King Ceolwulf of West Seax is strong and expands west against the Britons, north against Mercia and eastwards too. Thus he is an enemy."

I remained standing and as I listened, I marvelled again at just how many kings and kingdoms there were in this land that was once but a single Roman province. Would there ever be just one kingdom here again I wondered. I supposed that was unlikely given how splintered Britannia was now.

"Cissa's greatgrandfather was his namesake," Aethelberht continued, "the first Cissa, who conquered and founded the city of Cicestre amongst some Roman ruins and fortresses that lay close to the sea. Cicestre controls access to the lands of Suthseaxe. Ceolwulf has made it clear he is coming to take it, but Cissa is stretched defending his lands and I can send him little aid as I too am being hard pressed by troubles with Middle Seax. Yet I have promised to send Cissa a company of warriors."

Slapping his hands down on the arms of his throne, Aethelberht got to his feet and took a pace forward, running his gaze over me, my huscarls, now seated behind me, and our men, who were even now entering the hall and finding places at the bench-

23

es near to Guthred's men.

"That is a fine group of warriors you have there, Earl Cerdic. Reinforced by Lord Guthred and say a score of my own, and you have a company under your command."

I did not like the way this conversation was heading. I glanced at Hussa. He flashed me a nasty smile; he too had realised what Aethelberht was about to suggest.

"Prince Hereric, Earl Harald, Earl Cerdic and Lord Guthred: here then is my proposal. You take a company to Cicestre and stay there through the winter until Eostre, protecting it from all attacks that might come. Then we will talk again about a possible alliance."

I glanced back at Hereric, Harald and Guthred. They looked as shocked as I.

"Sire, I…"

Before I could voice my protest, Aethelberht cut across me with a smile. "Oh, you need time to discuss this. Yes, of course you do. You can tell me your decision in the morning. First though, I invite you, your men and your huscarls to join me tonight at my table. Eat and drink your fill and on the morrow we will discuss what I have in mind."

With that the king turned away.

I bowed and rejoined the others. "Nicely done, Cerdic, "Guthred mumbled, "now we are embroiled in a fight that does not concern us."

"I didn't ask for this!" I snapped back.

Lilla held up his hands to stop us arguing. "Sit down Cerdic," he patted the bench beside him, "and let's all calm down. After some food and ale we will all think more clearly."

As always, Lilla was right. Later, after drinking several goblets of Aethelberht's fine Cantiash ale and chewing at succulent roast chicken and freshly made bread, we were in a better frame of mind as we discussed the king's proposal. Should we refuse, saying that Cantia's wars and those of its allies were no affair of ours? Yet if we did, Hussa would use it as proof that we had no courage or honour. Moreover, if we would not assist Aethelberht in Suthseaxe he might well decide that he had no reason to risk his own resources and men in an attempt to get Hereric or Edwin onto the throne in Northumbria. As we conversed I was aware of Hussa sitting some distance away at another table. From time to time he would glance over at us, a smile of triumph on his lips. He knew the predicament we faced as much as we did. Eventually I drained my cup and slapped it down on the table. "We don't have a choice do we? I don't like it but we have to go and help defend Cicestre and then, hopefully, Cantia will support us."

Guthred's face darkened but he said nothing. Harald nodded, "I agree," he said.

Hereric also nodded. "So be it," he said, "we will tell Aethelberht tomorrow. Now pass the jug, I feel like I need more beer."

"After you with the jug, Highness, "I said, and filled up my own goblet. I felt like more beer too because I was angry. Angry at Hussa for his tricks that had dragged us to Cantia, and angry at the result. I was going to have to spend the winter in some godsforsaken land I had not even heard of before. That meant another Yuletide away from my family.

"Aidith is *not* going to be happy!" I mumbled to myself as I topped up my cup.

Chapter Three
Suth Seaxe
Winter 606

The decision now having been made we informed Aethelberht the following morning. Hussa, standing in the shadows to one side of the hall, watched us in silence, his dark eyes brooding, his mind no doubt pondering this move and what it now meant. I felt some satisfaction that now at least we could prove our worth to the Bretwalda and yet my brother did not seem perturbed by the thought. He was as cunning as an old fox and I was a bit concerned that he might have more irons in the fire, more plots in development.

I did not have much time to contemplate my fears. Aethelberht, having committed to giving aid to Cissa that autumn, gave us just a couple of days to resupply, replace broken equipment and make ready. His promised twenty warriors under a thickframed, baldheaded veteran called Wilfred, a few years my elder, joined our band – albeit reluctantly. Indeed, I had the feeling that none of these men wanted to be with us. That might cause problems, I mused. I would need to find a way to get them integrated with the rest of the company. Not that the rest were exactly united. The division started at the top with the dispute between Guthred and me, and was reflected by constant niggles and fallings out between Guthred's men and my own. The very night before we departed, Godric and Eduard almost came to blows when Godric called Cuthbert a 'grubby little thief'. Only Lilla held the peace – the one man whom it seemed everyone trusted. I was glad he had elected to come with us to Cicestre.

The winter was not far off and dark clouds hung above us when we set off for Suthseaxe. The route west threaded first through the high ground of the Cantiash downs, the city of Cantwareburh soon dropping out of sight behind them. Beyond this was the huge swathe of the Weald; a massive and incredibly dense forest that, according to Lilla, even the Romans had not fully pacified.

"There are villages deep in this woodland that are their own little kingdoms, "he told me. "No one can get to them and I imagine they like it that way."

"So how do you know about them then?" I asked testily.

Lilla looked at me like I was an idiot, "Cerdic, my dear fellow, I know about practically everything!"

I looked about us. We travelled, as ever, on one of the ubiquitous Roman roads. This one was more overgrown than most; ancient oaks and beech trees hung over the roadway, so we travelled in shadow for the most part, our horses swishing through colourful swathes of fallen leaves. Occasionally, however, the road climbed up onto elevated ground high above the bulk of the treetops. When it did so, we saw on either side of us, stretching to the far horizon, a sea of autumnal orange, red and gold. It was a beautiful sight. Here and there we could see smoke rising from fires deep in the forest – from some of Lilla's hidden villages perhaps. I thought about what life must be like for these scattered settlements, cut off and isolated. Then I thought about the world outside those hamlets, a world full of anger, rage and conflict. In that moment I envied them their sheltered lives, realising I would give any status I owned – or once owned, or might own in the future – to be there now with my family and friends, in a place where the cares of the world were far away.

Eventually our road dropped down to the Suthseaxe plain, the woodland fell behind and ahead of us was Cicestre. The world had returned and with it all its troubles.

Yet another Roman town, Cicestre was one of the first to be seized by the South Saxons who named it after one of their early kings. Just as in Cantwareburh, the Saxon settlers had looked on its tall stone walls and buildings with distrust. They had chosen to build the king's residence on the fields to the south rather than move into the echoing, tomblike houses in the city. Where a similar thing had happened in Eoforwic, the local British Eboracci tribesmen, who found themselves under Aelle's rule, lived on in the stone buildings, but here the local Regini tribe had abandoned Cicestre and allowed themselves to blend in with the Saxons, moving out of the city to live alongside them.

That had been a hundred years ago. These days a new king, Cissa, lived in Kingsham, as the adjacent Saxon settlement was now called. Meanwhile, Cicestre crumbled; trees and bushes grew up and nature encroached, conquering a fortress that no enemy had captured. So it was, as we approached from the east, that the walls looked more like trees and bushcovered mounds than bastions and gateways. The Roman roads in the area intersected in the centre of the old city and unlike the rest of Cicestre's streets, the Saxons did keep these fairly clear. At the crossroads stood a large civic centre – a forum – or so Lilla said. Under its shadow a few guards halted us, questioned us and then directed us on towards the southern road leading to Kingsham. We exited through another ivycovered archway and out into a palisaded enclosure. In the middle was a large hall with smaller huts and hovels clustered around it. We were greeted by the king's steward, who told us his name was Wynchell. Having introduced ourselves and arranged to settle our men, we followed him through to the main hall.

"King Cissa has gone north with the army to establish a winter base for them. Before he left he bade me welcome our allies from Cantia… "Wynchell paused, his gaze passing over Hereric, Harald, Guthred, Lilla and me,"…as well as you others from, er… further north. I am to explain what is required of you; it is a simple task really."

As he spoke he waved us across to a table where a cured hide was rolled out on its surface. I examined it. On it was drawn a map of the south east of Britannia showing the Weald, downs and main settlements, such as Cicestre and Cantwareburh. I cast an appraising glance over it, mentally comparing it with my own map that Lord Wallace had given me years before. Unlike mine, this one was no work of a Roman scribe but a crude attempt at best. Nonetheless, it showed enough to get a feel for the lay of the land.

"We are here," the steward said, tapping the symbol of a tower. I glanced to the east and saw that Cantwareburh had a similar symbol, as did the city to the north which I knew to be Lundunne. All fortified by the Romans. Then I looked further west and saw that another tower symbol lay beyond the western edge of the Weald and a little way inland. The roads from Cicestre ran along the coast and then up to that tower. I pointed it out and asked what it was called.

The steward shrugged, "Why, that is Witanceastre, the capital of West Seax."

I studied the map again. From Witanceastre the roads fanned out like a spider's legs. One leg came down to the coast to the west and thence east to Cicestre; one reached out eastwards through the Weald – presumably the area Cissa's army was in at present – and others headed towards Lundunne and other locations. It was a strong position and I could see why King Ceolwulf of West Seax was threatening to expand in all directions.

The steward tapped the map again. His finger was now pointing at a spot just to the west of Cicestre where a smaller, house-like symbol lay close to an inlet of the sea.

"That is Boseham. There is a large Roman palace or villa there, about half a mile or so from the road and up against the sea. It is enclosed and quite defendable. Any army trying to attack us here has to come past it. If a company of men can hold it for a while, it will prevent Ceolwulf attacking Cicestre, unless West Seax is happy to leave armed men in their rear. Indeed, a garrison there could pin down Ceolwulf for some time and enable King Cissa the chance to maybe attack towards Witanceastre."

He looked up, directing his gaze at Hereric. "That is your task, Prince Hereric. You are requested to take your company to Boseham, fortify it and hold it until Eostre, when we should know where Ceolwulf is heading. After that you should be able to return to Cantwareburh."

"If we are still alive," Eduard muttered from behind me, earning him a stern glance from Wynchell.

"Very well, we shall do as requested," Hereric replied.

"How are we to be provisioned?" Harald asked.

"You will find Boseham well stocked with ales and wines, salted meats and sufficient dried fruit and livestock for the winter."

Harald grunted. "When exactly does King Cissa want us to fortify this Boseham?" he asked.

"Why, right away to be sure," the steward replied.

I frowned. "Now? With the winter coming? Cissa can't be expecting an attack until the spring, surely?"

"I do not presume to question what my king expects or otherwise, "Wynchell reprimanded me. "I obey his orders. My understanding from King Aethelberht is that you are here to be of service to us. Is that true?"

Hereric answered before me. "Indeed it is and we shall be."

The steward was fractionally more respectful of Hereric than of me, inclining his head as he spoke. "The truth, Prince Hereric, is that Ceolwulf of West Seax has proven unpredictable. A winter attack is by no means impossible."

Hereric nodded. "Of course, then we will go at once."

We returned to our men who grumbled at the news that we still had a few miles to travel before we were finished. As I remounted my horse I leant across to Harald. "I am not sure that Cissa trusts us, nor, I fancy, does his steward."

Harald shrugged, "Doesn't have much reason to, I imagine."

"I suppose that much is true. Just the same, I am a bit anxious about all this. The border with West Seax lies just beyond Boseham and that puts us very much in danger's way."

"We have been in danger's way for ten years now, my friend," Harald commented.

A grunt from behind me told me that Eduard had been eavesdropping. "Yes Cerdic, why should today be any different?" he snorted.

I laughed at that and said no more. Yet inside me I still felt anxious about this 'simple task' that Wynchell had set us.

Slowed down by the carts that accompanied us, it took just under two hours to pass back through Cicestre and then across the flat land between the city and Boseham.

The villa was built close to the end of a long, narrow inlet from the sea and indeed, as we approached we could hear the cries of gulls circling nearby and smell the salt tang in the air. A small fishing village was clustered around the inlet and I could make out half a dozen masts. Then, shortly after we passed through a bank of woodland, the villa became visible through the trees.

Chapter Four
Ceolwulf
Winter 606

Hussa left Cantwareburh shortly after Cerdic. Accompanied by the dozen or so warriors and huscarls he had brought south from Northumbria, he rode to the coast and the port of Doverre. The weather was deteriorating as the winter storms approached and the sea was choppy and unappealing. A number of his men groaned at the thought of the sea voyage so late in the season and on such tossing seas.

"Quit your grumbling. It will only be a day's journey and then we will be safe in West Seax. We cannot get there by road – not without being seen by my brother or one of his princelings. Cheer up though; I am sure King Ceolwulf will be welcoming enough when I present Aethelfrith's tribute and gift to him. Now if you've finished griping, Rolf, take this bag of silver and go find us a boat. If it will make you feel better, by all means try and get one that doesn't look like it's about to sink!"

Hussa had chosen his followers carefully. Rolf was the oldest and probably the most experienced of the huscarls who had sworn to follow him. Each of them had something Hussa was able to use, be it value or skill. Most were men who, like himself, had no particular allegiance to country or king, but were ambitious for wealth or status. Perhaps too they were men to whom the fates had not been kind. Choosing them was not some form of weakness on his part, nor was it a show of empathy or sympathy for whatever misfortune had befallen them. No, it was more the case that men such as himself were willing to go that bit further to achieve what they wanted. It was that hunger and desire that gave them all strength; a willingness to accept sacrifice and hardship for the bigger prize.

Each of them had a history of which Hussa was aware. Rolf, for instance, had once had a family and land of his own. When Owain of Rheged had attacked Catraeth, Rolf's village had been overrun by the Britons. It had been a small community of shepherds who fed their sheep on pastures watered by the streams and waterfalls that ran down from the Pennines. Owain's army had slaughtered the villagers, including Rolf's family, and taken the sheep as plunder. After Catraeth, Rolf was yet another man with no master, no home, no money and no future.

When Hussa came to the attention of Aethelfrith and started to have rank and wealth of his own, he had sought out Rolf and taken him as his first huscarl. The man was grim, but much like himself, he had little to smile about. There was no doubt that Rolf was brave and although it was a far cry from shepherding, he had easily learnt the warrior's craft and fought willingly enough when he was asked. If ever there was a moment when Rolf showed pleasure it was when they fought the Britons, in particular those from Rheged.

"The boat he finds will be full of holes and stink of fish, I bet!" Wilbur said with a grin, making the other men chuckle.

If Rolf was grimfaced and sour in disposition, Wilbur was almost his opposite, using humour to deal with hardship. Wilbur had lost his wife and children to the same plague that had almost killed Cerdic's wife and son. Many villagers had died that year, either from the sickness or starvation, for the plague had left them with too few men to tend the livestock and gather the harvest before it spoiled. Hussa, who with his company had been billeted not far from Wilbur's village at the time, had witnessed the man's anguish as he burned his family's bodies. Once

33

the fires were out he had collected the ashes, placed them in clay pots and buried them deep on the outskirts of the village. Then he had collected an axe, sword and spear and presented himself to Hussa.

"Lord, take me with you when you leave. My family are dead and I have no food."

Hussa had stared doubtfully at the thin, lanky young man. "We are going north to fight the Britons, maybe even the Picts and Scots. If you come with me chances are you will be dead before winter."

Wilbur had laughed. "That will solve my food problems then," he had said with a smile.

Amused, Hussa had agreed to take him and now, along with Rolf, he was one of Hussa's most trusted huscarls.

Rolf returned a short while later. "I've found us a boat in Doverre harbour. The captain's a trader called 'Louis'. He's just brought a cargo of wine from the Frankish coast and has decided to winter here. He means to gather goods from along the uth coast ready for the spring sailing and is willing to take us as far west as Portusceastre."

Hussa nodded. "Good work. We can go overland to Witanceastre from there."

It was not a particularly pleasant journey and even Hussa, whose previous sailing experience with Cerdic had been comfortable enough, found his stomach churned. However, they arrived with no mishap and by the following afternoon were leading their horses off the docks at Portusceastre. Having enquired of the road to Witanceastre, they set off and a day later were approaching the city that was beginning to emerge as the capital of West Seax.

The stone walls that surrounded the town marked the place

as a Roman fortress. Like Cantwareburh and dozens of other towns and cities, the Saxons and Angles were gradually assimilating Witanceastre by building their own hovels, huts and mead halls inside and around the remains of the old stone houses. As with King Aethelberht in Cantwareburh, King Ceolwulf had his own large hall in the city surrounded by stables and workshops, and this was where Hussa led his men.

Ceolwulf had a proud lineage of warrior kings: his ancestors had sailed a fleet of ships to Britannia just over a hundred years ago. Landing on the south coast they had established the westernmost of the Saxon kingdoms. Hussa had heard that the first King of West Seax had been called 'Cerdic'. Indeed, now he thought about it, he was sure he remembered the story that his halfbrother had been named for this king. Quite why their father, Cenred, had chosen the king of a land so remote from his own, Hussa had never discovered. This warrior dynasty had expanded rapidly across the plains of southern Britain and seemed to be fighting almost everyone – Saxons as well as Britons – as they carved out their kingdom.

It was well known that Ceolwulf had aspirations to become the dominant power in the south. This meant he was a natural enemy to Cantia, Suthseaxe and Mercia. If Mercia and maybe even Cantia seemed to be moving towards opposition to Aethelfrith, then West Seax could in turn prove to be an appropriate ally to Northumbria. That had been Aethelfrith's thinking and the reason Hussa had travelled hundreds of miles to the south.

With the exception of Rolf, who walked at his side carrying a satchel, Hussa left his huscarls at the door and made his way up the centre of the great hall towards the king. Ceolwulf was perhaps thirtyfive years of age and with his fair complexion, blue eyes and blond hair, he was every inch the ideal of Angle and Saxon kinghood.

Smoke from a nearby fire pit hung in the air as they reached the far end of the hall. As both men paused to bow respectfully to the king, Hussa nodded at Rolf, who uptipped the satchel and poured out the contents. A glittering pile of golden artefacts tumbled onto the reedstrewn floor: coins, plates, cups and richly bejewelled items, necklaces and bracelets. Ceolwulf looked down at the treasure and then waved to one of his guards, who picked up several items and presented them to the king to examine more closely. Finally, he directed his gaze at Hussa.

"I am told that you are Lord Hussa, an emissary from Aethelfrith of Northumbria? "He paused, waiting for a nod of affirmation from Hussa before going on. "I am curious to know what interest Aethelfrith has in West Seax that would justify such a worthy gift."

"Your Majesty, I'm sent to express King Aethelfrith's supreme admiration for you and your kingdom. Like Northumbria, you have become powerful; perhaps the strongest kingdom in your part of Britain. My king likes strong rulers. He would propose an alliance between us to defeat our mutual enemies."

"Which enemies do you speak of?"

"Sire, it is no secret that West Seax desires to expand northwards into the lands of Mercia. Mercia is no friend of Northumbria. Indeed one of that nation's nobles, Ceorl, is known to have friendly dealings with the Deiran pretender, Prince Edwin. Meanwhile, to the east the land of Cantia stands poised to assist the other pretender, Prince Hereric."

"Cantia is not our neighbour and we need not seek trouble with it for your sake and that of your king," said a sourfaced, balding man who stood at Ceolwulf's right hand.

"This, Lord Hussa, is Lord Boyden, my chief advisor, "Ceolwulf said, his lip curling in a halfsmile. "He is a cautious man is Boyden, aren't you?"

36

"So men say, sire," Boyden replied.

"So, Lord Hussa, persuade him that we should ally with you and pick a fight with those we are not currently fighting and he in turn might persuade me."

Gathering his thoughts, Hussa bowed to Ceolwulf's advisor. "I understand, Lord Boyden, that you have no reason to trust me or my king…" he began, but Boyden interrupted, holding up a hand to silence him.

"Exactly so," he grunted. "So what can you do that I would know we can trust you?"

Hussa smiled because for this he had an answer. "I can give you some news of Cantia and Suthseaxe; news that you will wish to hear and that I wish to tell you."

Now Boyden and Ceolwulf did look interested, but Hussa remained silent allowing the tension to build.

"So tell us," Boyden snapped. "What news of Suthseaxe do you have… and how did you obtain it?"

"I learnt it from the very lips of King Aethelberht for I have not long come from his court. I was present when he sent a company of spearmen to help Cissa garrison his frontier against a possible attack by West Seax. More details I learnt by plying one of his officials with ale until he told me more than he should have. I know where the company is heading." Hussa grinned.

"Go on," the king said, his gaze now riveted on Hussa.

"It would seem that Aethelberht has demonstrated Cantia's support for Suthseaxe by sending a small company of experienced warriors to garrison Boseham, under the command of my halfbrother, Cerdic, who champions the cause of the Deiran princes and is seeking an alliance with Aethelberht on their behalf. Boseham is strategically placed to defend Cicestre against an attack by you."

Hussa coughed then cleared his throat before continuing, "Sire, such a move is designed to free up the Suthseaxe army so that it can operate freely, perhaps to strike at Witanceastre. Aethelberht's spies believe that you are fully engaged in your plans to move on Mercia or elsewhere. It seems to me that if you only feint an attack in the north and instead send several companies to Boseham, then you can capture it and sweep on to Cicestre."

Hussa fell silent as the king, exchanging glances with Boyden, carefully considered what Hussa had said. At length he spoke.

"I will weigh up your news and suggestion, Hussa of Northumbria, as well as this offer of an alliance with Aethelfrith. Whilst I do this you are welcome in my city and in my hall this winter. Spend Yuletide with us. Lord Boyden will ensure you and your men are found accommodation in the city."

Hussa bowed and he and Rolf withdrew. As they reached the doorway of the hall, Boyden caught up with them.

"Along with other duties, I am the king's chancellor and manage his estates. I will have you escorted to a house we keep in the city for the guests of the king. You are free to come and go around the city as you wish, and to eat and drink with others in this hall at night time."

The house provided for them proved to be spacious enough for all of Hussa's huscarls to sleep in the main room, with a separate bedchamber for Hussa himself. There was a resident steward to see to their needs and provide ale and mead for them all. There were also two women: the first was in her late fifties with grey hair. She was rather plump and went by the name of 'Nina'. The other was her daughter. She was rather different, being only twenty, with long, ravenblack hair. She was certainly of an appealing build and her face was attractive enough, but there was an intensity in her expression that immediately drew Hussa's attention. One of the huscarls, a coarsehumoured lad by the name of Octe, made some comment about being glad that entertainment had been provided for them.

Hussa spun round and glared at him, "Wipe that leer off your face. You will not touch either of the women; do you understand?"

"Your lordship has taken a fancy to her for yourself have you?" Octe asked with a snigger, falling into silence after a second glare from Hussa.

"You idiot! We are here to forge an alliance with West Seax. If we start misusing the women how well do you think that will go?"

"Of course, of course. I understand, my lord," Octe replied respectfully enough, but there was the slightest emphasis on the '*I understand*' that hinted Octe was implying there was something else going on here.

Hussa was about to rebuke him for insolence when the darkhaired girl came into the room carrying two large jugs of ale.

"My lord, would you and your men care for some ale?" she asked. Her accent was strange: a warm, deep sound Hussa could not quite place. He nodded and allowed the girl to pour the ale. Watching her for a moment, he was suddenly aware that his men had noticed his interest in her, but he did not care what they thought. He never cared what men thought of him. Not since... well... not for a long time anyway.

"What is your name?" he asked the young woman.

"Rowenna, my lord."

"Where are you from, Rowenna; Witanceastre?"

She shook her head. "No, my lord, I was captured in Dumnonia."

"So you are British?"

"I don't really know what I think I am, my lord," she said with a shrug. She then pointed at the older women who had brought some bread in for the men to eat. "My mother is, but I was very young when I was captured. It was King Ceawlin, the king's grandfather, who captured us – well, one of his thegns leastways. I now belong to King Ceolwulf and look after his guests."

"Like us?" Hussa asked. Rowenna nodded.

"What do you do for these guests then?" Octe asked lasciviously.

"I am a slave, sir. I do whatever I am asked to do by my master's noble guests."

"I like the sound of that!" Octe said, moving closer to Rowenna and reaching out a hand towards her breasts.

Rowenna put down the jug of ale on the table and waited for him to get closer still. Then, with a speed that astounded them all, she seized his outstretched hand and tugged, letting him stumble forward so that he tripped over her foot, banged his head on the table and ended up sprawled on the floor.

Octe groaned and rolled over, rubbing at his scalp. "What did you do that for? I was only being friendly."

"I said I did anything my master's noble guests wanted. I did not say all of his drunken huscarls too!"

"That was a nice move," Hussa said thoughtfully. "Bit unusual for a serving girl, I would say."

Again Rowenna shrugged. "I like to be able to handle any man who might come along."

Still on the floor, Octe snorted. "Well you can handle me any day lass," he smirked.

Hussa glared at him again, but before he could speak Octe

held up two hands. "Heh, I'm only kidding, lord. I can take a hint. I was just thinking that with winter coming a bit of comfort would not go amiss, that is all." Dragging himself to his feet he threw himself down on the bench.

Hussa gestured towards him. "Pour Octe some more ale, girl, he's had a nasty bump on his head," he smiled.

"Thank you, lord," Octe said as Rowenna moved to obey.

"Yes, well enjoy it; it's all the comfort you will be getting to-night!" Hussa retorted. The rest of the men roared with laughter as Octe's face flushed a dull red.

Yawning, Hussa finished his ale and climbed to his feet. "I am going to bed. Drink as much as you want tonight. I think we are safe here. Tomorrow, Rolf, take some men and silver and have all the armour and weapons repaired."

As he turned away, one of his men – Thomas, a lithe, agile fellow – produced a sheepbone flute and started up a lively tune. Soon the men were singing along, deep into their cups. Hussa left them to it and retired to his room, pulled off his tunic and britches and slid under the furs. For a while he listened to the men singing and then started to drift off, warmed by the ale. A little while later he heard the door open and shut and in the halflight made out the shape of the girl.

"What is it, Rowenna? I told you that you are not required to sleep with any of us. There is no need."

He felt her lift the furs and slide in beside him, her cool flesh naked against his own.

"I know I don't need to, lord. I want to."

He turned to face her, feeling himself stiffen. "In that case, so do I, "he said and kissed her.

The sex was enjoyable, of course, but there was more. There was a kind of offering and taking of comfort in the act. He had

41

sensed a sadness in her, and she in him and they each seemed to want to take some of that away from the other. It was not a feeling Hussa had felt before and he found that he wanted it to continue.

"Stay with me tonight," he said.

"If that is what you want, lord."

"It is, but only if you want it too…"

There was silence for a moment in the darkness before the answer came.

"Yes, I would like that. I will stay."

Chapter Five
Villa on the Coast
Winter 606

Compared to my childhood home, Boseham villa was sub-stantially larger and had once been very grand; more of a palace, in fact. It was positioned almost a mile south of the Roman road – which headed westwards out of Cicestre towards West Seax – and alongside the end of the inlet from the sea. Looking past the villa, across the flat wetlands that ran along the coast, it was obvious there were many inlets and waterways that dug deep into the coastline of Suthseaxe. As a result it would be impossible for an army to outflank the villa from the south. It would certainly be possible for West Seax to swing past the villa to the north, but in so doing it would leave a defendable fortress at its rear. Any army using the Roman road to attack Suthseaxe really had to take Boseham first.

As we left the Roman road, the hooves of our horses and the soles of the men's boots clattering on the pebblestrewn path that curved round towards the fishing village and the villa, I now gave my attention to the structure itself. It was perhaps seventy feet in length on each side and suffering the same decay we had become used to – two hundred winters had not been kind to most of Roman Britain. Stained by all those winter storms, the once white plastered walls were cracked and peeling. Above them the roof, which had once been covered by red tiles, now showed many gaps and cavities and in places had collapsed completely.

The path we followed led to an entranceway of impressive scale. As we approached the gate we were met by four men, their shield emblems showing they belonged to a company from the king's guard. They had clearly been expecting us. Their leader, a craggy old veteran who introduced himself as Randolph, bowed his head in respect and offered to show us round before he left.

"You are leaving?" I asked in surprise.

Randolph nodded. "Yes, my lord. My king commanded that we stay until you arrived and then I was to return to Kingsham," he replied as he led us into the villa.

"I don't think they trust us do they?" Harald said in an undertone, echoing my earlier words.

"Well, we're probably better off on our own anyway," I replied philosophically.

My companions and I dismounted and leaving our horses with our company of weary, footsore warriors, who welcomed the opportunity to rest awhile, we entered the villa. We followed Randolph through the wide gaps between tall stone pillars that supported the huge roof above us. The entranceway led on into an interior garden, some fifty paces long, which occupied the heart of the structure. Opening up onto this garden on all sides were a dozen or so rooms, their entranceways sheltered from the noonday sun by a colonnaded walkway. At one time it must have been very grand. The garden itself was overgrown, although it appeared that either Saxons or Britons had tried to maintain the kitchen garden as this had not completely returned to nature. Indeed, I could see quite tidy areas where onions, garlic and chives had been dug up and their leaves left as evidence of former crops. There was a hint of thyme and lavender hanging in the cold autumnal air, which suggested that somewhere these too had grown, but at this time of the year there was little left in the ground. The farmer in me was intrigued and I made a note to investigate the gardens and crops when I had the time.

With Randolph acting as guide we explored the rooms. Near

the entranceway was what had once been a small bathhouse, but here the roof had collapsed almost completely so the area was unusable. So too was much of the south side of the villa. Fortunately, the east side – and most importantly to us the north – was mostly intact. These would be the sides of the building that we would have to defend if an attack came from West Seax, so we explored these in more detail. There were kitchens, dozens of bedrooms and presumably other rooms in which to eat and receive visitors. Eduard and Cuthbert stared goggleeyed at so much space. I was perhaps a little less in awe than they, having at least some experience of living in such a building, but even I was impressed by the size of this complex.

All of us, including Lilla – although he would never admit it – were taken aback by the mosaics. Room after room had floors decorated with brightly coloured patterns and shapes that had been built from panels of coloured tiles and fragments of painted stones. There were fish, eagles and other birds, warriors, maids in pleasantly scanty clothing, and some very peculiar creatures that none of us, Lilla included, recognised. "Extraordinary, "he said as we bent to examine them.

Randolph shrugged. "The villagers are mostly Britons. They say that according to legend this place once belonged to a Roman emperor – there is even a statue down near the shore if that kind of thing interests you. "An expression of concentration passed across his face then he added, "Actually, it's there whether it interests you or not!"

Finally, he led us to the stores. True to his word, the steward had provided us with provisions, but these were not exactly generous. As we looked over the salted meat, grain, cheese, dried fruit and barrels of ale, it became apparent that there was probably only enough to sustain half our number for any length of time.

"Well, we're not going to get pissed very often are we?" Eduard commented drily, summing up the situation pretty well.

"We'll make do. There are woods around here which belong to the villa and which should allow for hunting," I said. "I guess we are also going to have to get used to eating lots of fish," I added, thinking about the fishing village close at hand.

Having finished our tour, Randolph departed with his men very soon thereafter and we settled in. Our first task was to ensure we had enough food to get us through the winter. I sent Lilla to the village to see what he could find. By performing a series of stories from the North, the bard soon had the villagers eating out of his hand. They willingly agreed to provide us with a weekly delivery of fish – fresh, or smoked if the weather prevented their boats from putting to sea – in exchange for which Lilla agreed to entertain them through the winter. Next, he went off to Cicestre and managed to negotiate a supply of ale and more grain as barter for a delivery of dried herbs and medicinal plants – these at least seemed to be in copious supply at the villa.

Meanwhile, I sent Cuthbert and some of his scouts out hunting. They spent several weeks seeking game in the woods between Boseham and the border with West Seax. This had two purposes, of course. He was able to bring us back frequent supplies of hare, deer and even pigeon to supplement the villa's meagre supplies. It also meant he could keep an eye on West Seax.

"We managed to get close to a town some miles beyond the border," he told me, returning from one expedition. "It's called Aemelesworp and it seems there is a small garrison there. "

"How many men?" I asked.

"Perhaps thirty."

"Probably doing the same job as us: watching the border,"

Harald commented. "I don't think we need worry about them for the present."

I agreed with Harald, but nonetheless I asked Cuthbert to maintain a vigilant watch on Aemelesworp through the winter months. The garrison's base might become the kicking off point for an invasion after all.

Whilst Cuthbert and Lilla were solving the problem of our supplies, I and the rest of the company turned our attention to the villa itself. Most of the decay and damage of the last two hundred years had been to the west part of the villa. As that was closest to the head of the waterway it was not a likely route of attack. Nevertheless, I wished us to fortify our position as well as we could, so I sent Eduard and other burly companions into the woods to gather timber for repairing the walls.

Here, Harald and Guthred were surprisingly useful. During the last two years of their stay in Cantwareburh they had seen how the monks repaired the stone walls of the church they were restoring. Although most of our people lived in wooden structures, there were some, both Angles and native Britons, who continued to live in the crumbling remains of Roman houses – much as my own family had done – and who attempted to maintain them as best they could. Having observed this, Harald and Guthred were able to give us a few suggestions on how to patch up some of the walls using the piles of stone, brick and tile that lay in and around Boseham. While that work was underway, I set some of the men to digging a ditch around the villa to increase the height advantage of those inside. By the combination of all this: the makeshift stonemasonry and the use of wood and ditch, we were able to make the villa relatively defendable. Certainly more so than it had been when we arrived.

When the work was done I walked down to the sea with Lilla

and examined the stone statue Randolph had mentioned. It was around fifteen feet tall and stood beside the shore. The weather had eroded the features, but it was still possible to make out that the face had been cleanshaven and the hair cut short. Around the man's torso the sculptor had carved what looked like a cloak.

"The locals say it is Vespasian, others think it is Trajan," Lilla commented.

"Who are they?"

"Who were they, you mean," Lilla gave me a look of disdain. "You are a bloody ignorant fellow aren't you?"

"So you have often told me," I retorted.

"They were Roman emperors hundreds of years ago. Maybe one of them built this place. Maybe he lived here."

As he spoke, a blast of freezing cold air hit us. I shivered, "Well we live here now – so let's go back to the villa and have some ale."

By Yuletide the winter storms had begun in earnest and the fields soon turned to impassable mud. It was clear there would be no campaign now for several weeks. So finally we relaxed and I allowed the men some days of rest, feasting and drinking. Fires roared in the hearths and Harald had even managed to get some of the furnaces working that drove hot air under the floors of the rooms.

With boar or deer roasting on the spit and the local ale and wine not at all bad, it should have been a hospitable enough winter, yet despite having many friends around me I felt maudlin and alone. I missed Aidith, Cuthwine and little Sian. I hated being away from them for so long, not knowing what was going on at home and how they were. So I drowned my sorrows in ale, drinking far more than was good for me as we waited out the winter.

Chapter Six
Rowenna
Early 607

"Ah, Lord Hussa there you are, "King Ceolwulf called out to him as he walked into the hall. "I have considered your report and was just about to send for you."

It was a few weeks after their arrival. Hussa's men had spent the time repairing equipment, resting and drinking a lot of ale. Many, including Rolf and Octe, had been out pursuing the women who frequented the taverns and brothels in Witanceastre. Hussa, meanwhile, had spent much of the time in his room with Rowenna. They had lain with each other many times, of course, but while that was thrilling and joyful, he had found to his surprise that he enjoyed their other shared moments and conversations as much if not more. As a result there was a lightness to his step and a warmth of contentment in his chest that he had never felt before. Was this happiness? Was this how Cerdic felt? If so, then maybe he envied his brother even more.

"Your Majesty, have you decided how we may be of service?" he now asked.

Ceolwulf nodded. "Yes, we will make use of your information. I am campaigning with my western companies over towards Dumnonia in the spring. I will leave the campaigns in the East to Lord Boyden. If Boseham is lightly defended, as you say it is, then it should fall easily enough. At the end of the winter, you will take command of an army of three companies whose purpose is to capture the fort there then press on to Cicestre. Boyden, meanwhile, will take the bulk of our warriors and lay an ambush for the Suthseaxe and Cantia's main army. He will draw them into West Seax but not engage them. Once news reaches them that Boseham has fallen and the supply lines from Cicestre are threatened, we can expect a degree of panic. Then, as they withdraw, he will fall upon them, harrying them all the way to Cicestre. Finally, he will crush them against the city of Cicestre, which you will hold."

Hussa considered the plan. Three companies against the one which Cerdic commanded would make for a good chance of success despite the fortifications of Boseham and his brother's skills.

"Well, Northumbrian?" Boyden asked. "Why do you hesitate? This is how you can prove to me your worth and win our trust. Do you not think you can succeed?"

"If you give me three companies and assuming Lord Boyden fulfils his part of the plan, then I will take the fortress, sire." Thinking about his brother, he added with a wolfish smile, "And I will have a lot of fun doing it."

"Then it is agreed. Bring your men to my tables tonight and we will celebrate."

"I will, sire, thank you." Hussa bowed and withdrew.

He and his men spent the winter mostly in Witanceastre. There were meetings with the king and Boyden, going over details of the attack. Hussa studied at length maps of the area around Boseham and the beginnings of a plan began to emerge. He travelled with Rolf to a small village just inside the border with Suthseaxe to assess the terrain in the area and to establish a base for the companies that would launch the attack.

At Yuletide he returned to the city and reported to the king on the development of his plan for attacking Suthseaxe and Cantia.

"I will confer with Lord Boyden on what you have told me," Ceolwulf said. "We will talk some more later."

50

Hussa returned to the house he occupied with his huscarls. He had something he wanted to discuss with Rowenna; something that had been building in his mind for some time to the extent that he could no longer ignore it.

Lying together in the contented aftermath of love making, he asked. "Did you say the king owned you?"

"Yes, I imagine so, although it is Lord Boyden I answer to. Why do you ask?"

Hussa paused, asking himself the same question. Just what was he thinking? Shrugging the question aside, he spoke without further thought. He just knew what he wanted to do; logic had nothing to do with it. "Then I will talk to Boyden tomorrow and make him an offer."

Rowenna gaped at him. "You want to buy me?"

He paused a moment then said, "No, Rowenna, I want to free you."

"You want to do *what?*" Rolf asked the next day as they walked through the centre of Witanceastre, the other huscarls trailing along behind. "

"You heard me, "Hussa said.

"I don't get it. She's a slave. One moment you are practically kicking Octe in the balls for trying it on with this girl and the next you want to buy her freedom?" Baffled, Rolf shook his head. "You don't have a problem drinking the king's ale or eating his meat, so what is the issue with using the women he provides for your fun?"

"That is different," Hussa replied.

Rolf frowned. "Don't see why. You're a lord; kings and lords can do what they want with women. That's what they're there for. Take my advice; just hump her and enjoy it!"

"Leave it now!" Hussa growled.

"I…" I said leave it! "

Rolf held up his hands. "Very well, but tell me this: you ask for my advice all the time, why not this time?"

"I ask your advice about battles… and sometimes beer. "

"Why?"

"Because you know a lot about battles and beer."

"I know quite a bit about women too."

"Maybe, but I make my own decisions about them – and I've had enough of this conversation. Now take the men on and get all the repairs done."

So saying, Hussa tossed Rolf a pouch of money that clinked with silver nuggets and old Roman coins, the latter stamped with the heads of the emperors and their names, like 'Diocletian' and 'Magnus Maximus'. The Saxons did not mint their own coins but were happy enough to use any they came across. Silver was silver after all.

"What about you?" Rolf asked.

Hussa pointed towards the bulky shape of Ceolwulf's hall. "I want to see Boyden and find out what he and the king think about the information we brought back from Suthseaxe."

"Very well, lord."

Deep in thought, Hussa walked slowly towards the king's hall. Like Rolf he had known enough women these past ten years. Each palace and lord's hall had brought with it any number of 'bed warmers'; gifts from King Aethelfrith or one of his lesser kings and nobles whose halls they travelled between. Hussa was no fool; given the opportunity he had seldom refused the offer. Each night had been fun enough and yet each morning had found him feeling empty; that in some way something was lacking.

Once again he thought of his halfbrother's cosy little family: of Aidith, whom he had once hoped might fall to his charms but who'd only had time for Cerdic; of their young son, Cuthwine. Hussa knew from his spies in Iago's court that they now had a baby daughter too. Family and home – that was what Cerdic had and he, Hussa, did not. Maybe that was why he had taken such pleasure in destroying their father's villa, the home he should have been part of but had been denied. He had killed Cerdic's mother too, the woman he had held responsible for that denial. Hussa grunted with satisfaction; now that was one woman he had not minded destroying. And yet, despite all this, Cerdic now had a new home and a growing family, while he, Hussa, had nobody; no wife to go home to; no place to call his own. He had sired no children – none that he knew of at least, but if he had they'd be bastards; rejects like himself. Thinking about it hurt. It was like probing an aching tooth.

Dismissing thoughts of Cerdic that made him feel increasingly depressed, Hussa turned his attention to the job in hand. He located the steward supervising the delivery of wine and ale to a storeroom beneath the king's hall.

"Lord Boyden," Hussa said, "I have a proposal for you."

Hussa returned to the house around dusk having spent the afternoon talking to the king and poring over plans for the campaign. He had also struck a deal with Lord Boyden and from him bought ownership of Rowenna. It had cost him twentyfive shillings and as he walked back to the house he wondered what on earth had come over him. As Aethelfrith's lieutenant he had become rich and twentyfive shillings was nothing to him. Yet, despite his new found wealth, Hussa was habitually careful with money. He did not waste it, choosing to repair items rather than buy them new, unless they were beyond repair and essential, so why had he just spent twentyfive shillings on this woman's ownership? Were her skills in bed so good? Was that it? Certainly there was no denying she had skills in that department, but that alone was surely not enough? What was it about Rowenna that had made him act so ridiculously out of character?

Rolf and Wilbur were standing outside the door and both looked sombre.

"What is it?" he asked them. "Why are you loitering out here?"

"We were waiting for you, lord," Rolf said. "She is in the hall and we wanted to talk to you first."

"She? Who?"

"Rowenna, my lord."

Hussa was mystified. "What about her?"

"When we had all gone out, Wilbur saw her leaving too."

"So what?" Hussa shrugged. "She no doubt had chores and errands to run."

"Yes, well it's where she went, lord," Rolf said.

"What do you mean? Where did she go?"

"She went across town to a house owned by the steward," Wilbur said.

"You followed her? Why?" Hussa was growing increasingly irritated.

"We were concerned you had fallen under a spell of hers and wanted to know a bit more about her," Rolf replied.

"So you were spying on her?" Hussa demanded, irritation turning to anger.

"We were not the only ones spying!" Wilbur retorted indignantly.

"What do you mean by that? You are suggesting Rowenna is a spy because she visits another house owned by Boyden? She belongs to him for Woden's sake… or at least, she did. Whatever's got into the two of you? Have you got nothing better to do?"

Rolf held up his hands to calm Hussa down, "Thunor's balls, lord, but will you not just listen a moment!"

Hussa bit back a curse. "Go on. I'm listening. And it had better be good!"

"While we were watching, Boyden arrived with a guest. We managed to get near. He left the door open and we saw them inside drinking together. Then Rowenna led this guest to another room. They were in there a fair while, if you catch my drift. When they emerged the man was smiling. He had another drink with Boyden then left. After he'd gone, Rowenna talked with Boyden for a while. We crept closer and overheard her speaking about the man she had 'entertained'. Turns out he's a wine trader. She told Boyden everything the man had said, including something about how he might cut the price of his wine because she had been particularly enjoyable and he fancied her services again. And then I heard her say something about you, though I didn't catch what."

Hussa's face was dark now. For a long time he said nothing, his face angled away, his gaze fixed on a distant building at the end of the street. Then at last he turned back to them.

"Come with me, I have to have a word with my new slave."

"So you bought her after all," Rolf asked.

Hussa nodded. "Yes, and if she is spying on us for Boyden, then I mean to get my money's worth out of her!"

Chapter Seven
Aemelesworp
Early 607

Not long after Yuletide the rains slowed and finally stopped, the weather turned colder and the frosts came along with sleet and snow, which piled into great drifts, cutting off the villa from the outside world for a whole fortnight.

True to form, Eduard had somehow managed to meet a pretty little darkhaired girl from the village and thereafter his winter certainly improved. "Put it this way, mate," he commented to me and Cuthbert, who was as miserable as I was at being away from his family, "I ain't finding it difficult to stay warm at night, if you get what I mean."

"Thanks a lot, Eduard. That makes us feel a whole lot better," Cuthbert replied, before volunteering to go out on another scouting mission to the border as soon as he could get through.

I doubted there was much need as it was deep winter. Even when the drifts had subsided I could not imagine an attack coming any time soon, but bored with the weeks we had spent cooped up in the villa, I decided to go along with him to use up some of the time. Aedann and Lilla felt the same, so it was that the four of us, muffled up in warm clothing, circled up through the woodlands before coming back down along the border, aiming for the road that we would then take home.

Sneaking over the border towards the West Seax village of Aemelesworp, where we knew there was a small garrison, we hid in a thicket nearby to observe the comings and goings. It seemed quiet enough at first, but as we watched and shivered, we noticed two things that disturbed us.

"Cuth," I said quietly. "I thought you said there were only around thirty warriors garrisoned here."

"There were last time I came this far," he replied.

"Well they seem to be breeding," Lilla mumbled dryly, "like mice."

He was correct; there were not merely thirty but now near a hundred warriors in the place. Lilla, of course, took this in his stride. "All part of the adventure that life is," he commented as we counted heads. I was not so happy and glancing at Cuth and Aedann I saw reflected in their faces the same worry that now gnawed at me. That number of warriors was far more than the defence of the area would normally call for.

Secondly, I had spotted two men on horseback deep in conversation. One I did not recognise, but he had an air of authority about him and was presumably the commander of the garrison. He was around my age, tall and muscular with long dark hair and a bushy beard. However, the other man was all too familiar and my jaw dropped at the sight of him.

"Woden's balls!" Aedann exclaimed, taking the words right out of my mouth. "What's that bastard brother of yours up to now?"

I shook my head. "I am not sure, but if he is telling them that the road to Cicestre is guarded by only one company, we might be in for a difficult time."

"How would he know?"

"Well he knew you were coming to Suthseaxe from Aethelberht as he was there when the Bretwalda gave us the task. After that, well, a bit of sneaking about would suffice. He'll have his spies. Maybe he bribed a court official in Cantia or else someone from the fishing village has been tattling I daresay," said Lilla.

"One hundred men – not an army is it?" Cuthbert speculated.

"No, but something's brewing and a hundred can grow," Aedann said.

"That is what worries me," I muttered. "Come on, let's get back to the villa."

We returned to Boseham and informed Hereric and the others. Straight away I sent Cuthbert with a message to Kingsham to say we had seen a hundred men gathering at a village near the border with West Seax. We also added the news that we had spotted an agent of Northumbria. I doubted that Cissa would have heard of Hussa and I was not sure yet what my brother's presence might mean, but one thing was for sure: wherever Hussa was, trouble was sure to follow swiftly afterwards. With a good deal of anxiety I waited to see what form that might take.

By now it was late on in the winter. The thaw had begun some days ago. The earliest plants were beginning to thrust up from the ground and leaf buds on the trees were noticeably fattening. It was, however, not yet spring and we had not expected any attack to come quite so soon, despite what Wynchell had said. Yet, only a week or so after Cuthbert had left for Kingsham with our message, he was back, short of breath and bearing alarming news. I was with Hereric, Harald, Guthred and Lilla when he burst into the villa.

"They are coming, Cerdic," he gasped.

"How many?" Harald asked.

"At least three hundred, lord."

"It seems your mice have bred some more, Lilla," I said.

He smiled, as always taking the news in his stride. Guthred on the other hand was scowling. "We should pull back, retreat to Cicestre and try linking up with Cissa's army," he urged.

I shook my head. "I disagree. We have been given this task and the villa is now as defendable a position as we are likely to find. Cicestre is crumbling and too big to hold. Here at Boseham is a good place to make a stand."

"We also undertook to hold the villa, Guthred," Harald pointed out.

"It does not matter what we have agreed to do," Guthred said. "It does our princes' cause no good if we do the honourable thing and then all die here. What do we care if West Seax and Suthseaxe come to blows? I say we withdraw and let them slaughter each other."

Hereric looked at Guthred and then across to me. He was not the brightest of our pair of Deiran princes – Edwin, his uncle, was by far the more intelligent – but like his father, Aethelric, Hereric did not want for courage. "We will stay," he said firmly. "We gave our word and if we run away now Hussa will have won."

Guthred glared at me as if my influence on the prince was unwelcome. Then he just nodded resignedly. "As you wish, my prince."

"How far away are they?" Harald asked.

Cuthbert thought for a moment, his face screwed up in concentration before he answered. "So many will not be able to travel as fast as I did, so I expect they will be another two to three hours, maybe."

"Well, if we are staying I suggest we get ready," Guthred said.

We deployed the men. Guthred and his sons went with a third of the company – thirty warriors – to the east side of the villa, which ran adjacent to the track coming down from the Roman road. I took my warriors from the Wicstun Company to the north side, whilst Harald gathered together the remainder of the men from Cantia along with his own huscarls. They took up position in the central garden to act as a reserve and stand by in readiness to rush to the support of whoever needed them most. I sent Prince Hereric to join them, but he followed me to a window in the north wall.

"Just where do you think you are going, Prince Hereric?" I asked him.

The young prince waved his sword at me. "I am going to fight," he said.

I snorted. "You bloody well are not. You can go back to the garden with Harald."

He frowned. "Why?"

"Because it won't do to get you killed, will it my prince?"

"Then you will just have to make sure that doesn't happen, won't you, Cerdic," he retorted loftily.

"My prince...!" I implored him.

"We are here to make an impression on these people, Cerdic. I can't hide away in the background. Princes of the House of Aelle must be seen to be willing to risk themselves if we are to ask others to fight and die for us."

I turned to Eduard in exasperation, but found he was nodding his head and grinning at me. "He's right, Cerdic."

"Oh... very well, as you will, I give in. But since you have a lot to say on the matter Eduard, you great ox, you have just volunteered for a job: you have to keep Prince Hereric alive!"

The grin dropped from his face. "Great. Thanks, Cerdic."

"Don't mention it. Come on, let's get ready."

Along the northern side of the palace the men of the Wicstun Company were occupying windows and gaps in the wall, which had been barricaded with rubble, wood and anything we could find from inside and around the villa.

Hereric moved to an empty window and Eduard took up his post alongside him. Aedann and I stood at the next window and Cuthbert, along with another couple of archers, crept up to the roof and positioned themselves on a rafter, bows at the ready.

I looked out of the window. There was a bare field outside, dug over after the harvest and divided by the northsouth track from more fields to the east. On the far side of the fields, maybe a hundred and fifty paces away, there was woodland. The trees extended out of sight to the east, arching round to join the great swathe of woodland that ran into the Weald to the east of Cicestre. To the south the trees thinned out and then stopped abruptly at the edge of the marshy land that capped the nearby sea inlet. This would be the battlefield, this strip of land between villa, forest and sea – here blood would be spilled between the stones, the woods and the water.

We waited. The worst part of battle is waiting. Oh, don't get me wrong – battle is terrifying and dangerous, but the actual fighting takes over and dominates everything so there is precious little room and time for thinking. But when you are waiting before the battle, thoughts come easily – too easily really. You worry about dying; you worry about pain and injury; you worry about those you might lose and those who would miss you if you were killed. The fear gnaws at the soul and tugs at the heart.

In the end, to fill the void I walked across to Hereric to ask him a question. Around us I could hear murmured conversation as other men distracted themselves and tried to occupy the time before their fate was decided.

"My prince…"

He looked up at me and I could see that he was pale, his hands trembling. He turned away, embarrassed that I should see his fear.

"It is all right, Hereric," I said softly, dropping the honorific and speaking as if to a family member, a younger brother perhaps. "We are all afraid. Only a madman does not fear battle and you are not a madman. Just keep your sword in your hand, your shield on your arm and face towards your enemy. The rest is down to the gods."

He nodded. "Were you going to ask me a question?" He asked after a moment.

I saw that the tremble had now gone and I smiled. "Yes, what is the real reason you wanted to be here at the forefront of the battle?"

He looked at me again, hesitating before he spoke. "You want the truth?"

I nodded.

"Because of your brother," he said.

His answer took me aback. "Hussa?" I frowned.

"I want to kill him. When my father died I was almost too young to fight, certainly too young to kill Hussa. But he it was who killed my father. I owe him a death... he owes me a life."

"You will have to get in line," Eduard muttered from Hereric's other side.

There certainly were a lot of folk in that villa who wanted Hussa dead, I reflected, and no one more than I. "We will do it together one day," I promised. "And maybe today is that day!"

"We can but hope," Eduard growled.

"Here they come!" Cuthbert shouted from the roof.

And come they did.

First we saw a couple of dozen scouts. They had pushed through the trees and were crouched down in the shadows for several minutes observing us, counting our numbers and assessing the defences we occupied. Then several slunk back into the trees to report what they had seen to their commanders. The remaining scouts watched us and we watched them and we both waited.

Then their main body arrived. At first we heard the stamping of their boots on the broken stone surface of the road. Then we saw the tips of their spears and their banners flapping in the breeze. From what I could see there were three companies, each carrying banners of red and yellow emblazoned with creatures of legend: dragons; twolegged wyverns with wings, and wingless, serpentlike wyrms. The noble houses of West Seax had taken these fearsome sigils as their own. We had all heard tales of such beasts living deep in the southern forests and having seen the Weald I could well believe it.

Finally, the men beneath those banners came into view: grimfaced, determined and wellequipped, many of them armoured in mail shirts and armed with fine swords as well as spears. This was going to be a hard fight, I thought with a grimace, glancing over at Eduard. He just grinned at me and hefted his axe. The great oaf was clearly relishing the battle that was about to happen.

The first company through the trees wheeled neatly to their right and ran down the wood's edge before coming to a halt. Then they turned left to face us and readied shields and spears. The next company mirrored the move off to the left of the road. The final part of the army formed up on the road itself, spilling out on either side of it.

A figure on horseback rode forward – the same man I had seen speaking to Hussa in Aemelesworp. He stopped thirty paces away and addressed us.

"I am Nerian, Earl of the Eastern Marches. Do I speak to the company of Hereric of Deira?" he demanded.

63

"Prince Hereric, son of King Aethelric commands here," I replied. This was technically the case, although each man here would have known that Harald and I were really in charge. I emphasized the prince's rank though.

Nerian turned to stare at me. "I have a message then for Prince Hereric. My lord, King Ceolwulf, would ask why you interfere in affairs that are none of your own. Our dispute over this land is with Cissa of Suthseaxe. Go now from here and no blood need be shed today. What does Prince Hereric say? "he replied, taunting us with the title. He was saying that Hereric really had no status. Kings had status, but an uncrowned son of a king – an Aetheling – was merely kingworthy. Hereric was one of several who might become king. Yet so far from home and with Aethelfrith in power in Northumbria there was little chance of that. Around me I could feel the restlessness in the men. Many were asking the same question. Why are we here? Would dying here today really help get Hereric or Edwin into power in Northumbria? I had to say something before the men's morale crumbled. Yet at that moment I could not think of anything.

I have said before that Aethelric was a bloody terrible prince and king but made good speeches and today it was his son who came to my rescue. Prince Hereric stood up so that his head and torso could be seen clearly in the window. Then he shouted a reply, clear and loud so that everyone in both armies would hear his defiance.

"I have given my word to defend this land. The word of a Prince of the House of Aelle. That word will not be broken. This means that this land today will be treated as Deiran land and Deiran blood will be spilt defending it if need be. You should go home, if indeed you desire no bloodshed this day."

Nerian glared at Hereric and then, without giving a reply, tugged on the reins, dug in his heels and galloped back to his men.

"Nice speech!" I murmured to Hereric.

"Really?" he said, blushing at the compliment.

"Really," I replied, and meant it.

Then the West Saxons started hammering spear on shield and we turned our attention back to our enemy. There was little prologue; none of the shouted insults and crude gestures that often precede battle as warriors work themselves into the fury they need to kill or be killed. After only a few moments of gathering their courage, they advanced in good order towards us. First the company north of the road moved off and marched across the field. I took the risk of getting hit by arrow or slingshot by poking my head out of the window in order to look to the east. There the second company had halted around fifty paces away from the villa then wheeled so as to face us.

I turned and signalled one of my men. "Run to Lord Harald and tell him they intend to hit us on both the north and east walls simultaneously. He must be ready to come to the support of whichever wall weakens."

The man nodded and ran off. Looking back out of the window, I could now see that the western company was also advancing towards us. The third company, with Nerian at their head, was waiting on the road, ready to exploit a breakthrough on either wall. I dropped back down, readied my shield and drew Catraeth, my short stabbing sword; one of the kind that had once been used by the Roman legions. Many years after it came into existence I had taken it off the body of the first man I killed. It was the best sword to use in close fighting.

When the enemy were thirty paces away Cuthbert and his archers let fly their arrows. All along the walls, our own men were using slings and arrows to pick off a few of the enemy in order to weaken the attack and begin to erode their confidence. Yet we knew the real test would come when the shield wall arrived. For me now, the battle had narrowed down to this one wall... this one company. I lost sight of the bigger picture and silently prayed to Tiw, God of warriors, that Harald had an overview, because now my job was simple – to keep a hundred West Saxons out of the villa with a mere twentyfive of my own men.

"Who was with me at Calcaria?" I called out.

Many men shouted. "Aye!"

"Who was with me at Catraeth?"

Again many shouted. "Aye!"

"Who was with me at Degsastan?"

They all replied, apart from Hereric. I glanced at him and added. "Who fought with me at Tre'r Ceiri, the City of the Giants?"

Now he too nodded and roared with all the others. "Aye, me!"

"Remember those fights," I shouted. "Remember how we won. We fought together, we were brave and trusted each other. Do the same and we will win today!"

Then I shut up because the enemy were charging!

Chapter Eight
Boseham
Early 607

A javelin flew through the window narrowly missing my head. I swore loudly as I ducked away from the opening. A moment later I was back there to find a gangly youth and a scarfaced brute clambering up the barricade. Two thrusts with Catraeth sent them both tumbling back into the shield wall, the youth screeching in agony and clutching a gushing wound on his arm, the brute, his throat slashed open, already dead. Glancing to my left I saw Eduard smash his shield into the face that had just appeared in the opening and then swing his axe, taking the man's arm off at the shoulder. I shouted in alarm as I spotted beyond him a West Saxon who had reached the top of the barricade and was about to throw his spear down at Hereric. The prince seemed frozen in indecision.

An arrow pierced the man's spear arm and he dropped the weapon. Whilst he was still struggling to pull a sword out of its baldrick, Eduard bellowed out an order to Hereric.

"Move yourself, Aetheling! Stab the git!"

That seemed to wake him up. He thrust up with his longsword, punching the blade through the man's belly and neatly pulling it out again as the man fell away, then stepping back to face his next foe. The young prince's training was at last taking over; he was not thinking now, just acting as a warrior should.

Close by me Aedann was holding back three men at once, his shield deflecting the thrusts of their spears and his skilful sword arm slashing back and forth. His opponents seemed none too keen to risk that arm and held back whilst Aedann taunted them, mixing Welsh swear words in with English at the same time, confusing, frustrating and infuriating them. Despite the fighting I found myself grinning at that.

In any battle you will find most men hang back. They won't run away, perhaps, but neither will they take too many risks. Aedann's foes were of this type. They grouped together, taking protection from each other and edging forward, caution being their watchword.

The next man I saw through the window in front of me was of a different sort. One like Eduard, who lived for battle, was fearless and knew a ferocity that few men experience. I had felt it on occasion in the heat of battle, but not often. I could tell that this man knew it every day. He had left his shield behind and wore no helmet. Indeed, not even did he take the protection granted by a shirt of mail. He wore only a linen shirt over his britches, ignoring the cold winter air as he roared at us. He bore a huge, twohanded sword, which he swung around his head as he stood atop the barricade, wide eyes glaring at us.

Hereric, abandoning caution in favour of recklessness, called out a cry of challenge and moved towards the man. He did not get far before Eduard tugged him back.

"Easy boy. Let him come at us. Then we gut the bastard together, eh?"

"Fancy your chances with me do you, Northumbrian?" the man taunted.

Eduard just grinned in response. "Try me," he said.

"I'll wipe that smirk off your face," the warrior yelled and came at Eduard, huge sword swinging. Eduard took the blow on his shield and hacked back with his axe, but by then the veteran was already moving back out of reach. Behind him three more warriors were climbing over the barricade. One gave a throttled cry and fell dead, one of Cuthbert's arrows sticking from his throat. I moved to intercept the other two, but had to dodge to one side as Eduard's foe leapt forward and aimed a blow at me. I deflected it with a frantic flick of Catraeth, but the warrior's huge blade knocked my sword out of my grip. Then Eduard was back at the man, axe and shield driving him away.

The other two enemy warriors saw my unarmed state and came at me, but they had failed to notice Wreccan, my longsword, swinging in a scabbard at my hip. I drew it and saw them hesitate at sight of that long blade. That pause gave me enough time to counterattack, impaling one of them and then, as I cut back out of the man's belly, taking the other in the throat with the return stroke.

I looked over in time to see Eduard slip on some blood and go down on one knee. His foe's eyes widened in triumph and he lifted the great twohanded sword ready to cut my friend in half. What he did not see, until too late, was Hereric darting in, his sword angled upwards aimed at the man's heart. As he thrust it home, the giant warrior stared at him, disbelief flashing quickly over his face before he collapsed, his lifeblood pulsing from his chest.

Eduard laughed as he climbed to his feet. "What was that about me looking after our prince, Cerdic? "he chortled as we recovered our position at the barricade.

Retrieving Catraeth, I left Aedann, Eduard and Hereric, backed up by Cuthbert, to hold our part of the north wall. I needed to check that the rest of our company were holding their positions. I darted through the interconnecting rooms, relieved to see that so far as I could tell we were keeping the enemy out of the villa, but not without cost. I was just about to retrace my steps when Godric came running to find me.

"Earl Harald asks that you come at once," he panted.

"What is it? Have they broken through the east wall?"

He shook his head and ran on ahead of me. "This way," he flung over his shoulder.

I followed, noticing at once that he was not leading me to Guthred on the north wall, but towards the west wall; towards the sea. We hastened on through a door into a gallery that ran along the west side of the villa. The room beyond had large windows which would once have let in the summer sunlight – warm rooms that the Romans would have enjoyed through the hot months. On this cold winter's day the sunlight was weak and a sea mist lingered on the flat ground that led towards the nearby inlet. Harald was in the room assembling his reserve.

"What is it?" I asked. "What's happening?"

Harald simply pointed out of the windows. Peering in the direction of his finger I made out several mistshrouded shapes on the water. A dozen or so small boats were being rowed towards us. As they came closer I saw that each held around ten warriors and standing in the prow of the middle boat, peering back at the villa, was Hussa.

"Woden's buttocks!" I cursed.

"Yes, indeed, the sly bastard has tricked us yet again, "Harald said. "If it were not for a runner sent from the fishing village to warn us, he might have made it to shore before we knew of it."

I glanced around. Harald had but five and twenty men. Having pinned us against the east and north walls, Hussa had then brought another company by sea to outflank us!

Harald and I looked behind us, back through into the villa's garden. We then looked at each other, both knowing we'd had the same thought: could we run? If we ran now – abandoned the villa and made a run for it before Hussa arrived – could we reach Cicestre and perhaps get help? Yet we knew at once that such a course of action was hopeless. We could never disengage the rest of the company. Oh yes, we two and a few others could get away, but at the price of letting the rest of our company perish. We let that faint hope die and grimaced at each other, both knowing that outnumbered and outflanked as we were, in all likelihood we would all perish, but we could not abandon our men. Nearby, Lilla stood watching us, not commenting, just observing, a half smile on his face.

"We stay!" I said.

"We stay!" Harald agreed.

I turned away and watched the boats row the last few yards and then beach on the gravel bank. The first few warriors leapt over the side and waded towards us. Harald's men took up positions at the windows and he and I joined them.

"Ah well," I said. "Maybe we can at least kill Hussa before we die."

The enemy had now formed up into a shield wall and marched forward, spears, swords and axes hammering against shields as they came on. We had no archers here, but we had Francisca throwing axes and Angon javelins. We made do as best we could, flinging them towards our foe. One or two found a target in the gaps between shields or struck unprotected arms and legs, and maybe half a dozen men fell wounded or dead. Yet it did not stop the others.

Hussa was in their centre now, his fine chain shirt shining in the winter sunlight, one arm pointing forward, his right hand grasping his sword. I recognised that magnificent blade. He had won it by beating me in a tournament when we were but seventeen, back in the days when I lived secure with my parents in the villa, while he lived in a hovel in the village with his mother, whom my father had got with child. My mother was enraged when she discovered his adultery and Hussa's existence was never acknowledged. At least, not in my mother's hearing! But on that distant day, when a tournament was held in the villa's grounds, my halfbrother had won – and it seemed he would win on this day too.

Fate – it mocks us. We believe we have control over our lives and yet we have none. We can plan it all out. We can see a direction that makes sense, and yet the gods and the Norns laugh at our mortal efforts and shatter our plans with a roll of their dice or a move of a pawn on their game board. Thus we came here to Cantia and on to Suthseaxe believing there was a reason to it all – part of a larger plan to return to Northumbria one day. Ironic then that we were now surrounded on three sides, outnumbered three to one and about to perish, all our mortal plans come to naught at the whim of the gods.

Which only goes to show how wrong a man can be. Maybe I could hear Loki's laughter. Yet if so it was not at me… it was at my brother, for at that moment, to the east of the villa a fanfare of horns sounded.

I turned to Harald and frowned. Was this another army come from West Seax to ensure our destruction? Clearly not, for while I had no way of seeing what was going on, I saw Hussa's reaction. He halted his warriors and ran along to the rear of his company. When he reached the end he looked east, along the southern wall of the villa towards the open ground beyond. Even at this distance I could see the colour draining from his face – or maybe I just imagined it – whatever, he stared in dumbstruck horror in that direction. After a moment he shouted orders and with his arms going like windmills indicated that his company should turn and retreat back to the boats.

"What the bloody hell is going on," I said, glancing across at Harald, who shook his head and shrugged.

"Let's find out," Lilla suggested.

Leaving the men to guard the south wall we ran back through to the gardens. As we entered I spotted Guthred and Frithwulf emerge from the north side and almost at the same time Eduard and Hereric joined us from the west.

"The company on the north wall are running, Cerdic," Eduard panted. "I thought we were done for. Half of the enemy were through the windows and we were fighting in the rooms and halls and then someone shouted something and quick as lightning they just turned and ran."

"What on earth…" I began, but Guthred held up a hand to stop me.

"Another army attacked them. We were doing as badly on the east side, I'd lost two men and too many others were wounded. I was about to order a retreat back to here when those horns sounded and from the woodland to the north a whole army arrived. They immediately launched an attack, but not on us. They were attacking the West Saxons. Smashed into their rear and slaughtered about half. The rest ran for it, leaving their dead on the field."

"Who? Who are they?" I asked, mystified.

"We saw two banners above the new army. One group fought under the banner of swallows on a field of blue…" Guthred answered.

"Cissa… the South Saxons? "

Ignoring my interruption he continued, "And the other under a red banner with a white horse rearing on its hind legs."

I gasped. "Cantia… that means Aethelberht? "

73

There was a movement over near the gate. The sole guard we had left there was talking to a group of men on horseback. He moved to one side to let them enter and as they passed out of the shadow of the archway into the sunlight we saw the banners Guthred had described. Next to the standard bearer carrying the red flag of Cantia, Aethelberht was riding towards us and beside him a young man with a red beard and intensely blue eyes. The Suthseaxe blue flag adorned by swallows flapped over his head, born by the steward we had met in Kingsham at the end of the autumn. The young man could only be Cissa, King of the South Saxons.

We all bowed in greeting as the pair approached.

"Hail, Prince Hereric of Deira," Cissa said. "I give you my thanks for undertaking the defence of this villa of Boseham. With your help we have smashed Ceolwulf's army. I have men pursuing them as we speak. They will not get away; we captured their camp before attacking here. We took gold, ale, food and slaves and will share them with you as reward, for this defeat will hurt West Seax and stop Ceolwulf's ambitions – for a while at least."

"Did... did you know he would attack here?" Hereric asked.

Cissa glanced at Aethelberht before answering. "We did not know with certainty. We expected an attack further north, possibly against Suthseaxe and Cantia, going around the Weald. King Aethelberht, however, came up with a plan to let West Seax believe the south road to Cicestre lay open, guarded only by a single company here at Boseham. As Aethelberht hoped, it proved too tempting and Ceolwulf attacked you. We had wintered not far away, far enough back from the border not to be seen, but not in Kingsham where I knew he would have spies. We also made it seem we were in the North by spreading false reports and lighting fires up there. Once we received your message of an

74

army gathering we knew we had him, but we had to wait till he launched his attack in order to surprise him."

I listened to Cissa but was looking at the Bretwalda and to him I directed a question. "When King Cissa says you let West Seax believe we were vulnerable here, sire, you mean you relied on Hussa telling them?"

Aethelberht shrugged and then nodded. "I had made a few assumptions about your brother," he said.

Lilla had been right. He had warned me that Aethelberht looked into a man's soul. We thought we were being tested, Hereric and the rest of us. And of course we were. We needed to demonstrate our courage, steadfastness and strength of arms. Boseham had proved we would do what we promised to do. Yet it was more than we who were being tested. Hussa was also being put on trial and, by extension, so was his master, Aethelfrith of Bernicia. The Bretwalda had taken the issue of Northumbria and boiled it down to what we and Hussa would do when we were both offered an opportunity, in our case to prove our worth, and in Hussa's case, to destroy us. Suspecting Hussa of doubledealing, Aethelberht had confided to him that Cicestre was vulnerable, counting on him sharing this knowledge with Cantia's enemy, Ceolwulf of West Seax. The wily Bretwalda had used my brother as a decoy and us as bate. Hussa's duplicity had enabled our victory at Boseham.

It seemed to me that the conflict in the North was drawing in more and more of Britannia and here at Boseham battle lines in the South were being defined. We now had a new enemy in West Seax and new allies in Cantia and Suthseaxe.

Deep in thought, I became aware that King Cissa was speaking to me. "Are you going to offer us a drink?" He asked. "We have brought three oxen to roast today. When you have dealt with your dead and wounded, let us celebrate our victory and talk about the future."

Fire pits were dug in the garden and the three oxen slaughtered and lifted above the flames. While the meat cooked we broke out the ale and wine in the main hall of the villa, to which more was added, brought in wagons from Cicestre. The drink was flowing and soon there was laughter and music. Lilla, who had been tending the wounded and dressing their injuries – although thanks to the timely arrival of the two kings, these were few – improvised a tale of the battle of Boseham and set us all as heroes in the piece, diplomatically including Cissa and Aethelberht.

Later, Cissa spoke to Hereric for a while and I overheard the words 'marriage' and 'grant of land'. It transpired that Cissa was proposing an alliance with our Deiran prince, this to be formalised by a marriage between Hereric and a princess of the South Saxons. Several names were mentioned, including that of 'Breguswith'. It was the first time I had heard that name mentioned, but not the last.

I sipped my ale and thought of my own wife, Aidith. With the battle won we could hope to return home and gods willing I would see her soon.

Chapter Nine
Hussa's Rage
Early 607

"Woden's balls! I had him! I had that bastard brother in my hands. That stinking villa had practically fallen to me. I had companies on three sides breaking in. A matter of moments, that's all it would have taken and they would have been on the run. I had Cerdic in my sight. He would not have got away, I can tell you that!"

Hussa threw a goblet of ale across the room so it smashed against the far wall. He and Rowenna were alone in the hall at Aemelesworp, the village inside the West Seax border from which he had launched the attack. His huscarls knew better than to stay near him when he was in this mood. Nothing made Hussa in a worse temper than losing, and of all people, losing to his brother in particular.

"What happened?" Rowenna asked softly.

Hussa glared at her. "Haven't you been listening to anything I have been saying woman?"

"Oh I have been listening, but you have been screaming so loud that I've understood hardly any of the words. Maybe if you stop shouting, calm down and tell me what happened?"

Hussa glared at her again but then took a deep breath in an effort to calm himself. "Look, I had three companies. One hit the north wall. One swung round to hit them in the east wall. I took the third on the boats and came from the west to outflank them. We had them! We had them surrounded."

"So what happened?"

"Boyden happened that's what."

Rowenna frowned. "What do you mean?"

"Well, you know the plan – I told you. He was supposed to be drawing Cissa and Aethelberht further into West Seax. The idea was to allow me time to take Boseham. He was only supposed to turn and move against them when Suthseaxe and Cantia heard of the fall of Boseham, and then he was to attack, harassing them all the way south. They would then be crushed between Boyden's army and my own, either at Boseham or in Cicestre. That was the plan. But we did not get that far did we? Boyden must have arsed it up because something went wrong and Cantia and Suthseaxe turned up at Boseham before I could take the villa. Boyden was nowhere in sight. Ten companies to three. I didn't stand a chance. I was lucky to get out of there with half of my men. Chances are Cissa's men are picking over the spoils in our camp even now."

"Well it wasn't your fault was it? I mean, if Boyden made a mistake…"

Hussa shook his head. "Boyden won't see it that way. And there is a serious chance that neither will Ceolwulf. Everything I tried to achieve here in West Seax could be a waste of time. After this disaster I will be lucky to get out of West Seax alive, let alone secure an alliance between Aethelfrith and Ceolwulf."

"But that is not what is bothering you the most is it?" Rowenna asked.

Hussa glanced at her and was surprised again at how perceptive she was. She certainly had skills; her understanding of what was going on inside a man's head was clearly one of her many talents.

"No. It's Cerdic. Every time he beats me it reminds me of… well, our past. How mother and I were so badly treated and how he always had all the advantages."

"You make him sound like some sort of spoiled child. From what you say there is more to him than that surely?"

"Oh, he is certainly a good man," Hussa replied, putting stress on the word 'good' and curling his lip. "In fact impossibly so at times. Even when the odds are against him, when any decent, sensible man would think about himself, my brother will put himself at risk – and even his family – out of duty and for his beloved Edwin."

"Now you make him sound like a saint!"

Hussa frowned for a moment. "Oh… you mean one of those men of God, servants of this Christ; holy men who can turn away from temptation and resist the lusts of the flesh?" Hussa's voice dripped with sarcasm. Then he paused and thought about Cerdic. "He is no saint in the way you mean, and yet as it happens I believe he is completely faithful to his wife, Aidith."

"Come now, he's a man, isn't he? Put a skilled woman in his bed miles away from his wife and then see how faithful he is," Rowenna said. "What man would not take advantage of the moment? Are you saying Cerdic would not?"

Hussa thought about this. "I'm not sure he would, actually. From what I know of him he is impossibly pure at times."

"If I was a free woman with my own money I would wager that in the bedroom he is no different from any other man. Yet you own me and I have no money of my own to wager," she said resentfully, for Hussa had failed to free her as he had said he would.

A nasty smile crept onto Hussa's face. "Tell you what; I'll take you up on that wager. You will go to Boseham, I will have a boatman row you close and then bring you back before dawn. Over there is a victorious army; they will all be drinking and whoring tonight. You are to find Cerdic and attempt to seduce

79

him. If you can get him into bed with you I'll make good on the wager and free you. What do you say?"

"I thought you told your men that you did not use women in this way!" Rowenna scowled. "And you promised to free me once before."

Hussa gave her a cold look. "Which shows how much of a fool I am. That was before I discovered you were whoring for Boyden and also acting as his spy. Did you think I wouldn't find out? You have your talents, Rowenna. I bought them and I will use them. Now you will spy for me. Do as I say. Go to the enemy camp, find out what you can about the alliance between Cantia, Suthseaxe and Hereric, then use your special talents on my brother," he leered at her. "If you are successful, I will again think about freeing you."

"You can't be serious!"

Now it was Hussa who scowled. "Do as I tell you, woman. Get yourself out of here and onto a boat. Oh, and don't think about running away. Remember that your mother is still in Witanceastre. I bought you. I could buy her too and life as my property could turn very bad for her. "

Rowenna stared at him. "You're threatening me? To think I rather liked you that first night. You seemed kind and gentle. In the end you are not much different from all the other thugs that Boyden had me entertain."

"Just bugger off and see if you can entertain my brother!"

"You're an evil bastard!" she screamed at him.

Hussa laughed. "Oh, just go. Any insults you fling my way I have heard before, believe me."

Rowenna got to her feet, gave Hussa a disgusted look then flounced out of the hall.

When she had gone, Hussa found a clean goblet and poured himself some ale from the jug. A few miles away his brother would be celebrating a victory surrounded by his friends. "And I have just sent him a woman!" Hussa exclaimed. Not that he cared about Rowenna, she was nothing to him, leastways that is what he kept telling himself. Why then was he fighting the urge to go after her and stop her from leaving?

Looking around the hall Hussa suddenly felt very alone. "Rolf!" he bellowed. He was going to get drunk and he needed a companion to do it with.

— Boseham —
Later that Night

In Boseham we celebrated our victory into the night. The wine and ale flowed and we drank and laughed. Cissa raised a great cheer by announcing that some women would be joining us – those they had captured from the West Seax camp. A good many were brought in and it was clear to me that they were camp followers – whores who have found a way to survive by using their bodies and skills for sex. I have captured women in the past and seen that for the most part they are terrified, screaming and running to get away. There are men who might take pleasure in that, but I have never been one of them. In my experience there is little enjoyment in coupling with a woman who does not want it and much to be had with one who does. The whores led into the hall looked bored rather than terrified. Obviously they saw our entertainment as their job, as if the defeat of their former masters was irrelevant, and truth be told it probably was to them. Churchmen in my later years would frown and look scandalised at the mention of camp followers, yet I too had learnt to

81

survive by using my body and skills as a warrior, why was it any different?

In any event, by that stage I was tired and drunk and giving thought to my bed – on my own I hasten to add. I was married after all and whilst I do not deny that after some months away from Aidith I was tempted by the thought of female company, I was not going to betray her trust with a twopenny whore. I got up to leave, but Eduard pulled me back down and insisted that I finish another flagon of ale with him. Then finally, really quite ridiculously drunk, I staggered to find my bed.

That night my dreams were wild. I dreamt of the battle. Hussa's face came into view, smiling and cunning. 'You won today, brother,' he said, 'but this is just a part of the fight and we have a long way to go yet. In the end the world will see you for what you are and I will have my revenge.' Coming half awake, I forced Hussa away from my thoughts, but as I drifted off again he was replaced by Aidith, Cuthwine and Sian. Behind them I could see flames and smoke. Our children were standing by Aidith's side and she was screaming and waving at me.

I called out to her in terror. Then the flames dissolved and I saw a shape moving towards me in the darkness, thin and lithe – a woman. "Aidith? Is that you?"

"Hush yourself," came the reply. "I am here now," and she slid in under the covers, pulling the furs and wool blankets over her nakedness, her hands now clawing at my tunic and my britches, her long black hair spilling over my chest.

Now, many years later, I look back at that moment and ask myself if I really thought it was Aidith; did I really think I was dreaming? Had the ale befuddled my mind so much that I really did not know what was going on, or had it stirred my desires so that when the woman climbed on top of me I just wanted her and forgot everything else, including Aidith? I will never know for sure.

It was all sweat and writhing bodies and thrusting… and then release. We were more like beasts than man and woman; that much I can recall. And when it was done I fell asleep and at last found oblivion, for I had no more dreams that night; none that I remembered at least.

When I woke next morning I was alone. No one lay beside me in the bed. Yet the chaotic arrangement of the furs and an elusive snatch of memory suggested something had gone on. Also, I was naked, which was unusual given my drunken state the night before when I would normally have flung myself fully clothed under the furs. My last clear memory was of drinking with Eduard before I came to bed. Had it been simply a dream of passion and lust and nothing more, or had a woman come to me and climbed into my bed? No, surely not. Months of abstinence, the tensions of battle and relief of victory, coupled with half a barrel of ale; that was all it was. I told myself I had imagined it all in a lustfilled dream. And yet one so vivid that I could still feel her hands on my skin, her midnightblack hair cascading over me.

In an effort to clear these images from my mind I shook my head. And wished I hadn't, for a herd of wild horses was galloping through it. I was also extremely thirsty, my tongue like a lump of sawn timber and the inside of my mouth like a cess pit. Getting out of bed I went to find a drink and a bucket of cold water. I gulped down some small beer and then upended the bucket over my head and, despite the winter weather, went out into the cold dawn air.

I felt someone come up behind me. It was Cuthbert. He gave me a strange look – a mixture of suspicion and uncertainty.

"You all right, Cuthbert?" I asked.

He tilted his head to one side and looked me up and down, making me suddenly conscious of my nakedness. "I am fine. What about you?" he said.

"What do you mean?"

"Last night when I got up for a piss I thought I saw someone going into your room. I..." he hesitated, "...I thought it was a woman. None of my business, of course, but I assumed she was one of the captured whores and I was a bit surprised. "He shrugged, "Not that it matters. Like I said, none of my business."

"Well actually, yes, it is. If I'd had another woman, I mean. You are married to my sister after all. That makes us brothers and Aidith your sister by marriage and you care about her."

He nodded, "Yes I do, the children too. I wouldn't want to see them hurt."

"Don't worry. I love them all more than my life. I would never be unfaithful to Aidith, even with a whore. I think someone might have come into my room last night, but truth be told I have no memory of what happened, if anything did happen... I was too pissed to know."

He held my gaze for a while. Not exactly judging me, perhaps reappraising me. Surprised maybe by what I had done... or rather, by what he thought I might have done. In the end he just shook his head and followed me into my room, waiting as I pulled on my britches and tunic. I was blue with the cold by this time, which had at least served to clear my head somewhat, though the wild horses were still galloping.

"Well, she is not here now," he said with a half-smile. "Anyway, Cerdic, have we done what we set out to do?"

"Yes... yes we have. More than we planned in fact. Not only have we forged an alliance with Cantia, we are also now allied to Suthseaxe."

"Then is it not time to leave? The ships will be putting to sea again soon."

"Yes, Cuth, it is time to go home."

Over the next few days we gathered our belongings together and the men and I prepared to take the first ship of the spring homeward bound.

It was time to go back to Gwynedd and Aidith. I thought no more about the darkhaired beauty. If indeed she had ever existed she went out of my head like a forgotten dream.

Chapter Ten
Witanceastre
Spring 607

"Well, what happened?" Hussa asked. It was the following afternoon. He had woken that morning with a dry throat, a raging pain in the head and feeling nauseous, to find he was lying on the floor in the great hall of Aemelesworp. Close by, Rolf was snoring heavily. Groaning, Hussa had dragged himself to his feet and then to the bench, where he had sat staring at a tapestry that hung on the wall opposite. It showed a hunting expedition: men with bows and slings pursuing boar and stag through the forest. Further on it depicted their return to the hall, carrying a boar and a deer suspended on branches. The hunters looked happy and joyful that their mission had been a success. Hussa stared. The tapestry stared mockingly back at him as if to ask him how his latest enterprise had fared.

It was as he was pondering this that the doors to the great hall opened letting in bright sunlight and cold air. Rolf groaned and rolled over to face the darkness at the end of the hall, but Hussa turned towards the light and saw Rowenna silhouetted in the doorway.

She stepped into the hall. "Awake now are we?" she asked, picking up some of the abandoned goblets and gathering them together ready to be washed later.

Hussa grunted. "Well, what happened?"

Rowenna stopped what she was doing and looked at him, presumably to ensure she understood which question he was asking.

"Are you sure you want to know?"

Hussa hesitated. Did he want to know what had happened last night at Boseham? A moment later he nodded. "I asked didn't I?" he snapped.

"Very well," Rowenna said, her face tightening. "I went to the enemy camp and it was as you said. The South Saxons were feasting and getting drunk. They had rounded up all your whores and were taking them into the villa. I was able to attach myself to them easily enough – after all, what is one more whore either way?" She glared at him.

"Just go on," he said wearily.

"I managed to get close to a group of the leaders. The way they were talking it seems you walked right into a trap they had concocted, drawing in the West Seax army then giving it a bloody nose."

Hussa frowned. "They are just taking the credit for Boyden's failure to engage them in the North."

"Well if you ask me, it sounded as if they had good reason to take the credit," Rowenna said, but Hussa ignored her.

"Who was there? Could you identify anyone in particular?"

"Well, I think one was King Cissa and one that Prince Hereric. They were talking about him marrying some Suthseaxe princess. That is all I could learn."

"Damn it! That means Hereric has gained the support of Suthseaxe. Aethelfrith will not like that." He frowned. "Did they say anything else?"

She shook her head. "No. Your brother's company, along with the men from Suthseaxe and Cantia were enjoying them-selves too much to waste time talking politics. By then they had consumed a lot of ale and… well, you can guess the rest."

"I do not wish to guess the rest!" Hussa said. "I want you to tell me."

Rowenna arched her eyebrows. "Well, the women went off with whichever men had the coin. "

"And you?" Hussa asked, suddenly nervous of the answer and cursing himself for asking.

"I wandered about avoiding grasping hands whilst I looked for your brother. In the end I discovered he had already gone to bed."

"Bloody typical!"

"He'd had a lot to drink, I think. Anyway, I joined him."

Hussa stared at her. "What do you mean, you joined him?"

Rowenna gawped at him. "I can't say it any plainer. Do I really have to spell it out?"

Hussa slapped his hands on the table in frustration, the sound almost waking Rolf, who stirred and rolled over onto his back. Shortly afterwards his snoring began again.

Breathing a sigh of relief, Hussa nodded. "Yes, Rowenna, you do."

"Pervert!" She retorted, but seeing his thunderous expression, added, "Very well. We humped. Or rather I humped him. He was hardly in a fit state! But yes, we did it. Your brother was well and truly 'seduced'... how much more detail do you want?"

Brushing aside her sarcasm, Hussa laboured the point. "So, you actually did it with him then? He succumbed to your charms?"

"I've just said so haven't I?" Rowenna rolled her eyes. "It wasn't difficult, the man was drunk. Charm had nothing to do with it, believe me. I have yet to meet a drunk who would refuse a naked woman if she got into his bed. You men are not the most discerning of creatures at times."

"That doesn't matter, "Hussa said. "I promised to think about freeing you if you proved me wrong. That was the wager. I confess that I did not expect you to succeed. However, it interests me to learn that Cerdic is not the saint I thought he was."

Rowenna raised a mocking eyebrow. "I couldn't say, we did not exactly have a conversation..."

He stood up and walked towards her. "Anyway, I will free you, it was our agreement. You can go where you will, be what you want to be. From this moment on you are no longer my slave. Now go."

She stared at him,

"My mother is in Witanceastre, I have nowhere else to go. Besides which, despite you being such a mean bastard, as it happens I would like to stay with you."

"I am not good company just now. In any event, I don't think I want a woman who has lain with my brother."

Rowenna glared at him. "But you told me to! It's what I do, or what I did. I spy, I seduce. You said you wanted me to do it for you."

"Yes, you whore, "Hussa's lip curled. "Fine. You want to stay? You can stay on in my household as a servant. To cook and clean and maybe sometimes to spy for me. But I won't have you by my side or in my bed. I don't want my brother's leavings."

"Bastard!" She slapped him across the face. "You're an utter bastard to use me and then abandon me in this way."

He caught hold of her wrist, the mark of her hand flaming on his cheek. "Raise a hand to me again, Rowenna, and you will live to regret it." He shoved her away from him, "Now get out of my sight."

Without a backward glance she stomped towards the doorway. At the same moment Wilbur stepped into the hall and had to jump to one side as she pushed on past him. "What's eating her?" he asked, watching her leave the hall.

Hussa ignored the question. "Well? What is it Wilbur?"

"A messenger from King Ceolwulf, lord. He wants you to report to Witanceastre immediately."

This was not a conversation Hussa was looking forward to. He grimaced, knowing he had no choice. "Very well, wake the men, prepare the horses. We ride at once."

After Wilbur had gone, Hussa wandered over to the door and looked outside but could see no sign of Rowenna. "Bloody woman!" he muttered, pondering on what she had told him and wondering how he might use what he had learnt about Cerdic to cause his brother the most damage. Still thinking about that, he turned away from the doorway and went to kick Rolf into life.

They reached Witanceastre that evening. Wilbur led the men and horses to the townhouse that had been left at their disposal, while Hussa, accompanied by Rolf, went to report to the king. As they walked up the hall they could see Boyden and his huscarls watching them from the shadows to the side.

"Ah, Lord Hussa, there you are," Ceolwulf said. "Your enterprise hardly met with outstanding success, did it. Seventy men dead or captured I hear. Boseham and Cicestre still in the hands of Suthseaxe. Not the victory I was promised."

"Sire, I confess we were not able to capture Boseham and the battle turned against us, but this was because the armies of Suthseaxe and Cantia unexpectedly arrived on the battlefield. We were outnumbered and outflanked. Our defeat would not have occurred had Lord Boyden undertaken his part adequately, as we had planned."

"You dare to accuse me?" Boyden shouted, moving out of the shadows and walking right up to Hussa until they were only inches apart. "You Northumbrian runt. You fail in your duty then dare to pass the blame to your betters."

Hussa turned his head and spat onto the floor. "You are not my better, Boyden. King Ceolwulf is my better, not you. You were supposed to draw the armies of Cantia and Suthseaxe into West Seax and then to ambush them as they marched to Boseham or Cicestre."

Boyden's face twisted with contempt. "The armies of Cantia and Suthseaxe did not march into West Seax. They did not in fact come particularly close to the border. My scouts reported that they hung back in the forests in northern Suthseaxe. At the time you were about to attack Boseham they were already on the march, away from the border and south towards you!"

Hussa shook his head. "That is not possible, unless they were expecting the attack..." he trailed into silence, becoming aware that they were all staring at him. Boyden was actually nodding.

"So you see how it looks, Lord Hussa, "the king said. "One perfectly feasible interpretation of these events is that you are in fact a spy from Cantia or Suthseaxe and came here to feed us false information, to draw an attack to Boseham and hand us a bloody defeat."

"No, that's not true!" Hussa exclaimed. "I've not lied to you! I am loyal to Northumbria and King Aethelfrith and it is he, my master, who wants an alliance with you. I am no spy."

Thinking on his feet, a thought occurred to Hussa and he spun around to point at Boyden. "You could still have attacked when the enemy was in North Suthseaxe. You could have launched an attack to draw them back at that point or to fall upon their rear. I still maintain you could have been more aggressive. Outnumbered as we were, we didn't stand a chance. You sent no warning. Did you let us fail on purpose?"

Now it was Boyden who spat on the ground at Hussa's feet. "You dare try to pass the blame to me again? I would gut you here and now were I not under orders from the king."

Ceolwulf was nodding. "Indeed, I am tempted to let him do it, Hussa. But I am surrounded by enemies. An alliance with Northumbria might be worth pursuing. I need to know, however, if I can trust you, Hussa of Deira. So this is what I will do: you and your men will confine yourselves to the house I have provided for you. I will investigate this matter further and get to the bottom of our defeat before I decide what to do with you."

The king now turned to address the court. "Lord Boyden, you will take command of the armies to the east in case Cantia and Suthseaxe launch an attack to follow up their victory. I must take command of the army to the west, for when Dumnonia learns of our defeat it may well try its fortune on our western border. You, Hussa, will stay here until we return at the end of the campaign season. Only then will I determine your fate."

"My lord, please, my men and I are innocent," Hussa protested, but Ceolwulf had turned away.

"Then you have nothing to fear from my investigation," Boyden said as his huscarls moved in to push Hussa and Rolf towards the doorway.

Frowning, Hussa stared at Boyden. "Your investigation?"

"Yes indeed. The king has asked me to investigate the Boseham affair further. He trusts me you see, Hussa. He has no reason to extend that trust to you! Now go until you are summoned."

Over the following days the king and his army marched out westwards to campaign against the Britons and Dumnonia. Boyden went east to take command of the companies watching the border with Suthseaxe. There was, however, no sign of offensive action by Cissa or Aethelberht. Content with having given West Seax a bloody nose and securing the frontier near Boseham, both kings stayed inside their borders.

For a week or two Hussa and his huscarls drowned their sorrows and got drunk most nights. But after a while, Rolf complained that he was starting to feel a bit flabby and in need of some exercise. Indeed, most of the men were putting on weight hanging around the house all day with little to do. So Hussa ordered them to drill and practise their warrior skills. Ceolwulf had not forbidden them arms, which in itself was at least a hopeful sign. Although they were closely observed by Boyden's men, providing they stayed within the city boundary they were left to their own devices. And so Hussa used up the summer months getting bored out of his mind with practice and drill.

It was high summer during the Northumbrians' house arrest, when Rowenna finally reappeared. Hussa was sitting alone in the hall sharpening his seax on a stone and pondering once again if he could have avoided his current predicament. He became aware that a shadow had fallen across him and looked up to see that his former slave had entered the room. For a while Hussa stared at her in silence. He had not expected to see her again and was not sure how he felt about her reappearance.

Finally, she broke the silence. "I have come back because I have news. I'm not sure you will want to know it. I am unsure how I feel about it myself."

"What news?" he asked, frowning.

In response she laid one hand on her abdomen. "I am with child," she said.

Chapter Eleven
Secrets
Spring 607

It was the time of the festival of the Goddess Eostre, coincident with the Christian celebration of Easter, when we arrived back in our little Welsh village in Rhufoniog. From some distance away we could hear laughter and then, as we closed in on the last hedgerow, we heard the noise of wooden weapons clattering against wicker shields. I glanced at my companions, Eduard, Cuthbert and Aedann, and we shared a knowing smile. I had strong suspicions as to what was going on and my theory was proven true a few moments later when a man's voice could be heard bellowing through the spring air.

"Get back on your feet Master Cuthwine. You should not have been so easy to knock over. Learn to stand better or I will have you run to the sea and back, earl's son or not!"

We knew that bellow. It was Grettir's. In his day he had been a fearsome warrior, but was too old now to campaign with us, much as he wanted to. He had been our trainer when we were growing up and we had all been in awe of him. Over the years that awe had turned into affection and the sound of his voice made us smile as we finally came round the bend in the lane and out onto the green in the centre of the village, which for now doubled as the extent of Edwin's domain. A long way from Deira, but a pleasant enough home for us all.

There, on the green, Grettir was training the young men, including the children of the village. One of them was my own son, Cuthwine. He had been born the year after the battle of Catraeth and was now eight years old. No, I had to correct myself. He was nine. I observed sadly that he would have passed nine while I was away during the winter and I recalled that just before I had left for Cantia, I had asked Grettir to start his training.

"Father!" my boy shouted as he saw me, and dropping his sword and shield, he ran across the green and jumped at me. I allowed the initial embrace and then held him away from me and let my face take on a stern expression.

"Now, Cuthwine, before we speak I must hear what Grettir has to say about you!"

The lad looked worried and biting his lip, glanced across at his instructor. Grettir never needed to pretend to look stern, the man was probably born with that expression, but he kept the tension of the moment lingering by very slowly walking across to us, his gaze never leaving Cuthwine. Finally he spoke and to be honest, it was not just Cuthwine who was holding his breath, I was as well and, I noticed, so too were my friends. We could all remember the fear the grey-haired old veteran had inspired in us.

"He has much to learn," Grettir said gruffly, "and he is rather clumsy, but he is determined and willing, so yes, I can make a warrior of him one day, possibly even a good one."

I breathed out. This was high praise coming from Grettir and I was filled with pride in my son. Cuthwine beamed and I gave him a punch on the shoulder. "Well done, now go find your mother and your sister!"

"We are both here, my husband," Aidith answered, emerging from the doorway of the hut we had taken over when we came here. Her green-eyed gaze passed over me, as it did whenever I had been away, noting fresh scars and wounds still healing. She relaxed as she saw I was not seriously hurt. By her side, tottering along in her shadow, came Sian. Now rising three, the little

95

girl looked almost like a miniature version of her mother, with those same green eyes and red hair, although hers was short and curly. "See, Sian, your father is back," Aidith said with a smile.

My daughter screamed in excitement and ran towards me. Halfway across the green she stopped and looked again, as if trying to remember who I was. Then, perhaps reassured by her brother's beaming grin, she apparently made up her mind that it didn't particularly matter and started to run again. I swept her up in my arms as she reached me and held her close.

Aidith joined us and studied me once more. She then leant in to kiss me, her red hair blocking the sunlight. As she did so, I had a brief recollection of dark hair falling across my face and different lips brushing my own... of rutting like a beast.

Having kissed me, Aidith stepped back a pace and looked me in the eyes as she always did, seeking that unspoken message that all was well, I was here to stay and our family life could resume once more.

Suddenly awash with guilt I looked away, unable to meet her gaze.

"Cerdic? Is something wrong?"

"Wrong? Of course not. What could possibly be wrong?" I gabbled, answering too quickly. Now I did look at her and saw that her expression was one of confusion, suspicion indeed that something was not quite right. I should tell her, I thought to myself. Just be honest about it. But I was too much of a coward. And anyway, what could I say? That I had been unfaithful to her in a dream? How stupid was that! So instead I avoided any discussion.

"I need to see Prince Edwin at once... important things to discuss. I will be with you all afterwards." And with that I hurried off towards the ale hall, which served as Edwin's residence as well as our meeting room. As I bustled away leaving my family on the green I chanced a look back. Aidith was staring after me, puzzlement and uncertainty written on her face.

It was, of course, a cowardly act. But I was still not sure quite what had happened on that drunken night in Boseham. With no woman in evidence the following morning – if indeed she had existed other than as a figment of my fevered imagination – I had no way of confirming that I had betrayed my marriage vows to Aidith. Cuthbert's observation of a woman leaving my room seemed evidence enough I suppose, but he could have been mistaken. The place was in darkness and he, himself, had not been entirely sober. I needed to know for sure what, if anything, had happened before I discussed it with Aidith. Not that there was any way to find out. It was all most vexing.

Prince Edwin was sitting at the same long table where he had been when we left for Cantia, and at his side stood Sabert. I blinked; it was almost as if in Rhufoniog time had stood still. However, it was obvious that time had passed and indeed, that it had been weighing heavily on Edwin. He listened to the tale of our adventure and battle without saying anything. And although in the end he congratulated us for progressing the alliance with Cantia and Suthseaxe and possibly even reinforcing it with his nephew's proposed marriage to a princess of one kingdom or the other, I could tell this news only agitated him more.

"So whilst you have been away heroically defending a villa against great odds, all we have done is sit out the long winter and then begin sowing the fields with wheat, oats and barley. No doubt you would have enjoyed it had you been here, Cerdic, but to me all this is just frustration."

I knew that without saying it in so many words, he was referring to my being more of a farmer than a warrior. It was the old insult that he had often applied to me in times gone by. I let it pass because actually he was right. I would rather have been here preparing the fields and celebrating Yuletide with my family than away making a name for myself – and for Hereric.

This actually was the problem: the rot I spoke about before. I was not alone in enjoying a rural idyll in the valley which we now called home. The men who had accompanied me to Cantia, as well as those who had stayed behind, were becoming accustomed to the peaceful life. Before Cantia I had not been consciously aware of it, but having returned home I started to observe these feelings all around me during that spring and summer of 607. In a word, it was contentment.

But not for Prince Edwin. He was constantly coming up with schemes to raid into Northumbria and spent many hours discussing how many boats we would need, how to provision those boats and where to find captains of sufficient skill to navigate around the south coast, past Cantia and right up to Northumbria. All the way through that summer he would summon us – myself, Sabert and veterans like Eduard, to listen to his plans. But whilst Eduard alone remained steadfastly enthusiastic and ready to jump off on each and every scheme, the rest of us always seemed to find some excuse to delay action.

It wasn't just me. Cuthbert and Mildrith were distracted by raising their first child – born not long after Sian – and with my sister now in her second pregnancy, Cuthbert would not want to leave her again. Aedann, after Bronwen's reluctant father had at long last given his consent – if not his blessing – to their union, was happier than I had ever seen him and preparation for their wedding and the subsequent celebrations distracted us further in that long summer.

Edwin, however, grew increasingly agitated and annoyed with us all. He did not even have the support of Sabert who, whilst not involved in a domestic life of his own, had no wish to go to war until we had the support we needed. He frequently confided in me his concerns over Edwin's state of mind.

"Each new plan is getting more and more wild, Cerdic. The other day he was talking about rowing all the way past the Scots and Picts to come at Aethelfrith from the North. He even suggested doing it during the winter storms because nobody would be expecting that!"

I nodded. I was fairly sure that Edwin's need to strike back against Aethelfrith and make some progress was made worse by the fact that his nephew, who seemed well placed to gain support from Cantia for an expedition against Northumbria before too long, was stealing a march on him. I mentioned this to Sabert and he agreed with me.

"Yes and whilst Iago is happy for us to have land here and to extend his hospitality and protection over us, and Cadfan continues to treat Edwin as a son, neither of them appear to have any appetite for directly challenging Aethelfrith. Not any time soon."

"Especially not when there is uncertainty over the attitude of Mercia, "I said. "Although we have a friend in Ceorl, whilst Pybba is king, Mercia will not challenge Northumbria."

"No, indeed." Sabert sighed. "What can we do, Cerdic? Without their support we cannot take the war to Aethelfrith. He is too strong and we are too weak."

"For the moment we just have to be satisfied with protecting Edwin and living here in Gwynedd," I answered.

And as I've said, there lay the problem. We were all a bit too happy to live peacefully in the valley and let another year go by… and then maybe another. Nobody, Edwin excepted, had any urgency or motivation to do otherwise.

As for Aidith, it seemed that I had managed to escape further consequences of whatever had gone on during that winter's night in Boseham, because nothing was said. We were all occupied in the spring with the business of sowing and planting the fields and with the lambing and calving, and I think that if she harboured any suspicion that things were not quite right between us, she buried them. After all, I was well, I was there with her and the children life was going on as normal.

That summer Mildrith went into labour with her second child. It was a difficult birth and the newly born infant, a boy, was sickly. Everyone thought we would lose him at any time and as a result Aidith was often occupied helping Millie to nurse him. In the end he did survive, but was a frail little thing, always seeming undernourished and nothing but a bag of bones. Cuthbert appeared to distance himself from the child and one evening, when we were supping ale with Lilla after a hard day's work, he confessed he was afraid to show his son affection because if he did and the boy died, he was not sure he could deal with it.

"All we have with any certainty is today," Lilla said. "What comes after no one can know for sure. So live each day and take what joy it brings. Don't deny yourself that joy by imagining something in the future that might never happen. That's my advice."

Cuthbert must have taken Lilla's wisdom to heart, for not long afterwards I saw him cradling his son and gazing deep into the baby's eyes, silently showing his love, whatever pain might follow if the infant lost his slim hold on life.

100

The harvest came round once more. We gathered it all in and began to prepare for another winter – a time when there was little work to be done and we could spend cosy dark evenings by the fire, enjoying the fruits of our labours. Yuletide passed and before long our inactivity began to pall and we looked for signs of spring. It was only then, without any warning, that Aidith asked me the question I had dreaded since getting home twelve months earlier. I say that, but in fact so much time had gone on with nothing being said that aside from a niggling feeling of guilt – and even that was fading – I had all but forgotten about it.

Sian was playing with the other children on the green. Cuthwine was drilling with Grettir. Edwin had taken Sabert, Eduard and a few of the other veterans to the ale hall to discuss the latest of his plans. I was sitting outside our hut watching the training whilst idly sharpening the edge of Catraeth with a whetstone, and Aidith was sewing up a hole in one of my tunics. Suddenly she dropped the tunic, needle and thread back into the basket on her lap and turned to me.

"Cerdic, did something happen whilst you were away in Cantia?"

"What?" I was so surprised by the suddenness of the question that I gawped at her. "Why do you ask?" I stumbled out the words after a few moments.

"Because you have been acting oddly ever since you got home. You seem to go out of your way to avoid talking with me when we are alone, and we don't..." she paused, her cheeks flushed pink and she looked down at her hands, "...well, you have not lain with me much in these many months since you returned."

She was right. We had not made love very often at all. Whenever she got close I felt guilty and not worthy. It did not seem right, not after what I had done or thought I had done in Boseham. Each time Aidith and I lay together I would see in my mind's eye a cascade of long black hair and dark eyes looking down into mine. Even if I hadn't actually done anything, I had certainly experienced extremely lustful imaginings about a woman who was not my wife. And so I had avoided intimacy, always claiming to be too tired and going straight off to sleep. Actually, that wasn't exactly a lie in those days of labouring in the fields.

"Cerdic, you are not saying anything. Did something happen when you were in Cantia?"

"No, I swear it! "I said, hoping she would leave the matter there so I would not have to lie to her, but she was too sharp for that.

"What about in Suthseaxe then?"

"What has Cuthbert said to you?" I asked, realising how it sounded the moment the words left my mouth.

"So, something did happen then. Are you going to tell me what?"

"I... I..." I stumbled over my words. "I think... I think there might have been a woman..."

"You think?" She screeched. "What do you mean you think? Surely even you can tell when a woman has hold of your prick?"

"I'm sorry... I..." but I got no further because at that moment the alarm horns sounded. I think it was probably the first and only time I was relieved to hear them.

"What's going on? "Aidith asked, forgetting her anger. "Sian, where are you? Cuthwine come here!" She was shouting across the green.

I was still grappling with what had just happened when the horns sounded from the south once more. In a daze, I struggled into my chain shirt and then buckled on Catraeth and Wreccan. All around me men were staggering out of their homes, grabbing swords and shields, spears and bows and assembling on the green.

Prince Edwin came running out of the hall with Eduard. "What is it?"

"Don't know," I shrugged. Simultaneously we turned and looked to the south east. Up in the southern hills, where we had summer pasture for the sheep, was an isolated farm. Not long after we first came here, two of the families, including four of our warriors, had asked Edwin if they could take over the place. He had readily agreed if in exchange they would keep watch. Their elevated location high up in the hills meant they had an uninterrupted view down the valley towards the distant sea – the route to the roads that came into Gwynedd past Caer Legion from distant Northumbria and the most likely route of any attack from Aethelfrith. Yet there was another route from which an attack might come, one we had never considered, obsessed as we were with Aethelfrith. The ridge to the south east marked the border with Powys, Gwynedd's southern neighbour. Powys had been at peace with Gwynedd ever since we had been in Rhufoniog, and yet it was an uncertain peace. An attack from that direction, over the hills, would take an army right past our outlying farm.

"Smoke! I see smoke!" Cuthbert shouted and pointed.

Chapter Twelve
Kadir
Late 607

He was right. Smoke was rising from the ridge line. From the amount of smoke this was no simple woodman's fire. The farm must be ablaze.

"Riders approaching!" called a man on watch at the edge of the village.

Moments later we heard the sound of hooves thundering toward us. A pair of riders burst into view, one slumped down over his horse's neck. They skidded to a halt on the green in front of us and I recognised two of the men who lived up on the farm. The leading rider, a man named Barton, inclined his head toward Edwin.

"My prince, we are attacked," he panted. "They came over the southern ridge. Warriors from Powys, Dogfeiling I think. It's the nearest to us. We held them back while our women and children escaped into the woods west of the farm. One of our warriors went with them, but another was killed. We had to flee or be killed ourselves. Tomas here was hit by a slingstone – his arm is broken I think."

I motioned to Grettir and he and Lilla came forward to see to the injured man while Barton, still catching his breath, continued speaking. "We got away while they were pillaging and setting fire to the farm, but I think they will soon follow us down here," he said.

"Are you sure? Where were they heading?" I snapped.

He blinked at me as if I had misunderstood his meaning. "Lord Cerdic, they were heading here, where else!"

"How many… how many are there?" Edwin asked.

"Two hundred at least. They will be here in a matter of moments."

Edwin paled at that news. "I have forty men here. We cannot fight two hundred."

I shook my head. "No we can't, but we can get the families away, down towards the sea, and you with them."

"The families yes, but I am not running!" Edwin exclaimed.

"My prince…" I started to argue, but he gave me a look that told me he would not be swayed. "Very well," I said resignedly. "Lord Sabert, I suggest you lead the families away and take two of my men along with Tomas here."

It was Sabert who now started to argue, but I cut him off with a wave of my hand. "We need to get the women and children to safety. That will give the men a reason to fight even at these odds."

Sabert nodded, drawing his sword. "Very well, Cerdic, but keep all the men. You need them. I am not so old that I cannot swing a blade." He turned away, already shouting for the women and children to gather to him. Cuthwine was with Sian and Aidith, but broke away to come running towards me, his little seax glinting in his hand.

"Go back to your mother, son!" I shouted at him.

He shook his head. "I have been training, Father, I should fight."

"No, not yet. You are too young."

"But Father…"

"I said no!" I bellowed with more ferocity than I should have used. He recoiled away from me. I reached out to clasp his shoulder, "One day soon, my boy. But not today. I need you to help Sabert get the women and children to safety. I will follow."

105

Still he hesitated.

"Go now!" I shouted once more and at last he scampered away. As he ran he looked back at me and then past me and I saw his eyes widen in dismay. He had just seen the first few warriors emerging between the huts at the northern edge of the village.

They spotted us and one of them, a youth with a bow in one hand and shield slung over his back, turned and shouted something behind him. Then he loaded an arrow onto his string, took up a position beside one of the huts and watched us.

"Form up!" I shouted.

Around me the shield wall was fast assembling. We placed ourselves in front of Edwin's hall. The running wolf banner of Deira was thrust into the ground outside it and the prince and I stood on the stepped entranceway. This gave us a slight elevation so we could stare over the heads of the company and direct the fight.

At the opposite end of the village green, the enemy were growing in number. They had three companies forming. As Barton had said, two of them appeared to be Welsh from Powys. More specifically, from the cantrief or sub-kingdom of Dogfeiling. That was the district of Powys that ran along the border to the south of Rhufoniog where our village was situated. It had its own king – a man called Morfael. The Dogfeiling House was descended from the kings of both Powys and Gwynedd, but was a branch more minor than the ruling families under Iago of Gwynedd or Cynan of Powys. Lilla had once explained this to me when we arrived in the village. When I told him I found all the names and kingdoms confusing, Lilla had smiled and patted me on the back.

"It's all that fighting, Cerdic," he had said. "All those blows to the head. It's making you dimwitted. It's a good thing you have a bright fellow like me to help you." Looking at my chagrined expression he had burst out laughing.

Dim-witted or not, I recalled the fact that Morfael resented his subservient status and dreamed of acquiring a larger kingdom. Was this attack part of that dream?

As I watched our foes getting into position, I noticed something different about the third company forming up alongside the Dogfeiling. From their outlandish clothing, small round shields and large swords, these were unmistakeably Irish. I looked across at Edwin. He too had spotted this.

"What is an Irish war band doing in a raiding party from Powys?" he asked.

I shrugged, having no answer. As the companies formed up, a group of three Irish walked towards us, arms held wide to show they were no threat. Two of them hung back – huge bastards with no armour, bare muscular arms and nothing on their feet. Each held a javelin in his right hand and a handful more at the ready in his left. Their clothing consisted of short, kneelength and tightfitting britches, which I had heard they called 'trews'. Over these they wore a sleeveless jacket, striped red and yellow and held closed with a bronze brooch. Fastened to the back of their left hands they each carried a buckler – a round, hidecovered shield with a central iron boss.

These two were clearly the huscarls – or whatever the Irish word was for house troops or loyal bodyguards – of the third man. I turned my attention to him.

If the huscarls were huge this man was a giant. He had to be almost seven feet tall. Every inch was taut with muscle; no flab or fat upon him. He, rather unusually for an Irish warrior, did wear armour: a fine chain shirt – probably the gift of a king – over which he had hung a green cloak fastened at the shoulder by an elaborately shaped pin in the form of a snake. His trews were anklelength and he was wearing boots. He too had a buckler but carried no weapons in his hand, although I could see a fine sword hanging at his side. I knew him for a warrior chieftain, one like Felnius whom I had killed in Tre'r Ceiri.

I walked forward flanked by Edwin and Eduard until we stood twenty paces apart from the Irish trio then I held up my hand, palm outwards. "Close enough, Irishman," I said in Welsh. "Who are you?"

"I am Kadir," he answered in English. He paused and then looked at me and smiled. "And you are Cerdic, son of Cenred and lord to Prince Edwin of Deira, who stands there by your side."

"I don't understand," I tried again in Welsh.

"Enough deception, Deiran. You are no more Welsh than I am. Your flag there is familiar to the Irish and to the Scots. I saw it myself at Degsastan where you slaughtered thousands of our people."

Ah, that made sense. No wonder he knew who we were. "You attacked us!" I retorted in English.

Kadir smiled at the small victory of my admission that we were who he thought we were. I sighed and asked a question. "Why do you attack Gwynedd, unprovoked as you are?"

"Unprovoked?" Kadir laughed. "Earl Cerdic, there is bad blood between my people and yours, that is provocation enough. "He now pointed at our small company of warriors who stood gathered around our limp banner. "We will again attack you, but today it is you who will be slaughtered, not us." He paused again. Clearly the man liked to let the tension build.

"Yet it need not be that way," he continued. "If you and Prince Edwin surrender to me, the rest of your men may go free."

I glanced across at Edwin then back at Kadir. "What happens to us if we agree?" I asked.

Kadir tilted his head. "What do you expect to happen to you?"

I shrugged. "I imagine we are to be killed," I replied.

"Well then, you will not be disappointed. You will not die at once, however. The one I work for wishes that pleasure."

"Can you please tell us who that is?"

Kadir shook his head. "That is by way of a surprise awaiting you."

Suddenly, Eduard took a step forward. "Enough talk! We will not hand over Earl Cerdic or Prince Edwin. Do your worst Irishman. "

Edwin and I both looked at Eduard, but it was the prince who spoke. "You are loyal to your master and to me, Eduard, but this is suicide. Better that you and the men live to see their families again than that we all die here today."

"Forgive me, my prince, but I don't believe this Irish bastard will let us go. In any event we all swore to protect you. Would you have us run from this place as leaderless men with no honour and no courage? We will not do that."

Eduard had spoken louder and louder so that the men behind us could hear what he was saying. Several started to strike swords and spears against shields showing their support of his defiance.

Kadir said nothing merely nodding his head. "So be it. It is better this way." And at that he turned and walked back to his men.

The three of us backed away and returned to our company.

"You should have let us go, Eduard," I said.

"Bollocks to that," Aedann said, hearing the exchange from where he stood amongst the men.

"What about the rest of you?" I asked. "You need not die today. Let Prince Edwin and me surrender. If you do, this Kadir promises you can go free."

"What Aedann said, Cerdic, is how we all feel. And anyway, I think it's too late now," Cuthbert answered, already readying an arrow on his bow. "Here they come!"

Horns sounded from the enemy and with a clattering of spears on shields they rolled towards us. They stopped thirty paces away – each wing well overlapping our own. Then they began hammering away on their wooden shields with axes, swords and spears, blasting at horns and shouting – trying to scare us. I could see our men looking around them, despair rising as they calculated the odds, knowing there was no way out of this. We would all die here. After a period of trying to intimidate us the enemy would charge in, and although we would take some of the bastards with us we would all perish. I could see no way out. Then it occurred to me that there was one possible solution. If I could kill Kadir then I might change the outcome of this day.

With any army, the willingness to fight comes mainly from a handful of leaders and veterans. Even in the Wicstun Company it was men like Eduard and Aedann who held the company together and drew less warlike men along with them. If a leader leads, the men will follow. That being so, I asked myself, what would happen if Kadir died? Would his army fight or might they lose heart? It was a gamble, but one I was prepared to take even if it cost me my life.

"What are you doing, Cerdic?" Eduard said, as I stepped out of the shield wall and into the open space between ourselves and the enemy.

"Kadir!" I bellowed over the noise they were making. "I challenge you. Come and fight me. Our men need not die here today if we decide the battle, just me and you."

His warriors fell silent and over in their shield wall I could see Kadir was looking me up and down. His men outnumbered ours three to one. There was no need for him to respond to my challenge. Yet all his men had heard me. To not respond could be seen as cowardice in some men's eyes, and for a warrior, to be seen as a coward was worse than death. That is why he hesitated to dismiss my challenge out of hand. Even so, he opened his mouth to speak and from his expression I was certain he was about to refuse. I needed to provoke him a little further.

"Fight me... unless you are afraid, that is!" At that the company at my back began jeering loudly, whistling, dropping their britches to show their arses to the enemy and calling out insults.

And that, of course, was enough.

The huge man stepped out of his shield wall and approached me. As he did so, the army behind him started hammering again. The Wicstun Company took up the beat and strove to match the noise. The racket around us was intense and yet neither of us paid much attention to it, instead we looked at one another, each of us weighing the other up.

I readied my shield and drew Wreccan, my longsword. Kadir had his sword sheathed whilst his right hand was grasped around a javelin. We circled each other for a few moments and then with a roar, Kadir threw the javelin towards me. His aim was good, but I raised my shield, easily deflecting the blow. As I recovered, Kadir had drawn his sword and now came running towards me. He piled into me with all the impact of a charging bull and I staggered backwards several steps, fighting to keep my balance.

111

Whilst I was at a disadvantage, Kadir closed in and thrust his sword towards my belly. I parried with Wreccan and then tried to smash my shield into his face. Despite his bulk, Kadir managed to dodge out of the way and as I staggered past him he swung his blade, catching me along the side of my chest. My chain shirt absorbed most of the blow, but I felt a rib crack and let out a cry of pain. The Irish and Welsh bellowed all the louder and Kadir smiled, realising he had the upper hand and knowing he would win this day.

I was gasping for breath, trying to recover from the pain of the blow when he came at me again, this time aiming a cut across my throat. It would have taken out my windpipe had I not stepped out of the way and deflected the blade with my shield. This time I countered with a thrust from Wreccan. It caught Kadir in the arm, slashing open muscle and vein so that the blood gushed down to his hand. He grimaced, but all it seemed to do was to enrage him further. Now the wild bull, infuriated by the pain, attacked without remission, slashing furiously with his sword and forcing me backward with his buckler, stepbystep. I parried each blow and tried to counter attack, yet I never managed to contact him again. Finally, his buckler smashed into my face, breaking my nose and sending me reeling to the ground.

The world was spinning around me; blood was trickling down my face and I was seeing stars as well as sunlight. I fought to focus on the huge form that now loomed over me. One that I knew was preparing to land the killing blow…

Chapter Thirteen
Rhufoniog
Late 607

Still blinded and seeing naught but darkness, I lay on the ground. For some reason I thought of my Uncle Cuthwine, and the stories of the battle in which he had died. I thought of Grettir knocked onto his back and Samlen one eye coming to kill him. He had not died that day because Aelle had arrived and saved him. Aelle was dead though and I knew neither he nor any of his kin would come to save me.

In the distance I heard horns sounding and in my dazed state I thought I was imagining Cuthwine's last battle, but a moment later the horns sounded again, this time much closer. As my vision returned to me, though hampered by my rapidly swelling nose, I saw Kadir still standing over me, his sword wet with my blood, but he was not looking at me. Rather, he was looking to the west. From that direction the horns sounded a third time and now they were joined by the thunder of hooves.

Kadir looked down at me again and his sword swung back as if preparing to finish me off, but as he did so one of his bodyguards screamed out some words in Irish and Kadir hesitated, then he simply spat at me and ran back towards his own lines. He shouted an order and the two hundred men that had raided into Gwynedd started to withdraw, in good order and still in formation, back towards the north end of the village. They had just reached the huts and the sloping ground beyond when horsemen burst abruptly into view carrying the banner of Cadfan, Prince of Gwynedd. Indeed, a moment later, Cadfan himself rode into the village accompanied by Cadwallon, his son.

Hardly able to believe I had somehow escaped death, I pushed myself up onto my elbow, grunting from the pain of my broken rib, various cuts and abrasions and my throbbing nose, but grateful to still be alive to feel it. I saw that despite the noise the horsemen were making, there were only about fifty of them. At the edge of the village Kadir paused and looked back, as though he was counting the odds and considering whether his larger army could still win this day. As he hesitated, a company of spearman under the banner of Rhun, one of the lords of Gwynedd, came into view following up the horsemen. Kadir clearly decided that enough was enough and with a final glare in my direction he barked out an order and his warriors withdrew up the slope.

Cadfan rode over towards us and Edwin left the shield wall to greet him. Struggling to my feet, swaying slightly, I stood still for a moment until the earth stopped moving, then I walked across the green to join them, bowing my head to Cadfan and Cadwallon as I reached them. Cadfan was in his prime, a strong warrior prince about five years older than I. His son was a little younger than Hereric, already almost full grown, broad in shoulder and showing signs that he would one day equal if not exceed his father's height.

Slipping out of his saddle Cadfan warmly embraced Prince Edwin, his adopted son and also his godson, having stood in the role of godfather when Edwin agreed to be baptised. A role which I knew the Christians took very seriously. Cadwallon, I noticed, remained mounted, his face expressionless as he watched his father greeting Edwin.

"It is very good to see you both, but what are you doing here?" Edwin asked.

Cadwallon snorted. "Rescuing you by the look of things. It is

114

good we arrived in time, isn't it." Although he was smiling as he spoke, Cadwallon's sneering tone did not suggest he necessarily believed his own words.

Either Cadfan did not notice or chose to ignore his son's insulting tone. "We came to fetch you to court. There have been attacks all along the border, not just here," he said. "The king is summoning all the lords. It might be war with Powys!"

A few days after the raid on Rhufoniog, with our families located and brought safely home and with a garrison reinforced by some of Cadfan's men to protect them, I was on the road once more. Prince Edwin, myself and five others, including my three closest friends, set off for Deganwy, the fortress of the kings of Gwynedd.

Deganwy lay between the peaks of a twintopped hill. Within the outer walls, the king's hall and lesser buildings stood on the high saddle of land between these two peaks in a superbly defensive position. It was four years or more since we had first laid eyes upon it. Back then we had been strangers and displaced refugees, distrusted and reviled by many of the Welshmen. Although it was apparent that some still felt that way about us, we enjoyed the protection of Cadfan and through him his father the king, so none dared to touch us.

By the time that Cadfan, Edwin and we others arrived, the court of Iago, King of Gwynedd, had already assembled, his lords seated on stools and benches in the king's hall. We took our places and waited.

Peering down at us from his chair, which stood on a platform at one end of the hall, Iago spoke first. He was ageing and his voice weak so we had to strain to hear his words.

"My lords, I have summoned you to a council of war. The tidings I must share with you are that I have received word of

115

a number of raids by Cynan of Powys that threaten the alliance between us."

Around the hall there was a low buzz of conversation at this news. Some, perhaps lords more removed from the border regions with Powys, even looked shocked. Others, whom I recognised as owning land along that border, sat in silence, faces grim as Iago went on.

"Indeed, there have been attacks all along the border – at Llyn and Arfon in the west, into Arlechywedd and Rhun in the centre and against Prince Edwin in Rhufoniog, and also into Tegeingel further east."

The volume of murmurs rose and Iago paused. He let the conversation die back down before proceeding. "Any one of these unprovoked raids might warrant fullscale war. Yet we have learnt that it is more than just random spite or aggression behind the attacks. News has reached us that concerns Prince Edwin."

Iago let his gaze linger on Edwin for a while before signalling a guard, who nodded his head and strode quickly from the hall. A few moments later he returned, escorting a middleaged man with thinning grey hair. The newcomer was a stranger to me and judging by everyone else's reaction, to the bulk of the court also. He came forward, bowed to the king and waited.

"This is a messenger from Cynan of Powys," Iago said. "He arrived here this morning. After the recent attacks I was minded just to lynch him, but the news he brings concerns us all." Iago directed his gaze to the man and said. "Repeat now what you told me earlier, but speak slowly for the benefit of our guests whose Welsh is somewhat lacking."

The messenger stared around the room for a moment before speaking. "I am Earl Hywel, from the court of King Cynan. I

116

bring an explanation of the raids that have occurred these last few days, along with an offer of peace. Gwynedd harbours an enemy of our race and as such brings the threat of destruction on all of us." Hywel turned to glance around the hall, his eyes lingering on us Deirans. "All of Wales has heard that Cadfan ap Iago has adopted as son Edwin, son of Aelle and a prince of Deira. My king does not approve of that decision, nor of you taking him and his company of Angles into your protection. The raids which have just occurred were intended to capture Edwin and remove a cause of dispute between us. Clearly this did not succeed as he still stands amongst you."

Hywel turned back to face Iago. "Sire, my king has sent me with a request. Hand over Edwin and his party and there shall be peace between us. My king will even offer recompense for loss of life, limb and property during the raids." He paused a moment before adding, "My king says one more thing. Our two lands have been friends more often than enemies. Do not let a vagabond Saxon princeling come between us."

I stood forward and asked Hywel a question. "Is this the do-ing of Northumbria? Has Hussa come to the court and requested Cynan take action? If so you need to know he cannot be trusted – neither Hussa nor Aethelfrith."

Hywel frowned at me. "You babble, Saxon. No Northum-brian has requested anything of my king. Know this truth: your race will never be permitted power or influence over mine." At that Hywel turned his back upon me.

Iago cleared his throat. "Very well, Lord Hywel, you have given your message. Return to your king with mine: we will consider his request and respond to him in due course. He must keep his armies on his side of the border or else there will cer-tainly be war."

As Hywel bowed and turned to exit the hall, the buzz of conversation rose to the rafters. Iago waited until the emissary from Powys had departed then raised his hand for silence.

"So we now have an explanation for the attacks of the last week. This court must decide how to respond."

Cadfan at once stood forward. "Edwin is my adopted son. I will not hand him over to Powys. But you are my king as well as my father and your word is law. Only you can overrule me," he said, his tone challenging.

Before Iago could respond, Cadwallon stepped forward. "This is foolishness, Father. I did not approve of Edwin's adoption then and I do not approve of it now. In my opinion, to place the security of our kingdom at risk to secure the safety of a mere fifty Saxons, enemies of our race, is no less than the height of folly."

"Be silent Cadwallon. You act like a jealous sibling. You are my heir, not Edwin. However, if I choose to take him under my protection for my own reasons that is none of your concern."

Cadwallon moved closer to his father and stared straight into his eyes. "It is my concern when this policy threatens the safety of Gwynedd. At the very least, Edwin and his party should leave and go to Cantia or some other Saxon kingdom. We do not want them here!"

"Enough!" Iago shouted. "I will not have my kin arguing in front of my lords. Cadwallon, your father granted protection to Edwin and these men and I approved of the decision in return for the service they did for us in the battle against the Irish. We do not understand why Powys now decides it wishes to meddle in our affairs, nor this interest in Edwin, but I will not hand over our guest so easily. However, nor do I wish war with Powys. I have decided on a response."

He paused to gather his thoughts and then spoke again. "Prince Cadfan, you will travel to Powys as ambassador. You will negotiate with Cynan and find a way to peace. Prince Edwin shall stay here with me. Earl Cerdic can go with you as representative of the Deirans...with Prince Edwin's permission of course," Iago said as an afterthought, looking enquiringly at Edwin. The prince nodded; he did not really have a choice.

Over on the other side of the hall I heard the scrape of a stool and a polite cough. All heads turned that way. It was Aneirin the bard. He was an old friend of Lilla's and I knew him well. It was a pity Lilla was not here, but he had gone off on his travels as he was wont to do.

Aneirin stepped forward and bowed to Iago. "May I speak, sire?" he asked.

Iago nodded. "Of course; a bard's views are always welcome in this court."

"Thank you, sire. I have a suggestion that might assist Cadfan's mission to Powys. The situation is tense and we need to talk Cynan round. As such I advise we enlist the help of Abbot Tysilio at Meifod."

Around the hall the response appeared positive. I saw Rhun nodding his head and I looked across at Edwin to see if the name meant anything to him, but could tell by his shrug that he had no more idea than I. Iago must have seen our confusion because he now spoke.

"Your idea has merit, Aneirin. Prince Cadfan, go now and prepare for the journey. Meanwhile, Aneirin will explain to Prince Edwin and his party who Tysilio is and why he may aid us. This council is over. "At this he pushed himself up from his chair. As he got to his feet the hall was filled with the sound of benches scraping on the floor as everyone stood and bowed to

119

the departing king. When he had gone, Aneirin came over to us.

"I take it you have not heard of Tysilio?"

We shook out heads and the bard rolled his eyes in mock exasperation. Lilla would know who he was, of course, and once again I wished he was here.

"Abbot Tysilio's monastery is at Meifod, one of the key spiritual sites in Powys. It lies in the foothills of western Powys."

I still did not comprehend. "How does that help us?"

"Well, before Tysilio became Abbot at Meifod, he lived for many years on Ynys Mon where he established a church and a community. He is a friend of the Royal House of Iago and will at least listen to us."

I could see the value of having a friend in Powys, but had my doubts as to what influence this churchman might have over King Cynan who, for reasons as yet unclear to us, had apparently taken affront to we Deirans. I said as much.

Aneirin looked at me as if I was an idiot. Then he smiled. "Oh, did I not mention that Tysilio is Cynan's brother?"

I shook my head. "No, you forgot to mention that bit, "I replied, thinking to myself that these bards were all the same; a touch arrogant.

I rubbed my hands together, this was much more promising. As brother to the King of Powys, the Abbot should indeed have some influence.

I smiled at Aneirin, "Ah, I see. You figure we get Tysilio to talk to his older brother on our behalf to try and persuade Cynan to leave us alone?"

Aneirin nodded. "Yes, but not his older brother. His younger brother. Tysilio was the older brother; the first son of their father, Brochwel Ysgithrog. "

Edwin frowned. "Yet he did not inherit?" Then he shrugged,

"Well, I guess that not all first born sons inherit."

This was true, but Aneirin was shaking his head so this was not the whole truth. "Tysilio was named heir, yet he had no wish to be king and left the court to join the church at Meifod under the founding abbot there. Brochwel was incensed and a warband was sent to bring his son back, but Tysilio fled north to Ynys Mon – which, as you know, is in Gwynedd − and there he remained until after Brochwel died, at which point Cynan became king. Some years later, an accommodation was reached between the two brothers. Tysilio renounced all claims to the throne that he had never wanted and Cynan permitted him to return to Powys where he was welcomed at court."

"So you think he will help us?" Edwin asked.

Aneirin shrugged. "Well, he represents the best chance to exercise some influence over Cynan."

"Well let's go see him then, "said Eduard, standing close by me. "What are we waiting for? "

Chapter Fourteen
The Boy
Late 607

The summer and autumn had come and gone and Yuletide was approaching before Hussa was summoned back to the king's hall. Months of sitting around, their fate hanging over them, had made the men bad tempered and sulky. Yet Hussa, who had his own preoccupations, had been unable to do much to relieve the tension.

He had not known how to respond to the news that Rowenna was pregnant and, given the apparent stage of the pregnancy, that Cerdic was most likely the father. He could have told her that he had missed her during the time she had been away. He could have said that he had taken to walking the city walls to look across the fields for a sign of her. He could have reported that he had spoken to her mother a dozen times a week – not to harm her, despite his earlier threats. Rather he had enquired of the old woman where her daughter was – not that Nina knew any more than he.

However, he told Rowenna none of this. He let her move back into the house, sharing her mother's bed adjacent to the kitchen and not his own, but he had fallen into a sullen silence and Rowenna, having resumed her duties in the house, fell back into the role of servant. Thus they adopted a habit of ignoring each other. Hussa could have told her then that his heart ached and that he longed to say how he felt, but did not.

Indeed, it had been a tiresome few months and his men were getting restless, so Hussa was both hopeful and at the same time anxious about meeting the king. He hoped to have the opportunity to build the alliance between Northumbria and West Seax; to have the chance to prove his value to Ceolwulf. However, there was still the matter of the failed attack on Boseham to discuss and there remained a strong possibility that Hussa and his men would either be expelled from West Seax or held accountable for that failure.

His hopes for the meeting were not helped when he walked into the king's hall and saw Boyden in close conversation with Ceolwulf. Nor was his mood improved when Boyden turned and flashed him a nasty smile. Nevertheless, he tried not to show his anxiety as he bowed to Ceolwulf and waited for the king's judgement.

Ceolwulf regarded him for a moment, his face expressionless. Then he spoke; "I have examined the conduct of the spring campaign in Suthseaxe. Your orders were clear: to attack the fortress of Boseham with three companies. Given those numbers, the expectation of victory was high. "He paused and Hussa, who did not like the way this was going, knew it was wise not to speak until he was given the opportunity.

"However," the king continued, "the unexpected arrival on the battlefield of several companies from Suthseaxe and Cantia would clearly change the outcome we had anticipated and that being so, I have concluded that our defeat at Boseham cannot be considered your fault. Further, on hearing accounts from the companies you led into battle, it does not seem that any blame should be attributed to you in regard to the failure of that campaign."

Hussa let out a deep breath of relief. "I am very glad to hear this, your Majesty."

The king frowned and held up his hand. "You will remain silent Hussa of Northumbria, I have not finished yet."

"Apologies, sire," Hussa mumbled.

"There remains the matter of your accusations against Lord Boyden. I have also examined the campaigns in his area of West Seax and Northwest Suthseaxe. It is clear that the armies of Cantia and Suthseaxe stayed well back from the border and would not be drawn into a confrontation by any of the series of raids that Lord Boyden, unbeknownst to you, actually launched across their border. Indeed, it appears that Cantia and Suthseaxe were keeping their warriors away from the border deliberately, to avoid any possible engagement with the main body of our armies in the East in order that they would be able to fall upon Boseham once your attacks were heavily committed."

Hearing this news, Hussa felt a sinking feeling in his gut. It seemed he had been duped. "What you are implying, sire, is that I have been used. Are you saying that Aethelberht fed me information about Boseham to see what I would do with it?"

Ceolwulf nodded. "Exactly so. It seems that he played you like a stone on a Tafl board. Yet all the reports I have heard of you, Lord Hussa, suggest that you are cleverer than that. Indeed, it was your actions at Godnundingham that men say allowed Aethelfrith into the Deiran stronghold. I find it interesting that your wisdom appears to have deserted you in the matter of Boseham. It seems to me that you were less than sharp and I wonder if anything was distracting you. What do you have to say about that?"

Frowning, Hussa thought about Rowenna and how he had been enchanted and perhaps even obsessed by her through most of the previous autumn. Had it distracted him so much he had not even considered the possibility that he might be walking into a trap set by Aethelberht? Then he recalled how he had reacted to the news that she was a spy in the employ of Lord Boyden.

124

Indeed, had he not been ruminating about that very thing as the boats approached the Boseham villa? It is true that maybe he had not been thinking completely clearly at the time.

Hussa became aware that Ceolwulf was staring at him, waiting for an answer. "It is possible that I may have been distracted, your Majesty," he admitted.

The king scratched at his beard. "So you will understand why there are many men in my council who have suggested we should not trust you; that we should send you away. Boyden is one such man."

Over at the side of the hall Lord Boyden grunted and nodded his assent.

"Nevertheless," the king continued, "I find myself in a situation of fighting wars on three fronts: in the East is Suthseaxe and Cantia; in the West the Britons and Dumnonia. In the North lies a confusion of different lands, including the isolated British kingdom of Caer Celemion and the Saxons of the Thames Valley, which wraps around that land. These Saxons have no king as such, just a succession of war chiefs. Taking that land and adding it to West Seax would do two things: it would surround this British kingdom, making it easier for us to take it in due course, and it would open the route to Mercia. An alliance between Northumbria, who border Mercia in the North, and West Seax who would then border it in the South, could make a great deal of sense. However, these operations are not easy to achieve and I have few men that I can spare on them. "Ceolwulf paused, was silent for a moment as though deep in thought.

Where was this going? Hussa wondered, apprehension clawing at his innards.

The king cleared his throat and spoke again. "Some of the warriors in the companies under your command at Boseham have said that you led them well, despite the outcome. Some fifty of these men have agreed to join your own company of Northumbrians. So, Hussa, this is what I propose: you will take this newly formed company north under my banner and by any means necessary bring the Thames Valley into the kingdom of West Seax. Do this and you will earn my favour. And then we will talk again about an alliance with your lord, King Aethelfrith. What do you say?"

Hussa did not reply at first. He was taken aback by what had just been said. With no more than one hundred men he somehow had to conquer an entire valley that was inhabited by thousands of Saxons. Nevertheless, this was an opportunity. If he could only pull it off it would guarantee the alliance and bolster his reputation immensely, both with Ceolwulf and more importantly, with Aethelfrith. He just had to work out how, in Woden's name, he could do it!

"Well?" the king asked, a touch of impatience in his tone. "I ask again: what do you say?"

Hussa met Ceolwulf's gaze and gave a slight bow, "I'll do it your Majesty, to the best of my ability, and I thank you for trusting me with this important campaign."

"Mm," Ceolwulf grunted. "Very well, in that case you and your men are once again welcome in my hall for Yuletide. I do not suppose you have had much cheer these last few months, but you must understand that it was necessary in the circumstances. Now, however, if we are again to be comrades in arms we will drink together." He smiled, "What say you to that?"

"Again, I thank you, sire."

During the weeks of Yuletide, Hussa, Rolf and others of his huscarls spent their days studying maps of the lands to the north and questioning anyone they could find who knew about routes, roads and fortresses in the Thames Valley. At night they enjoyed Ceolwulf's hospitality. Hussa noticed, however, that Boyden still held his distance, his expression distrustful and suspicious.

"Don't think he likes you, Hussa," Rolf observed one night as they sat drinking ale and eating roast boar.

Hussa commented acidly, "You are a perceptive man aren't you, Rolf."

About to respond, Rolf frowned, his attention caught by someone urgently gesturing at them from the doorway. It was the old woman, Nina. "What does she want?" he asked, getting up from the bench and making his way to the door.

Sourly watching him cross the hall, Hussa downed another tankard of ale. "Well, what is it?" he asked when Rolf returned a few moments later.

"You had better come, lord, it seems Rowenna has gone into labour and the baby comes quickly."

Hussa grimaced. None of his men, not even Rolf, knew about what had happened with Rowenna after the defeat at Boseham. Having no idea that she was likely carrying Cerdic's child and not his own, Rolf naturally assumed, as did they all, that he would be eager to welcome his firstborn son or daughter into the world. If the men knew the woman had betrayed him – leaving aside the fact that he had instructed her to seduce Cerdic, it still felt like a betrayal — and that his own half-brother had sired her child, would they expect him to show concern for the brat? Of course not!

All year Hussa had been avoiding thinking about the matter even though it was forever gnawing away at the back of his mind – always there, like a headache that would not go away. Now that the moment had finally come he was still not sure how he felt about this child. If it truly was not his, why should he care about it? Was it because there was the slimmest chance that it might be? He realised, as he drew himself to his feet and stumbled towards the doorway, that in fact it did not matter, for whatever he pretended to himself, he was terrified of losing mother or child, or both in what was always the most dangerous time for a woman.

As he hurried through the streets of Witanceastre, following along after Rolf and Nina, Hussa's mind was in a whirl. Reaching the house he could hear Rowenna crying out in pain. He wanted to go to her, but this was women's work and Nina had them wait in the hall whilst she went through to the bedroom she shared with her daughter. Hussa bit his lip as Rowenna gave a loud scream and then fell silent. He looked at Rolf, who laid a sympathetic hand on his shoulder holding him back. There was a pause and then another noise penetrated the silence: the high-pitched cries of a baby filling its lungs with its first breaths. A few moments later Nina came through to them cradling in her arms a small form wrapped in sheepskin.

"Here is your son, Lord Hussa. He is strong and wellformed."

Speechless, Hussa saw the top of the baby's head, streaked with blood, almost bald but dotted with dark hair. He leant over the bundle Nina proffered to him and studied the tiny, red, screwed up little face. The unfocused eyes that seemed to look up at him were like those he shared with Cerdic; their father's eyes. It could have been either himself or Cerdic as a baby. Hussa told himself that he knew this infant was Cerdic's, it had to be, didn't it? And yet, as soon as the old woman passed the child to him and he clasped it to his chest, an odd feeling of attachment grew within him. After all, this boy was at the very least his nephew; his own flesh and blood. Did it matter if it was not his own son?

Then, as soon as the thought had occurred to him he knew the answer. Yes, it mattered. It mattered a lot, but what was he going to do about it? Would he acknowledge the child as his own? Would he name it as his heir? He felt dizzy again, at first uncertain and then angry as he felt Rolf and Nina staring at him.

Hussa thrust the bundle back at the old woman, who looked up at him, confused. "What do you wish to name him, lord?"

"That's not for me to say, ask his mother. She... he... they are both welcome under this roof, but it is not for me to name him." He turned abruptly to Rolf, "Come on, back to the hall, I need another drink."

Rolf too was confused. The arrival of a healthy firstborn son was usually greeted with delight, but Hussa looked anything but delighted. Following him to the doorway, Rolf shrugged. "What's eating you?" he asked, but as Hussa turned and glowered at him, he fell silent.

Chapter Fifteen
Meifod
Spring 608

In the company of Aneirin and Prince Cadfan, who was lead-ing the embassy from Gwynedd, we took our leave of Iago and left Deganwy. With a few of Cadfan's men and my own four: Eduard, Aedann and two of the Wicstun veterans, we were a mixed party of Welsh and Saxon as we rode away from the fortress. Cuthbert was not with us. I had decided that he should spend some time with his family, especially given the frailty of his infant son, so I had sent him home with a message for Aid-ith; one that I hoped would take the sting out of my continued absence.

Our route took us down through bare grey mountains capped with snow, and then through valleys between gentler hills to the south of the high peaks. In these more modest uplands we passed cold lakes and waterfalls edged with ice. Cadfan had cho-sen a path that avoided the lands of the Dogfeiling and brought us to our destination from the north and west. Before entering the valley of Meifod, he had sent ahead a rider.

"The valley contains the hill fort of Mathrafal, which is the summer court of the kings of Powys,"Cadfan said. "Being in the foothills it is a good location for a cool summer palace but is not the ideal spot in winter or early spring. Our road takes us along the banks of the River Vyrnwy, past the fortress and so on to Meifod."

"King Cynan is at Mathrafal?"I asked anxiously. "I thought the whole point was to avoid seeing him until we had spoken to this Tysilio."

"It is unlikely, but that is what I am checking."

The rider returned soon with the news that Cynan was not at Mathrafal and that we had permission from the garrison's captain to proceed to Meifod. "The King is at Pengwern," he announced.

"Pengwern is the river fortress on the plains of Powys not far from the border with Mercia and more pleasant in the cold winter months," Cadfan explained.

As we passed Mathrafal, I observed that it was a palisaded fort with earth banks and wooden walls, lying snug up against the River Bawtry, which flowed east to join the Vyrnwy – the river we were following. I could see we were being watched from atop its battlements by a dozen curious guards. We crossed the Vyrnwy close to the confluence, rattling over a wooden bridge and onto the bare farmlands that lay on either side of the river. The fields were ploughed, but as yet no crops were visible above the bare soil.

About a mile or so beyond the river crossing we spotted Meifod. The site lay next to an orchard and a small lake fed by the Vyrnwy. On its banks was a circular wooden wall granting protection to the half dozen or so huts that clustered around a church. News of our approach had clearly gone ahead of us because at the gate we were met by a group of monks. When we drew to a halt, one of them stepped forward. He was a tall, whitehaired fellow with not an inch of fat on him. He leant on a plain staff and without speaking turned his head to gaze on each of us in turn. Finally he addressed us.

"Who comes to this holy enclave?"

"I am Cadfan, Prince of Gwynedd. I come seeking counsel of one who was once friend to my father, King Iago and his kin."

"I am Abbot Tysilio. I was and still am a friend," the monk answered. "So enter and be safe," he added.

131

I was at once impressed by this Tysilio. He showed no fear as we armed men approached him. Moreover, he was dressed in a plain monk's habit, had his hair cut like that of a common monk and bore none of the elaborate clothing and jewels that Augustine, his bishops and his churchmen customarily wore.

We rode through the gate and dismounted, whereupon some of the monks came forward to take our horses. I noticed one of them was staring at me and whispering something to Tysilio. The Abbot turned to look at me before moving to where Cadfan stood waiting. The two men had a murmured conversation then walked over to me.

Cadfan held out his hand toward me, "Lord Tysilio, may I formally present to you the Earl Cerdic of Deira. He is one of a group of Angles from Northumbria who are guests of my father."

The Abbot acknowledged the introduction with a nod. "As it happens, one of my monks was present at the meeting with the English bishops a few years back. He recognised you, Earl Cerdic, and it must be said that I am not best pleased to have pagans in this holy place."

"My lord," Cadfan said while I was still gathering my thoughts, "Prince Edwin, Cerdic's liege lord, is my own godson and a baptised Christian."

Tysilio looked sharply up at Cadfan. "So I have heard. There are many who do not approve of us sharing the gospel of Christ with men such as this. Men who have taken our lands, burned our churches and killed our people."

Cadfan nodded. "Just as there are many who argue that our reluctance to take the gospel to these men is what brought our downfall. Our pride meant we failed in our most important task; that of telling the lost and the damned the good news, as Christ Himself intended we should."

I figured that when the Welsh prince spoke of the lost and the damned he meant me. Conscious of Thunor's hammer hidden beneath my clothing, I glared at Cadfan, but remained silent.

Tysilio did not look convinced.

Cadfan tried again. "This man is sworn to the service of Prince Edwin who is baptised and saved. Is that not enough?"

"A wolf hidden in a flock of sheep is none the less a wolf, Prince Cadfan. Yet... I have an idea. A test."

"Test?"I asked.

Tysilio nodded gravely. "If God loves you even though you know Him not, then you will pass the test."

I hesitated then asked." "And if He does not?"

"Then you will fail, Earl Cerdic, and I will know you for a wolf!"

Nettled, I asked," Well what is this test then?"

Tysilio inclined his head towards a grove of trees that grew outside the monastery walls. "Come with me."

He led us all, monks, Welsh and Angle alike, to the grove of yew trees. Some were very old indeed, but it was to what I judged to be the most ancient that he led us. Some trauma must have happened to this yew in the perhaps seven or eight hundred years it had lived, for it was severely misshapen. One branch curved like the archway of a Christian church and had bent round in such a way that the end of it twisted around some of the tree's exposed roots lying above the ground. Thus it seemed to form an opening or portal and, from the Abbot's gestures, I guessed he intended me to walk through it.

Mystified, I turned to him and asked, "This is your test? Simply for me to walk under the branch?"

"That is the test," Tysilio confirmed.

I walked up to the tree and examined the branch. It seemed

133

ordinary enough: just a gnarled old tree bent over in an unusual manner, perhaps from a lightning strike at some time in the past.

I glanced at Aedann and Eduard to see if they knew something I did not, but their blank faces told me they were as puzzled as I was.

Cadfan too looked confused. "This man is brave, my lord. He has been of service to Gwynedd and is under my protection. If there is a hidden danger here then I would wish to know its nature."

Tysilio considered this for a moment then nodded. "Very well, I will tell you. Earl Cerdic and his companions are not the first Angles to come our way. A few months ago a group of traders from Mercia came this far. They mocked our God and doubted His power. They said they did not believe in miracles. I, praying that God would show His power, challenged the leader of the group, who was considerably older than his companions, to pass under that tree. He laughed at me as he walked into the archway, but beneath the twisted branch he was struck down and could neither move nor speak. God had answered my prayer and shown His power. The man died the next day."

"If he was an old man, though, maybe he had a seizure?" I suggested, trying to sound confident. After all, could their God really strike down a man passing under a branch? It seemed unlikely. Yet I was not as confident as I tried to appear. I had heard it said that the Goddess Freya held power over certain trees and that a man could not speak a falsehood when standing beneath them. Indeed, our ancestors had held trials under these trees for this very reason. If Freya could make a man tell the truth, was it not possible that this Christ could strike a man down?

I stared at the branch for a long time, trying to see if there was any sign of magic upon it. There was a slight movement in the gentle wind but otherwise it appeared an ordinary branch. I turned back to the Abbot. "So what will happen?" I asked. "You know already that I am a pagan. What will this test serve?"

"Pass under the branch," Tysilio said, "and we shall see if God chooses to strike you down. My monks and I will pray, and if God blesses your Prince Edwin and through him yourself, then you will pass through unscathed. If my God rejects you He will cast you down and we will know His Will. You will then have to leave this place… if indeed you are still alive and able to do so."

I didn't much like the sound of this! I stepped over to where Cadfan, Aedann and Eduard stood. "What do you think?"

Eduard answered first. "It's a tree Cerdic, that is all it is. A tree can't kill a man, not unless it falls on him and this old tree doesn't look like falling any time soon."

"What about magic, though? These priests have their own magic spells don't they Aedann?"

Aedann, who was, of course, a Christian, shrugged. "They would call them miracles not magic spells, Cerdic, but I have heard many tales of the priests as well as of the saints and what they can do. Best I can do is pray for you."

"As will I," Cadfan said.

"Very comforting," I mumbled to myself as I turned back. Nodding to Tysilio, I approached the branch and I also prayed. Not to his Christ, but to the old gods; the gods of my fathers who had brought us to this land and kept me safe at Catraeth and Degsastan and other places. Around my neck I wore Thunor's hammer, Tiw's spear and also Loki's snake. I touched them now as I asked for their protection from this Christian magic.

I stopped praying when I reached the branch. I had asked the gods to protect me. What would happen next was up to fate and outside my control. Yet one thing is always in a man's control:

135

the choice to do a thing or not to do it. Everything else is wyrd or fate. I was a man. I made the choice and firmly grasping the hilt of my sword, I stepped through the opening in the tree. And as a man I stood on the far side, peeping through squinted eyes, daring myself to breath. When the expected blow failed to arrive I turned to look at Tysilio.

He was studying me closely. I waited. Nobody spoke. After a few moments he nodded. "You passed the test, Earl Cerdic. My God has not rejected you and you are welcome at my fires," Tysilio said simply, then turning away he led his monks towards the monastery leaving the rest of us by the tree. I unclenched my fists and breathed out, releasing the tension within.

"Told you it would be all right!" Eduard chortled, slapping me on the shoulder before leaning in to look more closely at my face. "I wonder if these monks have some decent ale, you look pale, like you could use a jugful."

Aedann and Cadfan came closer. "He's right, you do look pale. Come, let us join our host," Cadfan said, setting off after Tysilio.

"You need not have been concerned, I told you I was praying for you," Aedann said quietly after Cadfan had left.

"I was praying too... to my gods."

"So?" Aedann said.

"So which ones were listening?"

"I have told you before that we Christians believe in only one God and it was He who answered my prayers," Aedann replied.

"Unless of course it was my gods who intervened and used their magic."

Behind us Eduard groaned. "I really am going to need some ale if you two are going to have a religious debate," he said, with such a hangdog expression on his face that it made us laugh. Still chuckling, we followed Cadfan towards the monastery.

Chapter Sixteen
Haiarme
Spring 608

"My grandfather moved the capital of Powys to Pengwern," Tysilio explained as we rode east out of the hills around Meifod and on to the plains that stretched away in all directions. "My family used to rule from Viriconium, the old Roman city on Watling Street. Then your people came and the city was hard to defend, so we moved."

Thinking of Eoforwic with its walls of stone, I was about to ask why, but Tysilio was apparently reading my thoughts, for before I could speak he added, "No walls at Viriconium. It was far from the threats of Picts, Irish or..." and now he nodded at me, "Saxons like you raiding across the sea. It was a trading settlement really. When the Mercians came, particularly when they captured Letocetum not far away, it was decided we needed a more defendable capital. The river helps with that."

I saw what he meant when we reached Pengwern. We had ridden along the north bank of the River Vyrnwy all the way to the point where another river joined it. Tysilio called this one the 'Hafren', but these days I know it by the Angle name of 'Severn'. The Romans apparently called it 'Sabrina', according to Lilla, who has since told me a tale of some water spirit living in it. Whether there was or was not a spirit in the water, the Severn was a wide river and a barrier to any army, whatever it was called. It formed a tight loop and a neck of land that was a mere three hundred paces across and led to a peninsular. Upon this was a hill and on and around this hill was a small city. It had been built of wood, for there was little stone nearby. Protected as it was by the river and with a wooden palisade across the narrow neck of land, this would be a hard place to attack.

All around Pengwern there were rich farmlands as far as the eye could see, full of fields ploughed and ready for the seed, separated by orchards and pasture. It would be a land worth fighting for.

Tysilio saw me appraising the landscape. "This is the Paradise of Powys. No harsh mountains, no deserts and no marshes. This is land made by God to feed man. Eden might as well have been here. My people will fight to defend it, Saxon, make no mistake of it."

For a moment I had a vision of these fields, orchards and farms ablaze with Saxon fire, its people's blood spilt by Angle blade. I understood why these Welsh felt so fiercely about their land. I shrugged. "I don't want your land, my lord, I just want a way to go back to mine."

"In that case, I bid you welcome to Pengwern, capital of Powys. We will see what is going on in my brother's head and try to sort it all out."

As he spoke we approached the gates. The battlements were well manned by apparently battlehardened men standing watch under the banner of the lords of Powys: a red lion on a field of gold. The road, lined on either side with houses and workshops, passed on up the hill. At the top stood a large hall – King Cynan of Powys's stronghold and winter palace. As we climbed towards it, the advantage of height enabled a view east. A single bridge headed that way, allowing the road from Pengwern to sweep down along the river to another crossing point close by an unmistakeably Roman city, all straight lines and white stone. Tysilio saw me looking that way.

"Yes, that is Viriconium. It is still inhabited but was not safe for the court of a king so it's a quiet market town nowadays. Shame that, for it is a pretty place."

We rode on to the king's hall and dismounted. Whilst some of Tysilio's monks and my men were seeing to the horses, another mounted party rode in. They were led by a young man of around twentyfive years and of fair complexion. As he dismounted, something about him reminded me of a younger Lilla. I mentioned this to Eduard.

"Some resemblance, I agree, but you know Lilla. He would say this fellow is not as handsome as he," Eduard replied with a wink. On my other side, Tysilio gave a delighted laugh, rushed over to the newcomer and embraced him. They exchanged some words and then Tysilio brought the young man across to us.

"This is my nephew, Prince Selyf of Powys, my brother's oldest son. Selyf, allow me to introduce Prince Cadfan of Gwynedd and Earl Cerdic of Deira."

Selyf inclined his head at the mention of Cadfan, a sign of respect for a fellow prince. When he heard my name, however, he flashed me a sharp look.

"Are you a companion of Prince Edwin of Deira, now in exile in the court of Gwynedd?"

"I am indeed, your Highness."

Selyf frowned. "My father may not be happy to know you are here, Earl Cerdic."

"Why is that, nephew," Tysilio asked. "Why the aggression to Gwynedd this past winter? Gwynedd and Powys have long been allies. Powys's fight has been with Mercia all along the Hafren, and with the kingdoms of Deheubarth to the south and west. The northern border was safe; a border with allies and friends. What has happened to change that?"

139

The prince gave a hollow laugh, "Would you believe it when I tell you that what changed everything was that my father got married?"

"Married?" I asked.

"I know he got married," Tysilio said. "I was there after all, but what has that got to do with this attack on Gwynedd? I don't understand."

"You were present at the marriage last year, true, but you have not been in court since then so do not know how things have changed. Mostly the changes are to do with the king's new wife. My father— " Selyf stopped talking abruptly.

"What about your father?" Tysilio prompted, but his nephew just shook his head.

"Not here," he said.

I thought at the time that he was anxious not to speak of his father the king in front of me and Cadfan, but thinking about it further, he was not looking at us but towards the king's hall. Standing on the steps looking around the courtyard was a women – a very beautiful woman. She was young, no more than sixteen perhaps. She wore a rich dress of red and blue trimmed with gold thread on collar and cuff. Her hair was partially covered, but copper red curls spilt out down her shoulders and back. She was easy on the eye no doubt, but for me the effect was marred by the suspicious glare she cast at our party and the scowl she wore on her pretty face. A moment later she turned and went back into the hall.

"Who is that?" I asked.

Cadfan grimaced. "That is the king's bride; that is Haiarme."

The name was vaguely familiar but I could not place it. Nevertheless, I felt a niggle of anxiety on seeing her.

"Come, I will introduce you to the king and try to argue for peace," Selyf said, leading Tysilio and Cadfan toward the hall.

Following them into the warmth, I saw fires burning in a number of fire pits and braziers dotted around the hall. By now it was approaching evening and the court was gathering in anticipation of food and drink. Curious eyes studied us as Selyf led us through the hall, many heads bowing in respect for the Abbot who accompanied us. Enthroned at the far end of the hall was Cynan. The warrior King of Powys was now in his sixties, yet of powerful build and imposing stature, albeit with a balding head fringed with white hair. He had little flab or fat on him.

"Seems like his young bride is keeping him well exercised, eh?" Eduard whispered with a smile, for once speaking softly so that only Aedann and I could hear.

"Father," Selyf said, approaching the king, may I present Prince Cadfan and party, guests of my uncle and here on embassy from Iago of Gwynedd in answer to the..." he hesitated "...to recent events."

In the murmur of conversation around us, I caught a few words: 'raids,' 'Angles,' and 'Edwin,' amongst them. All eyes were turned to us now as Cynan studied us. He got to his feet to clasp his son's hand and then embraced Tysilio, his brother. Finally, his gaze fell on Cadfan and the rest of us.

"Whom do we have here?" he asked.

"Brother, may I present Prince Cadfan of Gwynedd and his party," Tysilio said. "It is as Selyf says; they have come on an embassy from Iago."

We each bowed to the king. Cadfan stepped forward. "My father, King Iago, sends his greetings to you, noble King Cynan, and with them his wish for peace. I am here in an attempt to resolve any dispute between us."

Cynan grunted and then turned to retake his place on his

throne. "Tell me, Prince Cadfan, does Iago offer me what I ask for… the handing over of Prince Edwin of Deira and his ragtag band of followers?"

Cadfan shook his head, speaking carefully with as much respect as his voice could carry and yet with resolute tone. "Prince Edwin is my godson and adopted son, sire. He and his party are guests in Gwynedd. King Iago has extended his protection over them. As such we will not hand them over."

Cynan remained silent, staring at Cadfan who stumbled through his next sentence. "Sire, forgive me, but what is your interest in the Deiran exiles? Why are you so bothered about them?"

The king's eyes widened at the question. "Is it not enough that they are the enemies of our blood? Thieves who took from us the lost lands and killed or conquered our people. A better question would be why would you, prince of an ancient house, protect murderers and bandits?"

Cadfan glanced at me. "I have found they have more honour than we have been taught. Perhaps our two races can live side by side, Welsh and English, at peace."

"That will never happen!" Cynan exclaimed. "Our very blood calls out to us for revenge against them. How can you stand there and protect them? How can you trust them?"

I was starting to get more than a little nervous at this exchange. So far, only Selyf and Tysilio knew we were Angles and not Welsh. I noticed they were both keeping quiet, perhaps waiting for the right moment to let Cynan know about that fact.

"My experience of them as comrades in battle against the Scots and Irish has taught me trust," Cadfan replied. Then he took a deep breath, "However, your Majesty, leaving aside that matter, my father asks how we can resolve the present dispute and become allies once more."

As he was talking I noticed that Haiarme had appeared out of the shadows behind the throne, presumably from the royal quarters. What worried me, however, was catching sight of the two men who accompanied her; one I recognised as Kadir, the huge Irish warrior who had defeated me. Indeed, he would have taken my head had Cadfan not come to my rescue. The other man I did not know – broad-shouldered, though shorter than Kadir, and a little older. I whispered a question to Abbot Tysilio.

"Kadir is there. It was he who attacked us, but who is the other man with Haiarme?"

"Morfael. He is the lord of... or rather, the King of Dogfeiling. His armies attacked Gwynedd supported by Kadir's Irish."

So that was Morfael. Ultimately his men were used in the attack. Was this all part of his plan to get more power for himself? Seeing him side by side with Haiarme and Kadir worried me. Something was very wrong here. Some deeper plot. I turned my attention back to Cadfan and Cynan, who was shaking his head as he replied to Cadfan.

"I have already made clear how you can resolve it. Hand over Prince Edwin and his party. Did you not understand my message brought to you by Hywel?"

"I understood it, sire, but I ask again, why are you so bothered about them? They are no threat to Powys. Has Aethelfrith of Northumbria asked for them? Is that it? Is his envoy, Hussa, here?"

The king was on his feet again. "The world will end before I do a thing because an Angle has asked it!"

"Well then, your Majesty, why demand Edwin be handed over?"

Cynan turned to glance at Haiarme and his face softened. It

was as if forty years had suddenly fallen away from him and in that moment he looked like a lovestruck youth, the age I had been at Catraeth; the age I had been in fact when I first loved Aidith. It was clear he was besotted by his beautiful young bride.

He turned back to Cadfan. "I demand it because it is to be a wedding gift to my wife. I promised I would present her with the people responsible for the death of her father."

"Oh shit," I mumbled to myself, because I now remembered where I had seen that beautiful face before. It was four or five years before, and she would have been little more than maybe ten or twelve years old at the time, but I had seen her at the court of Áedán mac Gabráin, King of the Scots, when I had gone there with Hussa on a failed peace mission. I shivered at the memory, for it had led to months of imprisonment in a stinking hole beneath the stronghold of the Scots. Haiarme had been no more than a face in the crowd, but even at that age her striking beauty had attracted my attention. She must have been a person of high rank to have married a king like Cynan. If she had been a princess of the Scots, her father would have been a prince. Who?

My mind was in a whirl. Two princes of the Scots had died at the hands of the Angles. The young firebrand youth, Bran and his older brother, Domanghast, who had died at that fight in the stone circle. The fight that had kindled Áedán mac Gabráin's hatred of us. It was not our fault. In fact Hussa had started the fight and Aethelfrith had killed Domanghast, yet there was no denying that we Deirans had been there, and to a daughter who had lost her father to Angle blades, the difference between Aethelfrith's Bernicia and our Deira was a small one. In her eyes we were all Angles; all equally guilty.

I had never heard her name before now, but she had the same eyes and nose as her father. Haiarme was clearly Domanghast's

144

daughter.

"It wasn't us. We weren't responsible for him dying!" Eduard burst out in badly accented Welsh. I was fairly impressed he had followed the conversation, which was all in Welsh, but aghast and horrified at his outburst.

"Oh Woden's balls!" he mumbled, as all eyes, including those of Haiarme and Kadir, turned on him and then on the rest of us. As Kadir fixed his gaze upon me I saw his eyes widen.

"That is one of them!" Kadir pointed. "I almost killed the bastard in the raid. That is Earl Cerdic, one of Prince Edwin's chief lords and advisors!"

Haiarme burst through the group around the throne and in a startling display of speed, leapt forward and slapped me on the face before being pulled away by several of her handmaids.

"Murderer!" she cried. "You were at the battle where my father died. I will see you suffer!"

"Your Majesty, this man is one of my party. We have come here in peace!" Cadfan protested as the king's guards moved towards us.

"Father, you cannot do this!" Selyf exclaimed.

"Please, my brother, see sense," Tysilio pleaded.

It had no effect. Haiarme, whose handprint I could feel stinging on my cheek, was on her knees before Cynan.

"Fulfil your promise, my husband," she begged him.

"Seize the Angles," Cynan ordered, "They are to be put to death at once!"

"Oh Woden's balls!" Eduard repeated. "Sorry, Cerdic."

Chapter Seventeen
The Thames Valley
Spring 608

Rowenna had called the boy Hal. Its significance was not lost on Hussa. Firstly, the name started with an 'H' – just as his own name did. Her people would traditionally name their children in such a way that the names started with the same letter as their sire's. She was laying a claim on Hussa – telling him that Hal was his responsibility just as she was. She was also telling the world the same thing. Secondly, there was the name itself. It meant ruler, householder and leader. She intended the boy to have more than she had – to own and rule land and men. Hussa could make that happen, she was saying. If he so chose.

The symbolism was not wasted on his men either. Although they did not dare say anything, he would see them watching whenever the child was in the same room as Hussa. Waiting to see if he would recognise the child as his own. They were puzzled, that was clear, as the winter turned into spring and the child grew with the waxing days.

"I don't understand you, "Rolf said – the one man who would dare to speak his mind, whatever the consequences – "What is it you fear? Anyone can tell by looking at him that he is your son. I would be proud to have such a son. Yet you turn your back on him and the woman."

"I have not turned them out of my household. I have fed and clothed them."

"You know there is more to it than just that. Take him, acknowledge him, and name him your heir. That is what I would do."

Hussa glared at him. "What you should do is keep your nose out of my business. Go, make sure the men are trained and equipped and ready to leave tomorrow. We have a long march ahead of us and maybe fighting at the end so just do your job or I will find someone better."

Rolf stared back for a moment before nodding and turning away. Rowenna came over, carrying the boy. She sat on the bench next to Hussa and placed Hal between them. He was growing fast, Hussa noticed, already able to sit on his own. The baby looked up at him and smiled. Despite himself, Hussa felt a smiled curl his own mouth before he turned away and stared into the fire.

"So you go away tomorrow," Rowenna stated.

Hussa nodded, not taking his gaze off the fire. "Yes. I will leave one of the men as a guard and you may live in the house until I return."

"Hussa, what am I to you?"

Finally, he looked at her. "Not now… I do not wish to discuss this now."

"When then? A little over a year ago you took me to your bed. You treated me as your woman. Then you used me like a whore to seduce your brother and spy upon him and his people… "

Hussa slapped his hand onto his leg in frustration. "You were already a whore and a spy. I simply bought you and used you and then I freed you. You chose to stay. Be thankful that I continue to give you shelter and food."

"Is that all I am to you then? Just a woman you once used and feel obliged to keep?"

"It is all I can give you, Rowenna. If you want love, devotion, kindness, you picked the wrong brother. Cerdic can maybe give you all those things. I cannot."

147

"Cerdic has a woman and children already, and besides, I do not love him. It is you, Hussa, that I love."

Hussa shook his head. "Then you are a fool. Home, family; that is Cerdic's story. Not mine."

"It could be yours!" she cried.

Hussa got abruptly to his feet, saw Hal's gaze follow him, but ignored the plea in the little boy's eyes. With a sobbing hiccup, the child began to cry. His mother picked him up and held him close to comfort him as Hussa turned away, conscious of her glare boring into the back of his head as he strode from the room.

"So, where are we going and what is the plan?" Rolf asked. It was a week later and he and Hussa rode at the head of a column of spearmen – the mixed company of Hussa's own fifty men and thirty West Saxons that Ceolwulf had given him to command; fewer than Hussa had hoped for. They had left Witanceastre and taken a Roman road that had led them to the tiny village of Swinedunne, which lay near the intersection of two roads. Swinedunne was located in a woodland clearing and all around it the pigs and boars after which it was named rooted for food amongst the trees. The inhabitants had watched the West Seax warriors warily as they approached and turned onto the road that would lead them north east, towards the Thames Valley. Hussa had called out that they were here on the king's business, but the village Ealdorman did not seem to know or care which king or which kingdom they came from, just so long as the villagers were left in peace along with their pigs, it seemed.

"This road takes us into the upper Thames Valley," Hussa answered Rolf's question, pointing ahead of them. "Swindunne is the furthest north that Ceolwulf has reached and as you can see from the local inhabitants, it is by no means strongly held. Indeed, no one kingdom really holds this area. It's between Mercia and West Seax and other lesser kingdoms, British and Saxon."

Rolf sniffed. "Bloody confusing, if you ask me."

"It is that," Hussa replied. "East of here are the dense forests of Celemion. Ceolwulf is trying to surround it and to do that he needs the Thames Valley to join with West Seax. The Thames runs to the north of Celemion."

"I see," Rolf nodded. "So who holds the Thames Valley?"

"No one – leastways, no one king. According to Ceolwulf each community governs itself. The river proved an easy route for Saxons from Lundunne to push deep inland between the forests of Celemion and the Chiltern Hills. As they made their way up river, successive warlords built new towns or captured and subdued British settlements along the way. If you look at the map, you will see that from the furthest point inland the warlords reached, there are numerous small towns or villages strung out along the Thames: Doric, Garinges, Readingum and Wochinoes to name a few."

"So you're saying we take over one and move on to the next?"

"That's what I'm saying," Hussa said.

"With eighty men?" Rolf frowned in disbelief.

"Yes, well I am hoping persuasion might work."

"And if it does not, what then?"

"Oh; then we resort to deception."

"Sneaky tricks you mean?" Rolf grinned.

Hussa laughed. "My area of expertise wouldn't you say?"

"What if that does not work though?"

"Then we fight," Hussa said, a glint in his eye.

Rolf shrugged. "Just as long as we have a plan, I'm happy. So where do we start?"

"Doric; evidently it's Roman; they called it Durnovaria, so

Ceolwulf said."

They travelled along the road, north and east through woodlands, often following the chalky track that rose above the surrounding land. Hussa looked down at the track as they rode along it. It was not lined with stone like the decaying Roman highways, but a pathway formed over thousands of years by the tread of many feet – human and animal – in the chalky, rocky surface. Rolf must have noticed the same thing.

"It's old this road," he said. "Not Romanbuilt I mean."

"No. It's been here forever, leastways that's what the Britons in West Seax say. It's an old drovers' road running all the way to East Anglia, or so they say."

"I wonder how many have travelled along it – how many long forgotten kings and men?"

"Who knows? It's our road now and it's up to us to make sure we are not forgotten."

"That is down to wyrd and destiny," Rolf said quietly. "It's in the hands of the Norns, the Valkyries and the gods."

Hussa shook his head. "I don't believe that. I have made my own path and I am still making it." He turned to look at Rolf. The intensity of his stare made Rolf shiver and seeing it, Hussa asked. "Are you afraid, my friend?"

"Half the bloody time, yes. You are like a shooting star, consuming all in his path yet still bright with glory."

"You don't have to follow me."

Rolf shrugged. "I do if I want part of that glory!"

Three days later they made camp where the track, known as the Icknield Way, emerged from woodland south west of Doric. A little way ahead of them, where the path met and crossed first a Roman road running northsouth and then the River Thames, lay a settlement. It was a small Saxon village of two dozen huts.

Beyond the river in the distance were other Saxon villages. To the north the road crossed a loop in the Thames before passing over a lesser river into the small, walled stone city of Doric.

"This does not look easy, Hussa," Rolf said. "It's surrounded on three sides by water and on the fourth by a fortified wall."

Hussa nodded. "This is as far up the Thames as the Saxons have yet penetrated. The villages are Saxon, the city British. North of here, Mercia has yet to arrive in force, so the Britons hold on here, living side by side with the Saxons, who also do not have the strength to build a kingdom. Peaceful and harmonious coexistence forced by necessity."

"Peace that I take it we are here to destroy," Rolf stated dryly.

"Indeed. That north south road leads to Calleva. It is the first axis of attack on Celemion that Ceolwulf needs."

Hussa studied the scene for a while before turning to the company. "Ricberht!" he called out.

The leader of the West Seax portion of the company emerged from the ranks. "Lord Hussa," he replied.

"I am told you speak Welsh."

"Yes lord, from my mother. My father is Saxon though."

Hussa reached into his pouch and handed over two silver Roman coins.

"Take this and two men and visit the city. Find out the strength of any garrison and what you can about the defences. Be back here by dawn tomorrow."

Ricberht nodded and departed.

Hussa now turned to Rolf and passed him more coins. "Rolf, take Wilbur and another and visit the villages. Find out what you can about the mood of the Saxons. Would they support an attack on the city, that kind of thing. Again, be back tomorrow at dawn."

Rolf nodded and soon he and two others were striding across the meadows to the nearest village. Hussa looked at the sun, it was reaching midday. "Everyone else, set up camp, rest and eat. You may hunt in the woods to the west but go no closer to the river."

That night, Hussa's sleep was disturbed by dreams of the house back in Witanceastre. Rowenna sat by the fire cradling Hal. Then she turned to Hussa and passed him the boy. Hussa held him for a moment then suddenly swung round and threw the boy into the fire. The child screamed but it was now the hated face of Cerdic's mother that he could see burning in the flames.

He woke with a start and sat bolt upright, pulling his fur and cloak around him, staring into the embers of the nearby camp-fire and breathing heavily.

"Woden's balls, but what was that about?" he asked himself. After a moment he heard the sound of conversation between the guards and someone outside the firelight. The scouts were back. As they approached, Hussa rose, stirred the fire into life and threw on more wood. Gesturing them to take a seat and warm themselves, he waited for the report. Rolf spoke first.

"The first settlement is called Welingaford and is close by a ford over the Thames. At Welingaford there is just a small farm and half a dozen hovels. No more than thirty people live there. A mixed British and Saxon family who, I think, would not care for war and just want to be left alone to farm and breed their cows. The next village is called Benson and is very close to the city. It's a lot larger; more like two hundred there and some good, fit men, a number of which look like they can handle themselves. The Ealdorman of Benson - his name is Eorpwald - has no love for the Magistrate - that's what they call the one who rules the city - since he had Benson's son hanged for some dispute over a cattle theft. Neither Eorpwald nor his people want a battle, but they do resent the power of the city. The Magistrate rules the area like a Roman governor, as if it's still part of the Empire. I think the people of Benson might agree to join West Seax if that meant being rid of the overlordship of the city. I am not sure what I think of Eorpwald himself, though. I suspect he has an eye on the role of local warlord. Maybe if we take over Doric we can place Eorpwald in charge. After all, someone would need to be after we move on."

Hussa nodded. "True, but that would be Ceolwulf's decision, not mine."

"Of course, yet whoever you put in place would surely be considered by Ceolwulf?"

Hussa shrugged, accepting the point. "Do you trust this Eorpwald?"

"I'm not sure. He had the feel of an opportunist about him."

Hussa looked across at Ricberht. "What have you to say?"

"Lord, the Roman road from Welingaford goes north along the west bank of the Thames. There is a point when the river loops westwards. There the road crosses the Thames and then turns to cross the smaller river, the Thame, and so reaches the south gate into the fortress of Doric. It is well defended from the land side by a stone wall, which the Britons maintain and man. Yet the Thames side is set a distance back from the river beyond fields and meadows, and the stone wall there is not as well preserved. Indeed, there are gaps. I estimate they have forty armed defenders amongst a population of perhaps five hundred. There is something else, lord. As I said, the Roman fortress is placed more across the neck of the loop formed by the river rather than within it. So there is a gap of meadow land between river and wall of several hundred yards. Moreover, there are earthworks near there, an embankment or dyke across the loop."

"Part of the Roman city defences?"

Ricberht shook his head. "I don't think so. Looks older – maybe the Britons made it or maybe the Old People."

Hussa nodded. Another piece of this land created by people that were long forgotten when the Romans came. Just how old was this Britannia he wondered.

"What you are saying is that the river cannot be seen from the city because of the embankment?"

"Yes, lord."

"What about the river. Can it be forded at that point?"

"Yes lord. Not the Thames itself – we will need to cross that on the Roman road, but where the Thame meets the Thames there is a ford across the Thame. So we could cross to the meadows rather than use the road."

"I see." For a moment Hussa was silent, thinking through what Ricberht had told him. Then he asked another question.

"What about the people themselves and this Magistrate?"

Ricberht scratched at his chin before answering. "It is like Rolf said, the place seems to have carried on as if it was still part of Rome. We saw this Magistrate walking through the streets. He was dressed like in those paintings you sometimes see of Roman senators."

"He wears a toga?" Hussa said, surprised.

"Yes, and his guards are dressed like Roman legionaries, with scale armour and steel helmets. "

Rolf snorted. "Pompous ass, hanging onto the glory of an empire that's not been here for two hundred years. I say we string him up by his toga. "Around him the men laughed.

Smiling, Hussa waved a hand to silence them as he thought it all through. "I don't have any problem with that suggestion, if that is what is necessary. Yet I perhaps smell an opportunity here."

He stared into the fire and thought some more, then pointed at Rolf. "Send a message to this Eorpwald. Tell him that the overlordship of the area is his, providing he comes with as many men as he can to the city gates at dawn tomorrow and supports us in an attack. Then take half our men and make your way quietly to some woods near Benson. Remain out of sight. I do not want you to be seen or heard. At dawn tomorrow assemble near the city gates on the road from Benson to Doric. We will then see what Eorpwald does."

"I'm going to need more than half the company if you expect me to attack the city gates with or without the support of these Saxons," Rolf said.

Hussa laid an arm on Rolf's shoulder. "You are not going to be attacking the city gates my friend. Your job is to see what Eorpwald does. The city gates are my problem. Mine and Ricberht's. I'll take Wilbur too. But I am not going to tell you what we will be up to, just in case any of you are caught. What you don't know you can't tell. But do your utmost not to get caught, Rolf. Just remain hidden in the woods and be outside those gates at dawn tomorrow is all I ask."

Rolf looked extremely unhappy, but he set about kicking and bullying Hussa's men into action. Soon forty warriors had assembled and were marching away across the fields eastwards. After they had gone Hussa gave instructions to Ricberht to have his West Seax men ready to march at noon.

That afternoon, Hussa and Wilbur led Ricberht and his company of West Saxons, as quietly and stealthily as they were able, through the fields and copses between their campsite and Doric, aiming for the point at which the Roman road crossed

155

the Thames some miles to the south of the city. As dusk was approaching they left the road and headed across country until they reached a patch of woodland near the small River Thame. From the shelter of the trees Hussa peered in the direction of the city, now only a mile or two distant. He could make out the tops of buildings but could see no obvious high point where a man on watch might easily observe them, and anyway, in this diminishing light they would be hard to spot. He beckoned his men out of the woods and led them silently to the river.

At the point where the Thame approached confluence with the Thames, its course became extremely tortuous so that a series of small isthmuses protruded into the river. As the sun set behind the forest lands to the west, Ricberht led them along one of these narrow strips of muddy land. As he had reported, at the far end of the isthmus the river was indeed extremely shallow and fordable. The company passed across the river and assembled on the far bank to the north. East of the river a low ridge obscured their view of the city. They plodded across the damp marshy meadows until they reached the ancient earthworks.

Gesturing for the men to wait, Hussa clambered up the slope aiming for an elm tree growing at the top, which would provide him with cover. It looked almost as ancient as the earthworks, bowing like an old man over a depression in the ground. From beneath its branches he could look down on the city without being seen. He was now opposite the western wall, which lay a couple of hundred yards beyond the embankment. The stonework had decayed in the two centuries since the Romans left, yet like so much of their legacy, it still presented an impressive barrier to an attack. However, as Ricberht had reported, it did not prevent a small group of men traversing the wall, so long as they could approach stealthily. Hussa had given instructions earlier

156

in the day to carry drinking water in skins and to wrap shields and spears in cloth, fur and wool to muffle the sounds of them clattering together. For his plan to work, stealth was essential.

Satisfied with what he had seen, Hussa went back down the slope to the waiting men. "We will remain here until it is nearly dawn," he said quietly, "so I suggest you all get as much sleep as you can. And if anyone hears someone snoring you have my permission to slit his throat!" There were some muffled sniggers at that, but the men soon settled down.

Having set a watch, Hussa selected a spot for himself next to Wilbur, who was already asleep. He drowsily dozed, drifting in and out of sleep, but unable to settle completely, eager as he was to get on with the business in hand. Eventually, when the morning star rose above the horizon in the still dark eastern sky, he nudged Wilbur awake and motioned him to wake the others.

"Tell the men as quietly as you can to relieve themselves as necessary. They are to say nothing and make no sound. When everyone is ready, we will cross to the city," he said softly.

Not long afterwards he was leading them across the open fields to the wall. As there was no guard on this western section, they were able to climb the decaying stonework and haul themselves up onto the battlements. Once assembled they kept their shields and weapons muffled and followed Hussa as he set off around the perimeter. The eastern sky was now lightening, the yellow line on the horizon followed rapidly by a sliver of golden globe. It promised to be a fair day.

Hussa could see two guards silhouetted against the skyline. They stood on the battlements above the main gate in the south wall. Hopefully it would not occur to them to look round. He pointed at them and motioned his men to crouch down. He did likewise. And now they waited.

The Roman road, which approached the main gateway from its crossing over the Thame via the village of Benson, was fast becoming visible as the sun climbed the sky. Hussa peered down at it and along its length as far as he could see. In the distance he could now make out the rooftops of Benson one or two miles to the south. The road was empty.

He was just starting to wonder if Rolf had forgotten his instructions, when he saw him emerge with his half of the company from the shadow of some trees growing near the road. As they began to assemble near the city gates, Hussa looked around for Eorpwald's Saxons who were supposed to be joining them. At first he saw nothing. Then he spotted a glint of sunlight reflecting off a spear point or sword hilt. It was carried by a warrior standing at the edge of a copse close to the road and only fifty paces from Rolf's flank. As he watched, some thirty men in rather aged looking Roman armour emerged from the woodland and at their side were around as many armed but unarmoured Saxons.

Meanwhile, back at the gateway Hussa saw a man in a toga stepping up onto the battlements flanked by ten guards. It could only be the Magistrate and he had clearly been forewarned.

"Bastard! "Wilbur mumbled behind him and Hussa nodded. Rolf had been right to suspect Eorpwald of duplicity and opportunism. Given the choice of supporting their attack upon Doric or siding with the local British warlord sitting within the fortress, Benson's Ealdorman had chosen what he saw to be the less risky option, no doubt hoping for a reward and more power as a result.

The sharp-eyed Rolf had spotted the threat and bellowing out an order swung the company round with an ease that betrayed the experience of a dozen battlefields. Hussa heard him yell out the order to form a shield wall and an instant later a barrier of wood and iron faced the emerging enemy. Rolf's men were veterans, yet outnumbered and likely to soon be outflanked. It was time for Hussa to act.

"Stand up men and unbind your weapons. As loudly as you like, "Hussa commanded. Grinning and making as much noise as possible, Ricberht's forty men got to their feet. Hussa drew his sword, his beautiful, magnificent longsword, symbol of his triumph over his brother long years ago. It was on days like that one – days like this one in fact – when he had tricked an enemy who thought himself so clever, that Hussa felt like a god. Smiling, he gripped his shield and sword, pointed at the Magistrate and yelled, "Charge!"

He set off along the battlements at a run, followed by Ricberht, Wilbur and the rest of the company all shouting threats at the tops of their voices as they thundered along behind Hussa.

Ahead of them, the Magistrate and his guards turned with horror to see death descending upon them in the shape of a young warrior lord swinging a terrifying blade around his head.

Two of the guards, quicker thinking than the rest, tried to lock shields to form a rudimentary shield wall, but Hussa's momentum was such that as he smashed into their shields they were knocked onto their backs and with two vicious thrusts of his blade to their throats, they were dead in an instant

Ricberht and Wilbur were right behind Hussa and in the blink of an eye were amongst the Magistrate's guards, slashing about them with their own swords. Hussa jumped through the gap between two guards and now only one remaining warrior stood between him and the cringing Magistrate.

This warrior, however, was no novice. He parried Hussa's first attack with ease. Catching his breath, Hussa stepped back to consider his opponent. Clearly a veteran, he bore the helmet and uniform of a Roman centurion. Around and behind him Ricberht's men, whose warrior skills were vastly superior to those of their foes, were beginning to slaughter the other guards and as far as Hussa could see, were sustaining no damage to themselves. It was child's play in fact. The veteran saw it too. He grimaced as he looked around him and knowing the fight on the battlements was already lost, he lowered his sword.

Outside the gates, the Britons clad in ancient armour had halted their advance upon Rolf. Each of them was staring up at the battlements aghast at what he saw: their Magistrate outnumbered and clearly about to be killed.

"It is over, Magistrate," Hussa said. "We hold the city gate and we hold you!"

The Magistrate pointed down at his men outside the city. "Yet out there we still outnumber you, Saxon!"

"Maybe – but each of my men is worth two of yours and even if that were not true, you are up here not down there. In a moment your captain here will die and you will be next."

"I'm not afraid to die for my city," the Magistrate said, a defiant tone edging his voice. Not a craven then, despite his outlandish garb, thought Hussa.

"Maybe you are not afraid to die, Magistrate, but would you not rather live to rule your city and this area?"

"What trickery is this? I don't understand…" the Magistrate faltered staring hard at Hussa, clearly thinking he was being taunted before he was killed.

Hussa smiled. "Then let me explain. My name is Hussa. There is no trickery; I come here on behalf of Ceolwulf, King of West Seax. He claims all these lands from the Chiltern Hills to the sea. You control this city that once belonged to a mighty empire. We are building an empire once more. Join us. Have your men drop their weapons and no more of them will be harmed. Neither will you. Indeed, you will still rule the city, but on behalf of Ceolwulf of West Seax to whom you will owe allegiance."

The Magistrate looked down at the fields outside the city then back up and across the battlements. After a moment, he nodded his head and waved at what remained of his guards. With resignation they dropped their swords, which clattered onto the battlements. Then he turned and shouted a few words in Welsh to his warriors outside the gates, who commenced throwing down their weapons. The Saxons from Benson looked confused and bewildered as it sank in that they no longer outnumbered Rolf's company. Eorpwald, who was on horseback, tugged on his reins, kicked in his heels and galloped away southwards along the Roman road. Seeing this, some of the Saxons turned and ran; the rest dropped their weapons and held up their hands in surrender.

"Take the Magistrate and his guards below to the central buildings of the city," Hussa instructed Ricberht and his men. "I will follow shortly. Wilbur, come with me."

They descended the stairs to the gates, which had now been opened, and there greeted Rolf as he led his half of the company into the city.

Rolf stared at them for a moment, apparently unable to find the words he wanted to say. Finally he opened his mouth.

"Would somebody mind telling me what, in the name of Thunor's balls, just happened?"

Hussa shrugged, said nonchalantly, "Like I told you; a bit of fighting, some persuasion and the odd bit of deception."

Rolf laughed out loud. "Sneaky tricks you mean!"

161

Chapter Eighteen
East
Summer 608

"Locked up again! "I groaned. "All because of you and your big mouth!"

"Sorry Cerdic,"Eduard replied sheepishly.

"Well, boys, cheer up. At least we are not dead... not yet anyway!" Aedann commented as he looked out through the grill in the prison door of our cramped cell, the five of us taking up every inch of available space. "Mind you, that Cynan seems a little bit... unbalanced... don't you think? What about Haiarme? Merciful God but what a woman."

He was right of course, there was something wrong with Cynan. The King of Powys was practically foaming at the mouth as he screamed for our death, encouraged by his fierce wife. Cynan was known as a powerful warrior king who for thirty years had marched his armies the length and breadth of the Welsh lands. Indeed, whilst he clearly had a deep hatred for my people and had fought battles with Mercia up and down the Severn valley, as well as clashing with Iago's Gwynedd, the greatest of his wars and campaigns had always been against the other Welsh kingdoms of Deheubarth – which meant the southern lands of Brycheiniog, Ceredigion, Gwent, Builth and others. A confusing collection of would-be kingdoms that rose and fell, coalesced and broke apart.

Lilla had told me a bit about Powys and its king, and that he would often ride a chariot into battle. "Just like the chieftains of old, who fought the Romans," he had said. "They would charge hundreds of chariots at the enemy, using throwing spears and bows with deadly accuracy. No one uses chariots these days, except Cynan. He has a gleaming white one, so the stories go."

So, in his white chariot the King of Powys had conquered far and wide: a man to be feared and respected indeed, but now, it seemed, he had changed and was bellowing like a madman for our blood.

"This is more than mere politics. Haiarme has cast her spell over Cynan and he is totally under her enchantment," I said.

"Besotted he is, no doubt about that," Aedann said.

"Well, we have seen it before. Old men and young women I mean, "Eduard said. "One of my uncles once left his wife for a young Welsh slave. Made a total arse of himself over it. Nothing worse than an old fool besotted with a young woman."

"I thought we were about to be decapitated before Tysilio spoke," I said. "I am not sure about his God, but it is clear these Welsh hold their Abbot in huge respect."

That we had not been killed straight away was entirely due to the intervention of Tysilio, aided by Selyf. After we had been seized by Cynan's guards, Tysilio had told the story of testing my soul by getting me to pass under the tree at Meifod. There were gasps of awe and the bowing of heads in veneration to the Abbot. Clearly the fame of the miracle of the poor old Mercian trader being struck dead by the power of God had spread far and wide.

"God has spoken and this man is chosen by Him," Tysilio had then said.

"But he is a pagan, he worships false gods and demons!" Morfael objected in a hoarse gruff voice that reminded me of Grettir's. "Cerdic of Deira has killed many Christian folk, Welsh and Irish, I have heard the tales."

"He was at Degsastan and slayed hundreds!" Kadir shouted.

"Not quite hundreds…" I mumbled, more from a sense of getting the facts right than in an attempt to defend myself.

"Silence, pagan!" Morfael responded, moving towards me, but once again Tysilio was there between us, holding up his hands.

"The Bible teaches us that the Apostle Paul was not a Christian when he was chosen by God. The Almighty chooses men for His own reasons. My heart tells me that this man has a role to play in God's plan before he dies."

I cannot honestly remember ever being so pleased to be involved in any god's plan before that moment. I did not believe a word of it of course. All these years later, well… I have seen a lot and experienced a lot and maybe I have a more open mind then I did back then. Abbess Hild and Paulinus and others have had much to do with that in my later years. As for Tysilio, I sometimes wonder what he would think of the man I have become and the part I did play long after he had died. Maybe he is up there, in that Christian heaven, turning to the next saint and saying, "I was right. "But I digress. That is another story from many years later and for another day, perhaps.

After Tysilio had spoken, Selyf too had his say. "Whatever we do, Father, I urge caution. Prince Cadfan at least is an ambassador here from a former ally. We cannot fight all of the Welsh kingdoms at the same time. We face an alliance against us in the south and hostile Anglian lands to the east. We surely must make peace with Iago?"

Selyf seemed to be getting through to Cynan, for he nodded in agreement at that, but then Haiarme spoke again. "I will avenge my father and take retribution on those who caused his death. The men and their leaders must all pay," she insisted.

Cynan was nodding at that too. Was he becoming senile, I

wondered. A strong man with an iron will now struggling to keep up with events.

It was Cadfan in the end who managed to get through to him. "If Cerdic and Edwin and his companions are guilty of crime then justice must be done. But sire, I beg that you do nothing in haste now. Let us return to Gwynedd and bring Edwin and his men to a meeting to hear the accusations against them. Let witnesses be called and let us find the truth."

Looking straight at me, Kadir was shaking his head. "If they go back to Gwynedd, what is the guarantee that any will return?"

"Very well; let Prince Cadfan and his guards go to Gwynedd and I and my huscarls will stay here as hostages," I said, indicating Eduard, Aedann and our two veterans.

"So be it,"Cynan said.

That then was that. Cadfan and his Welshmen left for Deganwy to seek council with Edwin while I and my companions were led away into yet another prison cell. I did seem to spend more than my fair share of time locked up.

Actually, it was not as bad as it sounds, for a few days later Selyf managed to persuade his father to allow us to move into the prince's own quarters in another part of the fort, and although we were still under guard and unable to leave Pengwern, we were at least a lot more comfortable.

Soon after our confinement began, Cynan and most of the court migrated to the summer palace in the hills, which we had passed on our way to Meifod. Haiarme and Kadir went along too although Morfael returned to Dogfeiling.

For several weeks we were left in Pengwern under the supervision of Selyf whilst we waited for news from Gwynedd. Spring had turned to summer and as time went by I began to give thought to escape. I knew that no favourable answer would come back from Deganwy. Edwin would not willingly leave us captive and would agree to hand himself over to Cynan, but I could not see Sabert allowing him to ride into danger. Nor could I see Cadfan agreeing to hand over his adopted son. I did not blame either of them. Had the roles been reversed I would have been the same. Before too much longer it would be apparent to Cynan and Haiarme that they would not be getting fifty or sixty Angles, but just we five. The thought occurred to Aedann too.

"We are buggered aren't we?" he said one morning as, watched by two of Selyf's guards, we sat eating freshbaked bread and cheese washed down with ale. At least the rations had improved now that Selyf was our jailor. We had been restricted to stale bread and water before.

"Possibly," I replied quietly, hoping Eduard, who was sitting further down the table, was not listening. I did not want him hearing and then shouting out something. Subtlety was not one of his strong points.

"Come on, Cerdic. We both know that either Cadfan or Sabert will prevent Edwin coming. So when that mad bitch Haiarme figures it out we will be dangling from the nearest oak tree, you mark my words."

"Well then, we have to try and make sure she doesn't get the chance don't we?"

"How do you suggest we do that?"

"We escape and soon," I hissed.

"Escape!" Eduard boomed. "When?"

I glanced over at the guards and grimaced as I saw that Prince Selyf had walked into the room and from the expression of amusement on his face he had heard Eduard.

"Your man here asked when you were going to escape. Don't

166

you think you should tell him?"

"Your Highness, he sometimes gets carried away with wishful thinking," I said, with a glance at my old friend that I hoped was full of dark threat.

Eduard's face now was the picture of innocence. "What?" he said.

Prince Selyf laughed. "As it happens, the reason I ask is that I have come to help you escape. I just wondered if you had a better plan than riding out over the bridge today."

I gawped at him. "What?" I asked, not sure I had heard aright.

Selyf broke off a chunk of bread and chewed at it. "I have just returned from Mathrafal where we learnt that there has been an attack in the South. My father has taken the army down there to fight. That leaves Haiarme and Kadir alone at Mathrafal. They do not mean to wait for news from Gwynedd. I overheard them planning to come here and kill you all. I got out of there before them, but I am sure they cannot be far behind me. We must move quickly if I am to get you away from here."

I stood up at once, but then asked the question on my mind. "Why? Why let us get away?"

Selyf shrugged. "Mainly because I don't want a war with Cadfan and Iago. If you die that is what will happen – either as a direct result or when Iago refuses to send Edwin to us after hearing of your deaths and Haiarme persuades my father to attack. One way or another, I must stop a war with Gwynedd," he insisted.

I nodded. "Very well then, what do we do?"

The prince looked us up and down. "Reckon you could pretend to be farmers?"

I glanced at Eduard and winked before nodding at Selyf. "You know, I think we probably could."

Selyf's plan was pretty simple in the end and that made it a good one in my opinion. He had arranged for a local farmer to make a delivery of ale and cheese to the hall. The farmer came with a number of farmhands in three wagons. Once they had unloaded their goods Selyf took them into the hall and as it was getting late, invited them to stay the night. They were then liberally plied with ale and feasted. If the farmers were suspicious of the prince's generosity they had clearly decided to bury their concerns and just enjoy the moment.

Whilst the farmers were slipping into a drunken stupor, which Selyf reckoned they would not sleep off until well into the following afternoon, he had arranged for our quarters to be left unguarded. The two guards who should be watching our door had been instructed to help the farmers unload the wagons. The prince then persuaded them to enjoy a drink also and they did not argue.

Thus it was that before dawn, while it was still dark, we thanked Prince Selyf for his aid and generosity – I had no doubt that he would be in severe trouble from his father when our escape was discovered – and dressed in plain, worn garb that he had found for us, slipped out to where the wagons stood waiting beside the hall. By now our belongings, including our saddles and my swords, Catraeth and Wreccan, along with our amour had been deposited into the back of the wagons. Having been instructed by Selyf to do so, a couple of stable boys had already harnessed the farmer's draught horses. I was relieved to see them. Had the farmer used oxen, as was more usual, our journey would have been slow indeed. It seemed the gods were smiling on us. Our own lighter mounts had been bridled and roped to the back of the wagons, the reins knotted round their necks. A stable lad was not going to question his prince's orders, however odd they might seem, and I had no doubt Selyf would reward them for their silence. One of them stretched and yawned as we approached.

"Early isn't it?" Aedann said by way of greeting. As we had agreed, the rest of us nodded blearily but did not speak so that only Aedann's native Welsh would be heard.

The stable lad grimaced. "Yes indeed. Why are you up so early?"

"It'll soon be harvest time, friend, and the farm is a fair step away," Aedann said. "I want to get home today so we can pre-pare to bring in the barley. A farmer's work is never done," he added with a smile.

The lad yawned again. "Well, rather you than me," he said and waved us on our way as we clambered up onto the wagons. Aedann and I mounted the lead wagon, Eduard took the next and my other men the third. And we were off down the hill to-wards the bridge. Like the gate in the wall this was shut at night, but the bridge warden had been bribed and as we approached he pulled back the gate and we rattled across to the east side and then down the road towards Viriconium, surrounded by dark, silent fields. The only sounds were the gentle lapping of the river at its banks and the earliest bird noises. By the time we reached the old Roman city, however, there was much more sign of life. By now it was dawn and the city was waking for the day ahead, which promised to be a hot one as the sun rose in a cloudless sky.

We approached Viriconium from the west, our road taking us once more over the River Severn which, after we had crossed it on the bridge at Pengwern, had looped off to the north and then back down, so we had followed its west bank for the last mile or so. The road crossed a ford in the river, the waggons bouncing up and down on the stones of the river bed as we splashed across, pausing to let our sweating horses drink from the cold stream.

Next we passed through a modest embankment, but no palisade was in evidence, nor the stone walls of Eoforwic. It was not defendable as it was. A couple of Mercian companies could take this place in no time, I thought. I had no premonition that I would witness them do exactly that a lifetime later when, as an old man, I would see the place in flames.

It was not burning on that day, yet it was a hollow shell; a ghost of a town and a mere echo of what it had once been. Only a few hundred lived here now, not the thousands that had inhabited Viriconium in its time of glory. As we navigated the potholes of our Roman road, which was the western end of Watling Street, all about us lay the decaying corpses of buildings. In the centre of the city we passed the bulk of the forum building to our left and the bath house on our right. It was many lifetimes since men and women had bathed in this particular bath house and the forum's roof had collapsed, leaving cracked and weather-beaten pillars thrusting skyward. The bath house had been turned into a market with several dozen small stalls, each sheltering under canopies and awnings positioned along the outer wall, which the road passed, and around a courtyard on the far side of the wall.

We were eyed suspiciously by the market traders so I had Aedann jump down from the wagon and buy some wine, cheese, bread and salted meat to feed us on our way, reflecting again what a boon it was to have a natural Welsh speaker as one of my closest friends. I waved at a child who was sat on a pile of stone rubble eating an apple and she smiled back at me.

Aedann climbed back aboard as we left the other end of the

market and passed a priest leading some monks into a house, which appeared to have been converted into a church. He glanced up at me and I bowed my head respectfully as a good Christian might, remembering at the last moment to make sure my collection of pagan symbols on a thong round my neck did not slip out from their hiding place!

Beyond the church we passed a collection of abandoned temples, whose worshippers had been lost to the Christian god the Welsh now worshipped. I reflected upon this new god's power. I had seen something of the influence he was gaining over my own race in Cantia, and it was clear he had at one time also drawn Romans away from Saturn and Mars. Would the day come when this Christ triumphed over all or would he too in turn fall to other gods? As I record these my memories so many years later, I know the answer to that question, but I didn't know it back then.

I blinked and shook my head to clear it of these thoughts and concentrate on the task ahead. The sun was now climbing high in the sky and I wanted to be well past Viriconium come nightfall. Threading our way past the last few townsfolk going about their daily tasks we drove out through what was left of the outer eastern embankment. Here, Watling Street bent round to head east and we followed it, for as I had agreed earlier with Selyf, it was to the East that we needed to go.

"You cannot escape to the West or South as that will take you deeper into Powys and in any event, Haiarme and Kadir are coming from the West," he had said. "Nor is it safe to head to the North, the direct path to Gwynedd, for that way would take you through Dogfeiling whose inhabitants seem to be most close to Haiarme. No, it must be east to Mercia."

"Pybba of Mercia will not be happy to see us," I had replied 'yet we have an ally there in Lord Ceorl, maybe he will help us. Maybe we can seek passage or shelter with him."

As we drove eastwards, the farm lands once again stretched out on either side of us. Tysilio's 'Paradise of Powys' – fertile fields bulging with ripening crops and full of fat livestock. Tysilio was right to say that once the Angles beheld these bountiful lands they would want them. For now, and for some years yet, my race were some way away, but not that far and not forever.

The sun was sinking now, silhouetting in the west a high, isolated, flat-topped hill. From its shape I knew it was likely an ancient hill fort – one of those constructed by the Britons long before the Romans came, and abandoned by them during the centuries of Roman rule. This one I later learned was known as the Wrekin. In many places these old hill forts were reoccupied and fortified once more as a bulwark against the coming Angles and Saxons. I saw the glow of a fire from within the camp at the top; it seemed that here too the old forts were in use again.

We pulled off the road to camp for the night not far past the Wrekin, bringing the wagons up the slope of a gentle hill close by a belt of woodland and away from some marshy ground near the road. There was a small stream running into it so we were able to water the horses. Aedann and Eduard released them all from the wagons and roped them to a couple of trees leaving sufficient length of rope for them to graze.

As darkness fell it began to rain, so we slept under the wagons for shelter, taking it in turns to stand watch. I took the last watch and in the silence before the sun rose I watched the sky begin to lighten and the stars to vanish one by one. As I sat on the back of one of the wagons chewing on some bread and gulping a little ale, I noticed something moving on Watling Street to the west from whence we had come. I peered back down the road. At first it was just a movement, but from the elevation of the hill on which we were camped, I was soon able to make out the form of horsemen; maybe two dozen trotting towards us. They were maybe a couple of miles away, but it would not take them long to reach us. It might be quite innocent, of course, but I could see they carried a banner and I was not going to take that chance. Did I catch the hint of red? The banner of Powys was red, but so too was that of Dogfeiling!

"Wake up!" I shouted. "Get up quickly, we have to go."

"What is it?" Eduard grumbled.

In answer I simply pointed.

"Woden's balls!" Eduard swore.

"They will overtake us if we use the wagons," Aedann observed.

I nodded. The wagons had suited their purpose. Time to abandon them and our disguise as farmers. "Get your armour and weapons, release the draught horses and saddle up our own. Let's be on our way. Hurry!"

Speedily we pulled on our chain shirts and helmets and fastened our sword belts. Soon our horses were saddled and the five of us were mounted. The riders were now no more than a mile away. Eduard slapped the rumps of the draught horses so they scattered into the trees, then we turned our mounts eastwards and dug in our heels.

I had banked on our horses being fresh after a day of gentle walking behind the wagons and a full night's rest, and so they were. We set off at a gallop, widening the gap between us and whomever pursued us, for it was obvious now that we were being pursued.

After a while, one of the men shouted that the horsemen were closing again, so perhaps they had changes of mounts and were rotating them so as to keep up the pace. Not having spare mounts, we were forced to reduce our initial burst of speed, alternating our mounts' gait between a canter and a fast trot, but as it neared midday, they had begun to flag. At this point the rain returned, much heavier than it had been in the night and it soon became difficult to see far, which had the effect of slowing us down. This at least allowed the horses to recover a little and the rain cooled us all down. I had worried that we might be overtaken, but it seemed that our pursuers had also been forced to slow down.

All through that dreary and wet afternoon we pushed on, soaked to the skin and bone weary, our horses beyond tired and reduced to walking pace. Then, as we approached the ruins of another Roman town, its bath house and civic centre buildings crumbling and surrounded by the wooden huts of a more recent settlement, the rain stopped and the clouds cleared to reveal a red sunset, boding well for a fine morning. It also revealed that our pursuers were almost upon us.

Twenty horsemen, trotting along under two banners: the red kestrel of the Dogfeiling, and the white horse on a green field of Kadir, less than three hundred paces away and closing fast.

The weather might well be fine come the morrow, but I wondered if we would be around to enjoy it.

"Move it!" I shouted and dug in my heels, urging my mount to make one last effort. I eyed the ruins and settlement ahead. It looked familiar. Maybe if we could reach it we might put up a fight at least.

"Come on, move it!" I bellowed and the chase was on.

Chapter Nineteen
Wall
Summer 608

A head of us the villagers were watching us hastening towards them, pursued by a mounted warband. One of them was shouting something back over his shoulder towards the ruins. Beside him another had pulled out an ox horn, which he raised to his mouth. The horn sounded clear and strong and a moment later was answered by other horns more distant.

The horses were floundering as we reached the edge of the village and hurriedly dismounted.

"Who in Hel's name are you? "a thickset brute demanded in English. He was standing on the road at the entrance to the village, shield on one arm and handaxe in the other. Behind him more men were arriving, each carrying a shield and weapons, although for the most part these were farm implements or seax. These folk were English-speaking so we must have reached the border between Mercia and Powys.

"Well?" he asked.

I hesitated a moment. The last time we were in Mercia, the king here, Pybba, had been about to hand us over to my treacherous brother and it was only the intervention of Pybba's cousin, Ceorl, that had saved us. I had no certain idea how welcome we would be here. I had to say something though, and in the end I opted for honesty.

"Cerdic, son of Cenred, Earl of the South Marches of Deira, and my companions. We are known to Ceorl, the king's kinsman."

He gave me an odd look at that comment, but I did not know why. "So you are Angles then," he asked.

I nodded. "You too, I assume?" I said.

He nodded then held out a hand. I took it. "Magen of Wall," he said.

"Wall?"

"We call it Wall on account of the Roman wall here. The Britons who live amongst us say it has a Roman name: Letocetum, or something equally unpronounceable."

"Ah, yes. Thought I recognised the place. I have been here before. There is a well near here and some monks, am I right?" I said, recalling passing this way when we had first come into exile some three years before. We had come from the North then, not the West.

He grunted the affirmative and then stared back past me. The horsemen had arrived and were also dismounting and arming with shields and spears. I felt marginally better seeing they were not trained cavalry like the Gododdin, but just mounted infantry who use horses for transport but fight on foot. Even so, twenty-five fully armed and armoured infantry were more than a match for the five of us and I was not sure if the ill-equipped Mercians would intervene or if they did, how much use they'd be.

"What about these bastards? They Angles too?" Magen asked.

I shook my head. "Welsh of Dogfeiling and a few Irish Scot allies of theirs."

He ejected a gobbet of spit on the ground at his feet. "Hounds of that she witch queen then," he said.

Surprised, I was about to ask what he knew of Haiarme when Kadir stepped forward, pushing through his band of warriors. I had not spotted him before but he had clearly recognised me. However, it was to Magen that he directed his attention.

"We mean you and your villagers no harm," he shouted. "We merely want you to hand over these rogues and murderers for our justice."

Glancing at me, Magen asked, "What did you do?"

"Nothing to him. It's Haiarme that wants us. She blames us

Deirans for the death of her father, a prince of the Scots."

"Did you kill him?"

"No, nor did my men, but we were present when he died. The man who actually killed him is my enemy too."

Kadir was getting impatient. "Well, will you hand him over to face our justice or must I come and get him?"

Magen spat again. "This is Mercia, mate. Your justice does not apply here. You would be best advised to go home. As for coming to get him, I would not recommend it," he said, an edge of steel to his voice.

Kadir blinked, "You are joking aren't you? Ten of you and five of them against twentyfive of us."

The Mercian laughed. "I think your head count just went out of date, mate."

Behind us I heard the pounding of boots on the crumbling stone surface. I turned and saw a dozen more spearmen, these fully armoured and equipped with swords; two of them also had bows. In a moment they had joined the nascent shield wall and we now linked shields so that a solid barrier blocked Kadir's advance.

I could see his gaze roll over his opponents as he assessed us. He was weighing up his chances; twenty-five versus twenty-two was not such an attractive proposition. He frowned, coming to the same conclusion I had. We were formed up, pretty well equipped and holding a defensible position that he could not outflank. The odds were not great.

Now it was Kadir who spat towards us. "You will regret this, Mercian," he said. He turned and walked back to his horse. Mounting, he glared once more at us, then more particularly at me.

"You can't hide forever, Cerdic," he said.

Gesturing at his men to mount up, he tugged on his reins and wheeled away. His men clattered after him, but we stayed in position until we were certain they had gone.

Finally, I turned to Magen. "Thank you for that, we are in your debt. But why did you take the risk. You don't know us."

He shrugged. "You mentioned Ceorl and we are his men. He posted us out here with instructions, amongst others, to watch for any contact from Edwin of Deira, as well as for you. We were to let you through and get you to him safely. There is more, though. I don't particularly have reason to trust any Dogfeiling or their allies. Whilst we have been posted here there have been an increasing number of raids across our border, all apparently ordered by Morfael on the instructions of Haiarme. I have lost some good men. Anyway, I had better get you to the king."

I was alarmed at this news. "To Pybba? I regret to say that he is not exactly going to welcome us or be pleased to see us," I said.

Magen laughed. "Pybba won't have any opinion on the matter, you can take my word for it."

I frowned. "Why is that, then?"

"He died. His son, Penda, is too young to rule, so the Witan elected Ceorl as the new king. Tomorrow we will take you to him; he is in Tamwerth."

This was good news indeed. Mercia had not been hospitable to us when we were fleeing Deira back in 603. Indeed, only Ceorl had been friendly – a man keen on an alliance with Gwynedd so he could focus on the threat from Northumbria. Now we had an agreement with Gwynedd and with Pybba dead, Mercia and Gwynedd could be allies. That, just maybe, gave Edwin the hope of opposing Aethelfrith in battle. And if we won a victory, we could go home to Deira. My hand strayed to Thunor's hammer at my neck and I sent up a brief prayer to my gods. I had thought yesterday that they were on our side and now I was sure of it. "Yes," I said, "I definitely need to speak to King Ceorl!"

Magen proved an amiable host. Instructing a couple of stable boys to take care of our exhausted horses, he invited us to his camp just east of Wall. The Romans had, it seemed, built a fort there and the remains of this – a short wall and outer ditch housing several barracks – had been taken over by Magen's company.

"The border with Powys has become more dangerous of late, so Pybba, and after him Ceorl, decided to maintain a garrison here. It's not much, but its home to sixty men; their families live in the village of Wall, "Magen explained.

One of the barrack blocks had been turned into an ale hall and now it was after sunset, the garrison and their families were gathering for the evening meal. This was briw – a tasty stew of barley, carrots, onions, peas and beans and some lumps of gristly meat that I could not identify. Maybe not a feast, but my friends and I, poorly fed as we were and after a tiring day, were suddenly very hungry. We wolfed it down along with bread and ale, which was much stronger and sweeter than we were used to, but tasted good all the same. Then Eduard challenged Magen to a drinking contest.

The Mercian declined at first. "I have to set the watch soon," he said.

"You mean you're afraid you will be passed out, face down in your briw whilst I am still guzzling on the barrel," Eduard said.

Magen's men laughed at this, but there was more in the laugh than mere humour, as if they knew something Eduard did not.

"Erm… Eduard," I said tentatively, "maybe it is not such a good idea…" but by then Magen had filled two huge horns with ale and passing one to Eduard lifted his in a toast.

"May the best man win!"

To begin with they kept pace with each other well. Eduard started to gain in confidence after three full horns, but it was the confidence that ale gives a man, for after two more he started to look confused whilst Magen gulped away without any apparent effect. After two more, Eduard suddenly stood up and turned to me.

"Cerdic," he muttered.

"Yes," I replied.

"I think I should tell you something," he said after a pause, swaying on his feet.

"What?" I asked.

"I am going to be sick" he said. And so he was, all over the reed covered floor. He then slumped back onto his bench and slid to the ground.

Magen's men roared with laughter and all of us, except the now comatose Eduard, joined in.

In the morning we mounted up again. I had been afraid that we might have broken our horses' winds or that they would be lame after the hard ride, but in fact they had been well cared for by Magen's stable boys and seemed none the worse for yesterday's exertions. We rode with Magen and two of his men as escort, Eduard, moaning about his sore head, bringing up the rear.

"What on earth do they brew that beer from, do you think?" he muttered to Aedann, who winked at me and shrugged.

It took us half the morning to reach Tamwerth, stronghold of the kings of Mercia. We climbed the hill to the fort and entered the gates that we had snuck out of under cover of darkness a few years before. One of the guards at the gate gave me a suspicious glance and I wondered if he had been one of those whom Ceorl had arranged to be drunk whilst on watch so that we could get past him. If so, he would have been severely punished by King Pybba.

The hall of the kings of Mercia was largely unchanged since I was last there; except in one regard that is. We followed Magen through the outer doors, past armed guards and into the long chamber with its central fire pit and with tables and benches on either side. Then, at the end, sitting on the same highbacked chair wherein we had seen Pybba, was Ceorl. Dressed rather plainly for his rank, he was an austerelooking, middleaged man with greying hair, which was perhaps a little greyer than I recalled.

Magen and I stopped in front of him and bowed. Ceorl studied me for a while before speaking.

"So, you are back, Cerdic. Welcome. We have much to discuss."

"It seems so, your Majesty," I replied.

And we did. That night I was invited to sit at the high table next to Ceorl, with Magen on my right. Ceorl had no sons, despite being married many years, so on his other side sat young Penda, Pybba's son and, at least at present, the Atheling or kingworthy. The little lad was no more than four, maybe even three and he apparently had two younger brothers – mere infants. Pybba had left it very late to father heirs and as a result the Witan in Mercia had elected Ceorl, Pybba's cousin, as their king. Penda was excited by the entertainment that accompanied the meal – a juggler and a magician doing their acts, but soon grew bored when a harpist began playing, and yawning he toddled off with his mother, Pybba's widow.

After he had gone, a young woman stepped in front of us holding an earthenware jug from which she poured more ale for both Ceorl and myself, before bowing and retreating. With long golden hair and eyes of azure blue, she was certainly pleasing on the eye. The cupbearer for the king would usually be a close relative. As I've said, Ceorl had no sons, but he did have a daughter. I guessed this was she and that with his elevation in status, she was now a princess.

"Your daughter, sire?"

Ceorl glanced across the hall at the princess, who was now sitting back at the table and picking at a chicken leg.

He nodded. "Cwenburgh, my only daughter. It is of her that I wish to speak, amongst other things."

"Powys, being one of the other things?"

"Yes. As you recall from our last conversation, I desired peace with Gwynedd and Powys so that Mercia can focus on threats from Northumbria and its allies."

I frowned. "Allies?"

He sipped at his ale before answering. Meanwhile, the harpist had finished and around us everyone in the hall applauded. A bard stepped forward and began to tell the tale of Beowulf, one of our oldest tales. He did not tell it as well as Lilla, but its familiar rhythm and words worked its magic over the company, for soon most fell silent, enthralled by the tale of the battle with Grendel.

Next to me Ceorl stirred again. "I have news that West Seax is close to becoming an ally with Northumbria."

I pursed my lips at this unwelcome news. "My brother is in West Seax, stirring up trouble, or at least, he was last year."

Ceorl nodded. "My spies tell me that Hussa is Aethelfrith's ambassador there. He has been working on an alliance whereby West Seax and Northumbria divide Britannia into two: the North and the South. I fear that his words are finding a receptive audience."

I could now understand Ceorl's need to have peace with the Welsh of Gwynedd and Powys. "So this trouble with Cynan and his new wife is the last thing you need," I said.

He took another gulp of his ale and waved Cwenburgh over to refill it. She offered me more, but I declined. I wanted a clear head to concentrate on what the king was saying, and as I've said, this Mercian brew was remarkably strong.

"Cynan was fighting along his southern borders," Ceorl said, setting down his goblet. "These Welsh seem to be happy to kill each other just as much as we Angles are happy to slaughter other English. The pity of it is that I was just getting somewhere with diplomatic approaches when he goes and gets married."

"To Haiarme; the Scots princess?"

"Yes, and that is the problem. She is a Scot and blames all Angles for the death of her father Domanghast."

"So I hear," I said.

"I would not mind so much if a Mercian was responsible, but none of us was within two hundred miles of the bloody place when he got himself killed."

I pursed my lips. "Unfortunately I was there, but it wasn't us who killed him – it was Aethelfrith's and Hussa's doing. That matters not at all to Haiarme. She wants all of Edwin's party handed over and strung up and is demanding that Cynan delivers us to her."

"It makes no difference who was responsible. She is twisting Cynan to her will and what she seeks is revenge. Her personal guard are ScottishIrish, of course."

"But what about the Dogfeiling? Why is Morfael involved?"

"The Dogfeiling feel they are an ignored branch of the royal family of Powys. They hope to gain more power by being aggressive and proactive. Their lands border Gwynedd to their

183

north and parts of Mercia to their east. They sense the chance to regain lands."

It was as I had suspected. "It's quite a problem," I said.

Ceorl fixed me with a stare. I thought he had drunk too much but that stare was firm. "It's a problem that you and Prince Edwin must solve."

"Us?"

"Yes, because if you do this you can bring Gwynedd and Powys into an alliance with Mercia to oppose Northumbria and West Seax."

I shrugged. "Even assuming for the moment that we can, somehow, deal with Haiarme, Cynan, Kadir and Morfael and achieve peace, why would the Welsh trust us?"

"Because Mercia, Gwynedd and Powys would be linked by marriages."

I glanced at Cwenburgh. "Your daughter?"

He nodded. "Gwynedd and Powys are already linked by marriages I believe."

"Yes, Cadfan's mother was a princess of Powys."

"Then we will link Cadfan's family to Mercia," Ceorl said.

I nodded. "But Cadwallon is a little young for marriage. And besides, he does not approve of alliance with the Angles," I pointed out.

Ceorl shook his head. "I am not talking of Cadwallon. Is Edwin not now a son of Cadfan?"

"Yes, adopted by him."

"That it was adoption does not matter. He is legally Cadfan's son. A marriage between him and Cwenburgh would link Mercia and Deira, Powys and Gwynedd in a powerful alliance. Such an alliance could have the strength to oppose Aethelfrith. Return to your prince, Cerdic. Between you, you must find a way through the Powys problem and then this wedding can happen."

I glanced at the pretty young princess. She was wealthy, showered with gifts and owning jewels and fine clothes a peasant girl could only dream of. Yet which was luckier? The peasant girl would not be used in this game the gods played with us. I could almost imagine Loki chuckling with interest as he made his latest move and pushed Cwenburgh's piece close to Haiarme's in the chaotic game board we all occupied.

"Very well," I said. "I will head back to Gwynedd as soon as we are rested and provisioned, and go talk to Edwin. I am sure he will be delighted when I tell him of Cwenburgh. She is a beauty, sire."

Ceorl turned to look at her and his austere features creased in a proud smile. "Isn't she, though," he said, before downing his ale.

On reaching Gwynedd a week or so later we found that Edwin and Sabert were back in Deganwy, so I decided to head on there. Before I did, though, I figured I really had to spend some time with Aidith. Events had transpired to keep us apart for almost another year. The conversation we had been having had been interrupted by the arrival of Kadir and we had not had a chance to resolve the issue that was driving a wedge between us. In the chaos of the attack, we had sent the families away and by the time they had been located, I was already on the way to Deganwy at Iago's summons. In the letter that Cuthbert carried home for me when I sent him back from Deganwy, I had made no mention of how Aidith and I had parted, and having been involved with the embassy to Powys and imprisoned thereafter for several weeks, I had been unable to do anything about it. It had been yet another year when I was away more than I was at home and I dreaded what sort of a reception I would get.

Sian who was now approaching four, seemed very shy around me – I was not greeted this time by a screech and a hurtling child. She instead smiled nervously and went back to playing with a doll. Cuthwine, on the other hand, did hug me. My son was growing fast; Grettir told me he worked hard at his training and was coming along well. I made this comment to Aidith after we had finished our evening meal. She surprised me by slamming the crock plates down hard on the table.

"Don't you know why?" she asked in a tense voice.

"I don't understand…" I hesitantly replied. "All boys dream of war and battle. It is not as heroic as he thinks but I will tell him one day."

She was shaking her head. "That is not what he is dreaming of, you dolt. Don't you even know your own son?"

I frowned at her. "What do you mean?"

"He trains hard because if he does well he hopes you will take him with you when you go away. Cerdic, the boy needs his father. He misses you so badly and he thinks this is a way to be with you."

"Oh… I see," I said, uncertain what else to say.

"As for Sian, she could not remember what you looked like last week. She has given up asking if you will come back because when you do you are hardly ever here more than a day or so. And now that you are here she will still not have time to get to know you again because you are leaving tomorrow and who knows for how long this time." Aidith's voice broke as she added. "And every time you go away I never know if I will ever see you again."

Speechless, I stared at Sian. She was lying on the floor near the fire, wrapped up in her cloak and drowsily looking at the flames.

186

"Cerdic, what do we mean to you?" Aidith pleaded. "What do I mean to you?"

I went over and held her to me. Recently she was resistant or stiffened at my touch. This time, however, she allowed herself to fold into my arms.

"You mean everything. You must know how precious you are. I love you all."

She tilted her head to look me in the eyes. "Me? Do you still love me?"

"More than the world," I replied and I kissed her. It was the first time I had done so in over a year, and I kissed her in such a way as I had not done since returning from Suthseaxe. My guilt and anxiety about Boseham fell away and as I felt her respond, I wanted her more badly than ever before.

We moved into sleeping area and for the first time in what seemed like forever made love. We both needed it so desperately and for the moment we forgot the world; we ignored princes and kings; enemies and friends. There was no world. There was just us.

When we had finished she rolled over and turned to look at me. "Cerdic, we need you just as much as Edwin; just as much as Deira. Always remember that."

"I will," I said. I watched her as she drowsed into sleep. She was right. I was away far too often and for far too long. I had to do something about it. With renewed resolve I told myself that I would do something about it.

"So what you are saying is that we merely need to sort out the matter of a mad queen who wants us all dead; her senile, crazy husband who started a war to get at me; along the way deal with an ambitious rival monarchy; defeat an Irish warband and establish an alliance between races who have fought each other for years. Do all that and I get myself a royal bride and Ceorl will perhaps support my claim against Aethelfrith?"

"That is about it," I replied. "I know it won't be easy."

"On the contrary, it will be very easy. As it happens I was only just worrying about what we would do next week to keep busy. Now I know!" Edwin teased.

I could not help laughing, though in truth it was no laughing matter. When I had arrived back at Deganwy and gone to see Edwin and Sabert, I had filled them in on the situation and they had both been rather gloomy at the prospect. Not the opportunity of an alliance with Ceorl, but the lengths to which we would have to go to achieve it. It was clear, however, when we were invited to a general council meeting a few days later, that we had to come up with something.

Iago asked for reports from Cadfan and myself, which we duly gave. When the lords had been brought up to date with events, Cadfan spoke.

"Edwin is my adopted son. He and his people are under my protection. I will not hand them over to the so-called justice of Haiarme. Cynan is no longer in full control of his kingdom."

Cadwallon now stood. "With respect, Father, I oppose this position. You would risk war with Powys for a small band of exiles. It is madness."

Around us many nobles were agreeing with the young prince. At least half the council seemed to feel that our protection was not worth war. Gwynedd was divided between those supporting Cadwallon and those lining up behind Cadfan.

Iago lifted his hand and silence fell once more. "I granted these people protection. I would not happily remove that. Yet neither would I start a war. Prince Cadfan, Prince Edwin, you must find a way to resolve this matter without a war and find it before the winter ends! "

Edwin bowed. "I will, sire!" he said.

188

Chapter Twenty
Down the Valley
Summer to Autumn 608

After the capture of Doric, Hussa found the Magistrate, whose name was Septimus Maximus, most accommodating. He had the banner of West Seax raised above the man's house, which was the largest building in Doric and had been used as the council chamber. After inspecting the city and making some suggestions about the repair of the western wall, which had proven vulnerable to their own infiltration, Hussa left Doric under the administration of Septimus, but he also left Ricberht as a representative of West Seax, along with four of Ricberht's closest companions and huscarls, one of whom was sent to take control of the village of Benson.

Before leaving, Hussa asked Ricberht to name a good man from amongst the West Seax Company to replace him as their commander.

After thinking for a moment Ricberht said, "Tolan is a good warrior. He does not panic easily and is reliable as well as a bloody good man with a spear. I have seen him skewer three men in one go before now!"

Once the men had been rested for a few days, their equipment serviced and their provisions replenished, Hussa set off south along the east bank of the Thames. He took with him the twenty-six West Seax men and two dozen of Septimus's legionary warriors. This, along with his own fifty, now gave him one hundred men to continue the conquest of the Thames Valley.

The next significant town was Garinges, which lay around ten miles south of Doric. This was an important town to capture because it lay in a gap in a line of hills that included the Chilterns. These hills were home to the Chilternae, a tribe with mixed British and Saxon ancestors, who held the valleys and heights, their Saxon settlements curving around the Thames Valley following the course of the river. The Chilternae would have to be pacified or conquered one day, but that was not Hussa's job this year. Capturing Garinges was, as it was needed in order to gain access to the towns of Readingum, Wochinoes and others, all located in the lower Thames Valley. He only hoped that one hundred spears would be enough.

In the end his anxieties proved unjustified, for as they approached Garinges they could see that this was but a small Saxon settlement without the fortifications of Doric. It possessed a crude earthen embankment and a ditch, but no palisade, and unlike Doric, no stone walls. Moreover, there could not have been any more than twenty-five armed men to defend the town and surely they would assess the impossibility of their predicament. This proved to be the case, for as Hussa's company approached they were met on the road north of the settlement by three town elders, who held their arms wide to show they were unarmed. Behind them on a hastily erected flagpole flapped a crude representation of the West Seax dragon.

"I think they are surrendering, lord," Wilbur said.

"I think they are too," Rolf agreed.

They were both right.

The oldest of the three individuals stepped forward. "I am Jacob, Ealdorman of Garinges. We wish to avoid any bloodshed and having heard of your conquest of Doric, pledge our town to the kingdom of West Seax."

Hussa dismounted and approached the man. "I am Lord Hussa. How many men at arms do you have?"

"Twenty, my lord."

"Very well Jacob, this is what we will do. Ten of your men will join my company and accompany us on our campaign. The remainder will garrison Garinges. They will be under your command, as will the town. Obey my instructions and any others you receive from King Ceolwulf, and you will all be unharmed. However, rebel against the rule of West Seax and Garinges will be burned to the ground. Are my words clear?"

The grey-haired elder nodded vigorously, rubbing his hands together with anxiety. "Can I assist in any other way, Lord Hussa?"

Hussa nodded. "Yes; you can tell me if a man called Eorpwald came this way a week or two ago and where he might be found? I am keen to have a chat with him."

The three men exchanged glances, their anxiety plain to see.

"My lord, forgive us, but we do not know where the man Eorpwald is," one of the Ealdorman's companions said, earning him an angry glare from Jacob.

"So you do know who I am speaking about?" Hussa said.

The Ealdorman's shoulders slumped. "Yes, my lord, but he is not here. He arrived as you said ten days ago, full of news of the capture of Doric and how Benson was also under your control. He tried to persuade us to join him and march north, but we refused."

"Why? And don't give me any nonsense about loyalty to Ceolwulf and West Seax."

The man shook his head. "No, lord. In truth I did not think we had the strength to fight you and also I did not trust him."

"Wise decision and a truthful answer I think. Yet if you had the strength to fight us, would you?"

The Ealdorman gazed at Hussa in silence, his fear palpable. Rubbing his hands together to still their tremor, he drew a breath. Beads of sweat broke out on his brow before the answer came. "I expect we would, Lord Hussa, yes."

Hussa studied the Ealdorman for a moment. Despite his obvious terror, the man had courage. He shrugged, "I believe that too is a truthful answer. So tell me, what happened to Eorpwald after he left here?"

The third elder now spoke, "I think he went to Readingum, my lord," The other two nodded in agreement.

"Very well. We have an understanding. My king wants control of this valley all the way to the border with Middle Seaxe. I say again, assist me in this task and your people and town will be safe. Turn against me and we will burn it until there is nothing but ash in its place. Understood?"

The old men could only nod their heads.

"So then, we will stay here for a few days. Find us shelter food and ale. Tomorrow I will select the ten men to join us and they will train with us whilst I decide what next to do."

Two weeks later, his company reinforced by the ten strongest men from Garinges, Hussa set out again. He crossed the Thames to the west bank and then continued down a road that followed the river. Along the way they came across the small settlements, hamlets really of Belesduna and Pegingaburnan, which surrendered in much the same way as Garinges had. As before, Hussa recruited or pressed into service half the men of fighting age from each place and now had approaching one hundred and forty men. He created two companies, placing one under Rolf and the other under Tolan. Rolf he could trust to do what was needed, but he had yet to make a judgement on the latter. However, he soon became impressed with Tolan, for as Ricberht had said, the man never flapped or grew agitated. He just calmly did whatever was needed of him.

Hussa held back twenty men as personal huscarls and a reserve, foremost amongst these was Wilbur. By midsummer they were standing on high ground to the west of the settlement of Readingum.

"Arse!" Wilbur swore as they looked at the city.

Hussa thought he had a point.

Readingum lay in a fork between two rivers – the Thames, which passed it to the north, and the Kennet, which flowed from the south west to merge with the Thames just east of the town. A road from the south heading from Celemion crossed the Kennet and led on over the Thames. Between the two, sprawled along the road, lay the sizeable city of Readingum. It was Saxon, not Roman, so unlike Doric it bore no stone fortifications. Indeed, although much larger than Garinges, Hussa had expected it to be similarly open, so it came as a shock when, having made camp on the approaches to the city, Hussa and his captains went to look at it.

An attempt had been made to dig a ditch and to throw the displaced soil up onto an embankment lining the west side of the city. Barricades blocking the tracks in to the city had been built using carts, crates, barrels and chopped down trees. Hanging from spears all along the barricade were the pennants of captains declaring their intention to fight. Eorpwald's warning, it seemed, had been heeded.

"Looks like Readingum is determined to resist," Hussa commented. "Arse indeed!"

Hussa's army settled into their encampment and studied the city, trying to gauge how many men held it. Eventually they estimated the number to be around eighty. That meant that

Hussa outnumbered the defenders, but given the presence of the new fortifications any attack could be costly. He was pondering what to do when news was brought to him by Wilbur, who had taken a scouting party past the city to the east towards Wochinoes, which lay in the furthest reaches of the Thames Valley territories. Beyond Wochinoes was the land controlled by the Middle Saxons in and around Lundunne. Ceolwulf did not intend to challenge the Middle Saxons at this stage and had told Hussa that his final objective was Wochinoes. That being so, he had considered bypassing Readingum and heading straight to Wochinoes, hence Wilbur's scouting trip. The news that Wilbur brought, however, was surprising but also gave Hussa an opportunity.

"Sixty men from Wochinoes are marching on Readingum, lord. At their head is a familiar figure," Wilbur said.

"Eorpwald?"

Wilbur nodded, "Yes, lord."

"So Readingum and Wochinoes have formed an alliance. That means they will have as many men as we have and will probably try for battle." He pondered this for a moment then added, "Or maybe they will just wait it out until the winter comes."

"So do we attack now and try to take Readingum before Eorpwald arrives?" Rolf asked, eager for action.

"No, I don't think so," Hussa said. "I have a better idea."

Rolf grinned, "More sneaky tricks, lord?"

. "Perhaps," Hussa said, a glint in his eye.

Tolan was instructed to stay on the hill overlooking Readingum. His orders were to maintain the camp fires as if all of Hussa's command remained there. He was also to probe towards the city and make it seem as if an attack was imminent from the west.

"What do you mean to do, Lord Hussa?" Tolan asked.

"I mean to take Rolf's company and my own men and ambush Eorpwald's column," Hussa replied.

That night Hussa led eighty men on a long march through the darkness, across the Kennett to the south of Readingum and towards Wochinoes. Wilbur had identified a strip of woodland lining the road between Wochinoes and Readingum a few miles to the east. Scouts suggested that the men from Wochinoes would reach it the following day, so Hussa marched on through the night, arriving at his destination shortly before dawn. Sending Wilbur and his scouts along the road to watch out for the column, he ordered the remainder of his men to get some rest and regain their strength. They had little chance, for not long after dawn the scouts were back.

"Lord, they are coming," Wilbur panted. "They are less than a mile away!"

Hussa directed the men to take up positions on either side of the road, twenty or thirty paces back into the woodland. "Use the brush and undergrowth as cover and rub mud on your faces and hands," he commanded. "Stay hidden and be quiet until I give the order to attack. We do not want to alert them too soon."

Not long after everyone was in position, Eorpwald's column came into sight. They marched under the banner of a white swan on a black background, presumably the emblem of Wochinoes. Two men on horseback were at their head, one Hussa did not recognise, but the other was clearly Eorpwald. Hussa signalled to Wilbur, who loaded a stone into his sling. Beside him three archers fitted arrows to their bows.

"Now!" bellowed Hussa.

Wilbur let fly with the stone aiming it at Eorpwald, but at the last instant Benson's Ealdorman seemed to sense that something was up. He jerked his head around so that the stone missed him and instead knocked the Wochinoes captain off his horse. At the same time the archers released their arrows, one of them hitting the standard bearer who dropped the swan banner into the mud. Then, with a roar, Hussa and his men were up out of the undergrowth and charging forward from both sides.

The Wochinoes column was taken so completely by surprise that its men did not even have time to retrieve the shields strapped to their backs, never mind form a shield wall. Such was the shock of the attack that Hussa's company had absolute advantage and within a few moments a quarter of the enemy were dead or wounded. The fight went on a little longer before the Wochinoes Company, realising the inevitability of defeat, surrendered, their swords and spears clattering onto the road.

"Don't kill any more! Take them captive!" Hussa ordered.

"Woden's balls!" Wilbur cursed, pointing westwards along the road.

Hussa turned and saw a horseman riding hard towards Readingum. Eorpwald, ever the opportunist, had clearly abandoned his allies and left them to their fate. "A slow death for the bastard when we catch up with him, don't you think?"

Wilbur grinned and spat onto the road.

"What are our losses?" Hussa asked, casting his gaze over his men.

"A dozen wounded, lord. Three severely, but none dead."

"Good. See to the wounded."

Glad to have got off so lightly, Hussa watched as his men took control of their captives, forming them up into a long column at sword point, but all the fight had gone out of them and there was no resistance that he could see.

"Turn them around, we're going back to Wochinoes," Hussa ordered.

"Are you going to kill us, lord?" shouted a redhaired youth.

"Probably not, that depends upon you and your captain. Where is he?"

"He's over there," the red-haired youth pointed at a wounded warrior, who sat upon a tree stump holding his bloody head where Wilbur's sling stone had dented his helmet. He looked sick and pale but not likely to die.

Hussa went to stand over him. "What is your name?"

The man gave him a bleary glare. "I am Lord Woke. Who are you?"

"I'm sure Eorpwald must have told you. I am Lord Hussa of Northumbria. Here though, I represent King Ceolwulf of West Seax, who claims all these lands as belonging to his kingdom. I offer you a choice. Swear allegiance to Ceolwulf here and now and Wochinoes will join West Seax. Obey the king's orders and you will still be its lord and the men here will live. If you do not swear such allegiance I will give the order and here and now you and all your men will die."

Lord Woke looked up at Hussa and then across at his men. "Wochinoes has until now been a city that ruled itself. I, and my father before me, always knew the day would come when we would have to become part of something bigger. Either that or disappear forever. Perhaps that day has come and a decision needs to be made." With his head slumped in his hands, the man pondered the situation for a moment before he looked up again. "Very well, Lord Hussa. Come now to Wochinoes as honoured guests and we will surrender the city to you."

Later that day the people of Wochinoes looked on in surprise as Hussa led their lord and all his men into the middle of the city. There a banner was raised with the Wyvern of West Seax embroidered upon it and beneath it, Lord Wochinoes knelt to swear allegiance to King Ceolwulf.

"We will rest a week or two while our wounded recover, then resupply and march out to take Readingum, "Hussa said. "You and your men will assist us in that endeavour."

"Yes lord," Woke replied resignedly.

Some two weeks later a horseman arrived in the hall that had been given over to Hussa and his men. He was rain soaked having galloped hard through a late autumn storm.

"I come from Tolan at Pegingaburnan with bad news, my lord!" the man said as he took a goblet of ale from Wilbur and removed his wet cloak.

"Pegingaburnan? What in in the name of Loki's turds is he doing there? "Rolf asked.

"Well? What is this news?" Hussa asked impatiently.

"A few days after you had left for Wochinoes, Tolan received word that tribes have been gathering in Belesduna and Pegingaburnan in preparation for an uprising against us."

"Eorpwald's doing, I expect?" Rolf said. "Woden's testicles, damn that man to Hel! Should've killed the bastard while we had the chance."

Hussa shrugged. It was likely. The Ealdorman of Benson was proving to be, as the Christians might say, 'a thorn in his flesh'. How Loki must be laughing.

"Does that mean Tolan is outnumbered and cut off between them and Readingum?" Rolf asked.

The messenger nodded. "Afraid so."

"What about Garinges and Doric?" Hussa snapped, feeling as if all his work in the Thames Valley was unravelling.

"So far as we know we still hold them, lord."

198

Hussa thought about the town elders in Garinges. "Bastards had better have stayed with us or I'll string them up," he muttered to himself.

"My lord?" the messenger said, thinking he had missed an instruction.

Hussa shook his head, "Never mind." Turning, he addressed the warriors in the hall who were standing around looking on, waiting to hear the news and his orders. "We are going to Tolan. We will take back these wayward villages and make the people regret their rebellion. Be prepared to march at dawn. Get ready!"

There was a buzz of conversation as they jumped into action, assembling equipment and packing their sacks for the journey. Hussa turned back to the messenger. "Rest for a while, then I need you to return to Tolan with the tidings that we are on the way."

His face grey with exhaustion, the man looked longingly at the fire. "Of course, lord. Give me a fresh horse and food and I will set out before nightfall."

Hussa stared after him as the weary messenger went in search of food.

"What about Lord Woke? "Rolf's voice said in his ear. "Once we leave here will he rise up in rebellion too?"

"I dare say he might."

"So should we threaten him, warn him or kill him?"

"He has two sons, doesn't he?" Hussa asked.

"Yes, one of sixteen, the other a year younger."

"He cares for them, you would say?"

"What man would not love and care for his sons?" Rolf asked pointedly, looking Hussa straight in the eye.

Tempted to give Rolf a bloody nose, Hussa hung on to his temper. "We will take them both with us. Having his sons along will make Woke think about where his loyalties lie. We will also take half his men. We will need them. He has sworn allegiance, he cannot refuse. His boys can be given command of them, they are both old enough, although it goes without saying that Wilbur will actually be in charge. We need no threats or warnings here, Rolf. Woke will get the message. If not he will get his sons' heads back in a sack."

The year was already turning from late autumn to winter as they marched west, crossing the Kennet southwest of Readingum. The land they travelled across lay bare, cold and peaceful with that special quiet that winter brings. The world around them was settling down for the short days and long nights ahead. Only Hussa and his men were abroad with iron and steel, blood on their minds.

As they passed near the city of Readingum, Hussa sent out Wilbur to scout. "The fortifications are still in place," he reported on his return, "and it looks like they've taken advantage of Tolan's absence to clear the surrounding fields of crops and livestock."

"Probably got more men now too," Rolf suggested.

"Let's deal with the villages up river for now, then concern ourselves with Readingum," Hussa grumbled. "I can't be in two places at once!"

They reached the village of Pegingaburnan three days later and located Tolan. He had set up camp on a small rise to the south. A track led down to the village and the crossing over the Thames, which changed direction from flowing south to heading off eastwards.

Tolan spotted them approaching and hurried towards Hussa. "My lord, I am sorry to have brought you here but the number of warriors in the village are considerable. Fewer than mine but..."

"Not by many?"

"No lord, but they have also fortified the village and we believe they have good supplies of food, as well as access to the Thames."

"No shortage of water then," Rolf commented.

Hussa nodded, Tolan had acted wisely if conservatively. An adventurous commander might still have attacked and maybe, given enough guts and if fate was on their side, success would be theirs. Yet Tolan was not that man. Rolf maybe, but not Tolan. Clearly he had thought it best to play safe and keep alive the company Hussa had entrusted to him.

"Very well. Now, though, we have one hundred and eighty men in three companies."

"What is the plan, lord?" Rolf asked.

Hussa pointed at the village. "We attack the village."

"What terms shall we offer them?" Tolan asked.

Without taking his gaze off the village, Hussa snarled, "No terms. Everyone dies."

"My lord? What about the children... and the women?" Tolan asked.

Hussa just stared at him. There was a long pause.

"Yes, lord; everyone dies," Tolan said at last.

"It is necessary. An example must be made here, Tolan. Once Pegingaburnan burns, Belesduna will fall in line or know it will suffer the same fate."

Tolan looked across at Rolf and saw no help there. "Very well, lord, "he said and turned away.

Hussa now caught the expression on Rolf's face. "What?"

"I will follow you anywhere, you know that, but... "

"But what? "

"Women and children too?"

"You did not complain when I threw my half-brother's mother in the fire at their villa."

Rolf shrugged. "She maybe deserved it and besides, that was a personal grudge. Here though…"

For a moment Hussa stared at him then sighed. "Tolan," he called after the departing captain.

Tolan turned. "Lord Hussa?"

"Burn the village and kill the men. But do not pursue any woman or child who flees over the river into the Chilterns. They will carry fear with them and that will suffice."

Relief visible on his face, Tolan nodded.

"We attack at once!" Hussa ordered. "I want this place in ashes by nightfall!"

Chapter Twenty One
Winter's Cold
Winter 608

Shifting his position to scratch at a flea bite, Rolf swore softly. "I had hoped to spend Yuletide and the winter settled snuggly down in Witanceastre in some woman's bed, roast boar on my trencher and a barrel of ale within arm's reach. This is not exactly what I had in mind, lord."

He and Hussa were crouched in a frozen ditch inspecting the distant defences of Readingum. The sounds of Yuletide festivities and the enticing smell of roasting meat drifted to them from the city.

"Well that is fate for you," Hussa answered.

"Woden's buttocks is it fate!" Rolf snorted. "Boyden does not like you and he's the king's most trusted commander, so Ceolwulf listens more to him than he does to you. If we'd captured Readingum in the autumn, we'd be sitting at the high table in the king's hall right now, not freezing our bollocks off in this stinking ditch. Just because we didn't achieve everything we were supposed to and that bastard Boyden dripped his poison into the king's ear, we are requested – 'requested' my arse! – to stay here and watch this damned city. It's not right…"

While a disgruntled Rolf continued to grumble, Hussa blanked him out and studied the city, looking for a weakness while at the same time pondering on the events that had led him here. After Pegingaburnan had burned, news of his fierce response to rebellion soon reached Belesduna. As he had predicted, the result was a supplicant population and a leadership that had bowed to the inevitable. As his army had approached the town there was no disguising the hostility projected in his direction by the ealdormen. Even so, they had fallen to their knees and begged for their lives, pleading with him to spare the town and its people. He had let them sweat for a while, but had eventually extracted oaths of allegiance to King Ceolwulf of West Seax and let them live. Any further rebellion, he had told them, and they would be instantly and utterly destroyed. Satisfied, he had decided to remain in the town for a short time while he set about preparations for an attack on Readingum.

Belesduna lay beside the Roman road that led between Doric and Calleva in Celemion. Next to the decaying road stood a disintegrating villa and it was here that he elected to stay.

"You could burn that to make an example as a warning to the inhabitants," Rolf had suggested as they inspected it.

As Hussa considered this, the image of another villa in flames came to him and he heard again the screams of Cerdic's mother. They seemed to echo from the crumbling walls of this very building and despite himself he shivered. "I have burnt enough villas," he said. "I think I will live in this one for a while."

He had sent messengers through Garinges to Doric and others to Wochinoes and established that all remained loyal. Whether through fear or by deciding they were backing the right horse, the result was the same. Indeed, Ricberht sent word from Doric that he had recruited a dozen more warriors and as many skirmishers and was sending them to join Hussa's company. Gratified, Hussa had decided to wait for them to arrive, but in this he had made a mistake, for a couple of days later the winter storms arrived in earnest. After a succession of heavy downpours, the Thames and Kennet flooded, the fields became waterlogged and the roads churned into a quagmire so deep it was all but impassable.

As the water levels began to subside, the weather turned colder and the waterlogged land froze into wasteland of ice and snow. Hussa then sent a message to West Seax to say he was calling off an attack on Readingum until the spring.

Soon afterwards, a dozen mounted escorts had galloped into Belesduna. As they skidded to a halt in front of Hussa's temporary residence, the man who slid out of the saddle to face him was none other than his nemesis; King Ceolwulf's lieutenant.

"Is this as far as you have got?" Boyden's lips curled into a sneer as he viewed the crumbling villa. "What in the gods' names have you been doing?"

"We have captured five cities and towns and twenty or more hamlets and villages," Hussa replied grumpily.

Boyden gave a contemptuous bark of laughter, "Is that so? And yet the prize remains outside your grasp."

"Actually, I prefer Doric," Rolf commented by way of helpful intervention – or at least that is what he had intended. "Readingum is just a shit hole of hovels; Doric looks a lot prettier…" his voice trailed away as Boyden turned to glare at him then back at Hussa.

"I don't care what the city looks like. Readingum is the key to the Thames Valley and you don't control it do you, Hussa?"

"What did you expect?" Hussa shrugged, "Did you think all the settlements in the Thames Valley would simply roll over the moment we came into view? Some of these Saxons do not share your king's vision nor believe in West Seax's future as the dominant kingdom in the South."

Boyden's eyes narrowed. "Careful, Hussa, there are some of us who believe you have a deeper plan going on here. Maybe you're not just here to foster an alliance between West Seax and Northumbria. Perhaps Aethelfrith's true plan is to see division in the South – a gaggle of weakened kingdoms ripe for conquest when his time comes."

"What bullshit you do speak, Boyden. I only meant to say that the resistance here is stronger than perhaps some in Witanceastre would believe. These people are not just rolling over and submitting. I am having to take steps to enforce the king's will upon them. Rest assured that whatever I am doing is entirely intended to give to Ceolwulf control of the Thames Valley as he requires. I will tell him as much when I see him."

Boyden frowned, "And when do you plan that will be?"

"In case you hadn't noticed, Lord Boyden, winter has arrived! The campaign is over and I mean to return to Witanceastre with my report as soon as I am able. I will continue with the Thames Valley campaign in the spring."

"So that is what you plan is it?" Boyden sneered then shook his head, "Sorry to disappoint you Hussa, but you will not be welcome in Witanceastre this winter. That is what I came to tell you. The king requests that you remain here and continue to probe Readingum. Winter or not, if you find a weakness you are to act upon it. You are to go on with this campaign until the city falls to you and if it holds out 'til spring, then launch an attack with everything you've got. Ceolwulf will be probing at Basingstoches next year – it lies on roads leading to Calleva from the South. If you take Readingum and we can capture Basingstoches, then in the following year we will be in a position to launch a joint attack from north and south at the same time, thus splitting the country in two and taking Celemion."

Thinking through Ceolwulf's plans, Hussa did not reply at first.

"Is there a problem Lord Hussa?"

"I had hoped to visit Witanceastre for personal reasons," he said reluctantly.

"I'm sorry, but you will just have to wait until Readingum falls." Boyden looked up at Hussa and smiled, "Your woman and child were well last time I saw them. You have a fine son." His smile grew wider, "His mother tells me he is walking already. I daresay you are hoping to sire a sibling for him, eh? So now you have another reason to finish the campaign here as swiftly as possible. Heh call it an incentive!" he chortled.

Swallowing his anger, Hussa gritted his teeth. "What you are saying is that if I get on and finish this business swiftly I get to see Rowenna and... the boy."

"Isn't that what I just said?"

"So you would have no problem were I to hurry the campaign despite these treacherous conditions, almost certainly at the cost of more men's lives, just so I can get home to Witanceastre and my woman's bed?"

Boyden shrugged. "From what I have heard about you, Hussa that would not be exactly outside your character now would it?"

"You don't know me at all, Boyden. I do what needs to be done, but for a goal; a purpose, not for my own selfgratification."

"Well guess what, Hussa," Boyden shrugged, "in the end I don't give a tinker's damn how you justify what you do. Just get the work done and hand the king a victory. If you fail, you can kiss any alliance with Northumbria goodbye. So, do I return to him and tell him you agree to his request?"

Knowing he had no choice, Hussa nodded.

So it was that they spent a cold Yuletide listening in on the festivities at Readingum. Hussa had initially entertained the idea of a winter assault. He had hoped the ale and warmth inside their mead halls would lull the warriors of Readingum into carelessness such that they would weaken their defences and forego a watch on the outer walls. However, the lord of the city, perhaps assisted by Eorpwald, was in turn keeping a close watch on Hussa and his men, for at no point did the defenders appear to drop their guard.

One night, Hussa led a raiding party along the bed of a frozen creek that passed close to Readingum's outer defences, hoping to gain access and perhaps torch some of the buildings, maybe even open the main barricade so that Rolf could lead the other companies into the city. Yet, as they approached the walls there was a shout of alarm from the barricade and a flaming torch was flung down into the creek bed, followed by two more. Suddenly, Hussa and his men were illuminated and in plain sight. Before they could react, they heard the buzz of arrows. Two of Hussa's men were hit: one fell dead, an arrow piercing his throat; the other was skewered through the arm and bleeding heavily. Shouting that they should retreat, Hussa and his men scuttled back along the creek and out into the frozen night dragging the wounded man with them. Like a dog with its tail between its legs, they had no choice but to return to camp and lick their wounds.

After that Hussa did not attempt any more assaults. He set a close watch on the city, but withdrew the bulk of his companies back to the other settlements. Then he settled down to wait out the winter. He had plenty of time to prepare for the spring; build his companies; stack arms and equipment, and hone his plans to launch an all-out attack as soon as the winter had passed. And by the gods, when he eventually got into that city, the people of Readingum would know about it!

And as he waited so he brooded, thinking all the time about the woman and the boy.

Chapter Twenty Two
The Challenge
Early 609

"That's insane... my prince," I said.

"Can you think of any alternative?" Edwin replied.

I snorted, earning me a rebuke from Sabert. We were back in Rhufoniog, sitting at the long table in Edwin's ale hall. I shivered and pulled my cloak tighter around me. There was a fire burning in the fire pit, but it still felt cold on that late winter morning.

"Well? Do you have another plan?" Edwin asked.

I hesitated then said, "Practically anything would be better than you challenging Cynan's champion to a combat over his demands."

"I agree," Sabert nodded. "Everything we have done is about getting you or Hereric back to Deira and winning you the throne. You go and fight and you might be killed. What good will that do?"

"I want the throne. I want Aethelfrith caught and made to suffer for what he has done, "Edwin replied, eyes flaring to reveal his terrible desire for revenge.

"But...?" I started, for surely there was 'a but.'

"But I will not drag all our men, all our people to destruction for the sake of my ambition. My revenge can wait a while."

"There won't be any revenge, nor less a throne if you die," I retorted.

"What choice do we have? Iago will not risk war with Cynan, no matter what Cadfan's feelings are. He has been too far influenced by Cadwallon."

At Cadwallon's name, I saw another flash in those eyes. Cadfan's son, it seemed, had earned a place on Edwin's list. Whilst

Iago and Cadfan lived, Cadwallon could only influence and persuade, but one day he might be King of Gwynedd and if by then Edwin was King of Northumbria... I shook my head. That was a thought for another day. Edwin was still talking.

"If we do not go to Powys, Cynan will attack us here, urged on by Haiarme. Iago will let it happen and forbid Cadfan to intervene. One day of bloodshed and his troubles with Powys are resolved – and most likely the threat from Aethelfrith too."

"Well yes... but a challenge?"

"Cynan is a warrior king. Maybe he is going senile, maybe he is besotted by Haiarme, but at heart he is a warrior still. He cannot refuse a challenge. If I win he renounces his claim over us all. If I lose then he gets me, if I live, along with you two and anyone else who was at that stone circle when Domanghast died, but the families are left alone. So I'll fight and... if I win... then we are free. Honour would demand it."

"You think Haiarme would abide by that?" I asked.

"Good point, but we could leave. Get away from her influence," Edwin said.

"We could go on the road again. Go to Cantia maybe?" Sabert suggested weakly.

I frowned at Sabert. I didn't like the way this conversation was going. "If we did that, how long before all of Britannia heard we were running away? Difficult to raise support then."

Well we're not raising it now, are we," Edwin said, looking from me to Sabert, knowing that what he said was right. "So then, we send the challenge?"

I sighed, at a loss for what to say, apart from the obvious. "Very well, but not you. You need a champion. "I paused and looked at them both. "I will fight the challenge," I replied. "May the gods protect me now," I added.

Our messenger returned from Powys only a couple of weeks later – sooner that we had expected. Cynan had accepted Edwin's challenge, but had stipulated two conditions: firstly, the fight would take place in King Morfael's fortress at Dogfeiling and secondly, the entire Deiran party, including our women and children, were to witness it and, should I lose, the subsequent surrender of Prince Edwin and his Saxon lords, so that they would all know the penalties of betrayal.

"He's a cunning bastard," Sabert said. "I do not think we should agree to Dogfeiling. That means crossing the border into Powys. There is too much risk that Cynan will simply attack us when we get there."

"Not if Cadfan comes with two companies of his army, "I suggested.

Sabert shook his head. "Iago will not permit Cadfan to go to war over us."

I smiled. "But it won't be war. He will merely be escorting us in order to witness the combat. And if I get beaten, he can be relied upon at the very least to get our families to safety. Cadfan will agree to that, I am sure… if Edwin asks it of him."

Edwin nodded, "Very well," he said.

"All the same, my prince, you might want to keep it quiet from Iago and certainly from Cadwallon!"

So it was that at the time when Christians celebrate the death and resurrection of their Christ, and we the festival of Eostre, all our villagers – women and children too – left Rhufoniog and set off on the road to Dogfeiling. As we had hoped, Cadfan agreed to Edwin's request and he and his Welsh warriors – no fewer than three companies, including forty medium armoured cavalry – accompanied us. Together with the Wicstun Company and the prince's house troops, we were a considerable party on the road that day.

211

My mind went back to a similar march a few years before when it had been the Irish of Lleyn who demanded we be handed over. On that occasion, most of us were convinced we were going to be given over to the dubious mercies of the Scots. This time, however, our people knew the worst that would happen was that I would lose the fight with Cynan's champion; Edwin and his lords would surrender and the villagers would just have to go back to farming the land in Gwynedd under the lordship of Cadfan. Aidith, aware that if that were to happen I would likely be dead, was in a state of extreme anxiety, although she managed to put on a brave face for me and our children.

The route to Dogfeiling took us over a range of hills and south into the valley that was home to the resentful King Morfael and his people. It could have been a pleasant journey, for the frost of a few weeks before had gone, the sun was warm and spring was in full sway. For the younger children it was an adventure and many of them, Sian included, laughed and giggled as they played amongst the burgeoning spring flowers and fresh green grass, unaware of the threat that hung over us all. Aidith squeezed my hand and I tried to smile at her, but it was as if until that moment I had not really allowed myself to think about what I might lose this day. Not just my life – somehow that was not what worried me most – but the thought that I would not be there to watch Sian grow up or to teach Cuthwine how to fight or hold Aidith close, cut deep. The warmth of the spring sunshine, the beauty of the woodlands and the laughter of the children faded away and suddenly I felt cold and alone in a world of darkness.

The stronghold of the kings of the Dogfeiling was at Ruthin. Here, a decaying Roman fort lay on flat land not far from the base of an isolated, flat-topped, lozenge shaped hill. At one end

212

of this hill, a palisaded wooden fort dominated a straggle of huts and hovels that were dotted across the rest of it. The fight, however, was to take place in the Roman fort. This was smaller than the fortress and was, frankly, falling apart. Virtually none of the buildings had an intact roof and many of the walls had collapsed into the stone built barrack blocks. Between these blocks was a large open space and it was there, in that now weed covered, stony parade ground where Rome's warriors would once have drilled and practised their fighting skills, that I would duel with Cynan's champion for the future of our people. I was bowed down by the weight of the responsibility that lay heavy on my shoulders.

Morfael, his warriors and his court were already present under the banner of the Dogfeiling. They lined one side of the parade ground, so we naturally moved to occupy the other side. Not long after we arrived, we saw another company of warriors snaking down the hillside from the fortress. Above it flew the banner of Pengwern, Selyf's city, and now I spotted the Prince of Powys himself, riding a fine black stallion at the column's head. The company soon reached us and moved past the rear of Morfael's men to line the eastern side of the ground, over to our left.

Selyf dismounted and walked towards us. As he did so, Morfael, accompanied by two of his men, moved out to join him. Edwin glanced at me, his eyebrow lifted in an unspoken query. I nodded and we both walked forward to intercept them. Prince Cadfan followed suit and a moment later we all met up in the centre of the parade ground. I glanced at Morfael and then at Selyf, but it was Prince Edwin who spoke first.

"We have come here as we agreed. Are the conditions of the duel still understood?"

Prince Selyf nodded. "My father agrees that if you win he will drop his demands for you and all your people to surrender. If you lose, however, he will insist that you, your lords, and anyone else who was present at the skirmish where Domanghast died, are handed over for justice."

"What justice can they expect?" Cadfan asked, his eyes narrowing with suspicion. "Do not forget that Edwin at least is my adopted son."

Again Selyf nodded. "I will see to it that evidence is heard and the truth comes to light. You have my word, Prince Cadfan."

Cadfan then turned to Edwin. "Are you sure about this, my son? You do not have to go through with it."

Edwin reached out and placed a hand on Cadfan's shoulder. "Father, if I do not it will mean war with Powys. As your adopted son I feel loyalty to Gwynedd as I do to Deira. This way, there is a chance to resolve the problems that beset us without resorting to war. Cerdic will fight for us and if he wins, we are free."

"And if he loses?"

Edwin shrugged, "Then I will accept my wyrd."

Cadfan frowned, clearly puzzled by the unusual word. "Fate, Prince Cadfan," I explained. "It means fate. Edwin is saying he will accept his fate… as will we all."

Morfael eyed me up. "So you are to be the Angles' champion? It seems a lot of expectation has been placed on you."

"Yes," I said shortly. Looking around I added, "So then, where is my opponent? Where is King Cynan for that matter?"

"My father is coming," Selyf answered. "We stayed the night at Ruthin." He glanced up at the hill, "Indeed, he comes even now."

I followed his gaze and gasped. Coming down the hillside were sixty of the Irish that had accompanied Haiarme to Powys under the command of Kadir. The warriors, each almost as huge as Kadir himself, were a fearsome sight as they stomped towards us carrying their huge swords. Yet it was not that which had made me gasp. Just behind them was something I had heard stories about but had never seen. Few had in five lifetimes of a man.

A chariot of brilliant white was descending from the fortress drawn by a matching pair of grey stallions. Trimmed with gold so that it shone and sparkled in the sun, the chariot was a magnificent sight. The king held the reins, with Haiarme his queen at his side. Immediately behind them stood the Irish warlord Kadir, wearing his finest armour. So it seemed Cynan had chosen Kadir as his champion. Or had perhaps his queen made the choice?

"Kadir? I have to fight Kadir?"

Morfael's smile held no humour. "Indeed. Remind me, Lord Cerdic, how did that work out for you the last time?"

I did not reply; the bastard knew well enough that Kadir had beaten me into the ground and stomped on me. I glanced across at Aidith. She knew it too. I caught a slight shake of her head. "Don't do this, Cerdic," she was saying.

I shrugged, returning her look with one of helplessness. "What can I do?" it said.

I turned back to watch the white chariot, which was even now arriving at the fort. The Irish warriors lined up on the western side of the parade ground and Cynan halted the stallions in front of them. Then leaving Haiarme where she was, he and Kadir jumped out of the chariot and in a deliberate show of arrogance, strolled over to join us.

Acknowledging both Selyf and Cadfan with a nod of his head, Cynan ignored Edwin and me. "Are we ready?" he asked

215

Morfael.

"Yes, sire. We are all ready."

"Then the combat will begin in a few moments. Let the champions prepare and we will retire to watch."

We returned to our lines and I armed myself with Wreccan and Catraeth. Then I picked up a shield. I looked back at Aidith and tried to smile at her but only managed a tense nod.

"Good luck, Cerdic," Aedann said.

"Be careful," Cuthbert added.

Eduard patted me on the back. "This time just gut the bastard," he rumbled.

Turning away I stepped out onto the parade ground. As I walked slowly across to the centre, I felt the gaze of hundreds of eyes, all of them watching me. Lilla had once told me of the great arenas the Romans had built where men – usually captured warriors made slaves and known as gladiators – fought each other while others watched. 'Amphitheatres' Lilla had called them. In the largest, twenty thousand could watch as the gladiators fought and died for their audience's entertainment and for a chance at glory. To me it seemed barbaric, but Lilla said that many volunteered to fight in the arena for that glory and the wealth that went with it. For others, though, forced as slaves to fight, there was another motivation: the chance of winning their freedom by staying alive. Today I was not interested in entertainment, wealth or glory, but just that hope of freedom. 'Win today, Cerdic,' I told myself, 'and we will all be free.'

Kadir approached me from the other direction. Across his back he wore a scabbard holding a fearsome two-handed sword. On his left arm he wore a buckler, his fist clenched tightly around a handful of javelins. In his right hand he was holding a heavier throwing spear – longer than a javelin but not as heavy as the

216

type we used in a shield wall. It was all horribly familiar. He had the advantage of range over me for I bore no spear. His larger sword would also give him better reach than Wreccan gave me. My best chance was to get in close where Catraeth would be the master.

We halted forty paces apart and turned towards Cynan. The king had returned to his chariot and now grasped the front, leaning over to address the crowd. Sweeping his arm in the direction of Prince Edwin and our Deiran warriors, he shouted, "All Angles are our enemy! We fight them on our borders…" he paused as his men and those of Kadir and Morfael cheered.

As the cheers subsided, he continued, "…Yet there are some amongst these Angles who have done more. They stand accused of having ambushed and killed my queen's own father, Domanghast: a noble prince of the Dál–Riata, our allies in the struggle against the invader." Again he paused.

The cheers became curses and catcalls. Filled with anger, I shook my head. First at the accusations, which were plain falsehoods, and then at the irony of calling Áedán mac Gabráin an ally against the invader, for the Irish Scots were just as much invaders as we were. How truth is distorted by politics! Maybe a day would come when that was not so, but it seemed unlikely. At that moment it also seemed unlikely that I would live to see it if it did!

The king spoke again, "The Angles maintain their innocence and the King of Gwynedd and his son, Prince Cadfan, have offered them protection and argue for justice. Well I am a just and wise king, as you will attest." The cheers once more rose in volume and rebounded around the ruins.

This too felt ironic to me. Cynan may have been powerful once; a warrior king indeed, yet wisdom did not seem to be

217

one of his strongest traits. I saw him glance with adoration at Haiarme – and who has not given a lover a look of adoration after all? But no, the look he gave her was not solely one of adoration. There was intensity in it indicative of deep obsession and it seemed to me then that this once powerful king had slipped inexorably into madness.

"Yes, I am just," he went on. "My son Selyf has argued for a fair trial. He has suggested that not all the Angles are to blame, certainly not the women and children. Indeed, he questions whether any of the men here today are guilty. Well, today we will let God, the ultimate judge, decide. There will be a trial by combat. If my champion, Kadir, one of my wife's personal guard, wins then we will take into custody Prince Edwin of Deira, his lords, Earl Sabert and Earl Cerdic and any of their men who were present at the battle in that stone circle where the queen's father was murdered. If Lord Cerdic wins, however, then we must accept that God has declared their innocence and all will go free."

There was another round of cheering, and this time my own men took up the shout, calling my name and rattling sword or spear against shield.

Cynan raised his hand and the noise died away. "So be it. Let the combat begin. It will conclude with first blood from the torso or if one man is either knocked unconscious or unable to continue." He pointed at me and Kadir then sharply lowered his hand and shouted, "Begin!"

Kadir hefted the spear in his right arm, balanced it and then drew it back. I brought my shield across in front of me and braced myself for the blow. Kadir paused a moment and then moved away to his right. I turned to follow him, but it was a feint and he quickly doubled back and let fly with the spear.

He was strong and the spear flew like a stooping bird of prey towards me, but at the last moment I read the move and turned as quickly as he did, so his spear slammed into my shield and not into my chest, burying the head an inch deep into the wood.

I now had a heavy spear protruding from the blasted shield, weighing it down, making it difficult to move and manoeuvre. Meanwhile, Kadir tossed one of his javelins from his left hand to his right and prepared to throw it.

"Arse!" I cursed, hacking at the spear with Wreccan. It took three swings to knock it off and for those few moments my right arm was unprotected. Seeing this, Kadir tried his luck and threw a javelin at it. The point slid across my mail shirt gashing a hole in it and tearing my tunic, but did not cut my flesh. The blow still stung me though and I gave an involuntarily gasp, bringing cheers from the watching Irish and Welsh opposite us and shouts of concern and advice from behind me.

"Close on him, Cerdic; get stuck in!" Eduard shouted, his voice betraying his frustration that I and not he was Edwin's champion. I had a fleeting image of Eduard wielding his great axe and wondered if he would have made a better champion than I. No point now in thinking about it. I moved towards Kadir again.

As I approached two more javelins flew in my direction. One ricocheted off my shield and buried itself in the worn, crumbling stone of the parade ground. The other clattered off my helmet, stunning me for a moment so that all I could see was darkness and flashing lights. The fight had barely started and was already going the same way as the last one. I was a hardened, tried and tested warrior, yet I felt in that moment like a greenhorn; even more so when out of the shouts behind me I heard Grettir's voice, loud and gruff, yelling at me the way he always had when

I was just a lad. "Get on with it boy; attack the bastard!"

Swaying on my feet I heard Cuthbert shout, "Look out Cerdic!" In the nick of time my vision cleared and I could see that Kadir had used his advantage to close on me and draw his sword. I blinked hard three times and brought my shield up to take the first furious blow of that great weapon. The impact deadened my arm; it was numb and tingling now and unable to help myself I dropped my shield. Sensing victory, Kadir roared and his huge blade was falling again.

But this time Wreccan was in the way. I parried the blow and thrust my weight against Kadir pushing him back. As he staggered away from me, I shook my left arm to let the blood return, then tossed Wreccan to my left hand and drew Catraeth with my right, rolling my wrist so the point rotated a few times. Then I moved on Kadir with both blades at the ready.

He now had both his hands firmly gripped around the hilt of his great sword, the blade held close to his chest pointing to the sun, which even now was almost at its zenith over our heads and casting our squat shadows on the ground at our feet. We were both sweating and I noticed that Kadir was panting hard. His attacks thus far had taken a toll on me, yet had clearly tired him too. He was a big man, bigger even than Eduard. Big men tire more easily and that might be my best hope. It seemed my old trainer had spotted it too. "Keep him moving, boy!" Grettir shouted behind me.

I advanced on Kadir, Wreccan swinging in an arc towards his throat. He parried this with his sword and lunged at me in return. I planted my right foot and pivoting to my left let him pass me, then brought Catraeth around aiming to bury it in his chest or belly. Yet he had spotted the move and let his momentum carry him onwards and to the right. Catraeth gashed across his arm causing him to roar in pain, but it was not a mortal blow.

We stepped away from each other. Around us seven hundred throats were roaring and shouting at us. I glanced towards where I had last seen Aidith, but could not make out her face nor that of any of my friends. There was just a wall of faces and of noise.

Kadir approached again and took a huge swing at me. I managed to get Wreccan in the way, but the impact knocked it spinning from my hand. Now, though, I was moving in towards him, inside the reach of his vast sword. I stabbed hard forward with Catraeth, my Roman short sword, using it in the way it was intended when first it was forged; the way a hundred thousand Roman legionaries had done before me on their way to building their empire – some of them, maybe, on this very parade ground.

The point pierced Kadir's chain shirt. I had not struck him straight on, but rather across his flank. The razor sharp edge cut a gash down his side and blood gushed out, dropping like red rain on the ground. I lowered Catraeth, while behind me Angle throats erupted in a roar of triumph. The Irish and Welsh fell silent.

Kadir's eyes widened and he looked down at the wound. "You bastard!" he shouted and raising his great blade, moved to attack me again.

I stepped hastily backwards, raising Catraeth to parry the coming blow, but as I did so, a voice from the ranks of Welshmen boomed out, "Kadir, no! Wait!"

"What is it?" Kadir growled, glancing round, his sword poised to strike me.

"The fight is over!" Prince Cadfan replied, pushing out through his men and hurrying across the parade ground to join us.

"What?" Kadir's face flushed red with anger and disbelief.

"He is right," Prince Selyf said, now also leaving his own lines. "My father's conditions for victory were first blood from the torso. It is over, Kadir. God has decided. Cerdic is the victor. Both of you put down your swords."

Lowering our weapons, Kadir and I turned to face the white chariot only to see that neither Cynan nor Haiarme were watching us, both of them involved in an animated discussion. I saw the queen thrust her hand out towards Edwin and then clench her fist. Then I saw Cynan nod his head. Seeing it I felt a sudden chill, for in that moment I realised that the so called trial by combat was just an excuse. Cynan and Haiarme had not expected Kadir to lose, and certainly his victory would have made it easier for them, for it was clear they had never intended to let us go. Indeed, we had been afraid something like this might happen, which was why Edwin had asked Cadfan for armed support. It must have been obvious to everyone that Cynan was Haiarme's puppet; so under her spell was he that whatever she had said to him had persuaded him to go back on his word.

And so the order came. He pointed at Edwin and shouted his command to the massed companies of Irish and Welsh. "Seize the Angles, all of them, if they resist kill them."

"What is this?" Cadfan strode forward.

"Father, this is not right!" Selyf argued.

Cynan eyes were wild as he turned them on his son, a fleck of white spittle flying from his mouth as he shouted, "I am King of Powys, not you! Not yet! Until that day comes I command here and you will do as I say."

"Don't be foolish!" Cadfan said before Selyf could respond. "Do you want war, Cynan?"

"Yes!" came the reply, but not from Cynan. It was Haiarme

222

who screeched at us. "Yes, I want war. I want blood and death until all the Angles and any who aid them are destroyed. You heard your king. Attack!"

"Oh shit!" I said, turning back towards our own lines and dragging a bewildered Cadfan along in my wake. "Form up, form up!" I bellowed.

"Attack!" Screamed Haiarme again, and beside her Cynan cracked the stallions' reins across their backs so that the magnificent white chariot jerked forward, coming straight towards us.

Chapter Twenty Three
The Chariot Charges
Spring 209

I scampered back towards our lines. Cadfan ran alongside me and then veered off to join his Welshmen. "Form up! Form up!" I bellowed again. As I reached Eduard and Aedann I slipped past them, taking a spare shield from Cuthbert, who then scurried away to round up our few archers and slingers and clamber with them up some nearby masonry onto an elevated stone ledge. In a moment Cuthbert had readied an arrow in his bow and was taking aim. Around me the familiar clattering of wooden shields heralded the forming of the shield wall, the warriors' spears at the ready projecting outwards.

I turned to glance at the villagers. Aidith gave me a look that was both filled with relief that I still lived and anxiety about what was about to happen. She was holding Cuthwine back, the boy struggling to join me. Sian peered fearfully towards me from where she was taking shelter behind Aidith's skirts. Then the horns sounded to our front and Sian started back into hiding. Aidith gave me another terrified glance and then she turned away and herded the village women and children into one of the ruined barrack blocks.

Above us our running wolf standard fluttered in the sudden breeze that blew across the parade ground. To our right Cadfan had formed up his three companies of spearman but had himself mounted and joined the cavalry he had brought with him. I counted our numbers: three hundred spearmen; forty horsemen and a mere handful of archers. We were outnumbered by almost two to one.

Across the parade ground, Morfael was already forming up the companies of the Dogfeiling. Cynan's royal guard and Kadir's Irish, mounted and on foot, were also at the ready. To our left Selyf had joined his companies and they were also stood to, yet I could see that the Prince of Powys wore a very anxious expression. This was not a fight he had wanted, indeed, like Cadfan, he had hoped that today's duel would end the matter one way or another without war between Powys and Gwynedd, but that was not to be. He knew Powys outnumbered us here today and that the most likely outcome would be that all we Angles would die, but so too would many of the Welshmen from Gwynedd and indeed Powys too, for we would not go to Woden's halls without taking a lot of our enemy with us.

Cadfan knew his father's wish that Gwynedd and Powys should not fight; indeed, Iago would not want Cadfan's companies losing warriors to protect us. Yet Iago was not here and Cadfan was, and Edwin, his adopted son, stood by my side. I spotted Cadfan glance across at us and his expression was determined. Whatever his father wished, the Prince of Gwynedd would fight with us today.

It was madness, all of it. Men who had no wish to fight and die forced to do so because one old man was besotted to a state of madness with a much younger woman. And she, I then believed, was less than sane herself, so fixated was she on avenging her father's death. As I was thinking about this a sudden cacophony of horns sounded across the parade ground and the Powys companies started to move towards us. The Irish cavalry had already manoeuvred out onto the flank where they opposed Cadfan's mounted troops. The fight between the mounted men would most likely not last long and in any event probably would not swing the battle one way or the other today. No; the decision would be made in the shield wall and with Selyf's companies outflanking us on the left, I felt a growing sense of gloom about what the outcome would be.

There was a barrack block to our left and slightly behind us, adjacent to the one in which the villagers were huddled. "Wicstun company, pivot to the left! "I commanded and the men started shuffling backwards. Our right flank stayed fixed to the first of Cadfan's companies, but the left-wing now angled slightly backwards. This brought the fixed obstacle of the barrack block onto our flank, meaning that it would be difficult for Selyf's companies to break through and lap round us. I was only buying time, but we needed every advantage we could obtain.

A slingstone pinged off my shield and another clattered off the top of my helmet. The enemy slingers were pelting us with stones whilst their archers sent a volley of arrows into our ranks. Here and there the first injuries of the battle were already occurring. Our skirmishers traded arrows and slingshots with the opposition, but there were far more of them. Cuthbert himself aimed carefully, picking out gaps between shields; aiming at faces that were revealed and unarmoured necks and legs. Already half a dozen of the enemy had fallen wounded or dead to our missiles; we had probably had the best of the exchange of skirmishers, for whilst they had more archers than we, ours were more skilled. However, it was only a few moments later that the shield walls closed in and the main event could start.

Over on the right flank, the cavalrymen charged their horses at each other and were soon locked into a swirling melee. In its midst Cynan steered his chariot, flinging a javelin and then reaching out to stab with his sword at passing Gwynedd cavalry. Ahead of me Morfael's Dogfeiling warriors growled, cursed and roared at us. Then the shields collided, splintering spears and knocking men to the ground. The struggle of the shield walls had begun.

For the next stage of the battle my focus narrowed down to a few yards of space. Eduard was to my left, grunting and panting as he hewed around him with his axe. Edwin, on my right, staggered backwards from one blow to his shield then followed back with a slash of his sword that decapitated his opponent. Beyond Edwin, Aedann was shouting in Welsh at the enemy calling them all cowards and inviting them to fall at his feet. The struggle went on and on. At first we held them, but then the sheer numbers of the Dogfeiling started to tell and our shield wall began to buckle. Men took a step or two backwards and we were maybe only moments away from a rout that would end the battle.

'Damn Cynan!' I thought to myself. 'And damn Haiarme as well!' I was convinced they were both mad; only stark staring madness could have brought us to this pass. In that moment it occurred to me that maybe the only solution would be their demise. I yelled to Eduard to keep fighting and I pulled back out of the shield wall. I located Cuthbert and gestured for him to climb down from his perch and join me. As we ran to the right behind the companies from Gwynedd I told him what I meant to do. I realised that many of my men and those of the Welsh companies were already wounded, several most likely dead, but I pushed that thought away from my mind and tried to focus on my plan. Many more would die unless we could find a way out of this insanity.

When I reached the end of Cadfan's spear companies I had a clearer view of the cavalry melee. The Prince of Gwynedd looked magnificent in his gleaming chain armour and was easily the finest horseman in the battle, manoeuvring his animal around the enemy, confounding them and then dashing in to land the killing blow. However, it was not Cadfan I had come to seek out, for there, in the midst of the melee, still riding on his white chariot like the warrior chieftains of old that had fought against the Roman legions hundreds of years before, I spotted Cynan. Kadir was at his side, the wound I had inflicted upon him, apparently not especially serious, had been swiftly bound.

The sagas tell of the glories of combat, how warrior lords and kings should face each other like men, fighting on until fate decided who should win. You do not hear stories, generally, of kings and princes laid low by stones, javelins or arrows; such weapons are considered inferior, less glorious and perhaps not suited to the death of kings. Somehow, what I was about to try did not seem honourable, but then, Cynan was not honourable either and this course of action was, I felt, entirely justified, yet even so it went against the grain. "Thunor's hammer!" I muttered to myself before my resolve left me, and turning to Cuthbert I ordered, "Shoot the bastard dead and I'll give you and Millie a hundred gold coins!"

Cuthbert grinned, notched an arrow on his bowstring and took aim. "Cerdic, my old friend; this one I will do for free!"

I had my shield and Catraeth poised ready to defend my friend, but Thunor was, it seemed, on our side, for the two of us were left untouched while Cuthbert went about his work. Pursing his lips in concentration he took his time, swinging his bow to the left and to the right as he followed the movements of the white chariot.

And then he released the bowstring. The arrow, with the fate of so many hanging upon it, arched across the battlefield, straight and true like a bolt of fire from Thunor himself. It slammed into the throat of the King of Powys, who dropped like a stone to the floor of the chariot.

Quick as a flash, Cuthbert notched another arrow on the string and was aiming at Kadir, but the Irishman was too difficult a target. Fast recovering from the shock of Cynan collapsing, he grabbed the reins and whipped the horses to a gallop, steering them back through the melee to the rear lines where the queen stood watching the battle. Then he leapt down and helped by Haiarme, hauled the king's body out of the white chariot to lay him on the ground beside it. Cynan was not moving.

"King Cynan is dead! The King is dead!" I bellowed, gesticulating wildly in the direction of the chariot. Cuthbert joined in and then, a moment later, Cadfan also bellowed the news at the top of his voice. Ahead of us the king's company had started to fall back to take up position in front of Haiarme, Kadir, the white chariot and the body of Cynan. They were joined swiftly by Morfael. I noticed that none of them seemed particularly distressed by the death of the king. Clearly, his infatuation with his queen had not been reciprocated by Haiarme, who had eyes only for Morfael.

No man in his right mind wants to fight and die and as news of the king's death spread across the parade ground the battle began to falter, warriors lowering their weapons and looking to their leaders for orders. Kadir roared a command to his Irishmen. In a few moments they disengaged and were pulling back around the white chariot. Next, the companies belonging to Morfael pulled away from the shield wall, leaving my men gasping and panting for breath. A few in the company made to pursue them, but Eduard and Edwin roared at them to stand still.

On our left flank the companies of Prince Selyf were still engaged with our Wicstun men and were even now breaking through the barrack block in an attempt to outflank our warriors. Yet news of the king's death must have reached Selyf, for now I could see him looking searchingly across the battlefield. His gaze finally fixed upon Cynan's body where it still lay, having been hastily abandoned by Haiarme and Kadir, who for the moment were nowhere to be seen; nor was Morfael. And nor was the white chariot!

For an instant Selyf stood stock still, staring in obvious dismay at his father's supine form; then he opened his mouth and roared out an order. "Disengage! Disengage! Stop fighting at once!"

Slowly his companies withdrew, leaving a few bodies broken on the ground. Selyf hastened across the parade ground towards his father and with the fighting apparently ceased, Cadfan, Edwin and I joined him, each sheathing our weapons as we approached. For a few moments we stood in silence and looked down at the body of the king, the arrow protruding from his throat – though perhaps fortunately, Selyf was not to know it had come from Cuthbert's bow and at my order.

"I'm sorry for your loss, Prince Selyf," I said.

I wasn't, of course, but it's the thing you say, and I was at that moment sorry for Selyf; he looked stricken with grief, his eyes red with the strain of holding back tears.

"I loved him, Cerdic. He was a harsh man, even a harsh father at times and this last year or two since Haiarme came he changed from the man I knew, but he was still my father and I will mourn him."

Selyf stopped speaking and all around him we were silent, respecting his grief. After a few moments he glanced across the battlefield, "This battle was meaningless. Not only was it meaningless, but it should never have happened. It was dishonourable and good men have died needlessly because of it." He swallowed hard before continuing and looked at Edwin and Cadfan. "No fault attaches to either of you princes," he said. "Come, let us talk. I will send orders that Kadir and Haiarme are to be detained and that Morfael's men and Morfael himself should submit to my authority... for I am King of Powys now!"

Yes, so he was. That had not occurred to me until he spoke those words. Remembering how this very reasonable man had aided our escape from Pengwern a few months ago, I thought it augured well for the future.

It did not prove quite as easy as Selyf hoped. In the aftermath of the battle, Morfael's retreating companies had reached the path winding up to Ruthin and having done so, barricaded themselves into the fortress. When challenged they said they remained loyal to Dogfeiling and not to Powys, nor to Gwynedd and that Morfael's orders were to hold Ruthin in his absence, which they fully intended to do.

Meanwhile, the immediate pursuit of Kadir, Morfael himself and Haiarme had been blocked by the skilful retreat of Kadir's Irish horsemen whilst the rest of us were distracted by Cynan's death. So despite our best efforts, the passengers of the white chariot had escaped. That could not bode well for the future, I thought.

However, with Cynan dead and Haiarme gone, no one was left to pursue the claim against we Angles, so the new king agreed to dismiss the charges and release us.

Two of our Wicstun company had died in that brief, meaningless battle and another three had been severely injured, although not mortally. So it was in a subdued atmosphere that I went to find my family after the fight.

"It is over," I said to Aidith. "You are free to go and can return to Rhufoniog."

"Can we all go, you as well?" She asked. I hesitated and she frowned at the delay.

"What is it now?" She asked. "I thought you said it was over!"

"It is, it will be. I just need to go with Edwin to Pengwern for Selyf's coronation. He has asked us to be there. It will only be a matter of days and then I can come home."

"You promise?" I nodded and at the time it was not a lie. Selyf had decided to proceed towards Pengwern in order to be proclaimed king and had invited Cadfan and Edwin along. Eager to reforge an alliance with Powys, Cadfan agreed and naturally so did Edwin. I felt obliged to accompany them. With Cynan dead and Selyf now king, we should be able to come to an arrangement that would bring peace between Gwynedd, Powys and Mercia. Edwin might even be married by winter and an alliance that might bring him a throne could be forged.

When we reached Pengwern a few days later, however, it was to find that the troubles in Powys were nowhere as close to being over as we had hoped. Indeed, everything had just become a lot more complicated.

Chapter Twenty Four
Readingum
Winter 608

"So, how are we going do this, Hussa? "Rolf asked.

They were once again standing in woodland to the west of the fortified city of Readingum, which sat between the Kennett and the Thames. Smoke was rising from several dozen houses, workshops and ale halls. They could hear hammering and the sound of a saw echoing out across the surrounding meadows, covered now in spring flowers. The defenders were reinforcing the barricades. In some places sections of a palisade were being erected. It was clear that their builders had access to a good supply of timber.

To the east of the city, in the land running up to the confluence where the two rivers came together, were fields and copses, but Hussa suspected the defenders had sent parties across the Thames into the Chiltern foothills to obtain supplies of timber. The siege had been only partially implemented through the winter months and whilst Hussa had been able to cut Readingum off from any of the other Thames Valley settlements, the land to the north of the Thames belonged to the Chilternae – people of mixed British and Saxon heritage who clung to their hills and wooded valleys. Clearly the inhabitants of Readingum were on good terms with them. Either that or the supplies had been seized by force. Whatever, the partial siege appeared to have troubled Readingum not at all.

With the spring thaw, water levels had risen and the Thames was threatening to break its banks and flood the nearby meadows. That would make an attack upon the city more difficult, so Hussa was keen to get on with it as soon as possible. He had now assembled a significant army, having mustered almost every man of fighting age in the locality, leaving many of the settlements and towns with too few labourers to work the fields and plant the crops. If he was victorious he would send them home along with reinforcements to assist them. If he failed it could mean a famine along the Thames Valley. In such a situation, however, West Seax would probably abandon the campaign – and in any event, it would not be his problem.

Actually, it was the rising water levels that had given him his idea for the battle plan, which he now laid out to his company commanders.

"I have sent orders to Lord Woke to gather boats along the Thames below Readingum. I will take Wilbur's company to join the Wochinoes contingent. Rolf and Tolan will remain here and they will be joined by Ricberht, who is bringing all the fresh troops down the Thames Valley from Doric and below. I plan an attack on two flanks. Rolf will command the attack by land across these fields and over the barricades into the town."

Doubtfully, Tolen shook his head. "That will be a tough attack, Lord Hussa. Directly against a fortified position, I mean. We will outnumber the defenders it is true, but not by much. We will probably get in, but it could cost us at least half the men in our companies. "

Hussa held up his hand to silence Tolan. "If what I plan works out I am hoping that at most only half the city's defenders will be on those barricades."

"The boats?" Rolf said.

"Yes Rolf, the boats. I plan to land two companies at the confluence of the Thames and the Kennett. We will attack the city from the unfortified side – a bit like we did at Doric. This time, however, we will not do it stealthily; the plan will be to draw off as many defenders as possible. When we have pulled in as many as we can I will blow five blasts on the horn to signal you to attack. When you hear the horn, we will probably be deep in shit, so you must come as quickly as possible, you understand?"

Now it was Rolf who looked doubtful. "There's a heck of a lot that could go wrong with this plan, lord. What if you don't have enough boats? What if you can't draw off enough men to allow us to gain access over the barricades? You could get slaughtered before we can reach you. What if..."

Hussa waved his hands in front of Rolf's face. "Enough flapping about like some scared old maid, Rolf. Fate is made by the strong and the determined. Just be ready to attack when the time comes."

"And when will that time be?" Tolan asked.

"Eostre day. We will attack at dawn."

"Two weeks from today then," Rolf said.

"Indeed, "Hussa nodded. "Wilbur and I will leave tomorrow. We are going to march the long way round so as to avoid being spotted by the city. I plan to be in Wochinoes in five days from now, which will give me time to gather the troops from the city, inspect the boats and be ready to row upriver in time for the attack."

Lord Woke and his people had stayed loyal to West Seax. Whether it was the oath of allegiance the lord had sworn or the presence of so many of his men – and in particular his own sons – now absorbed into Rolf's and Tolan's companies, Hussa was not sure. Nor did he particularly care, but he was not blind to the hostile glares he received from youths and women as he rode into Wochinoes and along the main street to the lord's hall, though he gave no indication of that fact. His companion was less phlegmatic.

235

"I would not want to walk alone in this town after dark," Wilbur said with a shudder.

Glancing around at the stony faces and dark, resentful eyes, Hussa shrugged. "If the men fight well and Readingum falls, we can start releasing some of them a few at a time. They must respond to the summons for the battles in Celemion next year, however. We will need them all then. I will tell Woke this – he can tell his people if it helps to sweeten their mood. Sweet or sour, it matters not; their men will remain with us until after this campaign."

Wilbur shrugged. "You are the lord, Lord Hussa, and pressed men will fight if you have a hold over them…"

Hussa gave him a sharp glance. "I think I can detect a 'but' on the way into this conversation."

Wilbur screwed up his face as he attempted to make his point without using the 'but' word, then he relaxed into a smile. "However," he said triumphantly, "men with something to fight for fight better."

Hussa grunted, knowing Wilbur was right but not wanting to concede the point.

Lord Woke was accommodating and polite, if not exactly friendly when they reached the hall. They discussed the campaign plans and he affirmed his instructions. "I have two dozen boats collected on the river at Sonning and eighty spears ready to march in a few days, Lord Hussa. My men will fight for Ceolwulf."

"You have done well, Lord Woke – all that I asked and more." Hussa glanced across at Wilbur before continuing, "Though it occurs to me you may have done so for fear of what would happen to your sons and your men if you did not." He held up a hand to stifle Woke's protest. "Come now, such a reaction

236

would be only human. But the king and I would have men fight willingly for West Seax, not just out of obligation or fear. That being so, I would have you announce to your people that after Readingum has fallen your men will be released with a share of the plunder and a promise of more riches if they follow you and the king's banner into Celemion next year."

Woke looked stunned. "Are you saying that all the men will come home?"

"Those who live through the battle, yes."

"My sons too?"

Hussa nodded, "Your sons too."

Woke was still not convinced. "We have Ceolwulf's word on this?"

"The king is not here, Woke. I am and you do have mine." Hussa stuck out his hand then shrugged and added, "Obviously I can do nothing about those chosen by the Valkyries to feast in Woden's hall."

"No man can," Woke murmured, shaking Hussa's hand. Pushing back his chair he got to his feet and strode to the doorway. "I will pass on this news, Lord Hussa."

A few moments later the sound of cheering filtered into the hall and Hussa glared at Wilbur. "Happy now, you soft bastard?"

"I didn't say a word!" Wilbur said with a broad smile.

The oars rose and fell in and out of the cold water, disturbing the reflection of stars on the river surface, as the little fleet of boats made its way up river. Hussa sat near the prow of the largest vessel in which Lord Woke also sailed. Whilst Hussa was merely a passenger, Woke stood at the tiller and steered.

Staring out into the darkness, Hussa recalled tales of how their ancestors had used vessels such as this to cross the German sea and land all along the east and south coast, at first invited in as mercenaries and later coming as invaders and settlers. The days of the great migration were three generations and more in the past and had now all but ceased, so that most Saxons, save those along the coast, had never seen a boat let alone sailed in one. Yet the Saxons of the Thames Valley had used boats to settle deep into the heartland of Britain; as they saw it, the river was an artery linking them to the great markets in Lundunne and the wider world. Now, thought Hussa, the same boats would be used to complete their conquest by a larger power, that of West Seax.

As they rounded the last bend the first glow of the rising sun cut the dark eastern sky behind them and now Hussa could see silhouetted the shapes of the two dozen vessels that followed them. Ahead the river split. The broader Thames curved off to the right, whilst the narrow Kennet joined it at the confluence, which Woke now steered toward. On the far bank where the rivers met, a dense belt of woodland obscured any view of Read-ingum, though it was now but a thousand yards away.

They approached the bank as silently as several score oars could manage. The far bank seemed deserted at first. Then a patrolling spearman emerged through the trees and stumbled to a halt as he took in the scene, his bottom jaw falling open as he gawped at the small fleet of boats crammed with warriors coming towards him. Then he stirred into life and turned to get away intent on raising the alarm. Before he could reach safety, Wilbur had joined Hussa in the prow, his right hand a blur as he whipped his sling around and then, with a flick, the stone was gone. They heard a dull thud and a grunt in the direction of the fleeing sentinel as he collapsed into a gorse bush.

"Bloody good shot!" hissed one of the warriors behind Hussa.

"Two more!" Wilbur pointed, ignoring the compliment.

Looking to where Wilbur pointed, Hussa saw another spearman crouched by the body. Beside him stood an archer stretching his bow. The arrow streaked towards them, but the aim was wild and it plopped uselessly into the water ten feet from the boat. Before Wilbur could reply with another slingshot, the pair had retreated, shouting their alarm.

"Row hard!" With the need for stealth now gone, Woke's commanding voice bellowed from the rear and was taken up by the captains of the other boats.

The fleet surged forward and then, with a thud and a creak Woke's vessel grounded on the bank. Hussa drew his blade and jumped over the side, followed by Wilbur and the rest of the men in the boat. Around them the other boats were reaching the shore and men were disgorging onto the bank.

"My company! Follow me," Wilbur shouted and led the way through the trees, his own men, who had been in the leading boats, running at his heels, his standard bearer carrying his pennant of a tusked boar. Hussa held back, waiting for Woke's company to form up around him, his own pennant of a raven on a blue ground held aloft by his standard bearer. When they were ready, Hussa motioned them forward and set off after Wilbur with Woke coming after him, leading his company along the same bank.

The belt of woodland was only a hundred paces wide and they soon emerged into fields, ploughed and seeded but not as yet showing signs of growth. The sun had just reached the height of the treetops and they could now see the city of Readingum beyond the cultivated land.

Forming his company into a loose formation Wilbur led them across the fields. When he was about half way he shouted the command to halt. Hussa, who was coming across the same fields to catch up with him, saw why. It seemed the enemy sentinel had lost no time in raising the alarm. Spearmen were emerging from the city in number: fifty, one hundred, two hundred… all forming up into a shield wall. Once again, Wilbur shouted an order and his company condensed into shield formation and readied spears. Hussa could see he was outnumbered by more than two to one and would rapidly be outflanked.

Behind Hussa, Woke had reached the fields and was gazing at the ranks of enemy spearmen. Hussa could tell he was weighing up the situation and a horrible thought crossed his mind. If Woke now attacked Wilbur from the rear and the men of Readingum engaged from the front… well, he shrugged to himself, then it would all be over very quickly and it would merely be a matter of counting the dead. Did that thought pass through Woke's mind too, Hussa wondered. Woden's buttocks, he hoped not!

At that moment Woke barked out an order and his company moved forward. Hussa held his breath for a long moment before he realised that Woke's men were swinging around to join up on Wilbur's left flank. As they closed up and overlapped shields, Hussa nodded his thanks at Woke, who gave him a wry smile back. So he had entertained the thought. Was it fear for his sons that kept him loyal or the thought of plunder, or was it simply that he had a sense of honour? If they lived, Hussa thought, he would ask him. He pushed into the ranks between the two companies where his standard bearer was located along with his huscarls. There too was his signaller, ox horn held at the ready, head inclined in expectation of the order.

Hussa shook his head. "Not yet," he said.

The signaller stared at the large number of enemy shields and seeing there were enough to push Hussa's army back and maybe beat them, he looked at Hussa again, fear etched on his face.

"Wait! Not enough yet," Hussa grunted. "We need to pull in more."

In front of them the enemy horns sounded and the Readingum men roared as they advanced, spears to the front, coming straight at them. Slingshots and arrows from skirmishers now peppered their shields. Hussa signalled and Wilbur and others returned the barrage. A few men on either side were hit, their broken bodies falling onto the ploughed earth beneath their feet.

"Angle flanks!" Hussa ordered and the outer third of each company angled back to make it harder for them to be outflanked. "Hold here!" he added and the men braced for the arrival of the enemy shield wall, which soon came onto theirs with a crash, shattering spears and jarring bones with the impact. And rising into the air came the cries and screams of battle and the accompanying stink of shit and piss.

"Hold them!" Hussa shouted as he stepped back, pulling his signaller and four huscarls with him. Spotting a gnarled old tree stump in one corner of the field he climbed onto it to get a better view. In front of him Wilbur's shield wall was giving ground, the weight of the enemy numbers beginning to tell. They just needed to hold on long enough for… Hussa's line of thought ceased as he saw what he was hoping for: yet more armoured men piling out of the town. Set on slaughtering the invading army, the defenders had decided to throw more spearmen into the fight. Hussa ran his gaze over them, roughly counting their numbers. Three hundred men now faced his one hundred and sixty. That left maybe eighty more defending the west wall against three times that number under Rolf and Ricberht. He had them!

"Hold on, Wilbur! Not much longer," he bawled. "Now, signaller; blow five blasts and blow hard!"

As the sound of the horn wound into the air, Hussa shouted,

"Repeat it and keep repeating it!"

The signaller, red in the face with the effort, continued blowing five blasts on the horn until Hussa held up a hand to stop him.

Straining to hear over the pandemonium at hand, Hussa could make out nothing beyond the screams and shouting, the thud of blades on shields. Where was Rolf? Had his plan failed? What might have gone wrong? Had Rolf and Tolan fallen at the barricades? Were he and all his men doomed to die here in this field of mud? For a moment Hussa was almost overwhelmed with nausea, but just then there was the briefest pause in the hullaballoo of the shield walls and through it, echoing from the far side of the city, the answering horns from twenty signallers.

Thank the gods! Rolf was coming.

"Lord, watch out!" the signaller shouted.

Almost dizzy with relief, Hussa had failed to notice ten enemy warriors coming around the flank, looking to attack the rear of Wilbur's company.

"Follow me!" he shouted to his huscarls. Leaping off the tree stump and drawing his sword he charged towards the enemy. Around him his huscarls were screaming incoherently and Hussa too let the rage of the battlefield come upon him. He knew, with a certainty that grew with each battle, that there were few better swordsmen alive than he and he had a finer sword than many kings possessed. Somehow, the fact that it had been forged by a common blacksmith and not a royal armourer seemed more fitting with his own mundane background. Kings and bards spoke of fate and destiny woven by the Norns, but maybe there was room for a few men like himself to carve their own paths. Wasn't he doing exactly that right here and now?

242

He parried the first man's spear and then followed through with a stab to the throat. Stepping over the dying man he dodged to one side as another spearman tried to wind him with a shield blow. The warrior's momentum took him past Hussa who hacked at the back of the man's exposed neck, sending a spray of blood skyward and the man crashing paralysed to the ground. A third spearman took one look at him and backed away, dropping his spear and shield and holding up his hands. Hussa stepped up to him and ran him through with his sword. Today was not a day to show mercy, the numbers were still against them. Around him his veteran huscarls made short work of the enemy fyrd and soon the ten enemy warriors lay bloody at their feet with only one of his own men slightly injured. He had won this little fight, but the battle was turning against them. Enemy numbers were telling and Wilbur's and Woke's companies were in retreat, pulling back towards the shelter of the woods. Any moment now and it would be a rout. Time though for one last play of the game, Hussa thought and waved at his signaller who sent out a series of short blasts.

At the edge of the wood more men began to emerge. Only fifteen were visible but they were forming up around a standard. The enemy saw it too and halted their pursuit. What was this? Another company? Reinforcements? Hussa knew it was neither. It was simply the boatmen whom he had instructed before they sailed, just in case of this eventuality. Hearing the prearranged signal, they had pulled on the chain shirts and picked up the spears and shields he had provided and had brought along a sheet of sail cloth as an improvised banner. It was no more than a diversion and would not fool the enemy for long, but Hussa did not think he needed long.

Indeed, even now ranks of the enemy were shouting out, spinning round and pointing. Not at the fake company of boatmen but at Readingum, where Rolf, accompanied by Woke's own sons, had emerged from the city and was leading his warriors to attack the enemy's rear.

"Shield wall form up!" Hussa shouted. His command, echoed by Wilbur and Woke, was obeyed and his little army, together with the river men under their sailcloth banner, were advancing towards the fyrd of Readingum, whilst Rolf, now joined by To-lan and Ricberht, were hastening towards them from the west. The defenders of the city were trapped between them and in total disarray, not knowing which way to turn.

Hussa held up a hand and his companies halted, as did Rolf's and Ricberht's. "Men of Readingum," he shouted, "You have fought well. Some of you may want to fight more for the sake of honour. I tell you though, that if you do then you will die here. Some of us will too, but all of you. You are outmanoeuvred and outnumbered. No quarter will be given after this offer."

"What offer?" a voice shouted out from amongst the ranks.

"The terms are simple: surrender to me now. Readingum becomes part of West Seax and you swear allegiance to Ceolwulf as king. Half of any wealth in Readingum will be dispersed as plunder between the men in the conquering armies – their reward and your penalty for resistance. Then you will join us. Next year we are going to Celemion. You will take part in the fighting and if you live will share in the plunder of that wealthy British kingdom. Turn against West Seax at any time and your city will burn and its people will all be slain. Remember what I did to Pegingaburnan? That could be Readingum."

Amongst the enemy ranks there was a murmur of conversation. After a moment a tall, slender man stepped out and ap-

244

proached Hussa, arms held out to show he carried no weapon.

"I am Lord Verge of Readingum. I accept your terms. Maybe we made the wrong choice last year. We were deceived and persuaded by Eorpwald of Benson."

"He is a man that I would like to see personally," Hussa said, his eyes narrowed. "Bring him out."

"My lord," Rolf shouted over as he walked to join them. "I am sorry to say we saw Eorpwald and a handful of men gallop out of the city when it became clear we were winning. There was nothing we could do to stop him because we knew you were in a perilous position and would fall without our support. So we just had to let him go."

"Woden's arse! Don't tell me the slippery eel has escaped us again! He has the cunning of Loki. Where did he go?"

Rolf shrugged, "There is only one way he could go from here – to the forests of Celemion."

Hussa grinned, "Then next year we will have him." He clapped Rolf on the shoulder. "Well done, old friend. Come let us find Ricberht. I want to give him command of Readingum before we leave."

Rolf frowned. "Leave? Where are we going?"

"To Witanceastre of course, to see the king."

"Ah," Rolf winked. "And Rowenna too perhaps?"

Hussa's grin faded. "We shall see," he replied.

That was not, however what happened. At least, not immediately. It took some time to organise the garrison of Readingum, leaving Ricberht in command but with Lord Verge retaining his rank and post. Then Hussa fulfilled his promise to Woke and returned his sons, along with most of the rest of the companies from Wochinoes. Ever cautious, however, he saw to it that a portion of the men remained at arms under the eyes of Ceolwulf's

West Seax Company or his own men. That done, he checked on Pegingaburnan and Belesduna, Garinges, Benson and finally, Doric. Satisfied that the whole Thames Valley, from the Mercian border to Middle Seax was subdued and, for the present, obedient, he prepared to leave for Witanceastre just as summer was reaching its height.

It was then that Lord Boyden arrived.

Together with his huscarls Hussa was enjoying an evening meal in the Magistrate's hall in Doric, when a guard entered the hall and sought him out to tell him that King Ceolwulf's lieutenant was outside and demanding an audience with Lord Hussa.

"What does the bastard want now?" Rolf whispered as Boyden joined them in the hall. He looked curiously around at the pillars and statues and then threw himself down at a bench, poured himself a goblet of ale and scooped up a hunk of bread.

"Gods, but I am hungry. It's a long way round from Witanceastre to here. Be much faster when we take Celemion. About five Roman roads join at the city and go straight through the country."

"Yes, I know," Hussa said grumpily. "Is there a reason for your long journey? I am about to leave for Witanceastre myself."

Boyden shook his head. "No, you are not," he mumbled through a mouthful of bread.

Hussa frowned and struggled to control his temper. "Look, I have taken Readingum. The whole Thames Valley belongs to West Seax. What more does the king want of me?"

"The king is concerned about Mercia. He needs a free hand to act against Celemion."

"So?"

"So you are to go to Tamwerth, see King Ceorl and persuade him to keep out of the Thames Valley. "

"Ceorl is a friend to Cerdic. I am not sure he will listen to me. Besides, I have done as Ceolwulf asked. I'm overdue a rest!"

"Bollocks! "Boyden retorted, "You can forget that! You are to make Ceorl listen. Be persuasive. "

"That is it? "

"That is it. Go to Mercia and ensure they keep out of the Thames Valley whilst the business in Celemion is resolved. I don't think he would risk a premature conlict. Then you can return to Witanceastre and the king will discuss with you his plans for next year. I'm sure you will then get your just reward, Hussa."

"About bloody time!" Hussa glared at Boyden a moment longer before turning away.

"Rolf!" he bellowed.

"What?"

"Get the horses, we have to go north!"

Chapter Twenty Five
Empty
Summer 609

Not surprisingly it was Cuthbert who was the first to spot that all was not right in Pengwern.

"Something is wrong, Cerdic," he said, looking up at the fort as we rode towards it just behind Edwin, Selyf, Cadfan and their personal guard.

I glanced at him and then up at the city we were approaching. The smoke I saw rising was no more than I would expect at this time of day from cook fires and bakers and looked innocent enough. Then I realised there were no men on the battlements of the wall between the rivers, and that was unusual; even more alarming, the city gate was open yet no warrior stood by it.

"You are right, Cuth!" I said, nudging my horse forward to get to the head of the column and alert King Selyf, but at that moment he held up his hand to signal a halt. He had seen what we had seen and he and the two princes were staring up at the fortress. I joined them and suggested I dispatch Cuthbert and half a dozen scouts to investigate.

"Yes, thank you Cerdic," Selyf said. "It's probably nothing, but best to make sure."

When the scouts returned some while later, Cuthbert scampered over to where we waited on the road.

"Well?" I asked.

"The town is quiet, watchful even and no one is out on the street. It is as if they are afraid of something. I spotted a young lad fetching up water from a well and asked him if anything was amiss. He shrugged and nodded towards the fort. Something bad has happened in the garrison, he told me, but said no more, almost as if he feared talking to me. So we carried on up the hill to the fort. That too was deserted but we found half a dozen of the prince's… I mean King Selyf's men dead. They had been strung up and left to dangle. A few days ago I would say by the look of them."

"Are you saying the fortress is empty?" Selyf asked, incredulously.

Cuthbert nodded. "Yes, sire. Leastways we could not spot anyone there. I have to say we did not stay long after seeing the dead guards."

"I don't understand," Selyf frowned. "What is going on?"

"I suggest we find out," I replied.

We rode on up the hill towards the fort, our spearmen marching along behind us. Cuthbert's description had been accurate. The town was indeed exceptionally quiet with few signs of occupation: the wisp of smoke from some cook fires; here and there a door opening, a silhouette of someone's head revealing we were being observed, the door quickly slamming shut if the watchers realised they had been spotted.

We carried on through the gateway of the fortress, this too was open and there were no men on watch. It was here that we were greeted by the ghastly sight of the half dozen decomposing guards left hanging from the inside of the palisade.

Selyf dismounted and stood looking up at them, his face stony. Then he ordered them cut down and buried.

"They were indeed some of my own huscarls, left to guard Pengwern fort in my absence. If Haiarme did this, I want to know why."

Moving on, I and my huscarls split up to explore the fort while Selyf and the princes waited in the great hall surrounded by their guard, who stood alert and watchful, weapons at the ready.

The place was deserted; we found no huscarls or warriors of any kind, either dead or alive. Furthermore, the stores of ale, wine, grains and salted meats had all been removed. We did, however, come across a few slaves in the kitchens. One of them, an older, Angle woman who said her name was Elvina, told me some of what had happened. I took her up to the great hall and motioned her towards Selyf and the princes. She stood in front of them, shaking with fear and rubbing her hands together in anxiety.

"No need to be afraid, Elvina, nobody is going to hurt you," I said. "Just tell King Selyf and the others what you told me."

"It was four days ago, lord. Everything was quiet when that Queen Haiarme arrives with some of those Irish and some other Welsh. We all thought it was odd that there was no sign of King Cynan or Prince Selyf. Suddenly the orders come down to move all the provisions to carts in the courtyard and to be ready to leave immediately. Then some fighting breaks out and the next thing we hear is that some of the prince's men had been killed." Elvina's face was pale now, her hands trembling as she gave us her account. "We were scared and those of us that could went and hid in some of the stores. Don't think they knew where we were because they all took off."

"Why did you not cut down my huscarls?" Selyf asked angrily. "Why leave them hanging like criminals or worse?"

Elvina looked frankly terrified now and backed away from him.

"It's all right Elvina, just answer," I said softly. "King Cynan is dead. Prince Selyf is king now." She looked up at me for reassurance and I smiled at her. "Go on, Elvina, answer the king," I said, turning her to face him.

"Well, sire, truth be told we were scared. Too scared even to run and try our luck getting away, back to Mercia or wherever. We just hid down there in the kitchens and lived off what was left in the stores hoping you and King Cynan would come back."

"But you can't say why Haiarme killed my men?" Selyf asked, a little more gently.

"I think I can tell you that," someone chirped from the doorway. Recognising the voice we all turned. Lilla stood there. Beside him was Eduard.

"Found him locked up in the dungeons, Cerdic," Eduard said with a grin.

Glad as I was to see him, I was also shocked to find him here, my head teeming with questions. "Locked up? Why? Who locked you up? When did you get back? I thought you were still in Cantia with Hereric. What's going on?"

Although he was pale, dirty and unkempt – uncommonly so for Lilla – he was his usual sarcastic self. He smiled at me, a twinkle in his eye. "Now which question would you like me to answer first?"

"Who locked you up?" I asked again.

"Kadir did, on the queen's orders mind you."

I frowned. "Why?"

Lilla coughed. "I may have expressed one too many opinions about who should succeed King Cynan. I think I may have said Selyf should be king. Unusual for me of course, for as you know I tend to keep quiet and observe. It is just that Haiarme is seriously bonkers and she rubbed me up the wrong way... and as for that gross Irishman..."

"Of course Selyf should be king," I said impatiently. "He is the heir!"

Lilla shrugged. "Haiarme had another interpretation of the issue."

251

"What do you mean?" Selyf growled.

"I mean she maintained there is a prior claimant who she insisted would press his right to the throne."

Cadfan stepped forward. "Prior claimant? You can't mean...? You don't mean... Tysilio?"

Lilla nodded, "I do indeed."

This was greeted by stunned silence. It was broken by a shriek from Elvira, wideeyed she looked at Lilla and then at Selyf, "Shit!" she exclaimed.

Reminded of her presence, we all glared at her and she scampered away uttering obscenities, no doubt armed with the best gossip she would ever know and ready to divulge it to the other surviving slaves.

"I have to agree with her," Selyf said. "What are you talking about, Lilla?"

The bard was starting to relax into his tale, enjoying as he always did the attention it brought him.

"I happened to arrive at Pengwern from Mercia, aiming to head north to Rhufoniog to see Cerdic."

"Mercia? Me? Why?"

Lilla screwed up his face at the interruption. "There you go again; too many questions, Cerdic. Later, old friend, later. Anyway, as I was saying, I had hoped to rely on the hospitality of Selyf who has proven a good host in the past. I was alarmed to find, however, that the former prince was not here but instead found Haiarme and Kadir along with Morfael – all of them rather antagonistic to Angles, even bards! Not only that, but I walked in when a confrontation was going on between Haiarme and the captain of the prince's guards here in Pengwern. Haiarme ordered that every fighting man in Pengwern go along with her as well as all the slaves and food supplies here."

Lilla turned to Selyf, "I should tell you, sire, that your captain refused to take orders from anyone other than you."

Selyf nodded. "They are... were sworn to my service. And I to protect them," he added gloomily. "Pengwern was my fortress, which I held for my father when he was not here. These men were mine, provided in order to undertake garrison duty here. Haiarme had no right to demand that they leave."

"Well demand it she did, "Lilla said, "and in no uncertain terms. Then, when they would not comply, she started hanging them. A couple of the guards tried to resist but were cut down and thrown down the refuse pit. Haiarme then cajoled the rest to go along with her. She said that Tysilio was claiming the throne, as was his right, and that she was delivering to him his armies."

"I find it very hard to believe that my uncle would claim the throne," Selyf said. "Haiarme and the others are playing a game here. Yet to what end?"

"Sire," Cadfan said, "forgive me, but it may be best to discuss this later, since there is nothing we can do about it immediately. I am thinking we should see about provisioning the men and, if you'll allow, setting up camp to accommodate them."

"Don't know about anyone else, but I could do with a drink!" I chipped in.

"Yes, of course," Selyf said apologetically. "There must be some ale around here somewhere. I could use some myself. As you suggest, we'll meet in the hall later and discuss what is to be done."

We found out more about what had happened at Pengwern a few days later. Over the next day or so, provisions began to trickle into the fort. Selyf had sent messengers to all the nobles in the area, explaining his situation and requesting that they send a portion of whatever food and drink they could spare to the fort.

253

He paid for this with what treasury he had at hand and promised further payment later. In the meantime, scouts were sent out to locate Haiarme and Kadir, contact Tysilio and generally establish what was going on in Powys.

I spoke with Cadfan and Edwin about what our role should be. "I think we should support and stand by Selyf," I said. "Whatever Haiarme is up to, it is clear that Selyf on the throne of Powys provides us with the best chance of an ally here. Let's face it, Haiarme will hang us as she did those guards, given half the chance." Both Cadfan and Edwin emphatically agreed.

"Nor am I convinced that Tysilio is in any way involved with what has been going on," Cadfan said.

While we waited for the scouts to return I found Lilla and asked him why he had been heading north to find me. He took me to one side, finding a quiet room and shutting the door.

"Best what I have to say is not overheard."

My mouth felt dry. "What is it?"

"I left Cantia not long after Hussa. Having learned of Pybba's death, I wanted to re-establish contact with Ceorl. You know how it is with me... I travel simply; nobody questions my movements so long as I tell them stories. When I was in Mercia I stayed in Tamwerth with Ceorl..."

"How is he?"

"He is well, but stop interrupting me!"

"Sorry, go on."

"He had a visitor. Your brother was there Cerdic."

"Hussa? What was he there for?"

"I believe he wanted to offer Mercia a deal or ultimatum or something relating to the Thames Valley. I was not party to the details I have to confess," he said in an affronted voice. He was Lilla after all!

254

I reasoned that if it was not politics the bard wanted to tell me about, then Lilla's news must be personal. Was it about Hussa?

"He's not dead is he?" I asked with a sudden stab of anxiety. How odd, I thought, to feel worried about him. After all I had sworn to kill him more than once and yet... well, it's not ever that straightforward is it.

"No," Lilla snorted, "I'm sorry to say he is as fit as ever."

"Well what then?"

"It was Hussa, though, who had some news for me to share with you."

"Well?" I prompted him. The bard seemed rather hesitant to speak.

"He has a woman you know," Lilla said at length. "Her name is Rowenna." As he said her name he looked me squarely in the eye as if trying to gauge my reaction.

Now it was I who snorted. "Well good for him! That is hardly news, Lilla."

"She had a baby a couple of years or so ago."

"So I am an uncle then. Again, not exactly news. Hussa's problem is in his head. I daresay other parts of him work well enough."

"You are wrong on both counts."

I frowned. The man was making no sense. "Lilla, what are you saying, did this Rowenna have a child or not?"

He nodded. "Then why am I wrong? That makes the child my nephew or niece..."

"It was a boy."

"That makes him my nephew then. So I am an uncle."

"Hussa cannot have children, Cerdic. Leastways he says he has had enough practice with more than one woman and none of them has had his bastard yet. He said he has been with Rowenna

255

some long time and should have had a clutch of bastards from her before now, but has not; not one."

"Till now, you mean."

"Well, perhaps. There is another possibility. It seems Rowenna told him she was with only one other man in all their time together…" Lilla paused and looked at me pointedly, his eyebrow raised, "… around the time of Ceolwulf's campaign into Suthseaxe."

Suddenly I guessed what he was about to say. Gods I was slow wasn't I?

"Me? Surely not that one drunken night in Boseham villa. The night we threw back the army from West Seax?"

Lilla shrugged. "From what your brother said, it does seem a possibility. The woman knew your name."

It had not been a dream then. In my heart I had always known it, but had denied it so often I had convinced myself.

"Arse! Only once in my entire life have I slept with a woman who was not my wife… and I get her pregnant?"

"Some are more blessed by Freya and Frey than others," he observed.

"A pox on the gods of fertility then!" I muttered.

We were silent for a while as I absorbed the news and Lilla watched me without commenting. Then a thought occurred to me and I looked over at the bard. "What did Hussa want?"

"What do you mean?"

"Well, after telling you the news surely he wanted something from me? Was he threatening to tell Aidith unless I surrender Edwin… that kind of thing?"

"Would you surrender Edwin just to keep Hussa quiet?" Lilla asked.

"Well no, of course not!"

Lilla held his hands out. "Hussa knows that. He would not bother to ask. He knows you only too well, Cerdic. You are brothers after all."

"Are you saying he did not ask for anything, that he demanded nothing at all?"

"Not in so many words."

What is the git up to, I wondered. Then I had another thought. "What about the woman, this Rowenna. Why did she come into my room that night? Did Hussa put her up to it?"

Lilla shrugged, "I do not have that information."

"Well where is the woman now?"

"Somewhere in West Seax I believe. The boy too."

I thought about this. "Maybe I should try and see him. After all… if indeed he is my son…." I left the rest unsaid, my thoughts in a whirl as I considered the implications.

Lilla said nothing. What could he say? It was up to me.

We rejoined the others, with me carrying a heavy weight on my mind and dredging up unwelcome memories of dark eyes and jetblack hair. So it came almost as a relief when news finally arrived from the scouts. Haiarme, Kadir, Morfael, Kadir's Irish and the men they had taken from Pengwern had been located in Meifod. Haiarme had joined Tysilio. Other scouts brought additional news that Morfael's companies had abandoned Ruthin and also marched to Meifod. It seemed then that Tysilio was indeed gathering an army and did intend to rule as king.

"I still don't believe that my uncle wants the throne. He renounced it years ago," Selyf said when this news arrived. "He is a man of God and we are blessed indeed to have him. So to abandon all that and claim the throne seems too unlikely."

"Men change, sire," I commented.

Selyf shook his head. "Not men like Tysilio. God called him long ago and he has never wavered from that path."

"Well perhaps your god has changed his mind. Ours do a lot," I said, earning frowns from the Christians and a warning look from Edwin.

The final piece of news arrived a few weeks later. It came in the form of Morfael. He walked proudly into the hall and stood in front of Selyf, then gave only a slight inclination of the head by way of respect to royalty. You are not a king, he was saying, just a prince. Then he spoke, clear and loud so his words would be heard by all present and reach the common soldiers too.

"I come from the court of the King of Powys, Abbot Tysilio, who is in Mathrafal. He sends greetings to his nephew, Prince Selyf ap Cynan. Hear his words as I repeat them: 'A miracle occurred here in Meifod at the instant my brother Cynan fell in battle against the accursed Angles. He came to me in a vision in my cell. Brother, he said to me, I go now to be with our ancestors. Before I do so, I wish two things of you.'"

Morfael paused to glance around the hall, checking that all were listening. He need not have bothered, however, all eyes were turned to him. With a sharp nod, he continued speaking the words of Tysilio.

"'Firstly, it is God's Will that you succeed me as King of Powys. You were the rightful heir once. You renounced that to serve God, but God now requires you to step away from that role and protect his followers in Powys from the threat of the heathens and pagans who encroach daily upon us. When I, Tysilio, heard this I fell to my knees and wept, for I had no desire and hunger for the throne. But the angelic form of Cynan picked me up. It is because you are so humble that the Lord has asked this of you.'"

I glanced at Lilla. He gave an appreciative nod of his head towards Morfael and murmured, "He is not bad is he? Quite a good performance actually. I'll be out of a job!"

"The audience is certainly entranced," I muttered back, glancing round the room where the warriors were staring at him, eyes wide with wonder.

"The second thing Tysilio told us," Morfael went on, "is that Cynan said he feared for the safety of his beloved wife, Haiarme. So..." Morfael concluded, "Cynan asked Tysilio to take to himself as wife Queen Haiarme. Blessed be the words of our king, Holy Tysilio, and blessed be Cynan who is now with the saints. Blessed too is Haiarme, chosen by God to be queen again in Powys. Hallelujah!"

"Hallelujah!" The warriors chorused, whilst Selyf sat stony-faced on his throne.

Lilla turned to me, "Yes, a very good performance indeed!" he said.

Chapter Twenty Six
Aneirin's Mission
Autumn 609

After making his dramatic speech, which had so impressed all the warriors present and Lilla too, apparently, Morfael paused before delivering a final message to Selyf.

"King Tysilio is anxious to proceed with the marriage and also keen to receive an oath of loyalty from all the nobles and, of course, his kin. As such I am charged to relay a command to you Prince Selyf: you and all the nobles who follow you are to present themselves at Meifod in time for the feast of Easter, next spring. Oaths of allegiance will be taken after the wedding, which will occur at the same time. "

Morfael's face was a mask as he delivered this command. That said, I felt I could detect a slight curling at the corner of his mouth as a sign that he was enjoying himself immensely. The court fell silent and all eyes turned to gaze on Selyf. How would he react?

Selyf knew, of course, that what he said now was being listened to by the whole army: all the warriors as well as the nobles. So whatever he felt privately about all the things Morfael had just said, if he were to come out with it and refuse to agree, it was debatable what the reaction would be. He took a while to answer, no doubt attempting to find the right words that would give him some latitude in his actions. In the end he decided to keep it simple.

"Lord Morfael, I would be grateful if you could carry from me a message to my uncle, Holy Tysilio. I am a good son of the church and have never disobeyed any instruction that I have received from the Abbot, as was the case in the time of my father before me. If it occurred that the Lord God revealed his plans for Powys through the Abbot, then of course we have always sought to obey them. This is no different."

Morfael frowned. Selyf had actually said nothing much really and yet had appeared to agree to everything.

"Then you will come?" he asked.

"Of course, if that is the Will of God, then so be it. "Then, to change the subject he added, "You will be tired after your journey, can I offer you accommodation and refreshment?"

"Your offer of hospitality is most generous," Morfael said shaking his head. "However, there are still several hours of daylight left and I am needed back at Mathrafal as soon as possible, so I will be on my way. "He then gave a slight bow to Selyf and withdrew.

Once we were certain that he had indeed departed – I sent Eduard to confirm this – Selyf withdrew into his private quarters. A few moments later he sent for Edwin, Cadfan, Lilla and me. As soon as I had closed the door behind us Selyf threw himself down onto a chair and then, raising his hands, asked the question on everybody's mind "What do we do now?"

"Your Majesty…" I began, but Selyf raised a hand to interrupt me.

"Am I though? Am I the king, Cerdic?"

Cadfan was shaking his head, "How can you think otherwise, sire? It is clear to us all, I'm sure, that what we just heard was a farce and a fabrication. We all know Holy Tysilio – myself from the days when he was present at the court in Gwynedd. You from more familial links. Even Cerdic here has met the man. Let us ask him, as an outsider, so to speak. Cerdic what think you, is it likely that Tysilio would take the throne?"

I was about to say 'no' without thought, but the question deserved my consideration, so I weighed up everything I knew about the man who had made me walk under a tree and called on the power of his God.

"I don't think so," I replied at length. "I do not know him well, but he seemed to be a man of very strong beliefs; beliefs it is true that I myself struggle to comprehend, but I have seen such strong zeal before, both in men of the Christian faith and of our own religion. Such priests do not easily put that aside for ambition. I'm not saying they are all perfect, of course. We all know plenty of corrupt ones. Yet there are still many men who are utterly true to their convictions and if I know anything, I would say that Tysilio was one of those."

Edwin rattled his knuckles on the table. "Then it would appear, from what you are all saying, that if the Abbot has not claimed the throne he is being held against his will and made into a puppet. In which case, presumably it is Haiarme and the Dogfeiling king who are pulling the strings. We all know that Morfael resents his lowlier status and hungers for power. Doubtless Haiarme has promised it to him if he supports her endeavours."

Cadfan nodded. "I agree with Edwin, Selyf. I think it is likely that Tysilio is being held under duress. It is interesting that you are not being summoned to the wedding and the oathgiving until next spring, still several months away. Indeed, it has already been some time since Haiarme and her companions went to Meifod. I think Tysilio is exactly as Cerdic describes him. I believe he is holding true to his principles and refusing to comply with Haiarme. If she is to hold on to power, Tysilio needs to be in agreement and give his consent. Certainly if he is to take her as wife then he will need to give consent on that occasion!"

Selyf smiled. "My uncle can be as stubborn as my father was. I am sure that even Cynan's ghost could not persuade him to take a wife, least of all Haiarme. I am inclined to think she has not got her way yet and so we still have a chance."

His smile faded and he took a sip of mead from his goblet. "The problem is the army – how will they react if I refuse this summons to Meifod?"

Clearing his throat, Lilla now spoke. "Sire, enough of the warriors heard that speech for word of what has transpired to get to every man in the army by now. I can control an audience better than most men, and I can say that Morfael's performance today will still echo in all those men's minds. For them life is fairly simple. They are loyal to the king and they have a loyalty to the church. If they have come to believe that Holy Tysilio has been commanded by God Himself to take the throne then we are in a very dangerous situation. If you declare a claim yourself we could find ourselves in very hot water."

"That is what I fear, Lilla." Selyf gave a heavy sigh then addressed us all. "So then, what do we do?"

I scratched at the stubble on my cheek. "We need to find evidence that Tysilio is being held against his will and present that evidence to the army. Only then would they agree to follow you."

"So how will you get that evidence then?" Selyf asked.

"I won't, there is no way that I could get anywhere near Mathrafal. I'm lucky to have survived my last encounter with Haiarme."

"None of us Angles could easily just walk into Meifod asking to see the king could we?" Edwin said, looking at Cadfan, who shrugged and nodded, for aside from Selyf he alone in that group was not an Angle.

263

"There is a man who might be able to, though," Lilla said. "My friend and fellow bard Aneirin is welcome in all the courts of the Welsh kingdoms. If he could be persuaded to visit Mathrafal, he might be able to get this information for us. One of the reasons I was heading for Gwynedd, apart from to talk to you, Cerdic, is that I had heard Aneirin was going to be spending some time at Deganwy. I suggest that Cadfan, his army and Prince Edwin accompany me to Deganwy and we attempt to enlist Aneirin's services."

Cadfan nodded. "Sounds like a sensible plan, if Aneirin will agree. It also gets the Wicstun men home for the winter and Cerdic, you and your friends can get back to your village for Yuletide. I'm sure Aidith will be as eager to see you as you must be to see her?"

I glanced across at Lilla, who said nothing, and then I mumbled, "Yes my lord, but I feel I should accompany Edwin." In fact I was not sure Aidith would want to see me ever again, given the news I was carrying from Hussa. I had been debating with myself whether it was necessary to tell her and knowing I must, dreading the moment, so I seized on this possibility of delaying it for as long as possible.

A few days later we had made preparations and bade farewell, for the moment, to Selyf and to Pengwern. We marched north surrounded by the redgold colours of autumn. Eduard took the men straight home but Edwin, Cadfan and I went on to Deganwy. Here we were greeted by King Iago and Prince Cadwallon, who had put several inches on his height since I saw him last when he and Cadfan rescued me and our village from Kadir. The prince was growing into a man to be reckoned with.

As Iago summoned Cadfan forward I found it interesting to note that Cadwallon stood at the king's right hand – in Prince

Cadfan's own customary place no less. Was his influence in court growing along with his height?

"Greetings, my son. We are glad that you have returned to us," Iago said. "However, we would ask for an explanation about what we hear, that despite my explicit command, your companies fought a battle against Cynan in Powys. Moreover, you have dawdled in Pengwern and interfered with the politics of that country."

With a glance at Edwin, Cadfan proceeded to explain what had gone on in Powys. Cadwallon shook his head several time during the story, but Iago sat in silence and it was hard to know how he was reacting.

"So, my lord king, the battle was forced upon us by treachery and my subsequent involvement in Powys is entirely in an attempt to stabilise the country and return to us an ally."

Cadwallon interrupted the prince at that point. "Father, is it not rather the case that you allowed yourself to be drawn into the plots of these Angles. There would not have been a battle had you not gone to Powys."

With a dark scowl at his son, Cadfan retorted, "I have not been drawn into plots by anyone. My only aim is peace and to avoid the region falling into chaos."

"That is as may be, "Iago said. "From what we hear, King Tysilio is summoning Prince Selyf to attend the wedding to Queen Haiarme and to give his allegiance. That would seem to stabilise Powys would it not?"

"Well, probably but…"

"But nothing. Our involvement in the internal affairs of Powys are at an end. Am I making myself clear on this matter?"

Cadfan bowed, "Quite clear, sire."

265

As he turned to leave the hall he caught my eye. He said nothing but the expression carried many words: I cannot disobey my father again. If I am to be free to act in Powys it will be down to you to find the evidence we need.

I left the hall and went out to find Aneirin, knowing he would likely be hobnobbing with Lilla. The Welsh bard had been at Gwynedd for a few weeks by the time we arrived and was preparing to travel on southwards. When we put the situation to him, he fairly jumped at the chance to infiltrate Mathrafal. "Sounds like a bit of fun, actually," he said.

"It could be dangerous you know," I said. "If you are discovered spying, Haiarme will certainly execute you, bard or no."

"I am not inexperienced at putting myself in harm's way, Cerdic – you should know that."

"The Battle of Catraeth was certainly dangerous, I admit that. This, though, will mean you are acting on your own not surrounded by hundreds of warriors in bright blue armour."

"I'll be fine."

"Well I'm just saying if you go and get yourself killed, I will be supremely disappointed in you."

"Well then, I will just have to make sure I come back in one piece. I can't have Cerdic disappointed can I?"

He winked at Lilla and they both laughed.

Chapter Twenty Seven
Domestic Bliss
Winter 609

With Aneirin gone to Mathrafal and the atmosphere at court cooling considerably, I thought it best to return to Rhufoniog with Edwin. Despite missing Aidith and the children I was reluctant to return home. My heart was still heavy with the news that Hussa had brought and I knew I could not avoid facing it for much longer. I had hoped Lilla might have come with me for morale support, but he had elected for the time being to remain at Pengwern feeling that Selyf needed his support more than I did.

Riding home, my mind was chewing over my problem like a lump of gristle caught in my teeth. What should I do? Should I tell Aidith about my son – if indeed it was my son? The chances were that she would find out one day anyway; was it best coming from me now than someone else later. Hussa, maybe? She already knew that something had occurred when I was away in Cantia and Suthseaxe in the winter of 606. I was aware Cuthbert had inadvertently said something to Mildrith and no doubt my sister had told Aidith. More likely it was my behaviour when I got home that had raised her suspicions. Indeed, I had almost confessed at one point. She might not know the details but certainly she knew something had gone on. A child, though? That was a whole different issue! I remembered how my mother had reacted when she discovered my father had got a son on a woman from the village: Hussa! She never forgave him and I quaked at the thought of what Aidith's reaction might be.

She was already going to be in a bad mood. When she and the villagers had left Ruthin, I had promised to follow her home within a few days, but the long wait for news at Pengwern had meant we had been absent from home throughout the summer. Consequently, as we approached Rhufoniog we could see that the fields were heavy with grain and the orchards bulging with apples and pears.

We arrived home just as Sabert was organising the first harvesting. With the warriors absent for most of the summer, he had called upon the youths to assist him. There, in one of the top fields gathering in the wheat and preparing it for threshing in the barn, I spotted Cuthwine a few moments before he saw me. He had grown this summer and I felt that gnawing sense of missing out that I often did when returning home after a lengthy absence. For the hundredth time I wished I could just live out my days in such a valley as this, left alone by the world, the gods and kings and princes. I knew that is what Aidith wished for, yet I feared it was a forlorn hope. I walked across the field and hugged Cuthwine, enjoying the moment while it lasted. Then together we walked to the hut which we call home.

Sian was more enthusiastic than she had been during my last stay in Rhufoniog. She got up and embraced me, but she too was growing up and it was not quite the same as when she would hurtle out of the door when she saw me, letting out a squeal of delight and almost knocking me off my feet as she piled into me. This time, after an affectionate hug, she returned calmly to her sewing. I could see she was learning to repair her own dress and watched as she picked up her needle and thread without a glance back.

Aidith embraced me, but there was some reserve there, some holding back of her affection. I sighed. I was going have to get this out of the way sooner or later.

"Wife, we need to talk," I said.

She stepped back from me and I could tell from her expression that she suspected something of what I was about to say.

"Cuthwine, take Sian and go help milk the cows," she said.

"But Ma…" Cuthwine protested briefly, but one glance at his mother's dark face silenced him and he hustled his sister out of the door. Aidith went and sat next to the fire pit and stared into the embers. After a moment she looked up at me.

"Well husband, you have something to say to me?"

"I didn't mean to be away so long…" I started, but Aidith held her hand up. "I have heard the news," she said. "Given the circumstances I don't blame you for staying in Pengwern with Prince Edwin. But it's not about that is it?"

I shook my head reluctantly. "No, it's about that winter I spent in Cantia and Suthseaxe. Aidith please understand that I have never been unfaithful to you…"

"I knew it!" Her eyes flared with anger.

"Knew what? I just said I have never been unfaithful to you…"

"Until… that was going be your next word wasn't it? I have been a fool. All these years worrying about you away fighting your battles and winning your wars. But that is not what I should be worrying about. I should be worrying about you preferring to be away with other women to being at home with me!"

"No!" I said, shaking my head. "That's not the case! There have not been 'other women'. Just one. Just once. After our victory in Suthseaxe I got drunk. I mean really drunk, to the point where I didn't know what I was doing. I tried to tell you before, but Kadir's attack interrupted our conversation. Afterwards we seemed to be all right again, and I didn't want to upset you by bringing it up a second time. What would have been the point? I

269

wasn't even sure that what happened was real… in truth I actually thought she was a dream."

"Oh, so you dream about other women as well do you?"

I snorted at that. "Come on Aidith, everybody dreams, everybody thinks thoughts that perhaps they should not. All that matters is that they remain thoughts. You know that. Look me in the eye and tell me you have never dreamt of a handsome young warrior! We are none of us in control of our dreams."

She shrugged accepting this, but she was not done yet, her eyes still flashing with anger. "So what was she like, this woman who seduced you while you were under the influence of too much ale? Was it so much that you were incapable of pushing her off, or was it that she was so beautiful you didn't want to?"

I shook my head, "I honestly don't know… she could have been a troll for all I knew. Told you, I was drunk. I wasn't…"

"Cerdic, if you are about to say something like 'I wasn't looking at her face', this is not the time!"

"It was dark. I really don't recall much. All I remember is she had black hair."

"Men!" Aidith exclaimed.

She looked at me and somewhere in the back of her eyes I was sure I detected the merest glint of amusement. When she spoke again her tone was a little softer.

"So it was just the once?"

Now I was anxious she was about to forgive me before she had heard the full story and I would be right back where I started. "Yes… but…"

"But what?"

I gulped. "It's a bit more complicated than I made it sound."

"How so?"

"The woman… she was… is Hussa's woman."

Now Aidith's eyes were bulging. "You slept with your sister-in-law?"

"I don't think they are married."

"Oh, that's all right then I guess!" Her tone was acid, her lip curling with contempt.

"Aidith you are not making this easy."

"I am sorry. I did not realise I was supposed to make it easy for you. Well then, did you know she was Hussa's woman at the time?"

"No. I told you, I did not know anything much."

"So how do you know now?"

I bit my lip. "Hussa told Lilla."

Aidith stared at me. "Just how many people know about this? The whole army?"

"No! Hussa met Lilla in Tamwerth and told him."

"Then there is Cuthbert and Millie," she said.

Her words confirmed to me that Cuthbert had been indiscreet and told Millie about my night time visitor and she had said something to Aidith. Or at least hinted.

"I did wonder if my sister said something to you. Cuthbert told me he thought he had seen a woman come out of my room, you see."

Aidith shook her head. "No Millie did not say anything. She just was a bit odd. I asked if there was a problem with her and she said no, then I asked about Cuth, and she said no, not Cuth. Oh, Cerdic then, I said. She went bright red, so as a joke I teased her and asked if you'd got another woman on the side. Of course I didn't think it was true. I expected her to laugh, but she went all quiet and that was when I started to suspect, but I was not sure. And when I asked you what had happened in Cantia, you were all vague and off with me."

271

"Well I have not got another woman on the side, nor have I ever had one. Nor, indeed, have I ever wanted one. It just happened while I was drunk. One night that is all."

"So Lilla, Hussa, Millie and Cuth are all who know about it."

I shrugged "I may have mentioned something to Eduard..."

She glared at me.

"But Aedann doesn't know!" I added hastily.

"Well that's a relief, "she said dryly. "There is at least one of your friends who does not know about your conquests!"

"Aidith, please," I protested.

She frowned. "Two things I don't understand. Firstly, why would your brother, who hates you, share his woman with you? Secondly, why would Hussa tell Lilla about this? It hardly enhances his manhood to admit his brother slept with his woman does it?"

I didn't respond at first. I was thinking about her first question. I had a nasty feeling that Hussa, for his own devious purposes, had engineered this whole business. But why? To break up my marriage? He had always been jealous of everything I had, my family especially. As the silence grew, I felt Aidith's gaze on me. After a moment, she asked another question, and here we were at the nub of it.

"There is something else isn't there? Some other news? "

I nodded.

"Well go on... what is it?"

I rubbed my eyes and then pinched my nose.

"Well? "

The moment had come. I could no longer avoid it. "Hussa wanted me to know that I have a son. I mean a second son... it seems he is unable to sire a child..."

Aidith's face went pale. "A son by this woman?"

272

I nodded.

"Bollocks! "she cursed and stormed out of the door without another word.

'Well, I wasn't expecting that reaction!' I said to myself, then got up and followed her out. She was stomping out through the orchard to the east of the village when I finally caught up with her. I caught hold of her arm. "Aidith, please."

She shook me off. "Piss off and leave me alone."

Aidith almost never uttered an obscenity, now she had done so twice in a matter of moments. I put a hand on her shoulder. "Love…"

"Don't call me that. You don't get to call me that again!" she snarled, ducking out from under my hand.

"Be reasonable," I said, then winced as she thumped me on the chest.

"Reasonable! Why do I have to always be reasonable? You go off with Edwin for months on end and if I complain it's 'be reasonable.' You almost die in battle yet if I express concern you tell me 'be reasonable'. Now you sleep with Hussa's whore and it is I who am being unreasonable?"

Unusually for Aidith, who more often relied on sarcasm rather than volume when she was angry, her voice was getting louder and louder, such that she was now shouting at me. I could not think of a reply, for what she said was true, and so I just stared at her.

"Go away Cerdic. I don't want to hear any more about it. Just let me be." She turned away from me and without a backward glance, left me alone in the orchard.

I did as she asked and let her be. The days lengthened and cooled and I kept my peace. When around friends and the family she was civil enough and would speak when we needed to

273

about practical matters. Yet she saw to it we were almost never alone. At night I slept wrapped in furs on the floor by the fire, rising before dawn so the children were not aware of it. Once, when I tried to talk she simply shook her head.

"Not ready yet!" she said and went out of the door.

I asked Cuthbert once about what he had said to Millie. He gave me an anxious look and hesitated before replying, "Nothing really."

"What do you mean, nothing? I mean she found out about Boseham from Millie, which means Millie found out from you."

He eyed me again. "Well?" I prompted him.

"She was asking about what had happened in Suthseaxe, teasing me about what warriors get up to when celebrating victory, asking me about the women who hang around the camp and whether I'd been tempted. I got irritated and said something like there were no women at Boseham aside from one with long dark hair. Gods know why I said that, I should have kept my big mouth shut, but give Millie an inch… she kept pushing me and pushing me until I shouted that she should ask her brother not me. I think she did her own thinking after that. Sorry, didn't mean to bring such grief to my own brotherinlaw…"

"Well, in the end it was me who slept with the woman, not you, Cuth, though I was too drunk to know anything about it at the time and it meant less than nothing, but try telling that to Aidith! I have to square it with her before too long. I just need the right opportunity."

"Good luck with that,"he grinned.

I thought I had that opportunity a week later. It was Mōdraniht – Mothers' Night – the start of Yuletide and we had gathered together to feast in Edwin's hall. The hall was bright with candlelight and warm and comforting. As the cooks prepared to carve

274

the roast boar that spun on its skewer over the fire, Edwin had just called on the gods to bless everyone and keep us safe in the year to come; to bless our animals and our crops and then – and I think he had had a bit too much wine at this point – he called on Freya's blessing on the women that they might be fertile and have more children. Despite his baptism, Edwin rarely practiced Christian rites unless in the presence of priests or godly kings.

I happened to be looking at Aidith at that moment, hoping that in the celebrations she might feel mellow and perhaps be willing at last to talk. When Edwin mentioned children I saw her stiffen and the colour drain from her face. Then without a word she got up and left the hall.

I looked across at Cuthwine and Sian. They were playing with other children, all of them waiting eagerly for the roast pork. Quietly I got up and followed Aidith. I found her out in the cold, arms wrapped around herself and staring out across the star strewn skies at the shape of the constellation that represented the Goddess Frija, standing bright and brilliant just above the northern horizon.

"Aidith, please, what is it?" I asked, fearful she might turn and launch into a tirade as she had earlier that autumn. Instead, as she turned to me I saw that she had tears in her eyes.

"I am sorry," I said, "so very sorry."

"It's not the woman, or the one night you had with her that upsets me, husband. I know you love me and were not responsible for your actions that night. It's the child. When you said you had another son, all I could think about was your father and that women – Hussa's mother – and how your own mother was about it. I was there Cerdic… when she burnt, you know. I saw the hatred on Hussa's face that night and we all saw how she reacted to him. How much hurt and how much harm has been

275

caused and is still being caused because your father was weak and strayed from your mother's bed."

"What my father did was weak and wrong, yes, but my mother was not blameless. She was so bitter and unforgiving. It need not be like that for us, Aidith."

"Can you be sure? Or is this just the start of more hurt that Hussa has done to us. Burnt our home, driven us out and pursued us. And now he is trying to drive us apart. Will it never end?"

I tried to think of something to say to answer her fears but as I did I spotted half a dozen horsemen galloping hard across the frozen ground. Alarmed at these riders arriving so late at night, my hand went to my sword but before I could unsheathe it I recognised Cadfan at their head.

"Cerdic," he gasped, sliding to a stop in front of me, "I have come to call you to court."

"What, now? What has happened?"

"Aneirin has returned with news. Tysilio is definitely being held against his will by Morfael and Haiarme. *Now* we can act!"

Chapter Twenty Eight
Councils of War
Winter 609

The opportunity to talk further with Aidith was lost with Cadfan's arrival. The prince was persuaded to stay for a couple of days to enjoy Edwin's hospitality. Cadfan had stood as Godfather to Edwin, of course, but there was little of Christian tradition in the way we celebrated Yuletide. It was noisy and boisterous, but I don't think Cadfan minded, he even entered into the fun and games at times.

Cuthbert was persuaded to tell us some riddles. He had listened well to how Lilla did it, how he emphasized certain words and, when the riddle sounded lewd but had a common place answer, he would trick the foolish in the audience by movements and obscene gestures.

"A curiosity hangs by the thigh of a man, under its master's cloak," Cuth began, pointing down between his legs. I blinked. Was this the same man who as a boy had been too terrified even to speak to Millie? I glanced at my sister and saw that she was laughing and winking at him.

Cuthbert continued. "It is pierced through in the front; it is stiff and hard and it has a good standing place." The audience hooted and cheered. "When the man pulls up his own robe above his knee, he means to poke with the head of his hanging thing that familiar hole of matching length which he has often filled before."

The trick now was to work out the real answer and not be taken in by the innuendos. I scratched my head in thought, as did everyone else. Before I could think of a response Cadfan fell into the trap and shouted out.

"Sounds like a prick to me!"

Everyone laughed and he laughed too.

"No silly, it's a key!" my son Cuthwine shouted and everyone laughed again, and beneath the laughter I felt a certain quiet pride in my son; he was a bright lad.

It was probably a good thing that we had persuaded Cadfan to stay for a short break to enjoy the festivities at Rhufoniog because the atmosphere at Deganwy was significantly more grim and sober when we got there a week after Yuletide was over.

These Welsh did so love their holy men and got so very serious when they felt they were being threatened or mistreated. But what made the atmosphere more strained was that Prince Cadwallon was actively arguing against any intervention or involvement in Powys.

Soon after we arrived, Aneirin was summoned to the great hall and asked to recount to us the tale of his journey to Mathrafal. He walked in front of King Iago and bowed, inclined his head to Edwin and Cadfan and then turned to us all.

"I have just returned from a journey south into the hills of Powys. I went first to Meifod in search of news of Holy Tysilio. But I could not find him in the blessed community that he leads. His monks said he had left in the dark of night some months before, accompanied by just two of the brethren. He left no word to those who live with him, nothing to say where he was going, or why. Some weeks later they heard he was at Mathrafal, ruling as King of Powys."

"King!" Cadwallon shouted. "He is ruling as king. He has a claim to the throne, indeed a claim that is stronger than his nephew's, Selyf ap Cynan, for Tysilio was King Brochwel's oldest son. If he has chosen to take the throne then we should stay out of it."

Cadfan frowned at Cadwallon but did not disagree. "I concur that we should stay out of the politics in Powys… if, "he added, with a particular stress on that word that now made his son frown, "and only if this is truly the will of Tysilio."

Aneirin coughed to draw attention back to himself. "On that point, I have further information, if I may continue, your Majesty?"

Iago nodded. "Proceed."

"Having heard from the monks at Meifod that Tysilio had taken the crown at nearby Mathrafal fortress, it seemed only appropriate to proceed the few miles there. Now bear in mind that I am, I humbly suggest, well known in all the Welsh lands and even beyond and I trust I am welcome at many a court by many a prince and lord."

"Any king who did not welcome you would be a fool indeed, bard," Iago said, and there were rumbles of assent around the hall.

"His Majesty is too kind to a mere poet. But imagine, therefore, my surprise when I was not allowed access to the fortress. Indeed, I was ordered away by the Irishmen who were on watch there."

"Kadir's men no doubt," Cadfan murmured to me and I nodded. "Did you see any of the companies from Powys, Aneirin?" he asked.

"No," the bard shook his head. "The only Welsh I saw on guard were Dogfeiling. However, I snuck around the perimeter to where a river passes close to the rear gate. They were open and through them I spotted a monk come out of one of the huts and walk across the courtyard. Not Tysilio, but one of his brethren no doubt…"

279

"Grandfather," Cadwallon interrupted Aneirin to address the king and the bard, looking slightly annoyed, stopped speaking. "Nothing here suggests Tysilio is being held against his will."

"This is true, grandson," Iago nodded.

"But Highness, I am not finished yet," Aneirin said, a hint of impatience touching his voice. "There was a guard on the gates so I could not enter, but the monk came out of the gates to fetch water. He was challenged by the guard before being permitted to carry his bucket to the river. It was plain that all the while he was being observed, but by hiding behind a tree I managed to sneak close and was able to attract the monk's attention by tossing pebbles in the river at his feet. At first he was fearful, but I think he recognised me – I have stayed at Meifod once – and he came closer to stand under the tree where I was hiding. I asked him the whereabouts of the Abbot and he told me that Holy Tysilio was in one of the huts I had seen through the gates, that he is unharmed, but being held against his will until he agrees to marry Haiarme, which he is refusing to do. Unfortunately, I was unable to obtain any further detail, for at that moment the guard called out and the monk had to go lest I be discovered. When I saw the guard's back was turned to watch the monk returning to the hut across the courtyard, I made my escape, eager to reach you with this news."

"You are certain the monk said Holy Tysilio was being held against his will?" Iago asked.

"Absolutely certain, sire."

At this point Prince Cadfan stepped forward and addressed all the nobles in the hall.

"You have all heard what Aneirin has said. Holy Tysilio is well loved here in Gwynedd as in his native Powys. He is held prisoner and is being forced into marriage against his will to give Haiarme power as queen. It seems now more likely than ever that Haiarme and Morfael are in alliance and being aided by Kadir, and that they mean to use the Abbot to hold on to power. What more evidence do we need than this? The monk told Aneirin that Tysilio is unharmed, but who is to say that will not change if Haiarme loses patience with his continued refusal to wed her?"

At that there was a collective gasp and a buzz of conversation around the hall. Cadfan held his hand up and the noise subsided. "My lord king; nobles of Gwynedd; it is imperative that we send at once to Pengwern to give King Selyf this news and that we prepare to march on Meifod!"

Looking around the hall I could see that most were nodding in agreement, but inevitably, Cadwallon had to have his say.

"Yes, Father, if what the monk said is right, I agree. But we have all heard tell of Cynan's spirit visiting Tysilio and what it said to him. All our warriors have heard this too, and along with many in Powys they believe that God himself anointed Tysilio. Respected as Aneirin undoubtedly is, these men will need more proof than a bard's tale about what some monk said to him."

I saw Aneirin's face darken, his lips tightening with anger, but Cadwallon continued speaking. "They will need to see for themselves that Tysilio is truly being held against his will, to hear it from the Abbot's own lips, before they will march as if to war." Cadwallon shrugged and held out his hands, "But this is not possible and so the men of Gwynedd will not march – not on the basis of what we have heard here today."

Scanning the hall to see if the nobles agreed with him, Cadwallon caught my eye. He frowned, "What... what are you smiling at, Cerdic?"

"Forgive me for contradicting you, Prince Cadwallon, but I believe what you have said is incorrect. It is entirely possible that we could arrange to have Tysilio do just that, and with no risk to any Welsh lives. In fact it would be Angles' lives that would be at risk."

"How...? Angles' lives? You mean your own?" Cadwallon sounded confused, which made me smile all the more.

"Yes," I replied, "our own. You see, I have an idea..."

Witanceastre
Yuletide 609

Ceolwulf had no fewer than five boars roasting slowly over the fire pits that lined the centre of his great hall at Witanceastre. They had been slowly cooking all night and now were ready for the great feast that marked Mothers' Night at the start of Yuletide.

While the meat was carved, piled onto platters and taken to serve the king and his family at the high table, Hussa waited with Wilbur, Rolf and his other men, all of them crammed on the benches at one of the side tables. He was surprised when one of the serving women brought him a plate of pork and a trencher of bread and indicated that he should join the king at the high table. She led him to a space that had been made for him immediately opposite the king so that Hussa sat down facing Ceolwulf across the table.

As the noise of conversation and laughter grew in the hall and men began the feast, drinking the first of the many goblets of ale and mead they would consume this night, Hussa looked expectantly at Ceolwulf, who was chewing contentedly at a pork rib. Finishing it he turned and tossed the bone to one of his hounds sitting close by. He then turned back and regarded Hussa.

"I wanted to have the opportunity to thank you for the campaigns in the Thames Valley, Lord Hussa. As you know, there were some amongst my councillors who argued against putting my trust in a Northumbrian," Ceolwulf said, glancing along the table to where Lord Boyden could be seen sipping at his tankard of ale and watching the king talking to Hussa.

"Perhaps I did not get off on the right foot with Lord Boyden," Hussa said. "After Boseham I admit I was angry and felt betrayed. It seems I was wrong, but it does perhaps explain Boyden's reluctance to trust me."

The king nodded then reached for his tankard and took a deep draught of ale before continuing to speak. As men got stuck into their food, the noisy buzz of conversation subsided to a low murmur. At the far end of the hall a lyre player started up a tune. He sang a song about a wanderer sailing upon the icy sea, far from home and far from his companions and lord.

Despite the heat of the hall and the warmth of the meat and ale, Hussa felt a chill go through him. He had been away from Northumbria and his own king for more than two years. He felt himself to be that wanderer in a boat tossed around by the waves of fate. Coming here, his goal had been to conclude this alliance with West Seax as soon as possible so he could return to Aethelfrith, his best chance to gain power and glory. Then he thought about Rowenna and the child. What was their place in his dreams?

When the king spoke his voice seemed to come from far away, "You seem distracted, Lord Hussa."

Hearing his name, Hussa blinked, coming back into focus with a start. He smiled at Ceolwulf, "It is nothing, sire. I was just thinking that I came here to seek an alliance between Northumbria and West Seax. I hope I have been of service to you and to

West Seax these last two years. I would hope next year to return to Aethelfrith with news of an alliance between us."

Ceolwulf leant back in his chair and looked squarely at Hussa. "It is true that you have given me the Thames Valley, and I am pleased that you also appear to have had some success in persuading King Ceorl to keep his Mercian nose out of our affairs. Yet the campaign is not yet complete. So I have a proposal for you. Lead the Thames Valley armies in the attack on Celemion from the north and link up with my own armies and that of Boyden coming from the south. The aim is that we join up at Calleva, assault the city and finish what we started. Once that is done, I will have consolidated my position and I will have a clear access to the south of Mercia."

Ceolwulf paused to pick up another pork rib. Licking the fat off his fingers he tore off a mouthful of meat, the grease trickling into his beard. Waving the rib at Hussa he continued to speak as he chewed. "Any alliance between Northumbria and West Seax must involve how both nations deal with Mercia. To be able to contribute something to that conversation, West Seax must have easy communications to the Thames Valley and the border with Mercia. That means we need Celemion and its Roman roads. "

Hussa nodded, "I agree, sire, but must it be me who commands the Thames Valley Saxons?"

"You, Hussa, more than anyone, know the cities of the Thames Valley. You have an understanding with the lords of Doric, Readingum and so forth. It has to be you."

What Ceolwulf said was true and Hussa could not argue with the logic. "Very well. But if I do this, sire, if I lead the Thames Valley Saxons and others to Calleva, would you then agree an alliance with my king and let me travel north to inform him?"

284

Ceolwulf nodded and picking up his tankard he raised it towards Hussa. "It is agreed, "he said.

Hussa raised his own tankard and the drinking vessels clashed over the high table, sealing over food and drink an agreement that would cause blood and war.

"So, you have hardly been home a day and you have already agreed to leave again next spring and go back to your precious war. In fact, if you win next year you will be off north again to your king and your home in Northumbria, won't you."

Hussa tried to remain patient. "I am lieutenant to Aethelfrith of Northumbria, Rowenna. I came here with a mission. I am close to achieving what I was ordered to achieve. Of course I must then return to him."

Rowenna slammed down the wash basket she was holding, thumping it onto the table in the centre of their hall. One of the huscarls sitting at the far end of the table looked up at her and then hurriedly glanced away when he saw the stormy expression on her face.

Over near the fire her young son was playing with some wooden warriors, which Hussa knew Wilbur had carved for him. He studied the boy for a few moments. Hal had grown fast while they had been away, first in the Thames Valley and then in Mercia. Returning at last to Witanceastre, Hussa had been surprised by the boy's size. The lad did not recognise him and Hussa had said nothing directly to him. Wilbur, on the other hand, seemed to take to all children and they to him with equal enthusiasm. Somehow Hussa did not like that. He could not say why it irritated him. If the boy was not his, why should he care who the lad chose to befriend?

"What about Hal? What about me?" Rowenna was screeching. "Would you abandon us both? I thought there was a time when you loved me. Now we have a son that should bring us closer together, so why has it driven us apart? Don't you want a son?"

"The boy's not mine. I have told you repeatedly; I cannot sire children."

Rowenna glared at him. "Why are you so insistent about that? Why do you deny the evidence of your own eyes? Just look at him!"

Hussa stared across at the boy once more. When the lad had looked at him in the past Hussa had always seen Cerdic in his face, yet lately something had changed: the boy's features had sharpened as he lost his baby plumpness, and the colour of his eyes had darkened. Looking at him now, Hussa realised the child's face more closely resembled his own. Was it *possible*? Could Hal be his? While in Mercia he had bumped into Lilla and told him the boy was Cerdic's. Hussa was still not sure why he had done that. Why had he mentioned it at all? Had he just wanted to hurt Cerdic? Did it not hurt him too? He shook his head. He did not want this distraction. He did not want these feelings. He had lived all these years without the conflicts and anxiety that affection brings. Instead he had enjoyed power and influence. They were better, much better, he told himself. These distractions were disturbing; it had been a mistake to come back here. Shaking his head he got to his feet and turned toward the door.

"Where are you going now?" Rowenna snapped.

"Back to Doric to be with the army, not that it's any of your business."

"What? It's the middle of winter, three months before the campaign season starts? What will you do in Doric all that time?"

"Clear my mind and make ready for war, "he said, stomping to the door without a backward glance."

286

Chapter Twenty Nine
Spring Invasion
Spring 610

It had been a long winter and despite Hussa's professed intention to remove himself from Rowenna and her child, along with thoughts of home and family, he had found himself thinking about them most nights as he lay alone in his bed. He had tried taking a woman to the elaborately decorated bedroom that had been provided for his pleasure in the Magistrate's palace, and whilst it had been an enjoyable distraction – the woman was both beautiful and willing – it left him feeling hollow and even more aware of some as yet unmet desire and need within him.

"Damn you woman!" Hussa muttered as he rolled away from his concubine.

"My lord? Did I do something wrong?" she asked.

"No, nothing; I was thinking of someone else, not you, girl."

"What? Am I not good enough for you that you have to think of some other woman while I'm in your arms?"

"No... I mean yes."

Pouting she sat up in bed, naked; arms wrapped around her knees. "I don't understand."

"Neither do I," he said, his response bringing a frown to her flawless features. "Look, you were superb. I am just a bit... tired is all. Go to sleep now."

Slightly mollified, the young woman finally lay back down and turned away from him. After a few moments he could hear her breathing slowing as she slept, leaving him awake and feeling even more alone. He swung out of bed, walked across the room to the flagon of mead resting on a side table, poured himself a cupful and sipped at it. After a moment he slammed the cup down on the table.

"Damn the woman!" he hissed. "Damn the boy and damn bloody Cerdic and his bloody family as well!"

He walked to the high window, which boasted imported panes of plate glass – nothing but the best for the Magistrate's residence – and gave a view over the dark form of the River Thame trickling on its course past frozen fields to the nearby confluence with the Thames.

After a few moments, Hussa shivered and turned back to the warm bed and its comatose occupant, snoring slightly now, her mouth open.

"Won't this winter ever end!" he muttered, resigning himself to yet more weeks before the campaign could start. Gods, but he needed something to distract him!

As it happened, the following day he got his wish. Boyden arrived from Witanceastre with a message from Ceolwulf.

"You are to attack Celemion at Eostretide. You must plan your attack and begin preparing your army straight away; Ceolwulf wants you at the city gates no later than two weeks after Eostre. Do you understand, Hussa?"

Hussa nodded, "I understand. Tell the king we will be there."

When Boyden had gone, Hussa reached for his scrolled maps, unrolled them and set to work.

Hussa assembled the companies from all of the Thames Valley settlements and cities. Everyone responded to the summons, even the men he had demanded from the still scorched village of Pegingaburnan, which perhaps acted as both an encouragement and a deterrent to any of the leaders who might have considered

288

reneging on their agreement.

He had five hundred men under his command in six companies. Ricberht led the Doric company, Lords Verge and Woke their own companies. Rolf and Wilbur were each given command of a mix of the smaller settlements' contingents, Hussa's own men and the company he had brought from West Seax. Hussa himself held back his twenty best warriors, other than Rolf and Wilbur, as a personal guard. The weeks running up to Eostretide were wet with many heavy showers turning the ground to a quagmire. Thankfully, a few days before Eostre the rain stopped and the fields began to dry. That and his control of a Roman road from Belesduna and another from Readingum direct to Calleva was all Hussa needed to get underway.

As he advanced along the stone road, which was still in reasonable repair having been well preserved, the outlying settlements of Britons either surrendered or fled before him in the direction of the city. So it was exactly on schedule that he drew his army up at the edge of the forest surrounding Calleva and looked across a clear area of fields to the walls of the fortress city. The Britons closed the gates and prepared for a siege. So Hussa set up camp and waited for the return of the scouts he had sent out to circle the city and on to the south and the roads to Witanceastre. He had been in camp for a week when scouts returned with news that Ceolwulf had fought a battle against an army of Britons outside the small settlement called Basingstoches some miles to the South of Calleva and was now marching north towards the city.

"At last," Rolf said. "I was getting bored."

"At least you are alive when you are bored," Hussa replied.

"You need a hobby to keep you occupied," Wilbur commented, as he whittled away at another wooden peg, shaping it into a toy soldier. Was this meant for Hal? Hussa wondered irritably and then dismissed the thought, for what did it matter? The boy was nothing to him.

"Hobby my arse, it's a woman I need," Rolf grunted. "You play with your little stick, mate. I'm off to find some female company." So saying he wandered away towards the camp where, if his luck was in, he might find a camp follower.

The next day a messenger arrived from Ceolwulf, now camped to the south of the city almost exactly opposite Hussa's location. He sent orders for Hussa to commence an attack at dawn the following day and try to access the northern gateway into the city. Once the city's defenders were committed to an attempt to repel Hussa, Ceolwulf would then attack from the south and hopefully gain access against a weakened defence. It was a good plan, similar to Hussa's strategy at Readingum, but with a lot more men.

"So we are to be the sacrifice to win Ceolwulf his battle," Wilbur observed. He, Rolf and Hussa, along with the other captains, were assembled in Hussa's tent.

Hussa nodded. He could not disobey the order; he even understood it to an extent. In strict military terms it made a lot of sense. However, he was annoyed that Ceolwulf had misled him. In the conversation they'd had at Yuletide, the king had implied they would attack the city together, not that Hussa would have to sacrifice himself and his men first. Was this Boyden's doing – one final attempt to rid himself of Hussa whom he saw as a rival for the king's trust? Or was it perhaps that Hussa was being tested one final time to prove his value and worth to Ceolwulf before he committed at last to an alliance with Northumbria? Either way, Hussa knew he had no choice. He had to attack Calleva and hold the gates into the city until Ceolwulf attacked from the south and won the day.

A man's willingness to risk his life in a battle relates often to his motivation for fighting in the first place. The Thames Valley companies from Readingum, Wochinoes, Doric and so forth would obey orders and support an attack, but would not have the commitment or determination to win the battle. Hussa knew he could not risk putting them in the vanguard. Nor could he lead it himself, for if he fell at the first hurdle the men would lose heart and the battle would be lost even before it had properly begun. The vanguard, with all its risks and chances of death or glory, would have to be given to a commander he trusted and whose men were reliable. It had to be Wilbur.

"Wilbur, I'm going to have to ask you to lead this attack. Your company has the highest proportion of our own men in it along with Ceolwulf's own veterans. I am pinning our hopes of victory on an attack by you."

Wilbur nodded but said nothing. He knew the risks would be immense, but he understood why Hussa had asked it of him.

"May the Valkyries watch over you," Rolf said in his gruff voice, laying a hand on Wilbur's shoulder.

"I hope I will not be seeing any of them today!" Wilbur replied. He then patted Hussa on the shoulder, "Don't look so glum, my lord, somebody has to go first and it should not be you." That said, he walked away to brief his company.

At dawn, Wilbur's men dressed in all the armour they could gather and assembled in close formation. With their shields interlocking they set out across the fields towards the northern gates into the city. Behind them, Hussa deployed the Readingum and Wochinoes warriors on the left flank and the Doric company to the right, whilst his own personal guard and Rolf's company – after Wilbur's the strongest and bravest – followed Wilbur down the middle.

As the army advanced, a hail of slingshots and arrows from the walls soon began to inflict the first of Wilbur's casualties. Those who fell, either dead or wounded, were left lying in the fields. Hussa's skirmishers responded with projectiles of their own, but given the protection granted the enemy by the city's walls, this was unlikely to be effective. All he could hope was that it might keep the enemy skirmishers' heads down.

Wilbur's men were now nearing the gates. These were set back between walls that curved into a short channel. As a result, the city's defenders could fire down onto the flanks and the rear of Wilbur's company as it compressed and funnelled into the narrow passage. Trapped on either side by the tall stone walls, Wilbur's men could not manoeuvre or dodge and many fell to the arrows and slingshots that came from behind.

The only hope for survival was to smash down the gates and get inside. So from within their ranks a huge tree trunk, which they had felled and prepared the night before, was brought forward to pound repeatedly against the gates. In response, the skirmish fire from around the gateway intensified and more men fell. Worried that Wilbur was one of them, Hussa strained to catch a sight of him, immensely relieved when he saw his friend's face contorted into a shout as he bellowed out a command to keep ramming. The tree trunk continued to batter the gates, any of its wielders who fell instantly replaced from the ranks. Finally, with a rending crash the ram broke through, shattering the ancient wood of the gates into large, jagged splinters. With a roar Wilbur's men charged forward to pull at the wreckage until there was a hole big enough for them to scramble through and then, as one, they surged into Calleva.

292

They did not get more than a few paces into the city before they were halted by a volley of arrows from a line of archers, then blocked by a solid shield wall that had formed just inside the gateway. Above the racket of shouts, thuds and screams, Hussa could hear Wilbur bellowing for his men to form their own shield wall. And so, in the narrow space behind the gateway, the struggle of shield wall against shield wall began.

Wilbur had done well to gain access to the city, but the attack had cost his company dearly. Possibly as many as half his men were dead or soon would be in that death zone around the city gates. Depleted and exhausted by their efforts, the remaining men, struggling to find the strength to hold on, were gradually being forced back towards the gateway.

Hussa could hear Wilbur bellowing at his shield wall to hold firm, but there was a touch of futility and panic in his voice as it became clear his warriors were losing the battle.

Suddenly, Wilbur's voice was cut off and Hussa could neither see nor hear what had happened to his friend.

Drawing his sword and looking across at Rolf, who stood only a few yards away, Hussa raised his voice and roared, "Prepare to attack! The city gates must be taken!"

Chapter Thirty
Attack on Mathrafal
Spring 610

Iago, Cadfan and even Cadwallon agreed to my plan. It was simple enough and as far as they were concerned, had the major advantage that no Welshmen, apart from my close friend Aedann and the bard, Aneirin, would have to risk their lives. The risk was all being taken by me and a body of selected men – all of them Angles.

Several weeks after Yuletide, we assembled the companies and set off on the road to Pengwern. There Selyf was ready for us, a message having been sent via Aneirin not long after Yule. The spear companies of Gwynedd and Powys would march with us to Mathrafal, but this was not considered provocative, nor would it be seen as a prelude to war. After all, the message brought to us by Morfael in the autumn had not merely invited Selyf to attend Tysilio's wedding, but had insisted upon it. At the end of winter, on the eve of Eostre, Tysilio was set to marry Haiarme, and Selyf was expected to pay homage to the couple as king and queen. It was therefore fitting that he and all his nobles and warriors, as well as his friend and ally, the Prince of Gwynedd accompanied by his own company of warriors, should attend to witness and bless the occasion.

To further ensure that we did not appear to be prepared for war, our armour and shields were loaded onto carts and carried along behind each company, rather like Lilla had done before the battle at the City of the Giants, albeit covertly. Riders bearing gifts for the betrothed couple raced ahead of us to announce to Mathrafal that we were coming.

Both Selyf and Cadfan, who was leading the companies of Gwynedd in his father's stead, had also brought along a large number of musicians: drummers and hornists in the main, who began to play as we approached Morfael's fortress. So we marched to the sound of horns and drums along the riverside road between the holy enclave at Meifod and the royal castle, supposedly to honour the union we had come to witness. In fact it was intended to provide sufficient distraction so that all eyes in the fortress were directed upon the Welsh spear companies, who approached Mathrafal dressed to celebrate the wedding and making a joyful noise. Indeed, for the bulk of them this was exactly what they were truly expecting: that we were marching to a royal wedding and that for them it was a holy day, so the atmosphere was one of jubilation.

We – Prince Edwin, Aneirin and I, together with my own and Edwin's personal guard and the Wicstun company – needed the distraction because in actual fact, we had already left the column. We had deliberately positioned ourselves at the rear and dropped back so that we were able to slope off without attracting the Welsh spearmen's attention, for our plan would fail if questions were asked and word got out of what we proposed to do. Cadfan and Selyf knew, of course, but not their companies. The only other people who knew were the monks of Meifod. After Yule, having taken news of Tysilio to his nephew, Aneirin had gone on to the abbey to explain the situation and ask the monks to aid us. Horrified to learn of their Abbot's predicament and anxious to help him and their two captive brethren, they had readily agreed.

They now led us across a bridge over the River Vyrnwy and then through forest paths on the far side, looping east of Mathrafal and finally coming back to the river a mile or so to the south of the fortress. Here the monks helped us locate a ford, which brought us back across the river to the side where we needed to be. There they left us. Sworn to secrecy and with their blessings on our endeavour, they returned to their abbey from which they would later emerge purporting to attend the union of their Abbot and Haiarme.

As the sun set on the eve of the wedding we reached the forest edge south of Mathrafal on the top of an elevated section of land that ran along to the base of the fortress. We were facing the western side of the fort, a palisaded wall mounted on an earth embankment. North of Mathrafal, across a dirt road, Selyf and Cadfan had set up camp. Already dozens of camp fires were lit. We could see men milling around, hear them laughing and enjoying each other's company as they broached kegs of mead and ale.

To the south of the fort, running down to the river, we observed a low, damp meadow dotted with trees. "Over there is where I hid and could see into the south gate," Aneirin pointed, "but we won't see it from this angle as it faces the river."

Prince Edwin and I looked to where he pointed. The prince nodded, "When it is dark and the festivities have died down we will make our way there," he said. He turned to me, "And then, Cerdic, it is up to you."

I made no comment; I was only too well aware of what I had to do, which was to lead a small band of men: Aneirin and six of those closest to me whom I knew could be relied upon, namely Eduard; Cuthbert; Aedann and three of my veteran warriors. The plan was to gain access to the fort, locate the Abbot and smuggle him to some high point where he could clearly be seen and heard. All relied on two assumptions: firstly, that Holy Tysilio was not so closely guarded that we would be unable to get him out of his hut without alerting Morfael, Kadir and their men, and secondly, that he would confirm he had been held against his will, did not want the crown and had no wish to marry Haiarme. Hopefully, upon hearing this, Selyf's and Cadfan's Welshmen would attack Haiarme and her allies. Otherwise, the only help we could rely on would be Edwin, his huscarls and the Wicstun Company, all of whom were going to wait near the riverbank until we gave the signal. I did not think we could sneak an entire company through the gates, but we would certainly need their support if fighting broke out, which was why I had asked Edwin to keep them close and on standby to come to our aid.

It was a very risky plan and now we were about to embark upon it I felt the doubts come rushing in. "I hope you are right about all this, Aneirin. Are you certain that monk knew what he was talking about?"

I saw the moonlight glint off the bard's teeth and knew he was smiling. "Of course I am," he said, reminding me of Lilla. What was it, I wondered, that imbued bards with such confidence. I wished some of it would rub off onto me!

"Because if you are not," I added, "I will have kidnapped an anointed king and held him under armed guard. I doubt even Cadfan could protect us in that event. The entire Welsh army would turn against us!"

Aneirin's smile wavered a little but soon rallied. "You just need to have a little bit of faith, Cerdic."

"I just want the bloody Abbot to be where he is supposed to be!" I grumbled.

"That's Holy Tysilio to you, Angle," Aneirin reprimanded me, but his teeth were still glinting I noticed.

We waited, listening to the sounds of revelry from the Welshmen's camp and watching the bright light from their fires whilst we shivered under the trees on the edge of the cold, damp forest. Above us the moon rose into the starlit sky. Slowly the noise from the camp fell away and the camp fires began to die down. Eventually, well into the night – maybe not that long before dawn – the only sounds we heard were the haunting cries of owls hunting for their prey.

I turned to Edwin. "I think it's time, my lord prince," I murmured. He nodded and signalled to his men. Trying to be as quiet as possible we all got to our feet. I'd had everyone wrap wool and furs around spear points, hilts of swords and blades, as well as our shields. I hoped this would muffle the sound of our equipment as we moved through the darkness.

Walking out from under the trees we emerged onto the meadow that ran along the riverbank. The next couple of hundred yards were risky. We were completely exposed and although the moon was starting to set behind us, its light and that of the stars would still reveal us should a guard happen to look over the palisade. I hoped they had all had sufficient alcohol to keep them non curious and mellow, but there was always a risk that some sergeant at arms took his job so seriously he had not drunk ale this night; right now he might be standing watch observing us. My hand went unerringly to Thunor's hammer on the thong around my neck and I prayed to my gods: 'If one such is there, please make him look the other way.'

The moments dragged by as we padded across the meadow. Every creak of our belts and every clank of our equipment seemed to echo through the night. Nevertheless, we finally reached the trees that grew near the water's edge only fifty paces or so from the gate.

"This is where I hid," Aneirin whispered.

I nodded, waiting until Edwin and his warriors had all arrived and taken up position behind the trees, which provided some cover, though not a lot. The prince waved to me and I raised my hand, then turned my back on him and led my six

298

men and the bard towards the gate.

I let Cuthbert scuttle on ahead. He always chose not to wear armour or other heavy equipment that would impede his archery, nor did he carry a shield. Apart from his bow – his most lethal weapon by far – his only other defence was a short seax. He also carried a signalling horn thrust into his belt. I was anxious about his lack of armour but he was a natural scout and could move stealthily and silently far better than any man I knew. He paused to examine the gate, then after a moment, he reached up with one hand and latched on to the top of it, then heaved himself up using knots and kinks in the wood to support his feet. Soon he was over the gate, dropping out of sight behind it.

I felt my heart pounding in my chest as I waited for the cry of alarm that would happen as a guard discovered Cuthbert and perhaps a following cry of pain as a blade was thrust into his body. Yet the gate opened a few moments later with a slight creak and Cuthbert was standing there waving us on.

My men and I made haste to join our companion. As we reached him he signalled us to be quiet and then pointed across to the other side of the courtyard. Sitting on a barrel and leaning back against the wall, spear resting idly by his side and shield abandoned on the floor, was one of the guards who should have been standing watch. He was dead to the world, snoring gently, a tankard still clutched to his belly. I surmised that he had drunk too much this evening. It was as I had hoped: the gift of fine, strong ale Cadfan had sent in to the garrison earlier that evening seemed to have been well received. I let out a breath but then caught myself relaxing too early. I reminded myself that there were still several hundred guards here somewhere in the long, low barrack huts or sleeping in the great hall, which stood across the courtyard from us. Clearly we were still in considerable danger.

"So where is the Abbot?" I hissed at Aneirin.

"Over there," he replied, pointing at a group of low round huts near the stable block. "I'm fairly sure it's that one nearest the stables."

"Thank the gods no one seems to be guarding it, apart from the drunk on the barrel," I muttered, peering around the shadows the moonlight cast in the courtyard. We made our way across to the hut Aneirin indicated. I tried the door and found that it was locked.

"Cuth," I whispered, "see if that guard has some keys."

Cuthbert scampered across the courtyard to the guard and gently padded at him, checking the pouch that hung from his belt. There was a low clink of metal as Cuth retrieved some keys and either that or a sensation of movement roused the guard. He opened his eyes and looked straight up at my friend. "What the...!" he exclaimed.

"Sorry about this and all," stammered Cuthbert as he swung his fist and punched the bemused guard on the jaw. One thing about an archer is the strength of his bow arm; the man's head clunked against the wall behind him and he slumped lower down on the barrel, hopefully unconscious. Cuthbert was shaking his hand as he joined us "Ouch, that hurt," he hissed.

"You will have to get Eduard to show you how to punch a man," I grinned, taking the bunch of keys from him and trying one in the lock. It took several goes and I was beginning to fear these keys were not for the huts when at last one fitted. Relieved I turned the key and felt the lock give. The door swung open.

"Who are you?" I heard Abbot Tysilio say, his voice raised

in alarm.

"Hush my lord, please be quiet," I said softly, moving into the flickering light from two torches that weakly illuminated the interior of the hut.

There was a pause then a familiar figure loomed out of the shadows towards me and peered into my face. "I know you, it's Earl Cerdic isn't it?"

Then he spotted Aneirin standing in the doorway beside me. "You're the bard... it's Aneirin isn't it? You spoke to one of my brethren some weeks ago didn't you? What are you doing here?"

"I did, sire," the bard said softly. "He told me what had happened. We have come to help you and —"

"Not now, Aneirin," I snapped. "Questions must wait until later. We have to get out of sight until daybreak." I beckoned the men into the hut and was pulling the door closed when Eduard stopped me.

"What about him?" He asked, pointing at the guard, still lying unconscious on the far side of the courtyard. "At any moment he might come round and raise the alarm and if that happens..."

"You cannot kill the poor man," Tysilio suggested. "He is only following orders."

I shrugged. "I guess we could bring him inside the hut with us, tie him up and gag him," I suggested.

"Yes, but if there is a change of guard and he is missing from his post that will also cause alarm," Aedann suggested.

"Well then, one of us must take his place, obviously," I said, "and it has to be me."

"No," Aedann said. "Not you; me. I am Welsh after all and could pass as one of the guards better than anyone else. It may

301

be that they don't all know each other by sight. No offence, Cerdic, but it can't be you, your Welsh is too strongly accented to pass as your native tongue. Besides, we can't risk you. Aidith would never forgive me," he grinned.

"We don't know if the guard is Welsh. He might be one of Kadir's Irish," I argued.

"That's possible, but I'm still the best bet. Don't worry, if things go wrong I'll come running for help as fast as I can."

I reluctantly agreed to his plan and Aedann went off to take up position at the foot of the steps to the palisades. Eduard and Cuthbert dragged the guard, who was coming round slowly and moaning, into the hut. "Sorry, mate," Eduard grunted, cracking the poor fellow on the chin once more.

We looked around for something to secure him. "Here, "Tysilio said. "Will this do?" He handed us a rope halter, frayed and covered in cobwebs, which must have been abandoned by some stable boy. He then ripped a strip of dirty linen off the bottom of his robe.

"Perfect," I said, binding and gagging the unconscious guard and laying him in the corner of the hut.

That done, we pulled the hut door to, but I did not lock it because I wished to be able to exit in a hurry as the situation required. Now we waited for the dawn. In the dark hut I sat down on the dirt floor next to the Abbot.

"I need to know what happened, lord. Did Cynan really come to you after his death and ask you to take the throne?"

Abbot Tysilio shook his head sadly. "That woman is mad. She will stop at nothing to hold on to power. But there is more to it than that. She really does hate your kind. Blames you all to the last Angle, Jute and Saxon for the death of her father. I made the mistake of speaking out on your behalf if you recall. I'm afraid she did not take kindly to that. After my brother

302

died in the battle, I think she saw her opportunity." "And Morfael?" I asked. "What about his part in all of this?"

"Well, she and Morfael are lovers. I don't know how long it's been going on. I suspect, though, that it started before Cynan was killed. The Dogfeiling have long felt they have been left out of power and this was an opportunity for them to be right at its heart.

Eduard whistled and looked at me. "If Morfael was humping Haiarme, the next heir to Powys might even be his son! I know they would have to pretend it was the Abbot's here, but it would be Morfael's blood running in the child's veins. Then, if something were to happen to Selyf and Tysilio, who is to say the Dogfeiling would not be nominated as guardians of the young prince, with Morfael ruling Powys with Harmaine?"

"What you say is right, young man," Abbott Tysilio nodded gravely. "Lust for power has always been more potent than lust for flesh," he said. Then he sighed. "So you know how I have ended up in this hut – locked up but kept alive to be a puppet when the circumstances required it."

"We guessed, and having spoken with your monk, Aneirin confirmed it, yes," I said. "And what about this wedding – do you mean to go through with it?"

Tysilio held up his hands. "They threatened to kill every last man in my enclave and every woman and child in Meifod town – the village that supports our church. I do not mind what they do to me, but I cannot have the death of one hundred people or more on my conscience. I was praying and hoping that an opportunity would arise where I can speak out and tell people the truth."

I nodded, "Well I think I can help you there." I told him about our plan and he smiled.

"I heard the voice of the Lord, saying, 'Whom shall I send, and who will go for us?' Then said I, 'Here am I; send me'."

"Huh?" I said, perplexed.

"It is marvellous and wondrous how God works His plan. You are the answer to my prayer, Cerdic."

I shook my head, slightly affronted. "No offense, my lord Abbot, but it was my bloody idea, not your god's."

"You passed the test of the tree; you have been touched by the Lord, Cerdic. Whether you like it or not, you are chosen for His purpose."

"I am bloody not!" I protested.

Tysilio smiled. It was an irritating, knowing smile. I recalled what Selyf had said about how he and Cynan had always followed God's word as relayed to them by the Abbot. Did he really have a channel to the Christians' god? Was I really a part of his plan? I found the thought of this god looking down at me and choosing me for his tasks unsettling, as well as presumptive, and I touched the pendants around my neck, hoping my own gods would not be offended.

Tysilio saw the gesture but did not make an issue of it. "What has happened to your two brethren?" I asked to change the subject.

"They are in another of the huts, but are not locked in. They have been told that I will be punished if they attempt to escape," he said with a grimace. "We are permitted to pray together each evening... Vespers," he added. For a moment he was silent, and then asked, "How long until dawn?"

I got up and walked over to the door, opening it slightly. Outside it was still very dark, but there was the faintest hint of light towards the east. I turned back to him. "Soon," I answered, "very soon."

I saw Tysilio smile in the shadows. He seemed about to say something, but just then we heard the sudden bark of a command

304

out in the courtyard. I risked peeking out of the doorway to where Aedann was standing at the top of the stairs. He was leaning on the palisade gazing out towards the same dawn sky. Now, though, he turned to look at where the shout had come from. I looked in the same direction and felt my throat tighten as I recognised Morfael, King of the Dogfeiling; Haiarme's lover. He was accompanied by four other guards and was looking up at Aedann.

"I said where is Alfonwy and who are you? Answer me!"

"I am one of the guardsmen from Powys. Evan is my name?" Aedann said hurriedly. It was a weak response at best and Morfael was having none of it.

"Bollocks!" he said, peering closer "I know you, I've seen you before. You're one of those bastard Angles belonging to that usurper, Prince Edwin."

Aedann slapped his thigh, put his head back and roared with laughter. "I'm not a bastard Angle you bloody fool," he spluttered. "I'm a bastard Welshman!"

It was a good effort and for a brief moment Morfael looked uncertain, but then he turned to his accompanying guards. "Get him," he pointed. "And search the courtyard, there may be others here."

I drew Wreccan, releasing the hilt from its covering of sheepskin. It was time to act, dawn or not.

"Come on," I said to the others. "Aedann is in trouble." I turned to the bard, "Bring those torches, Aneirin, and then get the Abbot up onto the battlements. The rest of us will take care of the guards. Cuthbert, as soon as we get up there and have secured our position, you start blowing your horn as loud as you can; got it?"

I stepped out of the door. "This is it lads, we're neck deep in shit, let's see if we can wade out of it!"

Chapter Thirty One
Battle in the Fort
Spring 610

We charged out of the door of the hut and across the courtyard, yelling incoherent threats and challenges as we ran. Morfael and his guards were taken completely by surprise and as a result we smashed into their rear, knocking the warriors down with our shields and laying about them with axe and sword. By this time, Aedann had joined us. Seeing he was at a disadvantage Morfael backed off towards the hall while we carried on by and galloped up the stairs to the palisades. Aneirin, carrying the torches, was following with the Abbot. As soon as they had joined us on the battlements, I placed two of my veterans at the head of the middle set of stairs to block access. To avoid being attacked from the rear, I sent Aedann and Eduard along the palisade to block the northern set of stairs. Cuthbert and the other veteran I sent in the other direction to block the southern end. Then I took a torch from Aneirin and started waving it wildly in the air. At that point I spotted a flag fluttering in the breeze. It bore Morfael's symbol and so seemed oddly appropriate. Reaching up with the torch, I set it ablaze.

"Cuth, NOW!" I bellowed.

Cuthbert brought his horn to his lips and blew hard. A long, loud blast followed by three short ones echoed out into the dawn. This was the signal to Edwin and the rest of the company that we needed their help. I heard a shout as Edwin called the men to follow him and a moment later the Wicstun company banner was visible in the fast lightening skies as the men charged towards the gate. Meanwhile I was jumping and shouting and

306

waving my arms and the torch like a lunatic, and Cuthbert was blowing his horn to gain the attention of Cadfan's and Selyf's camp to the north of the fortress.

Below us, shouting and screaming, Morfael had reappeared. He had been joined by Kadir, his Irish guards, the Dogfeiling spearmen and a number of the Powys fyrd, who had been forced to join them. They were all staring up at us, confusion written across their faces as they saw the Abbot was with us.

Suddenly, a voice cut through the crisp dawn air, "Angle scum: they have captured Holy Tysilio. Rescue the king and kill the rest!" It was the unmistakeable screech of Haiarme, the queen. And once more Morfael rallied his men around him and they charged towards the stairwell in an attempt to gain access to the battlements and the Abbot.

Meanwhile, Kadir had rallied his Irish troops and was taking them towards the gateway where even now Edwin could be seen entering, surrounded by his own huscarls and the Wicstun Company.

Cuthbert let fly with an arrow killing the first of the Dogfeiling warriors who attempted to reach the palisade. A second arrow took out the throat of the man behind him, and then Morfael's warriors were engaged with my two veterans at the top of the stairs. I readied my sword in expectation of joining them.

I thrust the torch at Aneirin. "Keep trying to attract the attention of Cadfan and Selyf," I shouted. "Their warriors need to be drawn here so they can see for themselves that the Abbot is held against his will. Only then will they join us in this fight."

The bard nodded, and passing one of the torches to the Abbot, seized the horn from Cuthbert and began blowing it repeatedly, at the same time waving the other still blazing torch above his head.

307

Both my veterans at the stop of the stairs were hard pushed to repel the Dogfeiling warriors now trying to rush them. A spearman almost at the top succeeded in knocking one of my men back with his spear stave. Before I could wade in to help, another followed up with a sword swing, wounding my man in the arm. He dropped his shield and now a follow up thrust stabbed him in the chest. I saw him go down on his knees, struggling to breath. The other veteran was heavily engaged with another spearman and could not help. Leaping to the stairs, I thrust Wreccan into the Dogfeiling's throat, and then reaching down to my wounded man I grasped his tunic and dragged him back against the palisade. I now saw that in all the chaos Tysilio's two brethren monks had found their way up onto the battlements and were with the Abbot. Hastily I drew their attention and one of them, seeing what had happened, came scurrying over to minister to my man, who was now bleeding profusely. Leaving him in safe hands, I took up position beside my remaining veteran atop the middle steps.

I glanced left and right and saw that Eduard and Aedann were heavily engaged against a score of spearmen who were attempting to gain entry to the northern end of the palisade. Meanwhile, my other veteran and Cuthbert, who had discarded his bow and was now wielding a captured spear, were holding back a small party attempting a similar climb up the southern stairs.

At the gate Edwin and the Wicstun Company were now toe to toe and shield to shield with Kadir's fearsome Irish, but were heavily outnumbered, as indeed were we on the battlements. This is it, I thought. The next few moments will decide all of it. Then we could all be dead or, just maybe, we might have won. It seemed unlikely, but as Aneirin had said to me, 'You just need to have a little bit of faith, Cerdic.'

Then I no longer had time to think, I just had to act and I was deflecting a shield blow with my own shield and swinging Wreccan at the head of a warrior in front of me. To my side, my companion was grim-faced and determined. He and the other two veterans had fought with me many a year, ever since the time we escaped from Calcaria. a long time ago now. Had it been ten, eleven years or could it even be twelve? Could it really be that long? It seemed to me that I had been fighting forever. Was this how it would always be? Was I doomed to see my family only very occasionally? Was Loki that interested in me to keep me so occupied? Did Edwin really need me as much as he seemed to? Was I really that important? Surely the world would survive if Cerdic took a day off once in a while?

It is odd what thoughts run through one's head as one is wielding a blade and slashing at an enemy, splattered with his blood and covered in gore. I took a deep breath and stabbed the man in front of me in the neck. He dropped his shield and clutched at his throat as blood came gushing out, then he tumbled off the stairs. He was soon replaced by another Dogfeiling, a vengeful expression on his face and a fearsome two-handed axe in his hands. Yet another warrior, yet more fighting…

Above me the horn was blowing stridently as Aneirin tried desperately to draw the attention of the Welsh camp. Then the horn stopped. I chanced a glance in that direction suddenly afraid the enemy had won through to the battlements, but it was not that. Abbot Tysilio had moved to the bard's side and was leaning over the wall looking down at something or someone on the far side of the palisade. And then he began to speak, his voice clear and loud even over the din of battle, which was extraordinary in itself. I suppose he had plenty of practice at projecting his voice when leading his monks in prayer in those lofty churches with their high ceilings.

At the sound of his voice the battle simply stopped! All men paused to listen as if under some spell. You could do no other

309

– so powerful was the magic in his voice. Even to me, a dyed in the wool pagan as I was at that time, it seemed there could be no other explanation than that he was a conduit for the power of his god. I realized then why the man had such a hold on these people. They called him 'Holy' and who was I to argue?

"Men of Powys! Men of Gwynedd! I am Abbot Tysilio of Meifod. Hear my words. You have all of you been deceived. I am held here against my will! The treacherous Haiarme, my late brother's queen and her lover, Morfael, King of the Dogfeiling, have joined forces with Kadir and his Irish in an attempt to seize control of Powys. They plan to use me as a puppet to rule through me, forcing me to marry my brother's wife, in itself a great sin condemned by God. I now call on all Christians to do God's Will. I name my nephew Selyf ap Cynan as true King of Powys. As I once did many years ago, I again renounce the throne that was forced on me, to serve God as your Abbot. I have no desire to be king and no intention to marry this adulteress, traitor and witch, Haiarme. Now rally to your king, men of Powys. Side with us on this holy cause, men of Gwynedd. A blessing upon the men of Deira who have risked their lives to rescue me! Now, all of you, seize the pretenders and free me!"

There was a ferocious roar from beyond the palisade. Moments later there was a clattering and banging at the main gates to the north as Cadfan, Selyf and their warriors, who had come out of the camp and listened to what Tysilio had to say, tried to gain access.

Suddenly I heard a shout and Morfael appeared in front of me, his face flushed with anger as he forced his way up the stairs to face me.

"Bastard!" he spat at me, "I will make you pay!"

Then he charged at me, thrusting a great spear at my throat.

310

I brought my shield up and deflected the blow, which was so forceful that it shattered his spear. His momentum carried him on into me and knocked me over onto my back. My shield went spinning away and I lost a grip on Wreccan. Morfael was clambering back to his feet. He tossed away the broken spear, drew a hand axe and hewed at my face.

Abandoning the attempt to retrieve Wreccan I thrust out my hand and seized Morfael by the wrist. He spat down at me as we struggled: him trying to release my grip on his wrist so that he could finish me off, and me worming my other hand downwards towards my belt, my fingers clutching the hilt of Catraeth. We struggled for what seemed forever, but it could have been no time at all because none of my men reached me before I had drawn Catraeth out of its scabbard and thrust it upwards into Morfael's belly.

Blood suddenly gushed out of the king's mouth soiling the front of my tunic and chain armour. Rather than pained, he looked outraged that his plans had failed. Then he collapsed down upon me, let out one last gasp and was dead. I struggled to breathe until the weight of his body was removed as Eduard heaved him off me.

"You all right Cerdic?" he asked as he pulled me to my feet. I nodded and glanced around me. All attempts by the Dogfeiling to gain access to the battlements had ceased. Looking over towards the main gates I realised why. Cadfan and Selyf had got into the fort and with their spearmen were now surging across the courtyard driving back Morfael's warriors. In the middle of the courtyard a body of confused Powys fyrd had formed into a circle. These men had been in the companies of Selyf at Pengwern until they had been marched away by Haiarme. Now they changed sides again, rallied together and began attacking the rear of the Dogfeiling warriors. Over at the southern gate, Edwin was driving back Kadir's Irishmen, forcing them onto the spears of the fyrd. It was only a matter of time before this battle was won. No more plays on the board. No dice left to roll.

Then I looked around searching for Haiarme and Kadir. I could not see either of them. Were they already dead?

I got my answer a few moments later as the stable doors suddenly burst open and there stood the white chariot, flanked by half a dozen mounted Irish warriors on each side. In the same way that Haiarme had seized Cynan's throne, she had now taken over his battle cart, the reins held tight in her hands. Standing next to her, clutching an armful of javelins, was Kadir. Haiarme cracked the reins on the stallions' backs and they burst forward, the white chariot hurtling across the courtyard towards the southern gateway. This engine of war, a relic of an earlier age, now smashed through the ranks of the Powys fyrd scattering them in panic. Onward it galloped, driving through the Irish warriors, Kadir showing no concern that it was his own men now falling, crushed under the wheels. Finally, it reached the Wicstun Company.

"Let it through! Let it through!" I shouted and heard the command echoed by Edwin. The company split down the middle hurling themselves to left and right in desperate attempts to get out of the way of this white beast of steel, wood and iron drawn by two snorting greys, the horses as white as the vehicle they pulled. Then the chariot was through, turning southwards along the river, picking up speed across the meadow then vanishing into the forest we had rested in only a few hours before.

I stumbled down from the battlements and located Edwin. The remnant of Kadir's Irish and the Dogfeiling, their leaders either dead or deserting them, were dropping weapons and surrendering. A great cheer went up as the men from Powys, Gwynedd and my own Angles realised the day was ours. We had victory and we had achieved what we had come here to do. Edwin was shaking Cadfan's hand and then that of Selyf as I and the Abbot joined them.

Tysilio embraced his nephew, his eyes glassy with unshed tears. Then he stepped back, and said urgently, "We must pursue Haiarme and Kadir! If they get away they can rally support in the south of Powys. We cannot let them do that; they must be captured before they get too far."

Edwin turned to me. "Much of what has happened has been because of this woman's hatred of us, Cerdic. It should be us who finish it!"

"Agreed," said Selyf. "Pursue and capture them. Kill Kadir if you must. But bring Haiarme back. She has much to answer for."

"You will find horses in the stables, Cerdic," the Abbot said. "From what I gather, Morfael kept a good herd."

I nodded and then was running towards the stables gathering up my friends as I did so, all but my three veterans, all of whom had been injured in the fighting on the stairs, though I was happy to learn their wounds were not mortal. In fact, given the severity of the fighting on the battlements, I and my closest friends had got off very lightly with barely a scratch between us, though I had a nasty bruise where Morfael had thumped me with his shield. In the stables we chose six good looking horses and quickly had them saddled and bridled. So it was that Aedann, Eduard, Cuthbert, Aneirin, Edwin and I mounted and set off in pursuit.

"Let's run the bastards down," I shouted as I dug in my heels and we were away.

313

Chapter Thirty Two
Gateway
Spring 610

"Follow me!" Hussa roared as he led his huscarls forward towards the gate. Rolf echoed his command and brought his own men across to follow Hussa's. Woke, Verge and Ricberht responded to the cry and stirred their companies into life, leading them forward across the muddy fields.

Ahead of him Hussa could see Wilbur's much depleted company struggling to maintain a foothold at the gateway. Wilbur's standard seemed to falter in their midst and a moment later it fell into the swirling melee. Of Wilbur himself Hussa could see no sign. By now arrows and slingshots from the walls were pelting Hussa's and Rolf's companies, forcing them to raise their shields over their heads for protection as they ran forward. The advance, however, was swift. In an attempt to reach the walls as fast as possible, Hussa had abandoned the tight shield wall formation for a more open, flexible one. This meant they could move quickly yet were more vulnerable. Beside him he heard a cry as a huscarl struck by an arrow went tumbling to the ground. A moment later a slingshot ricocheted off his own helmet. "Keep going, just keep going!" Hussa implored them.

They pushed on down the bloody passageway that led to the shattered gate, stepping over the bodies of the dead and wounded. As Hussa reached the rear ranks of Wilbur's company, many frightened faces turned to him, panic stamped on their features. One young warrior started to back away from the gateway, crying out to him in terror, "It's no good, my lord, we can't break through them. We are beaten!" His words infected those around him and as their panic took hold, several warriors began retreating. Hussa had been in enough battles to know this was a dangerous moment. Once Wilbur's company started to run it would be nigh on impossible to stop it developing into a rout, and all the sacrifice to gain the gateway would have been in vain.

"No! No retreat. Follow me!" Hussa roared at them, pushing his way through the ranks, followed by his own huscarls. Shouting words of encouragement he reached the point where the front rank of Wilbur's company, shields locked, were holding back a superior number of Britons who were pushing out of the gateway. As Hussa paused for a moment to catch his breath the man in front of him was cut down by an axe blow and fell gurgling to the ground at Hussa's feet. The Briton wielding the axe, a huge warrior with a swirling black beard and wild eyes, looked ready to jump into the breach.

With a roar Hussa leapt into the gap himself and let his momentum carry him forward so his shield's iron boss smashed into the man's face. Stunned, the Briton collapsed backwards into the ranks behind and Hussa followed up, hewing to the left and the right with his sword and slamming his shield boss into another man's belly. Beside him his huscarls laid about them, stabbing and hacking away so that soon a dozen Britons were dead in the gateway.

Behind him Hussa heard cheering from Wilbur's beleaguered survivors as they rallied. Reinvigorated they followed Hussa and his huscarls forward. In their midst Rolf burst through their ranks, thrust a spear through the neck of another enemy warrior and drawing his own sword, came to stand beside Hussa.

Suddenly the resistance in front of them faltered and then vanished altogether as the remaining enemy warriors at the gateway turned and fled back into the city. With a triumphant cheer Hussa's companies charged after them.

Stepping through the gateway, Hussa looked around him and took stock. It was then that he saw the man who had double-crossed them at Doric; warned Readingum against them and stirred up rebellion in the Thames Valley. Eorpwald! Finally he had caught up with the conniving bastard. In the same moment Hussa spotted Wilbur.

There, just inside the gateway, a road ran along the inside of the wall. On the far side of this road another street led off towards the centre of the city. Blocking the entrance to this street was a company of Britons who were well equipped and still in good order, and at their head, wearing a fine chain shirt and helmet, stood Eorpwald. The bodies of many of Wilbur's company lay at his feet. Wilbur himself was amongst them, one motionless hand still clutching his axe, blood pooling around his body, and yet Hussa was sure he could see the slight rise and fall of Wilbur's chest. He was still alive! Eorpwald stood over him grinning and wiping the blood from his sword on Wilbur's tunic.

Incensed, Hussa leapt forward. "Bastard!" he roared. "You should have joined us when you had the chance."

Eorpwald smiled at him. "I like to be on the winning side," he said.

Hussa laughed, but there was no humour in it. "So do I," he said. "The difference is I know how to tell who is going to win and who is going to lose!" He glanced over his shoulder at his army then pointed at Eorpwald and bellowed out an order, "Attack at once, kill them all, but leave that double-crossing bastard for me!"

The roar was deafening and now even the companies of Wochinoes, Readingum and Doric could sense possible victory and with it the chance for plunder and gain. They surged through the gateway, some spreading out left, others right, down the road beside the wall, but most charging forward towards the

316

Britons. With a clash of swords and shields, battle was rejoined and Hussa found himself face-to-face with his enemy. He barely had time to look down at Wilbur's body before Eorpwald was swinging his sword towards Hussa's throat.

With a flick of his own sword, Hussa parried the blade and then feinted with his shield as though about to slam it into Eorpwald's chest. His enemy recoiled from the threat of the iron boss and Hussa followed up, swinging his sword to catch Eorpwald across his abdomen. Even the finest chain shirt was no match for that magnificent blade. It opened up a gash from which blood started to gush. Eorpwald shouted in pain, but his anger at being wounded only appeared to give him more strength. He counterattacked, hacking back at Hussa with unbelievable power, his face suffused with rage.

The clash of their blades numbed Hussa's arm and he dropped his sword, which went spinning away from him. With a cry of triumph, Eorpwald closed in for the kill. Hussa grasped the hilt of his seax and drew it, holding the short blade up in a desperate attempt to fend off the blow from his enemy's sword. The first swing knocked the seax out of his hand and now Hussa was defenceless apart from his shield. Stepping backwards to avoid the next attack, he slipped on the pool of Wilbur's blood and crashed to the ground next to his friend's body.

Eorpwald's eyes opened wide with glee in anticipation of victory. He stood across Hussa, about to thrust down with his sword and make the kill. Looking death in the face, Hussa felt a moment's regret, but no fear as he resigned himself to the inevitable. Then, beside him, Wilbur stirred into life.

With a desperate surge of effort Wilbur dragged himself up onto one elbow and lifted his axe. Swinging it he chopped deep into Eorpwald's shin before slumping back onto the ground.

Eorpwald screamed in agony and fell to his knees. Hussa lunged forward, grasped the wrist of the man's sword hand and shook it violently so that the sword flew out of Eorpwald's grasp and spun away. With his other hand Hussa seized Wilbur's bloodsoaked axe and buried it deep into Eorpwald's neck. There was a brief moment of horror in the man's eyes and then he tumbled to the ground, thrashed his arms for a moment and died.

Around him Hussa's army started cheering, some of them pointing along the road that led to the city centre, all waving their weapons in the air in celebration. The enemy were scattering; Britons fleeing in all directions pursued by vengeful Saxon warriors.

Dragging himself to his feet, assisted by a smiling Rolf, Hussa stared around and tried to work out what was going on. A moment later, he saw the reason for the men's jubilation. Marching down the road from the centre of the city came two companies from West Seax, their standard bearer carrying the banner of their king. Ceolwulf himself rode at their head and beside him rode Lord Boyden.

The companies halted just yards away and Boyden and the king rode forward to where Hussa stood, still reeling from his fight with Eorpwald. Ceolwulf leant down to grasp his hand in greeting.

"Well done, Lord Hussa, well done indeed. Your fight here allowed us to gain access to the south gates with few losses. How about you?"

"Not had a chance to do a head count yet, sire, but we suffered huge losses gaining access to the gate. Wilbur's company in the vanguard was decimated..." As he spoke his friend's name, Hussa forgot all else. He turned abruptly away from the king and rushed to where Wilbur lay. Rolf was already there,

318

kneeling beside the wounded man and supporting his head. Hussa could see that Wilbur was terribly wounded and had lost a lot of blood from the deep gashes in his chest and abdomen. He was still breathing, but his breath was becoming shallower with every passing moment.

Hussa fell to his knees beside him. "You won the day for us Wilbur. And you saved my life. I shall never understand how you found the strength to do that, but I thank you." Hussa felt tears coming to his eyes as he realised there was no hope for his brave friend.

"Do not weep for me, Hussa," Wilbur said, his voice barely above a whisper. "I will save a table in Valhalla and wait for the day you and Rolf join me there..." Slowly he moved his arm, stretching his fingers towards the pouch at his belt, his face creased with agony. "I want you to have these..."

"Here, let me, my friend," Hussa said. Untying the pouch he emptied the contents onto his hand. Three short lengths of wood and a small whittling knife fell into his palm. Two of the wooden pieces had been whittled into rough shapes, but the third was finished, finely carved into the figure of a warrior.

"Give it to the boy," Wilbur murmured. "Look after him, Hussa, he's a good boy."

"You were like a father to him," Hussa said.

Wilbur gave a slight shake of his head. "No, I was not, I was his friend. It is a father he needs, Hussa, and I cannot be that for him now. It has to be you." He reached down and closed Hussa's hand over the pieces of wood. "Promise me..." he said weakly and then his head slumped back against Rolf's chest. One last gasp of breath rattled in his throat, and he was gone.

Tears rolling down his cheeks, Hussa stared at Wilbur for a moment and then bent forward and whispered in his ear, "I promise."

Dashing his tears away with the back of his hand, Hussa tucked the pieces of wood and the knife away in his own pouch and getting to his feet, nodded to Rolf then walked slowly back to Ceolwulf.

"Our losses have been heavy, sire, "he said, "but the victory is ours. I have done as you asked. Do we now have an alliance? "

The king nodded. "I will gladly ally with Aethelfrith of Northumbria if men such as you lead his armies, Hussa. Yet, would you not ask for more – perhaps some personal reward for the victories you have won for me?"

Hussa looked across at Lord Boyden. "Just one request, sire. I would ask that Lord Boyden releases the mother of Rowenna from servitude to him and lets me buy her freedom."

Lord Boyden raised a surprised eyebrow. "I had heard rumours that you had fallen for the woman Rowenna. Yet is that all the reward you would wish in return for a victory such as this? The freedom of an old woman? Rowenna is already yours."

Reaching into his pouch, Hussa's fingers curled around the figure Wilbur had carved for Hal. He had known many victories. He had won wealth, honour and titles, and he hoped for more victories in the future and more power under his king, Aethelfrith of Northumbria. Yet oddly, on this day, on this battlefield, all of that seemed remarkably less important than the small wooden warrior in his hand and the boy who waited for it with his mother, not many miles away.

"Yes," Hussa nodded, "that is all I wish."

"Very well," Boyden said with a laugh of bewilderment, exchanging glances with Ceolwulf. "The mother is yours along with the house you lived in, and I hope for friendship between us in the future, Hussa, for after today I would gladly have you as a friend and would be a fool to keep you as an enemy!" Leaning down from his saddle, Boyden extended his hand.

Hesitating, Hussa looked at it for a moment, then he smiled and clasping Boyden's hand, shook it. He became aware of Rolf at his elbow and turned to him. "Come, let us burn our friend and send him to Valhalla. Our work is done here."

"Are we finally going back to Northumbria then?" Rolf asked.

"Yes," Hussa nodded, "but first there is one thing I need to do in Witanceastre."

Rolf frowned, "And what might that be?"

"I intend getting married."

His face breaking into a wide smile, Rolf laughed. "And about bloody time too, mate!"

Chapter Thirty Three
Pursuit
Spring 610

We galloped across the meadow, following the trail left by the white chariot and the accompanying riders. They had been travelling fast and at first we had no sight of them. Eventually the woods came to an end being replaced by more farmland further up the valley. Sharp-eyed Cuthbert gave a yelp and pointed, shouting, "There, I see them about a mile ahead!"

I squinted in the direction that he gestured. Sure enough, several fields ahead of us, beyond a small hamlet, we could see the glint of white as the sun reflected off the chariot.

"Come on!" I shouted, digging in my heels.

We forced the horses on in pursuit. The Irish were good riders, but the chariot was slowed as it crossed muddy fields, freshly ploughed and ready for the spring sowing season. Gradually we closed in upon them. I hoped to take them by surprise, but Kadir glanced in our direction, spotted us and shouted out a command. Eight of his horsemen broke away, circled round and came charging back towards us.

As they closed upon us, they drew their swords and we did likewise – except for Cuthbert. Skidding to a halt he slipped off his horse and in an instant had an arrow out of his quiver and nocked on his bowstring. The riders were thirty paces away now and we charged towards each other. Before we could reach them, Cuthbert had let fly with two arrows and two of the riders went down screaming with pain. Now our numbers were matched; each of us had one opponent.

I galloped straight at a man of about my own age who was guiding his horse using only his knees. In both hands he wielded a huge, two-handed sword. He was strong and I knew that if the edge of his blade connected with mine at the speed we were travelling, it was very likely he would cut me in two. However, such a blade is heavy and unwieldy and as we closed upon each other I ducked underneath it and then slashed across his chest with Catraeth, opening up a grievous wound.

He dropped his sword, lost his balance and went tumbling to the ground; his snorting horse veered away, its reins trailing in the mud. Spinning round, I paused to control my own excited mount, and then, as the Irish warrior climbed to his feet clutching his chest, I passed him one more time and with a swing of Catraeth, took off his head.

Aedann was circling another Irishman who was armed with shield and axe, both horses pirouetting around each other as their riders stabbed and sliced at their opponent. I've always felt that Aedann was the best swordsman in the company, he was also a very good horseman and he proved both now. As I watched, he checked his mount then lunged forward, the point of his sword passing between the top of the man's shield and his chin, punching through and coming out of the back of his neck. The precision of the stroke in such circumstances was remarkable.

Aneirin was not a seasoned fighter, although he had, of course, ridden with the Gododdin. Right now he seemed to channel all the experience he had gained on that day ten and more years ago, as if he was back once again fighting in that horrific battle. He dug in his heels and used the full weight of his horse so that his spear landed hard and true on his opponent's chest, skewering him and sending him hurtling backwards across the meadow.

Eduard had managed to pick the biggest of the Irish. Rather than bothering with sword and axe play he had launched himself from his saddle like some flying beast and knocked his opponent off his ride and down onto the muddy ground. There they rolled under and over each other, both having lost a grip on their weapons so that they now were using knees and elbows, hands and teeth, to punch, jab, bite and throttle each other. As they struggled I stepped towards them, but then I noticed that Edwin was in trouble.

The prince's foe had been armed with a spear and its point had taken Edwin in the shoulder. The wound was serious and he had dropped his sword. Now he guided his horse with his knees, using his shield in an attempt to protect himself. I turned away from Eduard and charged towards Edwin's opponent. Before I could reach him an arrow hit the Irish warrior in the back and he tumbled from his seat onto the ground, where I finished him off with a stab to the heart. I raised a grateful hand to Cuthbert then turned back to Eduard. My big friend was blue in the face, his opponent's hands locked around his throat. I moved towards them, but Aedann reached them before me. Tugging the Irishman's head back by his hair, he slashed the man's throat open with his sword and tossed him to one side.

At this point I helped Eduard up and we stood for a moment, breathing hard. Then I noticed that Cuthbert had remounted and was trotting over to us. "Come on! "he said as he urged his mount on past us. "We're not done yet!"

"Wait for us," I shouted and Cuthbert reluctantly reined in.

"Aneirin, see to the prince!" I bellowed over my shoulder at the bard, for Edwin was bleeding profusely from his wound and although he was protesting weakly that he could manage, it was clear he would be more hindrance than help. He realised this too and with a pained expression, waved me away as Aneirin strode towards him. The bard was reaching into the pack he carried, which was crammed with potions, sphagnum moss, herbs and salves, together with clean, folded strips of linen. I knew Edwin was in safe hands.

By now Aedann had mounted up, along with a wheezing Eduard. So, leaving the wounded prince and the bard, the four of us continued the pursuit.

The fight had not taken many minutes, but it had allowed the chariot and the remaining four mounted warriors to make considerable ground. They were now a mile ahead of us again. As we galloped after them we observed the chariot turning up the slope of a hill, Haiarme whipping the greys towards the crumbling remnants of an old fort at the top. It was clearly another of those that had been built by the Britons before the Romans came and abandoned centuries ago. As we neared we saw there was a pathway leading around the fort to an opening in the embankment. Elsewhere the slopes to the hilltop were steep and it was apparent that Haiarme and Kadir had decided to make a stand in the most defensible location they could find.

We followed them up the path and round until we reached a position fifty paces away from the opening. Now we could see them. The white chariot was standing in the gateway flanked on either side by two riders. Haiarme glared down at us, reins grasped tightly in her hands, whilst Kadir stood beside her, javelins at the ready.

"What do we do?" Eduard said. "They outnumber us by two and have the height advantage – and I don't much fancy that chariot riding up my arse do you?"

I considered the chariot. This was the only one I had ever seen. Lilla had told us tales of how the Britons, when they had fought the Romans in ancient times, had possessed dozens of such devices. I could well imagine how terrifying they would be hurtling towards the lines of foot soldiers. But he had also said that they would not normally charge through the shield walls the Romans had deployed in, for such a thing would be suicide to their horses, however devastating a blow it would be. Typically then, they would swirl, circle and engage the Romans using javelin and bow from the back of the fighting platform. Only when the Romans' formation was disrupted would the Britons then plunge on into their midst and lay about them with sword and spear. Here though, there was no room for manoeuvre – no place for Haiarme to circle and so it was a simple faceoff. Our horses were more manoeuvrable and if she did attempt to charge we could get out of the way but, of course, I did not want her escaping. The chariot was fearsome but it relied upon the horses as a means of propulsion. The horses were clearly the weakness in the design. And our Irish foes did not have a bow between them.

"Cuthbert, how many arrows do you have left?" I asked.

He answered by holding up the two remaining arrows in his possession.

For a brief moment I looked at the pair of brave, magnificent greys and it broke my heart to give the next order: "One in each of the horse's chests, Cuth, you understand?"

He nodded, slid off his horse and advanced a few paces towards the gateway. Then he brought out his bow, nocked an arrow onto the string and presented it towards the enemy. Now it was Haiarme who looked alarmed as she realised that with the horses dead their chance of escape was gone. With no warning she cracked the reins on the greys' backs and they surged forward. She was going to charge us!

However, from a standing start it takes time for chariot to get speed up, particularly one whose wheels are clogged with mud; and Cuthbert was not a slow man with a bow. So as the horses descended the path towards us, gathering momentum, he let fly one arrow and then the second. Two arrows arched across the air towards the white chariot and with unerring accuracy plunged into the beasts' chests. The greys screamed in agony, reared up and crashed over backwards. Coming up against their thrashing legs the chariot slewed; the traces broke and it launched into the air, leaping over the white horses and plunging on, it descended the slope and hurtled off the pathway, careering down the hill-side. Then it hit a rock and was brought to an abrupt halt, tipping onto its side. Somehow the white chariot's occupants had managed to cling onto the rail until that moment, but the force of the sudden stop had sent them tumbling over the top of the vehicle to roll further down the hill.

Kadir was on his feet in an instant. Still clutching his javelins, he moved to stand between us and his mistress, who was curled in a heap on the ground. It had all happened so quickly that the four Irish horsemen were still sitting motionless in the gateway, their mouths open.

"Aedann, Eduard, Cuthbert keep the horsemen occupied! "I shouted. Tugging on my reins I pulled my horse round and started down the steep slope towards Kadir. The huge Irish warrior regarded me with contemptuous eyes as I approached, but I could see he was unsteady on his feet and he made no attempt to meet me. Mounted, I had the advantage, but I was not prepared risk my horse by charging down the uneven slope, and so I slid off its back and on foot began to close upon Kadir. I had my shield and Catraeth. I had left Wreccan behind at Mathrafal, having failed to retrieve it after my fight with Morfael such had

327

been my haste to pursue Harmaine. I regretted it now.

Before I reached him I glanced back up the slope. My three friends were facing off against the four warriors, who now rode their horses at a trot out of the gateway. Cuthbert had no arrows left and had only his seax with which to defend himself, but as I watched he scuttled over to the white horses, still squealing and thrashing, their backs broken. He swiftly put them out of their misery, drawing his seax against their throats, but that was not his sole purpose. Grasping the arrows I could see still protruding from their chests, he began to tug and cut them free from the clinging horseflesh. My other two friends were still mounted, but Eduard, having lost his axe was, like Cuthbert, all but defenceless apart from his seax, which he now held in front of him. Aedann had his sword, but the odds looked hopeless. A few moments later the enemy horsemen reached them and their fight for survival began. Meanwhile I had my own fight to consider. I turned to face Kadir.

"Have we not been here before, twice now in fact, Cerdic son of Cenred? Have I not defeated you both times? Whatever the stupid rules of that duel might hold to be true, we both know I would have killed you."

"Time for that to change then," I answered. "And anyway, last time it was a draw."

Kadir snorted. "You go on believing that, if it makes you feel better." He took a step towards me swinging his great sword. "How about we treat this one by way of a decider?"

I sized up my opponent. He was still huge, had the advantage of size and bulk and strength. We were probably matched in skill. But there was today one element that had been missing before or maybe two: he was still looking a little dazed from his fall, although I was fairly sure he would overcome that. More importantly, being further up the slope I had the advantage of height. It wasn't much, but I intended to use it.

I charged down the hillside. As I did so I brought my shield round in front of me and held Catraeth out to one side ready for a thrust. Kadir steadied himself as he saw me advance at a run towards him. The great sword was held high, both hands clutched tightly around the hilt. He intended taking one great sweep at me, which given my momentum I would not be able to avoid.

What it came down to was luck and chance – or maybe wyrd and fate. In the end so are all things in life. We do our best; plan all that we can; put in place contingencies for all those 'what ifs'. But after all of that, the gods look down upon us, Loki rolls his dice and men's fate is decided. Today Kadir and I were those men. And today the dice were in my favour.

I reached Kadir. He swung his sword. The sword smashed into my shield, the great blow shattering it, numbing my arm and breaking a bone in my wrist that if I lived would take weeks to heal. But I hurtled on into him, knocked him onto his back and we tumbled away down the hillside. The pain in my arm was excruciating, but I focused on one thing alone. I brought Catraeth round as we fell and angled the point towards Kadir's heart. We went over each other one more time and this time I felt the point puncture his chest and I drove it home hard.

As we came to a rest, his huge body over mine, he let out a gasp. "You won, Cerdic!" Those were his last words.

Covered in his blood I struggled to free myself from beneath his huge body. A shadow fell over me. I looked up to see the face of Haiarme twisted into a scowl. In one hand was a short, curved dagger which she now placed against my throat.

From the corner of my eye I could see that back up the slope my three friends had somehow won their fight and I guessed Cuthbert must have used the two arrows he had retrieved from the horses. Yet they were too far away to intervene and I could have wept. After all my struggles and my victory today against the great Irishman, I was destined to die at the hands of this woman. How Loki must be laughing!

Haiarme glared at me, the madness bright in those beautiful eyes. "It's your fault, Angle, "she hissed. "Everything is your fault! I had Powys in my hand. I would have led it into Mercia. We would have retaken all the lands lost to your kind. I would have had my revenge on the people who killed my father. You spoilt it all! Just as your kind have always spoilt it since I was a child. Well I can at least kill you, who were present when my father died! "I felt the blade cut into the skin of my throat....

Something hard thwacked into Haiarme's temple; her eyes glazed over and she fell back unconscious, dropping the dagger.

Eduard grunted as he heaved Kadir off my chest, releasing me. "What a heavy son of a bitch!" he commented as he reached down to pull me to my feet.

"Thanks Eduard," I said, patting him on the shoulder. He grunted, "Don't thank me thank Cuth," he replied pointing up the hill.

Cuthbert stood at the side of the road looking down at me. His bow was abandoned on the ground. I could see his sling hanging from his hand, his face split in a great grin. So it had been a sling-shot that had felled Haiarme. I had forgotten he never went any-where without his sling, which he occasionally used for hunting.

"Haiarme?" I said, turning to where the small form of the Queen of Powys lay unconscious. Eduard walked across and crouched down to check her pulse.

"Her heart still beats. I don't think her skull is shattered. She will recover I guess," he said, using her belt and his own to bind her wrists and ankles.

I grunted and then looked at Eduard properly. For the first time I noticed the blood on his torso and arms. "You're wounded! Is it bad?"

"Oh no, I am all right, it is not my blood, Cerdic. That is Irish blood. Aedann is hurt though, come on."

My eyes widened with the news and I followed Eduard back up the slope. Aedann was lying on the ground between the two foes he had clearly killed. In the fight one of them had slashed his abdomen. "How bad is it?" I asked him.

"The cut is wide," he gasped in pain, "but not too deep. I'll live, God willing."

I reflected on the fact that his god like our gods seemed particularly interested in whether we men lived or died. Perhaps it would be better if the whole lot just pushed off and let us get on with it ourselves!

I heard a shout and looking towards the bottom of the hill saw two men on horseback.

"It's Aneirin and Edwin." Cuthbert said, handing me Catraeth, having retrieved it from Kadir's body.

"They took their time," I said, but I was smiling, not having expected them to follow us. It must mean that Edwin's injury was not as bad as I had feared. As they neared us, I pointed towards Aedann and Aneirin at once slid off his horse, dropped to the ground and went to work, delving into his pack for bandages and salve to dress Aedann's wounds. Meanwhile I had Eduard strap up my broken wrist.

When we were ready we tied Haiarme onto the back of one of the Irish warriors' horses and leading the other three, we rode away, leaving Kadir, his warriors and those beautiful white horses to the ravens that were already gathering in the skies above us.

As we reached the bottom of the hill, I looked back to see the outline of the fort and the upturned white chariot sticking up like some sort of shattered memorial on the hillside.

Chapter Thirty Four
Conclusions
Summer 610

Arriving at Mathrafal we found that the army had consolidated its hold on the fortress. Selyf had moved in to the castle and his banner flew over the battlements, which now his men patrolled. Cadfan and the Gwynedd companies were still in camps around the fortress. The defeated fyrd were corralled inside the courtyard and sat around looking miserable. Several of them spat and hissed in the direction of Haiarme as she rode in to the castle and was led towards the hall, her hands bound.

"Miserable lot of bastards are they not?" Eduard said, nodding towards them.

"What will happen to them do you think?" Aedann asked. "After all, they didn't have much choice but to follow who they thought was king did they? And they changed sides at the end."

I think Selyf will be lenient with them providing they swear allegiance to him," I said.

"With Tysilio giving his blessing to Selyf as king I don't imagine many will argue," Aneirin commented.

Next to the fyrd were the survivors of the Dogfeiling. These were Welsh and from Powys but were loyal to the Dogfeiling king, Morfael, who was dead and so now, presumably, to his heir, whoever that was. Their fate was less certain. How would Selyf deal with them?

Finally, in a separate, much smaller ring of fences was the remnant of Kadir's Irish warriors who stood looking defiantly outwards at their captors. As we passed them, they spotted Kadir's severed head, which Eduard had taken and was carrying. They now also spat, but it was towards us, not Haiarme. One of them shouted a dark threat in Gaelic as we rode on by.

"They, however, I don't think Selyf will be so generous with," Cuthbert commented as we dismounted outside the hall and pulled Haiarme off her horse. The queen had not spoken a word since her capture, but it was as well that looks could not kill!

Inside the hall, Selyf and Cadfan were in conversation with Tysilio. Lilla was also present, having turned up in our absence. He nodded at me as we entered the hall, then all fell silent as they regarded Haiarme. Selyf walked over to her and the two stared at each other for a moment before the woman spoke.

"What right have your thugs to capture me and murder my guard? I demand that you arrest these Angles and release me. I demand—"

"Enough!" bellowed Selyf. So fierce was his expression that Haiarme, despite her defiant attitude, actually took a step back. Selyf appeared to be struggling to control his anger. Finally he continued in a quiet voice. "Queen Haiarme, you have been brought here to answer for all that has transpired in Powys this last year. Take her over there," he ordered his guards and Haiarme was moved to a bench at the side of the hall, her wrists still tied.

Selyf turned away from her and addressed the whole hall. "Before we deal with Haiarme I must decide what to do with the men who followed her and her dead lover, Morfael. They are Powys men, but they are also Welshmen who have betrayed their country. They lie imprisoned right now in the courtyard."

There was silence as we waited for his judgement. "The fyrd from Powys who were marched here under some duress and against their will, I lay no blame upon," he continued. "Send guards immediately to release them and let them move freely amongst us, providing they undertake to swear fealty to me. This night I will receive the oath of loyalty from them all and they will be treated no worse for what happened here. That is my command."

There was no argument from anyone on this. It was a fair and popular decision and would help him establish his rule securely, which he so clearly needed to do.

"Next, we come to the Dogfeiling. Their king is dead. Bring in Morfael's brother, Eiludd from amongst the captives."

There was a pause whilst guards went to find this Eiludd. They returned with a young man of no more than twenty who was wounded. He arm was hanging in a sling and wrapped in bloodstained bandages. He was clearly in some pain but there was still defiance in his eyes as he approached Selyf, for like his people he was defeated but resentful.

"You are Eiludd, brother and heir to the lands of the Dogfeiling?"

"I am."

"You and your men followed your brother here and so supported the usurpation of the succession of the crown from my father to me. You were therefore complicit in the deception that Holy Tysilio had claimed the throne. Do you deny this?"

Eiludd shook his head. "For myself I deny nothing. I was aware of all the details and helped my brother in his quest to gain power. The men, however, were bound to us by oaths and are loyal. Deal with me as you will, but I ask that you spare the lives of the brave warriors of the Dogfeiling."

Selyf considered this for a moment. He walked over and had a whispered conversation with Tysilio and Cadfan and then returned to his high chair.

"We accept your argument regarding the loyalty of the men to their lord. We will not hold any responsible. However, as heir to Dogfeiling and now king, you are responsible. My judgement therefore is that you and five of your men will return with us to Pengwern and there you will stay as hostages until I am satisfied of your loyalty. You will be well treated and be able to receive visitors and send messages pertaining to the administration of Dogfeiling, but such messages will be inspected. You will also swear allegiance to me this evening. The rest of your men may go home to their wives and families."

Eiludd nodded. He said nothing but there was relief on his face. He had perhaps feared that a more severe penalty was likely for him and his men. I wondered, had the position been reversed, whether he would have acted so leniently. I doubted it.

"Return now to your men," Selyf instructed and Eiludd actually bowed before leaving.

"I am not so sure about the wisdom of that, "Edwin whispered to me. "Leaving a rival dynasty intact and its leader alive might come back to bite Selyf or Powys or us."

I shrugged. It did not seem to be our problem. Looking back from later days I am forced to concede Edwin had a point. That though is another story for another time.

Selyf turned and signalled that Haiarme should again be brought forward.

"So then, it is finally over," Selyf said, addressing the former queen. "You, a Scottish princess, have been the cause of civil war in this kingdom, leading to many lost lives. You never loved my father, but encouraged him to seek vengeance in your name, risking his life for your sake in a war he never really wanted. You took Morfael as your lover, falsely imprisoned Holy Tysilio and forced him to take the throne against his will, planning to become his wife so you and Morfael could control Powys in his name. Do you deny any of this?"

Haiarme stood proudly in the hall, staring defiantly back at the young king. She shook her head. "I deny nothing. I saw a chance for power and I took it. I saw a chance for revenge and I grasped it."

Shaking his head Selyf turned to the rest of us. "Some might say that as a child Haiarme was unhinged by her grief and that none of this would have happened had her father not been killed in her formative years. Yet we all suffer such losses; we all grieve over loved ones; it does not turn us all into power grasping criminals such as this woman became." He paused, looking around the hall. Several heads were nodding in agreement. "So then, "he went on, "we must decide the fate of Haiarme."

Lilla stepped forward. "I have information that might be relevant to this discussion," he said.

Selyf nodded that he should continue.

"I have been travelling in the North these last few weeks and was recently at the court of Áedán mac Gabráin. I have to report to you that the King of the Scots is grievously ill. He is thought to be dying and unlikely to live beyond the end of the year. Perhaps he may not even see the summer."

Despite her earlier defiance, Haiarme gasped. I could tell that she was genuinely shocked by this news. There was darkness in her soul, of that there was no doubt, but there was feeling too. No doubt of that either.

"Prince Cadfan, what would you do with Princess Haiarme?" Selyf asked, dropping any reference to 'queen'. She did remain, however, a princess of the Scots.

Cadfan pondered this for a moment before answering. "I would consider sending her to an isolated monastery to live out

337

her life. There she would not be able to do any more harm."

I exchanged glances with Edwin and knew he was thinking what I was thinking. There were no monks alive who could hold onto Haiarme, however remote their monastery. It was no solution.

Selyf nodded and then turned to Edwin. "So, Prince Edwin, what would you do with this woman? She has caused much sorrow in Powys, but in enmity she has set herself particularly against you and your people."

Edwin took less than a moment to reply. "I would send her home immediately, before her grandfather dies."

There was a collective gasp of surprise at this remark. Many were shaking their heads in disbelief. Selyf pointed at Haiarme as if to make sure we were all talking about the same woman. "You would not punish her? You would let her go, just like that. Perhaps you are taken by compassion for the fact that her grandfather is dying and her own father is already dead?"

"No, sire, it is not that, Edwin said. "We must take action to show that I and my people are strong and that any who go against us and fail to defeat us will suffer at our hands. Send her back to the Scots, but execute all the Irish who came with her, place their bodies in a boat and send her home surrounded by the corpses of her bodyguards and the head of Kadir, to show they were of no use to her. Strip off her fine raiment and dress her in rags. Soil her with ash and then let her return to the Scots, a symbol of the failure of her efforts here. Let Áedán mac Gabráin witness for himself the result of his final attempt to defeat us, for I have no doubt that he was behind what she sought to achieve or that over the years he has stoked her need for vengeance to the point of madness. Let him die with the knowledge that he has failed; let all men know that if they try to oppose us

338

a similar fate will befall them."

There was silence in the hall at the pronouncement. I stared at Edwin in amazement and now a chill came over me. He was a strong and natural leader and a brave warrior, but inside him there was something more: a desire for revenge and retribution that was disturbing. Was he, like Haiarme, being driven insane by his need for vengeance? It worried me. However, looking around the hall I saw that many men were nodding their heads and I recalled that some of them would have lost brothers, fathers and sons in the fighting that Haiarme had provoked. So maybe Edwin was right and maybe he possessed something that kings had to possess to be successful: a streak of ruthless vindictiveness. Which is why I would never be fit to be a king, I reflected. I wondered if Hereric had it too yet somehow I doubted it.

After a moment of silence, Selyf, who like me had been staring at Edwin a flicker of doubt in his eyes, suddenly nodded at Haiarme's guards; "So be it!" he said. "Take her away."

Her face pale, the princess was dragged away to witness her guards being executed.

"I believe that concludes the immediate business," Selyf said.

"Not quite," Tysilio said, as he now came forward and addressed the hall.

"My part in what has transpired these last two years must be considered and punished if it is found that I have transgressed."

Around the hall there were gasps of shock and surprise. These emotions were shared by King Selyf. "Uncle... Holy Tysilio, no fault in what occurred falls upon you," he said.

Tysilio shook his head. "Would that were so, my nephew. Truly, though, whilst I was used by Haiarme and Morfael to their own ends, I am afflicted with guilt that maybe I could have done more to prevent what occurred."

339

"I cannot see how," Cadfan said.

"I agree, Prince Cadfan, neither can I," Selyf said.

"Yet still I feel I should have done more," the Abbot insisted.

"I will not punish you, Holy Tysilio," Selyf said. "Put away your guilt, it is entirely misplaced."

Tysilio shrugged. "In which case I must punish myself and to that end, this is what I have decided. Whilst I remain here in Powys I am forever a hidden threat and challenge to your authority. Anyone who wants to seize power could use me as Morfael and Haiarme did. So I should leave Powys."

There were cries of "No!" from all around the hall at this, but Tysilio just shook his head. "It is no good arguing with me, I have made my decision. I will depart and travel south to Frankia or Britannia Minor perhaps; and there serve God as best as is possible whilst I have breath in me."

Selyf hesitated for a moment and then he nodded. "So be it," he said in a regretful tone. "Then our business here is done," he concluded.

Our business in Powys was also done. Yet we accompanied Selyf and his army back to Pengwern where we attended the delayed coronation at which Tysilio himself officiated. Then, whilst the celebrations were continuing he got up and with little ceremony simply left. I happened to be returning to the hall after a call of nature and bumped into him on his way out.

"So I leave now, Cerdic, son of Cenred."

"Right now?" I asked. "Just like that?"

"Indeed. I would not overshadow the celebration of my nephew's coronation. Besides which, I can feel the call of God to start on my next task across the sea. I doubt we will meet again in this lifetime. I thank you for what you did in Powys. God has marked you for a purpose, my young Angle friend: remember the tree."

"Yes, about the tree. It was just a trick wasn't it?"

Tysilio just smiled and started to walk away.

"Well, wasn't it?" I shouted after him.

The Abbot turned back one last time. "Not all mysteries have an answer, Cerdic. Some things must be taken on faith. My blessings will always be upon you and your family and friends," he added and was gone.

After being crowned, King Selyf addressed some comments to Edwin. "You and your followers have earned our gratitude and friendship here in Powys. You may consider yourselves our friends and allies and have our support and offer of shelter in the coming years."

"We thank you, sire," Edwin bowed.

There would still be negotiations and agreements to be reached, of course, but the door was open for what we had come here to do. Powys was now our friend and through us a peace with Ceorl's Mercia was made possible.

We left Powys a few days after the coronation and returned to our homes in Gwynedd. Ceorl had promised an alliance underpinned by marriage if we resolved the enmity and hostility of Powys and this we had done. So it was that in the autumn of that same year – the year that Christians called 610 Anno Domini – we, with our wives and families, found ourselves standing in the shrine to Woden and the other gods at Tamwerth to witness the marriage of Prince Edwin of Deira to Princess Cwenburg of Mercia, Ceorl's daughter. That marriage brought an alliance between Mercia and the princes of Deira, and through it a larger alliance with Gwynedd and Powys. The vagabond prince who had left Deira in 604 now commanded the support of the armies

341

of three kingdoms and he now had a princess who might one day be queen. I watched as she handed him a sword and asked for him to use it to protect her and their children.

As the words that bound them were spoken, I recalled my own wedding. I too had taken the sword that Aidith had offered me. I too had taken those same vows and I did try to protect my own from the dangers of the world and the many enemies we had made. Yet Aidith was right that the world drew me from them too often. Maybe the time had come to resolve that.

After the ceremony I walked with Aidith through the gardens around the temple. For a moment we were alone and I turned to her now and took her hands.

"What is it?" she whispered.

"I am wondering if I do enough to fulfil those vows I took to protect you and our family. If you ask me to I will leave Edwin and go with you and our children somewhere quiet where the world will not disturb us."

She studied me for a moment and then laughed, but it was a soft and kindly laugh that held no malice. I felt her arm loop around my waist. "Somehow I think that the world would find us, nonetheless."

"True," I grunted.

"Besides which, you took vows to Edwin too. I love you, Cerdic. I want as much of you as I and the children can have… but I love all the parts of you. You are the man I love because of all that you do. You would not be Cerdic if you abandoned Edwin, any more than if you abandoned me and the children."

We kissed. It seemed the right thing to do, but as I felt her lips brush mine, a slight shadow passed over the moment and I drew back.

"What is it?" Aidith asked.

I had been thinking before of Cuthwine and Sian, but now I was thinking of another child I might have sired. Was he truly in the hands of my nemesis: my greatest enemy, my half-brother, Hussa? How was he treating the boy? I recalled the moment some years before when he had spotted young Cuthwine at Deganwy. I remembered the look in Hussa's eyes – a mix of longing for what I had and threat that he might take it away – it was as if a cold hand had clutched at my heart and now, considering that moment again, I shivered.

Aidith frowned. "What is it?"

"I was thinking of the boy Lilla told me about... my son, perhaps." I felt her stiffen and shook my head. "I love only you, Aidith. The woman meant nothing and still means nothing, but what if he is my son? Is it right to leave him with Hussa? You know what he is capable of. Might he use the boy to get at me... at us?"

Now it was she who gave a shudder and as she gazed into my eyes I knew she was thinking back to the burning of the villa and my mother's gruesome, agonising death. Her face softened, "If he is a son of yours then he is a part of you, Cerdic, and haven't I just said I love all parts of you? If you need to find him... go my love, with my blessing. Just promise me you will return."

"You know I will," I said. I might have added, 'So long as I'm alive,' but there was little point. Aidith knew that only my death would keep me from her.

"When will you leave?" she asked.

"The sooner the better I guess; maybe tomorrow. I will head south to West Seax and find the boy and make sure he is safe and well before I come home."

If you need to bring him back with you, do so, "Aidith said. "We cannot allow history to repeat itself, Cerdic. We cannot let your son turn into another Hussa."

I held her close to me and breathed in the scent of her hair. What had I ever done to deserve this woman? I must have done something right.

"If you will leave tomorrow," she murmured, "let's forget the wedding feast and go to our room. I doubt we'll be missed. I want you to hold me close tonight."

"That was pretty much my plan," I said. Then I kissed her again.

Chapter Thirty Five
Home
Summer 610

Below them in the harbour, the ship that had carried them bobbed on the outgoing tide. Seagulls cried out as they circled and swooped overhead and plunged to snap up fish from the waves or pick up food from the detritus at the port. On the wooden ramparts of the clifftop fortress of Bebbanburgh, the banner of Aethelfrith flapped in the wind. Hussa led the way, riding along followed by Rowenna, Rolf and twenty of his huscarls. Hal sat in front of Hussa, dozing and snoring softly. His hands were folded in his lap and he clutched two wooden warriors, one carved by Wilbur and the other by Hussa himself. They were the boy's prized possessions.

In the courtyard of the fortress, Aethelfrith was training with his men, his chest bare and covered in sweat as they circled him. One stepped forward and lunged with a training blade and Aethelfrith knocked it from his hand before catching him on the back of his neck. As the man groaned and stumbled away the King of Northumbria saw Hussa and walked over.

"So you are finally back, you have been busy, I assume?"

Hussa scooped up Hal and then slid from his saddle, putting the now wide awake little boy on the ground where he stared up wideeyed at Aethelfrith. Hussa bowed towards the king. "I am sire; I apologize that it took so long but we have our alliance. West Seax will attack Mercia when we do. I hear that Edwin has married Ceorl's daughter."

Aethelfrith nodded. "Yes, we have just received that news too. However, I was not talking about that. I did not mean about

345

West Seax, I expected no less from you. We will deal with Mercia in turn. With them, Gwynedd and Powys and all the fools who would support Edwin of Deira, including your brother. But when I talked about being busy I meant the woman and the child."

Hussa held out his hand and Rowenna stepped forward to take it, smiled at him and then bowed to the king. Hal now mimicked his mother, bowing as well. Then he smiled shyly at Aethelfrith and offered up a wooden soldier. The king crouched down, took the soldier and examined it before returning it to Hal with a smile, patting him on the head with the words, "I can see that he is a Northumbrian warrior."

Standing back up, he gestured at the woman and the boy. "I take it these are your family, Hussa?"

"Yes, sire. May I present Rowenna, my wife and Hal..."

Hussa paused and then smiled at Rowenna "...my son."

The End

Historical Note

As with every book in the Northern Crown series we are dealing with a time period of which very little is known. Documentary evidence is scanty at best and not likely to increase. However, archaeological work goes on and is revealing new evidence that helps to improve the picture we have. In the end, a fiction writer has to sift and select from the evidence and come up with a coherent story based on the facts as we understand them.

Kent was the oldest Anglo-Saxon kingdom where, according to tradition, brothers Hengest and Horsa first stepped onto the shores of Britain with three boat loads of warriors – traditionally the first of the Anglo-Saxons. In the early 7th Century it was the most powerful kingdom and its ruler, Aethelberht, was considered a Bretwalda or Lord of Britain, extending authority over much of the English-speaking parts. In Aethelberht's time Kent had just become the first Anglo-Saxon kingdom to become Christian after the Augustine mission was accepted there. Aethelberht had been a pagan, but his wife, Queen Bertha, was a Christian and the daughter of the King of Frankia. Possibly the invitation by Aethelberht was a political move, but he soon threw his support behind Augustine and his successors. At the time of Cerdic's and Hussa's visit, it is likely that the old Roman church of St Martins was being repaired and was in use again, the beginnings of a monastery were going up and a start was being made on the early church from which the great Canterbury Cathedral would eventually emerge in the city.

Much of my description of Canterbury comes from excellent material produced by The Canterbury Archaeological Trust, which makes great maps and reconstructions.

There was certainly a conflict between Sussex and Wessex at this time as a battle around 607 is recorded in the Anglo-Saxon Chronicle, the source of much of what we know. We don't really know who won this battle, but it seems that the boundaries of Sussex and Wessex may already have been established. Chichester was a crumbling Roman city and the Saxons under Cissa lived in a nearby settlement.

The villa I portray at Boseham is heavily influenced by ruins of the magnificent palace at Fishbourne. This was possibly the largest Roman palace in Britain and probably at one point the dwelling place of a Romano-British tribal leader who backed the Romans. It has some amazing mosaics and the modern day museum is well worth the visit. I would have loved to have used Fishbourne for the scene of the battle, but alas it burnt down in the 3rd Century and was levelled. There is, however, evidence of a smaller villa under the modern day church at Boseham and so in my story that became the site of the battle. Recently, another large palace has been found in Wiltshire (again buried beneath the soil for more than fifteen hundred years, lending credence to the possibility of a number of such structures surviving, particularly in the south.

Wessex was at the time an emerging power. Ceolwulf is the latest of a succession of warrior kings who descend from a king coincidentally called 'Cerdic'. Wessex was expanding, particularly west against the Britons of Dumnonia and north – ultimately bringing them into conflict with Mercia. Before they could reach the Mercians, however, they absorbed a string of settlements along the Thames Valley and then (possibly later) a British enclave that was believed to have existed into the 7th Century around modern-day Silchester. This is a small fairly obscure village, but it is close to the ruins of Calleva Atrebatum which in Roman times was an important city. Straddling various east-west and north-south roads, it would have been a trading hub. Today it has mostly returned to the land, but you can still walk the perimeter and find the walls. The north gatehouse is particularly well preserved and so I had some good evidence on which to base the battle there. Of the city within, nothing remains other than odd bumps in the ground. The lands above are now home, rather oddly, to a small number of Alpacas – creatures most definitely not native to the area!

Moving north to Powys, I mention a number of locations and individuals. Again after all these centuries the evidence is scarce. I am indebted to correspondence and material sent to me by the Centre for the Study of Ancient Wales. They pore over all the material that does exist, such as the poetry, triads, Anales Cambriae, etc., and try to construct some idea of what occurred. Being academics, they are understandably reluctant to say what happened, but rather prefer to relate the various theories. As an author, of course, I needed to take a view of what sounded plausible and what would make for a good story.

Pengwern is an enigma. It might refer to the whole area of Eastern Powys or perhaps to just one location like a city. I was fairly convinced by the idea that Pen means 'head of' in Welsh, and wern related to the River Severn. The name Severn comes from the Celtic name *sabrinn-â, which then developed to become Sabrina to the Romans; Hafren in Welsh and Severn in English. Wern could be a corruption of these, in which case we have 'Head of the Severn'. Modern day Shrewsbury lies close to the source of the Severn, has been linked to the name and today even boasts a Pengwern rowing club, so maybe I am not far wrong.

Meifod is today a small village, but once was the site of a monastery and ancient church still named after Saint Tysilio. I visited the modern day church and there is an ancient tomb-stone dating to not long after his time.

Mathrafal is today an abandoned earth fort. It was apparently built in either the 6th or 7th Centuries. It was certainly the court of Powys in later centuries, before returning to obscurity and may well have been in use at the time of my story.

Cynan is thought to have been a son of Brochwel Ysgithrog and the father of Selyf, who may have succeeded him. He is sometimes referred to by the epithet 'Garwyn', possibly 'Car-wyn', which has been explained as meaning 'of the White Chari-ot'. Cynan is the addressee of a poem ascribed to the poet Talies-in. Here he is presented as a warlord who led many successful campaigns throughout Wales: and mostly against the Welsh rather than the English.

Tysilio was a 6th to 7th Century Celtic saint, also said to be the son of Brochwel Ysgithrog. He is mentioned again in the 'Life of S. Beuno'. From this we learn that St Tysilio wished as a lad to embrace the religious life and left his family and went to Meifod to be instructed by the abbot Gwyddfarch. His father disapproved and supposedly sent a warband to bring him back. Tysilio fled to the shore of the Menai straits in Gwynedd and there founded the church of Llandysilio. After his return to Mei-fod, in his brother Cynan's time as king, he became Abbot there.

After the death of Tysilio's brother, his sister-in-law, Queen Haiarme, (a different source gives this woman the name of Gwenwynwyn, but I thought that was too close to Gwynedd – not to mention Arthur's Gwenevere!) desired to marry Tysilio

350

and place him on the throne of Powys. Objecting to both proposals, the saint refused and found his monastery persecuted by the state. So he travelled across sea to Saint Sulac in Brittany, where he established a second monastery.

Who was Haiarme? Well there is a suggestion that she was indeed the daughter of Domanghast and granddaughter to Áedán mac Gabráin. The great King of the Scots seems to have gone into a decline after his defeat at Degsastan and eventually died in a monastery around 607 to 610.

Edwin did marry Cwenburg the daughter of Ceorl, and Hereric married also married a princess named 'Breguswith' but we don't know if she was Welsh or English. However, by circa 610 the princes have gained more support for their cause. It is possible that some form of alliance to counter Northumbria was forming around Gwynedd, Powys and Mercia. The scene is set for a major show down.

Edwin and Aethelfrith, along with Hussa and Cerdic look likely to meet again.

The story will continue in book 5 of the Northern Crown Series.

The Hourglass Insitute Series

Book One - Tomorrow's Guardian
ISBN 978-0-9564835-6-0
Time Travel Sounds like fun until you try it.

Tom Oakley experiences disturbing episodes of déjà-vu and believes he is going mad. Then, he discovers that he's a "Walker" - someone who can transport himself to other times and places.

Tom dreams about other "Walkers" in moments of mortal danger: Edward Dyson killed in a battle in 1879; Mary Brown who perished in the Great Fire of London; and Charlie Hawker, a sailor who drowned on a U-boat in 1943. Agreeing to travel back in time and rescue them, Tom has three dangerous adventures, before returning to the present day.

But Tom's troubles have only just begun. He finds that he's drawn the attention of evil individuals who seek to bend history to their will. Soon, Tom's family are obliterated from existence and Tom must make a choice between saving them and saving his entire world. Tomorrow's Guardian is a Young Adult Fantasy Novel.

The Nine Worlds Series

Book One - Shield Maiden
ISBN: 9780956810373
This is the world as it might have been if the stories been true...

Shield Maiden is a Historical Fantasy Adventure For Children of Ages 9+

Anna is a 12 year old girl growing up in a Saxon village in 7th century Mercia. Her life changes when she finds a golden horn in the ruins of a Roman Villa. Soon an ugly dwarf, a beautiful sorceress and even her own people are after her.

What powers does the horn have and why does everyone want it?

And why is Anna the only one who can get a note out of it?

About Shield Maiden

Shield Maiden is the first book in The Nine Worlds series in which the historical world of Anglo-Saxon England meets the mysterious world of myths and legends, gods and monsters our ancestors believed in.

This is the world as it might have been had those stories been true...

Won a Silver Children's Literary Classics Award in 2012.

The Praesidium Series

Book One - The Last Seal
ISBN: 9780956810397
Gunpowder and sorcery in 1666...

17th century London - two rival secret societies are caught in a battle that threatens to destroy the city and beyond. When a truant schoolboy, Ben, finds a scroll revealing the location of magical seals that binds a powerful demon beneath the city, he is thrown into the centre of a dangerous plot that leads to the Great Fire of 1666.

"an awesome array of characters which definitely included the good, the bad and the ugly, and an amazing plot!"
" This young adult historical fantasy had me totally engrossed and I would recommend it to anyway who loves historical fantasy/fiction (especially British) whether you're a teen or an adult. "
FIVE STARS
The Slowest Bookworm

"Denning has a real thirst for historical knowledge and this certainly shines through in his books, with his descriptions of London in 1666 making you feel as if you were in the middle of the raging fire."
YA Yeah Yeah

Winner of a B.R.A.G. Medallion

Lightning Source UK Ltd.
Milton Keynes UK
UKHW010722070223
416609UK00002B/741

9 780956 483591